FutureCrime

FutureCrime

An Anthology of the Shape of Crime to Come

EDITED BY

Cynthia Manson & Charles Ardai

DONALD I. FINE, INC.

New York

Copyright © 1992 by Davis Publications, Inc.

All rights reserved, including the right of reproduction in whole or in part in any form. Published in the United States of America by Donald I. Fine, Inc. and in Canada by General Publishing Company Limited.

Library of Congress Cataloging-in-Publication Data

Futurecrime: an anthology of the shape of crime to come / edited by Cynthia Manson, Charles Ardai.
p.   cm.
ISBN: 1-55611-312-9
1. Science fiction. 2. Crime—Literary collections. 3. Crime—Fiction.
I. Manson, Cynthia. II. Ardai, Charles.
PN6071.S33F8   1992
808.83'876—dc20   91-55185
CIP

Manufactured in the United States of America

10 9 8 7 6 5 4 3 2 1

Designed by Irving Perkins Associates

Grateful acknowledgment is made to the following for permission to reprint their copyrighted material:

RYERSON'S FATE by Doug Larsen, Copyright © 1989 by Davis Publications, Inc., reprinted by permission of the author; A KIND OF MURDER by Larry Niven, Copyright © 1974 by The Conde Nast Publications, Inc., reprinted by permission of Robert P. Mills, Ltd.; VRM-547 by W.R. Thompson, Copyright © 1989 by Davis Publications, Inc., reprinted by permission of the author; all stories previously appeared in ANALOG SCIENCE FICTION/SCIENCE FACT, published by Davis Publications, Inc.

DOGWALKER by Orson Scott Card, Copyright © 1989 by Davis Publications, Inc., reprinted by permission of the author; ONE-SHOT by Lawrence Watt-Evans, Copyright © 1990 by Davis Publications, Inc., reprinted by permission of the author; THE INCORPORATED by John Shirley, Copyright © 1985 by Davis Publications, Inc., reprinted by permission of the author; THE ENERGIES OF LOVE by Kathe Koja VanderSluis, Copyright © 1989 by Davis Publications, Inc., reprinted by permission of the author; THE BARBIE MURDERS by John Varley, Copyright © 1977 by Davis Publications, Inc., reprinted by permission of Kirby McCauley, The Agent; all stories previously appeared in ISAAC ASIMOV'S SCIENCE FICTION MAGAZINE, published by Davis Publications, Inc.

THE NOT-SO-BIG SLEEP by Terry Black, Copyright © 1990 by Davis Publications, Inc., reprinted by permission of the author; story previously appeared in ALFRED HITCHCOCK'S MYSTERY MAGAZINE, published by Davis Publications, Inc.

THE TERCENTENARY INCIDENT by Isaac Asimov, Copyright © 1976 by Davis Publications, Inc., reprinted by permission of the author; SHOW BIZ by Robert Bloch, Copyright © 1959 by Davis Publications, Inc., © renewed 1986 by Davis Publications, Inc., reprinted by permission of Harry Altshuler; I ALWAYS DO WHAT TEDDY SAYS by Harry Harrison, Copyright © 1965 by Davis Publications, Inc., reprinted by permission of Robert P. Mills; all stories previously appeared in ELLERY QUEEN'S MYSTERY MAGAZINE, published by Davis Publications, Inc.

MECH by C.J. Cherryh, Copyright © 1991 by C.J. Cherryh; THE WORLD AS WE KNOW IT by George Alec Effinger, Copyright © 1991 by George Alec Effinger; LAY YOUR HEAD ON MY PILOSE by Alan Dean Foster, Copyright © 1991 by Alan Dean Foster.

CONTENTS

Introduction

The day the first law was enacted is the day crime was born.

Humans had been killing and robbing each other for ages, but now a name was given to the darker side of human activity. Since then, humans have proven themselves extraordinarily resourceful in finding ways to break the rules they create to keep each other in line.

Each new advance in technology has brought with it opportunity for criminal enterprise. Who would have thought that Alexander Graham Bell's great invention, the telephone, would become an instrument of harassment and fraud? Who could predict that trains, automobiles, and airplanes would facilitate the getaways of countless fugitives? Who knew, when computers first sprang into existence, that computer theft, espionage, and vandalism would sabotage computer networks?

As surely as the future will bring new forms of technology, it will bring new forms of crime—*FutureCrime*, if you will, hence the title of our book.

If there is any genre ideally suited to examining crime, it is science fiction. Science fiction deals with how societies change, crime fiction with how people break society's rules. New societies necessarily advance new rules to be broken and, therefore, generate new crimes.

It is no wonder then that so many science fiction writers write about crime. Some of the genre's best-known novels are crime stories. Isaac Asimov's first robot novels are detective stories; Harry Harrison's Stainless Steel Rat series is about an intergalactic con man; Mary Shelley's Frankenstein brings to life a vicious and calculating murderer; and George Orwell's 1984 focuses on a "thought criminal" in what is surely a criminal society.

Similarly, science fiction short stories frequently turn to the subject of crime, as you will see from the stories in this collection. They deal with crimes of global significance, as in Isaac Asimov's "The Tercentenary Incident" and Lawrence Watt-Evans' "One-Shot," which address the problem of assassination. They deal with local crimes, as in John Varley's "The Barbie Murders." They explore domestic violence, as in Alan Dean Foster's grisly tale of retribution, "Lay Your Head On My Pilose." They consider crimes of the most intimate nature, such as the strange and horrible violation John Shirley describes in "The Incorporated."

SF crime stories are about murder, as in Larry Niven's "A Kind of Murder." They are about infiltration and theft, as in Orson Scott Card's "Dogwalker." They are about fraud, as in Terry Black's "The Not-So-Big Sleep." In short, they are about every sort of crime, but always with a new slant, new problems arising out of new realities. The killing in C.J. Cherryh's "Mech" *appears* to be an ordinary domestic homicide; the various thefts in George Alec Effinger's "The World As We Know It" *appear* to be just so many petty crimes; but with *FutureCrime*, things are not always as they appear to be.

As we go forth into the future a world of crime as yet unknown awaits us. Our guides will be the visionary science fiction writers of tomorrow, exploring not just the brighter side of human ingenuity, but the darker, more frightening side as well.

—Cynthia Manson
Charles Ardai
Fall, 1991

SHOW BIZ

BY ROBERT BLOCH

Imagine: when Robert Bloch wrote this chilling story back in the winter of 1958, its premise was pure science fiction. Or, to put it another way, speculative fiction. Remember, he wrote it before the explosion of public relations and media manipulation we live with today— before, not to put too fine a point on it, Ronald Reagan. . . .

FLORIAN AND CARTER stood at the rail of the yacht, staring out over the harbor. The bay was a bowl of moonlight in which a black dot bobbed.

"Here he comes now," said Florian. "You go below and keep out of sight."

"Sure it wouldn't be safer if I stuck around?" Carter asked. "You know how these crackpots are. I don't like this cloak-and-dagger routine, the way he insisted on coming out alone at night—"

"I'll handle him," Florian said. "Just run along and leave everything to me."

Carter left. Florian watched the rowboat approach, tossed out a line as it heaved to, and waited while its occupant clambered up the rope ladder to the deck.

The newcomer was a squat, gray-haired man, wearing heavy bifocals and carrying a worn leather brief case.

"Good evening," said Florian. "You're Professor—"

"Please," murmured the visitor. "No names."

Florian shrugged. "As you wish. But we're quite alone, I assure you. I sent the crew ashore for the night, just as you insisted when you phoned to set up this appointment."

"I know all this may seem melodramatic to you," the Professor told him. "But when I've explained, you'll understand the need for absolute secrecy." He cleared his throat. "I told them at the school that I was taking a leave of absence. Nobody knows I'm here. Nobody must ever know."

"You have my word," Florian said. "Now, shall we go into the cabin and get down to business?"

He led the way. The interior of the cabin resembled an executive's office, complete with intercom, teletype, and a battery of phones on the big steel desk. Florian slid into a seat behind the desk and waved the Professor to a leather lounge chair. "Drink?" he offered.

"Thank you, no." The Professor smiled bleakly. "After spending nearly six months trying to set up a meeting with you, I'm impatient to proceed." He unzipped his brief case. "It's an ironic paradox that the head of the largest public relations organization in the country has no time to see the public. But I assure you this interview will be important—to you, to myself, to the entire nation."

The Professor pulled a bulky manuscript from his brief case and placed it on the edge of the desk.

"Here it is," he said.

Florian frowned. "A book?"

"That's what it started out to be," the Professor answered. "When I sat down to write, three years ago, I intended to produce a text on political science. And then the idea came to me."

Florian started to reach for the manuscript but the Professor shook his head. "Don't touch it," he said. "It isn't a book now —it's a bomb."

"You mean you've developed a formula for some secret weapon?"

"In a way. Actually, it's neither new nor secret—but by carrying existing methods to their logical conclusion, I've created what might well be called a weapon. Of course my field is political science—"

"And mine is public relations," Florian told him. "What has all this to do with me?"

The Professor leaned forward. "How would you like to run this country?" he asked softly. "How would you like—*to own the world?*"

"Really, now—"

The Professor tapped his manuscript with a blunt forefinger. "Here's the blueprint," he said. "The perfect combination of political science and applied public relations that will do the job."

Florian sat back. "I'm afraid I'm not too impressed," he murmured. "After all, I've read a few books myself. *The Hidden Persuaders. The Lonely Crowd.* It isn't exactly news to me that voters can be manipulated by advertising and mass psychological techniques. In fact, our organization has been active in political campaigns behind the scenes for some years now. I know a little something about how to sell a candidate as if he were a piece of merchandise."

The Professor nodded. "We've come a long way," he said. "Less than a hundred years ago, Abraham Lincoln sat in his room at the home of Judge Wills in a dusty little Pennsylvania town, on the evening before the dedication ceremonies of a soldiers' cemetery, working with a pencil on the final draft of the Gettysburg Address. Today, our candidates and holders of political offices work with a staff of consultants—ghost writers, gag writers, idea men to feed them material; psychologists to mold their personalities into ideal father-images for the masses; advertising agencies to devise their slogans and conduct their campaigns with television spot-announcements in place of speeches; press secretaries to control or even write their public statements once they take office."

"I know all that," Florian said.

"And you probably know, too, that the old-fashioned political campaign is a thing of the past. There's nothing spontaneous about the rallies or the handshaking tours any more—every movement is planned and rehearsed. Presidential conventions are staged like Broadway shows. TV appearances require the services of a producer, a voice coach, camera and lighting experts, make-up artists, and little men with teleprompters."

Florian yawned. "So what?" he said. "Everyone knows how candidates are selected nowadays. Take a man with a clean record, a good safe middle-of-the-road attitude, and then package and sell him to the consumer with tested techniques. You can teach him how to smile and how to talk. Hell, that's been done by public relations outfits all over the country ever since television came in. And they use everything from soft-sell for the liberals to pure corn for the yokels, complete with hillbilly bands and dancing girls." He lit a cigar. "What you're trying to tell me is that political science is dead and show biz has taken over. Is that it?"

"That's what gave me the idea," the Professor said. "When I began to study just these things you've mentioned. How the people from the entertainment world have gradually infiltrated politics as advisors, producers, technicians. How they've tried to train our politicians and office holders to behave like actors. And it occurred to me then—why not *use* actors?"

Florian sat up. He put his cigar in the ashtray. "What's that, again?"

"I said, *why not use actors?* You said yourself that almost any man who starts with a clean record and a noncommittal attitude can be built into a political figure by means of present-day psychological techniques. The trick is to teach him to speak, to handle himself properly when on public display. So why waste time with tired old men or egotistical prima donnas who can't cope with their roles? If politics is show business, why not put the right actors into the parts to begin with?"

The Professor stood up. He began to pace the floor, and Florian followed him with his eyes.

"Think of the possibilities," the Professor went on tensely. "No more hit-or-miss campaigning. You cast men for public offices just the way you'd cast them for a show. It's just the matter of building the proper psychological image for any given locality. Prefabricate the right character and select the type of actor who fits that role—the Courageous Leader, the Elder Statesman, the Champion of Minority Groups, the Man from the Prairie, the Fighting D.A., the Boy Wonder."

Florian's eyes narrowed. "Is this what you've written about?"

The Professor nodded. "I told you I had a blueprint," he said. "It's all down in detail—analysis and methodology. You scout the country for likely prospects. Of course it will cost money and most of the preliminary work will have to be conducted in the utmost secrecy—but then, the big political organizations are used to that. The men who control them would be willing to put up the finances if we could guarantee success. And they'd be willing to wait, too. Naturally, we couldn't expect to take over the key offices in the nation overnight. We'd be starting from scratch, with unknowns. But the point is, we'd have a tremendous advantage: *our* unknowns would be real actors. They'd look the part, sound as convincing as big-time commercial announcers. We could bring them up the ladder fast. Aldermen, judges, then members of the state legislatures, then on to governorships, the House of Representatives, the Senate, the important appointive offices, the Cabinet, even the Presidency itself—oh, it might take fifteen years before we had a working majority in all the right places, but think of what power we'd wield then! And I tell you, the time is ripe for just such a move. I can feel it coming—it's inevitable! The public is already more than half sold on just this type of candidate, synthetically created. We can give them the real thing and take over the country!"

The Professor sank back into his chair. "Well?" he said.

Florian shook his head. "You're crazy. Absolutely stark, staring mad." He gestured at the manuscript. "If that's what you've been writing about, I advise you to burn this."

The Professor snatched the bulky sheaf and shoved it into his brief case. "All right," he muttered. "If you don't see it, I'm sure somebody else will. There are other public relations outfits, you know. Maybe they're not quite as big or quite as important, but I assure you any one of them could be or will be if they listen to my proposition."

"I take it, then, that you intend to present this idea elsewhere?"

"Naturally. It may take another six months to get a hearing, but I'm willing to spend the time. Because I believe in this idea. I believe that anyone with the vision and enterprise to carry out my methods can rule this nation, and eventually rule the world."

Florian sighed. "Nothing I can possibly say would dissuade you? You're sure of that?"

"Absolutely sure."

The Professor started to rise—but he never made it. Florian opened a desk drawer, pulled out a small revolver, and shot the Professor right through the center of his forehead.

CARTER CAME RUNNING in. "Oh, my God!" he muttered. "You did it!"

"Don't panic," said Florian. "We'll put the body in the boat and tow it outside the harbor. Then we'll sink the body with weights and turn the boat adrift. It will look like an accident —if anyone ever finds out. He assured me no one knew he was coming here, so we won't be implicated."

"It's risky," Carter murmured.

"Of course. But there was no choice."

"He knew?"

Florian nodded. "Yes, he'd even written a book about how to do it—figured it pretty accurately, too. It was his idea that a public relations outfit, with well-heeled backing, could turn a gang of professional actors from unknowns into key political figures in just about fifteen years. And he'd hit on most of the methods, too. So you see, I had no choice." Florian grimaced and pointed at the revolver. "It was either a matter of using that or of telling him you and I got the same idea and started working on it a few years ago."

Florian glanced at his watch. "Which reminds me, there should be a call coming in from Washington any minute now.

Maybe I'd better stick around. You can handle the body alone, can't you?"

Carter made a face. "I suppose so. But tell me, why do I always get stuck with the dirty work?"

Florian smiled at him. "That's show biz," he said.

THE INCORPORATED

BY JOHN SHIRLEY

From Robert Bloch's eerily prescient tale of PR manipulation, we move to an extrapolation into the distant future on the same theme. How far would the Powers That Be go to keep their secrets secret? John Shirley offers a disturbing answer in a story that brings new meaning to the term "intellectual property."

KESSLER WAS WALKING east on Fourteenth Street, looking for something. He wasn't sure what he was looking for. He was walking through a twilight made raw by a mist-thin November rain sharpening the edge of a cold wind. The wind slashed at his acrylic overcoat. The street was almost deserted. He was looking for something, something; the brutally colorless word *something* hung heavily in his mind like an empty picture frame.

What he thought he wanted was to get in, out of the weather; he felt a vague resentment to the city of New York for letting the weather modification system break down again. Walking in rain made you feel naked. And acid rain, he thought, could make you naked, if you wore the kind of synthreads that reacted with the acids.

Up ahead the eternal neon butterfly of a Budweiser sign glowed sultry orange-red and blue; the same design since sometime in the 20th century. He angled across the sidewalk, pitted concrete the color of dead skin, hurrying toward the sign, toward the haven of a bar. The rain was already beginning to burn. He closed his eyes against it, afraid it would burn his corneas.

He pushed through the smudged door into the bar. The bartender glanced up, nodded, and reached under the counter for a towel; he passed the towel across to Kessler. The towel was treated with acid-absorbents; it helped immediately.

"Get any in your eyes?" the bartender asked, with no great show of concern.

"No, I don't think so." He handed the towel back. "Thanks."

The tired-faced men drinking at the bar hardly glanced at Kessler. He was unremarkable: round-faced, with short black hair streaked blue-white to denote his work in video-editing;

large friendly brown eyes, soft red mouth pinched now with worry; a standard print-out greyblue suit.

The bartender said something else, but it didn't register. Kessler was staring at the glowing green lozenge of a credit transferral kiosk in the back of the dim, old-fashioned bar. He crossed to it and stepped in; the door hissed shut behind him. The small TV screen on the front of the phone lit up, and its electronic letters asked him, DO YOU WANT CALL, OR ENTRY?

What did he want? Why had he come here? He wasn't sure. But it felt right. A wave of reassurance had come over him. . . . Ask it what your balance is, a soundless voice whispered to him. A soft, maternal mental whisper. Again a wave of reassurance. But he thought: something's out of place. . . . He knew his mind as a man knows his cluttered desk; he knows when someone has moved something on his desk. Or in his mind. And someone had.

He punched Entry and it asked him his account number and entry code number and security code. He punched all three sets of digits in, then told it he wanted to see his bank balance. It told him to wait. Numbers appeared on the screen.

$NB 760,000.

He stared at it. He punched for error check and confirmation.

The bank's computer insisted that he had seven hundred and sixty thousand NewBux in his bank account. There should be only four thousand.

Something was missing from his memory; something had been added to his bank account.

They tampered with me, he thought, and then they paid me for it. Who?

He requested the name of the depositor. The screen told him: UNRECORDED.

Julie. Talk to Julie. There was just no one else he discussed his projects with till they were patented and on-line. No one. His wife had to know.

Julie. He could taste her name in his mouth. Her name tasted like bile.

JULIE HAD BEEN home only a few minutes, Kessler decided, as he closed the door behind him. Her coat was draped over the back of the couch, off-white on off-white. She liked things off-white or battleship grey or powder blue.

She was bent down to the minifridge behind the breakfast bar. She stood up, a frosted bottle of Stolichnaya in her hand. "Hi, Jimmy."

She almost never called him Jimmy.

Julie came out with a vodka straight up and a twist of lime for each of them. He'd learned to like vodka because she did. She padded across the powder-blue rug in bare feet, small feet sexy in sheer hose; she was tall and slender and long-necked. Her hair was the yellow of split pine, cut short as a small boy's, and parted on the side. She was English, and looked it; her eyes were immaculate blue crystals. She wore her silk-lined, coarse-fiber, off-white dress suit. The suit with no shoes. She looked more natural in her suits than in anything else. She had "casuals" to wear at home, but somehow she never wore them. Maybe because that would be a concession to homelife, would almost be a betrayal of the Corporation Family. Like having children. What was it she said about having children? *If you don't mind, I'll continue to resist the programming of my biological computer. When DNA talks, I don't listen. I don't like being pushed into something by a molecule.* He took off his coat, hung it up, and sat down beside her on the couch. The vodka, chilled with no ice, waited for him on the glass coffee table. He took a drink and said, "There's seven hundred and sixty thousand NewBux in my bank account." He looked at her. "What did they take?"

Her eyes went a little glassy. "Seven hundred and sixty thousand? Computer error."

"You know it's not." He took another sip. The Stoly was

syrupy thick from being kept in the freezer. "What did you tell Worldtalk?"

"Are you accusing me of something?" She said it with her icy Vassar incredulousness then, like: I can't believe anyone could be so painfully unsophisticated.

"I'm accusing Worldtalk. You're theirs. They do as they like with you. If Worldtalk says it's not productive to have kids, if Worldtalk says it's not *teamplaying* to have kids, you don't have kids. Even when their disapproval is unnecessary: You wouldn't have had to quit your job—I can understand you wanting to have a career. We could have had the kid in a hired womb or an artificial womb. I would've taken care of it during the day. If Worldtalk says listen for Usefuls, you listen. Even at home. They don't want employees, at Worldtalk, they want to *own you.*"

"It's pointless to go over and over this. Worldtalk has nothing to do with my decision not to have children. I worked eight years—"

"I know it by rote: You worked eight years to be assistant New York manager in the country's biggest PR and advertising outfit. You tell me *having children* is demeaning yourself! Eight years you licked Grimwald's boots! Going to Worldtalk's family sessions, letting them psych you up after work for hours at a time, co-opting your instincts!"

She stood up, arms rigid at her sides. "Well, why not? Corporation families *last.*"

"It isn't a real family. They're using you. Look what they got you to do! To *me.*"

"You got some seven hundred thousand NewBux. That's more than you would ever have made on any of your hare-brained schemes. If you worked for a corp you'd be making decent money in the first place. You insist on being freelance so you're left out in the cold, and you should be grateful for what they—" she snipped the sentence in two with a brisk sibilance, and turned away.

"So we've dropped the pretenses now. You're saying I

should be grateful for the money Worldtalk gave me. Julie—
What did they take?"

"I don't *know!* You didn't tell me what you were working on—and anyway I don't believe they took anything. I—god damn it."

She went to the bathroom to pointedly take her Restem, making a lot of noise opening the prescription bottle so he'd hear and know it was his fault she had to take a tranquilizer.

BASCOMB WAS DRUNK and drugged. The disorder of his mind was splashed onto the room around him: the dancers, the lights, the holograms that made it look, in the smoky dimness, as if someone was there dancing beside you who wasn't. A touristy couple on the dance floor stopped and stared at another couple: horned, half human, half reptiles, she with her tongue darting from between rouged lips; he with baroque filips of fire flicking from his scaly nostrils. The touristy couple laughed off their embarrassment when the deejay turned off the holo and the demon couple vanished.

Bascomb chuckled and sucked some of his cocaine fizz through a straw that lit up with miniature advertisements when it was used; lettering flickering luminous green up and down its length.

Sitting beside him, Kessler squirmed on his barstool and ordered another Scotch. He didn't like Bascomb like this. Bascomb was young, tanned, and preppie; he wore a Japanese Action Suit now, a kind of clinging, faintly iridescent jumpsuit. He was used to seeing Bascomb in his office, a neat component of Featherstone, Pestlestein, and Bascomb, Attorneys at Law, friendly but not too friendly, intense but controlled. My own fault, Kessler told himself: chase the guy down when he's off-work, hassle his wives till they tell me where he hangs out, find out things I don't want to know about the guy. Like the fact that he's bisexual and flirting with the waiter.

The bar was circular, rotating slowly through the club, leaving the dance floor behind now to arrive at the cruising rooms. As they talked it turned slowly past flesh-pink holographic porn squirmings and edged into the soft music lounge. Each room had its own idiosyncratic darkness, shot through with the abstracted glamor of the candy-apple red and hot pink and electric blue neon tubes running up the corners to zig-zag the ceiling like a time-lapse photo of night-time city traffic.

Bascomb turned on his stool to look at the porn and the live copulation; his mouth was open in a lax smile. Kessler looked over his shoulder. Again in the dimness the holos were nearly indistinguishable from the real article; a drunken swinger tried to fondle a woman with four breasts, only to walk through her. "Do we have to talk here?" Kessler asked, turning back to the bar.

Bascomb ignored the question. "The bottom line, Jim, is that you are a nobody. Now if you were, say, a Nobel-Prize-winning professor at Stanford, we might be able to get you your day in court, we might get a Grand Jury to investigate the people at Worldtalk . . ." Talking without taking his eyes off the intermingled porn and people. "But as it is you're a mildly successful video editor who makes a hobby of working up a lot of media theories. Every day some crank looking for attention announces a Great Idea has been stolen from his brain, and ninety-nine percent of the time they turn out to be paranoid or a liar or both. I'm not saying you're a paranoid or a liar. I believe you. I'm just saying I'm probably the only one who will."

"But I have the seven-hundred-sixty-thousand—"

"Did you request the name of the depositor?"

"Unrecorded."

"Then how are you going to prove a connection?"

"I don't know. But I know an idea was stolen from me. I want it back, Bascomb. And I can't work it up again on my own from scratch—I wouldn't know where to begin; it was all on a disk, and in paper files. Both are gone. They took all my notes, everything that could lead me back to it . . ."

"Sucks," Bascomb said sympathetically. They had rotated into the lounge; people on couches watched videos and conversed softly. Sometimes they were talking to holos; you knew when you were talking to a holo because they said outrageous things. They were programmed that way to ease the choking boredom of lounge bar conversation. "I want it back, Bascomb," Kessler repeated, his knuckles white on the rim of the bar.

Bascomb shrugged and said, "You haven't been in this country long; maybe you don't know how it works. First off, you have to understand that . . ." he paused to sip from his cocaine fizz; he became more animated almost instantly, chattering on: "you have to understand that you can't get it back the way it was taken. Whoever it was probably came in while you were asleep. Which adds credence to your theory that Julie was involved. She waits up or pretends to sleep, lets them in, they shoot you up with the receptivity drug. The beauty of the RD is that it works instantly and not only makes you cerebral-program receptive but keeps you sedated. They put the wires and tubes in through the sinuses, but they don't damage anything. They've got lots of microsurgicals in the big box they've brought with them, right? They look at the screen they've set up that translates your impulses into a code they can understand. They get some dream free-association maybe. But that tells them they're 'on line' in your brain. Then they put a request to the brain, fed into it in the form of neurohumoral transmitter molecules they manufacture in their box—"

"How do you know so much about this?" Kessler asked, unable to keep the edge of suspicion out of his voice.

"We get a case like yours once or twice a year. I did a lot of research on it. The ACLU has a small library on the subject. It really gets their goat. We didn't win those cases, by the way; they're tough . . ." He paused to sip his fizz, his eyes sparkling and dilated.

Kessler was annoyed by Bascomb's treating his case like a

curiosity, a conversation piece. "Let's get back to what happened to me."

"Okay, uh—so they made a request to the biological computer we call a brain, right? They asked it what it knew about whatever it was they wanted to take from you, and your brain automatically begins to think about it, and sends signals to the cortex of the temporal lobes or to the hippocampus; they 'ride' the electrochemical signals back to the place where the information is stored. They use tracer molecules that attach themselves to the chemical signals. When they reach the hippocampus or the temporal lobes, the tracer molecules act as enzymes to command the brain to simply unravel that particular chemical code. They break it down on the molecular level. They extract some things connected to it, and the chain of ideas that led to it, but they don't take so much they make you an idiot because they probably want your wife to cooperate and to stay with Worldtalk. Anyway, the brain chemistry is such that you can ask the brain a question with neurohumoral transmitter molecules, but you can't imprint on the memory, in an orderly way. You can feed in experiences, things which seem to be happening now—you can even implant them so they crop up at a given stimulus—but you can't feed in ready made *memories*. Probably because memories are holographic, involving complexes of cell groups. Like you can pull a thread to unravel a coat fairly easily but you can't ravel it back up so easily . . . Look at that exquisite creature over there. She's lovely, isn't she? Like to do some imprinting on her. I wonder if she's real. Uh, anyway . . . you can't put it back *in*. They take out, selectively, any memory of anything that might make you suspect they tampered with you, but lots of people begin to suspect anyway, because when they free associate over familiar pathways of the brain and then come to a gap—well, it's jarring. But they can't prove anything."

"Okay, so maybe it can't be put back by direct feed-in to the

His mother's wind chimes. His mother standing on the front porch, smiling absently, watching him play, and now and then she would reach up and tinkle the wind chimes with her finger. . . . He swallowed another tot of vodka to smear over the chalky scratch of loneliness.

"You really ought to get some sleep, Jimmy." A faint note of strain in her voice.

He was scared to go in there.

This is stupid, he thought. I don't know for sure it was her.

He forced himself to put the glass down, to stand, to walk to the bedroom, to do it all as if he weren't forcing himself through the membranes of his mistrust. He stood in the doorway and looked at her for a moment. She was wearing her silk lingerie. Her back to him. He could see her face reflected in the window to her left. Her eyes were open wide. In them he saw determination and self-disgust and he knew she had contacted them and the strangers were going to do it to him again. They would come and take out more this time, his conversation with Bascomb, his misgivings. They would take away the hush money they had paid him since he had shown he was unwilling to accept it without pushing to get back what he had lost. . . . They would take his argument with Julie . . .

Go along with it, he told himself.

That would be the intelligent solution. Let them do it. Sweet nepenthe. The pain and the fear and the anger would go with the memories. And he would have his relationship with his wife back. Such as it was.

He thought about it for a moment. She turned to look at him.

"No," he said finally. "No, we don't have enough between us to make it worthwhile. No. Tell them I said next they'll have to try and kill me."

She stared at him. Then she lay back, and looked at the ceiling.

He closed the bedroom door softly behind him, and went to the closet for his coat.

They hadn't taken the money yet. It was still there in his account. He had gone to an all night banking kiosk, sealed himself in, and now he looked at the figure, $NB 760,000 and felt a kind of glow. He punched for the telephone, and called Charlie Chesterton.

The screen asked him, you want visual? No, he told it, not yet.

"Sap?" came Charlie's voice. "Huzatunwushant?"

Wake Charlie out of a sound sleep, and he talked Technicki. He'd said, *What's happenin'? Who's that and what do you want?*

"Talk standard with me, Charlie. It's—"

"Hey, my man Kessler, what's happening, man! Hey, how come no visual?"

"I didn't know what you were doing. I'm ever discreet." He punched for visual and a small TV image of Charlie appeared below the phone's keyboard. Charlie wore a triple mohawk, each fin a different color, each color significant; red in the middle for Technicki Radical Unionist; blue on the right for his profession, video tech; green on the left for his neighborhood: New Brooklyn. He grinned, showing front teeth imprinted with his initials in gold, another tacky technicki fad. And Charlie wore a picture t-shirt that showed a movie: Fritz Lang's *Metropolis,* now moving through the flood scene.

"You went to sleep wearing your movie t-shirt, you oughta turn it off, wear out the batteries."

"Recharges from sunlight," Charlie said. "You call me to talk about my sleeping habits?"

"Need your help. Right now, I need the contact numbers for that Shanghai bank that takes the transferrals under a code of anonymity. . . ."

"I told you man, that's like, the border of legality, and maybe over it. You understand that first, right?"

Kessler nodded.

"Okay. Set your screen to record . . ."

BASCOMB'S OFFICE WAS too warm; Bascomb had a problem with his circulation. The walls were a milky yellow that seemed to quicken the heat somehow. Bascomb sat behind the blond-wood desk, wearing a stenciled-on three-piece suit, smiling a smile of polite bafflement. Kessler sat across from him, feeling he was on some kind of treadmill, because Bascomb just kept saying, "I really am quite sure no such meeting took place." He chuckled. "I know the club very well and I'm sure I'd remember if I'd been there that night. Haven't been there for a month."

"You weren't enthusiastic about it, but you ended by telling me we'd take 'em on." But the words were ashes in Kessler's mouth. He knew what had happened because there was not even the faintest trace of duplicity or nervousness on Bascomb's face. Bascomb really didn't remember. "So you won't represent me on this," Kessler went on. Only half a question.

"We really have no experience with brain tampering—"

"I could get the court files to prove that you have. But they'd only . . ." He shook his head. Despair was something he could smell and taste and feel, like acid rain. "They'd tamper with you again. Just to make their point."

He walked out of the office, hurrying, thinking: They'll have the place under surveillance. But no one stopped him outside.

CHARLIE WAS OFF on one of his amateur analyses, and there was nothing Kessler could do, he had to listen, because Charlie was covering for him.

". . . I mean," Charlie was saying, "now your average

Technicki speaks standard English like an infant, am I right, and can't read except command codes, and learned it all from vidteaching, and he's trained to do this and that and to fix this and that but he's, like, socially inhibited from rising in the ranks because the socio-economic elite speaks standard good and reads—"

"If they really want to, they can learn what they need, like you did," Kessler said irritably. He was standing at the window, looking out at the empty, glossy ceramic streets. The artificial island, a boro-annex of Brooklyn anchored in the harbor, was almost deserted at this hour; everyone had either gone into the city, or home to holo, or into a tavern. The floating boros were notoriously dull. The squat floboro housing, rounded off at the corners like a row of molars, stood in silence, a few windows glowing like radarscopes against the night.

But they could be watching me, Kessler thought. A hundred ways they could be watching me and I'd see nothing.

He turned, stepped away from the window. Charlie was pacing, arms clasped behind him, head bent, playing the part of the young, boldly theorizing leader of radical politicos.

The apartment was crowded with irregular shelves of books and boxes of software and cassettes and compact disks; Charlie had hung silk scarves in The Three Colors, blurring like multicolor smoke. "I mean," Charlie went on, "you can talk about our job security but it's a sham—"

A warning chill: and Kessler turned, looked out the window. Three stories down she was a powder-blue keyhole shape against the faint petroleum rainbow filminess of the street. She was looking at the numbers.

She might have guessed, he told himself. She met Charlie once. She might have looked Charlie's address up in ref disk. She went to the front door. Charlie's bell chimed. He went to the screen and looked. "It's your wife," he said. "You want me to tell her you went overseas? Japan?"

"Let her in."

"Are you kidding, man? You are, right? She was the one who—"

"Just let her in." She got it from the address list, he told himself. There was a cocktail of emotions in him. There was a relief at seeing her, shaken in with something that buzzed like a smoke alarm, and it wasn't till she was at the door that he realized that the sensation was terror. And then Julie was standing in the doorway, against the light of the hallway. She looked beautiful. The light behind her abruptly cut: an energy saving device sensing that no one was now in the hall; suddenly she stood framed in darkness. The buzzing fizzed up, and overwhelmed the relief. His mouth was dry.

Looking disgustedly at Kessler, Charlie shut the door behind her.

Kessler stared at her. Her eyes flickered, her mouth opened, and shut, and she shook her head. She looked drained.

And Kessler knew.

"They sent you. They told you where to find me," he said.

"They—want the money back," she said. "They want you to come with me."

He shook his head. "Don't you get sick of being puppeted?"

She looked at the window. Her face was blank. "You don't understand."

"Do you know why they do it, why they train you in that Americanized Japanese job conditioning stuff? To save themselves money. Because it eliminates unions."

"They have their reasons, sure. Mostly efficiency."

"I know. What's the slogan? 'Efficiency is friendship.'"

She looked embarrassed. "That's not—" She shrugged. "A Corporate Family is just as valid as any other. It's something you couldn't understand. I—I'll lose my job, Jimmy. If you don't come." She said *lose my job* the way Kessler would have said, *lose my life.*

Kessler said, "I'll think about going with you if you tell me what it was . . . what it was they took."

"They—took it from me too."

"I don't believe that. I never believed it. I think they left it intact in you, so you could watch to see if I stumbled on it again. I think you really loved them trusting you. Worldtalk is Mommy and Daddy and Mommy and Daddy trusted you . . ."

Her mouth twisted with resentment. "You bastard. I can't—"

"Yeah, you can. You have to. Otherwise Charlie and I are going out the back way and we're going to cause endless trouble for Worldtalk. And I know you, Julie—I'd know if you were making it up. So tell me what it was, what it really was."

She sighed. "I only know what you told me. You pointed out that P.R. companies manipulate the media for their clients without the public knowing it most of the time. They use their connections and channels to plant information or disinformation in news-sheet articles, on newsvid, in movies, in political speeches. So . . ." She paused and went on wearily, shrugging off her irritation. "So they're manipulating people, and the public gets a distorted view of what's going on because of special interests. You worked up an editing system that sensed probable examples of, uh, I think the phrases you used were 'implanted information' or 'special interest distortion.' So they could be weeded out. You called it the Media Alarm System." She let out a long breath. "I didn't know they'd go so far—I thought they'd buy out your system. In a way they did. I *had* to mention it at Worldtalk. If I didn't I would've been . . . disloyal." She said *disloyal* wincing, knowing what he would think.

But it was Charlie who said it: "What about loyalty to Jim Kessler?"

Her hand fluttered a dismissal. "It doesn't matter at this point whether it was wrong or right. It's too late. They *know.* . . . Jimmy, are you coming?"

Kessler was thinking about the Media Alarm System. It didn't sound familiar—but it sounded *right.* He said, slowly,

"No. You can help me. What they did is illegal as hell. If you testify, we can beat them."

"Jimmy, if I thought they—no, no. I—" She broke off, staring at his waist. "Don't be stupid. That's not—" She took a step back, and put her hand in her purse.

Kessler and Charlie looked at each other, traded puzzlement. When Kessler looked back at Julie, she had a gun in her hand. It was a small blue-metal pistol, its barrel tiny as a pencil, and that tiny barrel meant it fired explosive bullets. *They* had given it to her.

"Do you know what that gun will do?" Charlie was saying. "Those little explosive bullets will splash him all over the wall." His voice shook. He took a step toward her.

She pressed back against the door and said, "Charlie, if you come closer to me I'll shoot him." Charlie stopped. The room seemed to keen ultrasonically with sheer imminence. She went on, the words coming out in a rush: "Why don't you ask him what that thing in his hand would do to me, Charlie. Shall we? Ask him that. Jimmy has the same kind of gun. With the same goddamn bullets." Her voice was too high; she was breathing fast. Her knuckles white on the gun.

Kessler's arms were hanging at his side, his hands empty.

"Lower the gun, Julie, and we can talk," Charlie said gently.

"I'll lower mine when he lowers his," she said hoarsely.

"He isn't holding a gun," Charlie said.

She was staring at a space about three feet in front of Kessler's chest. She was seeing the gun there. He wanted to say, *Julie, they tampered with you.* He could only croak, "Julie—"

She shouted, "Don't!" and raised the gun. And then everything was moving: Kessler threw himself down. Charlie jumped at her, and the wall behind Kessler jumped outward toward the street.

Two hot metal hands clapped Kessler's head between them and he shouted with pain and thought he was dead. But it was only a noise, the noise of the wall exploding outward. Chips of

wall pattered down; smoke sucked out through the four foot
hole in the wall into the winter night.

Kessler got up, shaky, his ears ringing. He looked around,
and saw Charlie straddling Julie. He had the gun in his hand
and she was face down, sobbing.

"Gogidoutere," Charlie said, lapsing into Technicki, his
face white.

"Get off her," Kessler said. Charlie stood up beside her. "Julie, look at me," Kessler said softly. She tilted her head back,
an expression of dignified defiance trembling precariously in
her face. Then her eyes widened, and she looked at his hips.
She was seeing him holding a gun there. "I don't have a gun,
Julie. They put that into you. Now I'm going to *get* a gun. . . .
Give me the gun, Charlie." Without taking his eyes off her, he
put his hand out. Charlie hesitated, then laid the gun in Kessler's open palm. She blinked, then narrowed her eyes.

"So now you've got two guns." She shrugged.

He shook his head. "Get up." Moving stiffly, she stood up.
"Now go over there to Charlie's bed. He's got black bedsheets.
You see them? Take one off. Just pull it off and bring it over
here." She started to say something, anger lines punctuating
her mouth, and he said quickly, "Don't talk yet. Do it!" She
went to the bed, pulled the black satin sheet off, and dragged
it over to him. Charlie gaped, and muttered that the cops
would come because of the explosion and would hold you for
days and weeks till they were sure of what had happened, but
Kessler had a kind of furious calm on him then, and he knew
what he was going to do, and if it didn't work then he'd let the
acid rain bleach his bones white as a warning to other travelers come to this poisoned well. This woman. He said, "Now
tear up the sheet—sorry, man, I'll replace it—and make a
blindfold. Good. Right. Now tie it over my eyes. Use the tape
on the table to make the blindfold light-proof."

Moving in slow motion, she blindfolded him. Darkness
whispered down around him. She taped it thoroughly in place.
"Now am I still pointing two guns at you?"

"Yes." But there was uncertainty in her voice.

"Now take a step to one side. No, take several steps, very softly, move around a lot." The soft sounds of her movement. Her gasp. "Is the gun following you around the room?"

"Yes. Yes. One of them."

"But how is that possible? *I can't see you!* And why did I let you blindfold me if I'm ready and willing to shoot you?"

"You look weird like that, man. Ridiculous and scary," Charlie said.

"Shut up, Charlie, will you? Answer me, Julie! I can't see you! How can I follow you with the guns?"

"I don't know!" Her voice cracking.

"Take the guns from my hands! Shoot me! Do it!"

She made a short hissing sound, and took the gun from his hand, and he braced to die. But she pulled the blindfold away and looked at him.

Looked into his eyes.

She let the gun drop to the floor. Kessler said, softly: "You see now? They did it to you. You, one of the 'family.' The corporate 'family' means just exactly nothing to them."

She looked at his hands. "No gun. No gun." Dreamily. "Gun's gone. Everything's different."

Siren warblings. Coming closer.

She sank to her knees. "Just exactly nothing to them," she said. "Just exactly nothing." Her face crumpled. She looked as if she'd fallen into herself, some inner scaffolding had been kicked out of place.

Sirens and lights outside. A chrome fluttering in the smoky gap where the wall had been blown outward; a police surveillance bird. It looked like a bird, hovering in place with its oversized aluminum hummingbird's wings; but instead of a head it had a small camera lens. A transmitted voice droned from a grid on its silvery belly: *"This is the police. You are now being observed and taped. Do not attempt to leave. The front door has been breached. Police officers will arrive in seconds to take your statements. Repeat—"*

"Oh, I heard you," Julie said, in a hollow voice. "I'll make a statement all right. I've got a lot to tell you. Oh yeah." She laughed sadly. "I'll make a statement . . ."

Kessler bent down, and touched her arm. "Hey . . . I—"

She drew back from him. "Don't touch me. Just don't! You love to be right. I'm going to tell them. Just don't touch me."

But he stayed with her. He and Charlie stood looking at the blue smoke drifting out the ragged hole in the wall; at the mechanical, camera-eyed bird looking back at them.

He stayed with her, as he always would, and they listened for the footsteps outside the door.

DOGWALKER

BY ORSON SCOTT CARD

A wiseass computer expert living in a body that's half cybernetics and half little boy teams up with an ex-pimp to score big in an on-line heist. All they need is a fingerprint and a password—or so they think. A moving and uncharacteristic story from the author of Ender's Game *and the* Tales of Alvin Maker *series.*

I WAS AN innocent pedestrian. Only reason I got in this in the first place was I got a vertical way of thinking and Dogwalker thought I might be useful, which was true, and also he said I might enjoy myself, which was a prefabrication, since people done a lot more enjoying on me than I done on them.

When I say I think vertical, I mean to say I'm metaphysical, that is, simular, which is to say, I'm dead but my brain don't know it yet and my feet still move. I got popped at age nine just lying in my own bed when the goat next door shot at his lady and it went through the wall and into my head. Everybody went to look at them cause they made all the noise, so I was a quart low before nobody noticed I been poked.

They packed my head with supergoo and light pipe, but they didn't know which neutron was supposed to butt into the next so my alchemical brain got turned from rust to diamond. Goo Boy. The Crystal Kid.

From that bright electrical day I never grew another inch, anywhere. Bullet went nowhere near my gonadicals. Just turned off the puberty switch in my head. Saint Paul said he was a eunuch for Jesus, but who am I a eunuch for?

Worst thing about it is here I am near thirty and I still have to take barkeepers to court before they'll sell me beer. And it ain't hardly worth it even though the judge prints out in my favor and the barkeep has to pay costs, because my corpse is so little I get toxed on six ounces and pass out pissing after twelve. I'm a lousy drinking buddy. Besides, anybody hangs out with me looks like a pederast.

No, I'm not trying to make you drippy-drop for me—I'm used to it, okay? Maybe the homecoming queen never showed me True Love in a four-point spread, but I got this knack that certain people find real handy and so I always made out. I dress good and I ride the worm and I don't pay much income tax. Because I am the Password Man. Give me five minutes with anybody's curriculum vitae, which is to say their auto-psychoscopy, and nine times out of ten I'll spit out their pass-word and get you into their most nasty sticky sweet secret files. Actually it's usually more like three times out of ten, but that's still a lot better odds than having a computer spend a year trying to push out fifteen characters to make just the right P-word, specially since after the third wrong try they string your phone number, freeze the target files, and call the dongs.

Oh, do I make you sick? A cute little boy like me, engaged in critical unspecified dispopulative behaviors? I may be half glass and four feet high, but I can simulate you better than your own mama, and the better I know you, the deeper my hooks. I not only know your password *now*, I can write a word on a paper, seal it up, and then you go home and *change* your password and then open up what I wrote and there it'll be, your *new* password, three times out of ten. I am *vertical*, and Dogwalker knowed it. Ten percent more supergoo and I wouldn't even be legally human, but I'm still under the line, which is more than I can say for a lot of people who are a hundred percent zoo inside their head.

Dogwalker comes to me one day at Carolina Circle, where I'm playing pinball standing on a stool. He didn't say nothing, just gave me a shove, so naturally he got my elbow in his balls. I get a lot of twelve-year-olds trying to shove me around at the arcades, so I'm used to teaching them lessons. Jack the Giant Killer. Hero of the fourth graders. I usually go for the stomach, only Dogwalker wasn't a twelve-year-old, so my el-bow hit low.

I knew the second I hit him that this wasn't no kid. I didn't know Dogwalker from God, but he gots the look, you know, like he been hungry before, and he don't care what he eats these days.

Only he got no ice and he got no slice, just sits there on the floor with his back up against the Eat Shi'ite game, holding his boodle and looking at me like I was a baby he had to diaper. "I hope you're Goo Boy," he says, "cause if you ain't, I'm gonna give you back to your mama in three little tupperware bowls." He doesn't sound like he's making a threat, though. He sounds like he's chief weeper at his own funeral.

"You want to do business, use your mouth, not your hands," I says. Only I say it real apoplectic, which is the same as apologetic except you are also still pissed.

"Come with me," he says. "I got to go buy me a truss. You pay the tax out of your allowance."

So we went to Ivey's and stood around in children's wear while he made his pitch. "One P-word," he says, "only there can't be no mistake. If there's a mistake, a guy loses his job and maybe goes to jail."

So I told him no. Three chances in ten, that's the best I can do. No guarantees. My record speaks for itself, but nobody's perfect, and I ain't even close.

"Come on," he says, "you got to have ways to make sure, right? If you can do three times out of ten, what if you find out more about the guy? What if you meet him?"

"Okay, maybe fifty-fifty."

"Look, we can't go back for seconds. So maybe you can't get it. But do you *know* when you ain't got it?"

"Maybe half the time when I'm wrong, I know I'm wrong."

"So we got three out of four that you'll know whether you got it?"

"No," says I. "Cause half the time when I'm right, I don't know I'm right."

"Shee-it," he says. "This is like doing business with my baby brother."

"You can't afford me anyway," I says. "I pull two dimes minimum, and you barely got breakfast on your gold card."

"I'm offering a cut."

"I don't want a cut. I want cash."

"Sure thing," he says. He looks around, real careful. As if

they wired the sign that said Boys Briefs Sizes 10–12. "I got an inside man at Federal Coding," he says.

"That's nothing," I says. "I got a bug up the First Lady's ass, and forty hours on tape of her breaking wind."

I got a mouth. I know I got a mouth. I especially know it when he jams my face into a pile of shorts and says, "Suck on this, Goo Boy."

I hate it when people push me around. And I know ways to make them stop. This time all I had to do was cry. Real loud, like he was hurting me. Everybody looks when a kid starts crying. "I'll be good." I kept saying it. "Don't hurt me no more! I'll be good."

"Shut up," he says. "Everybody's looking."

"Don't you ever shove me around again," I says. "I'm at least ten years older than you, and a hell of a lot more than ten years smarter. Now I'm leaving this store, and if I see you coming after me, I'll start screaming about how you zipped down and showed me the pope, and you'll get yourself a child-molesting tag so they pick you up every time some kid gets jollied within a hundred miles of Greensboro." I've done it before, and it works, and Dogwalker was no dummy. Last thing he needed was extra reasons for the dongs to bring him in for questioning. So I figured he'd tell me to get poked and that'd be the last of it.

Instead he says, "Goo Boy, I'm sorry, I'm too quick with my hands."

Even the goat who shot me never said he was sorry. My first thought was, what kind of sister is he, abjectifying right out like that. Then I reckoned I'd stick around and see what kind of man it is who emulsifies himself in front of a nine-year-old-looking kid. Not that I figured him to be purely sorrowful. He still just wanted me to get the P-word for him, and he knew there wasn't nobody else to do it. But most street pugs aren't smart enough to tell the right lie under pressure. Right away I knew he wasn't your ordinary street hook or low arm, pugging cause they don't have the sense to stick with any kind of job.

He had a deep face, which is to say his head was more than a hairball, by which I mean he had brains enough to put his hands in his pockets without seeking an audience with the pope. Right then was when I decided he was my kind of no-good lying son-of-a-bitch.

"What are you after at Federal Coding?" I asked him. "A record wipe?"

"Ten clean greens," he says. "Coded for unlimited international travel. The whole i.d., just like a real person."

"The President has a green card," I says. "The Joint Chiefs have clean greens. But that's all. The U.S. Vice-President isn't even cleared for unlimited international travel."

"Yes he is," he says.

"Oh, yeah, you know everything."

"I need a P. My guy could do us reds and blues, but a clean green has to be done by a burr-oak rat two levels up. My guy knows how it's done."

"They won't just have it with a P-word," I says. "A guy who can make green cards, they're going to have his finger on it."

"I know how to get the finger," he says. "It takes the finger and the password."

"You take a guy's finger, he might report it. And even if you persuade him not to, somebody's gonna notice that it's gone."

"Latex," he says. "We'll get a mold. And don't start telling me how to do my part of the job. You get P-words, I get fingers. You in?"

"Cash," I says.

"Twenty percent," says he.

"Twenty percent of pus."

"The inside guy gets twenty, the girl who brings me the finger, she gets twenty, and I damn well get forty."

"You can't just sell these things on the street, you know."

"They're worth a meg apiece," says he, "to certain buyers."

By which he meant Orkish Crime, of course. Sell ten, and my twenty percent grows up to be two megs. Not enough to be rich, but enough to retire from public life and maybe even pay for some high-level medicals to sprout hair on my face. I got to admit that sounded good to me.

So we went into business. For a few hours he tried to do it without telling me the baroque rat's name, just giving me data he got from his guy at Federal Coding. But that was real stupid, giving me second-hand face like that, considering he needed me to be a hundred percent sure, and pretty soon he realized that and brought me in all the way. He hated telling me anything, because he couldn't stand to let go. Once I knew stuff on my own, what was to stop me from trying to go into business for myself? But unless he had another way to get the P-word, he had to get it from me, and for me to do it right, I had to know everything I could. Dogwalker's got a brain in his head, even if it is all biodegradable, and so he knows there's times when you got no choice but to trust somebody. When you just got to figure they'll do their best even when they're out of your sight.

He took me to his cheap condo on the old Guilford College campus, near the worm, which was real congenital for getting to Charlotte or Winston or Raleigh with no fuss. He didn't have no soft floor, just a bed, but it was a big one, so I didn't reckon he suffered. Maybe he bought it back in his old pimping days, I figured, back when he got his name, running a string of bitches with names like Spike and Bowser and Prince, real hydrant leg-lifters for the tweeze trade. I could see that he used to have money, and he didn't anymore. Lots of great clothes, tailor-tight fit, but shabby, out of sync. The really old ones, he tore all the wiring out, but you could still see where the diodes used to light up. We're talking neanderthal.

"Vanity, vanity, all is profanity," says I, while I'm holding out the sleeve of a camisa that used to light up like an airplane coming in for a landing.

"They're too comfortable to get rid of," he says. But there's a twist in his voice so I know he don't plan to fool nobody.

"Let this be a lesson to you," says I. "This is what happens when a walker don't walk."

"Walkers do steady work," says he. "But me, when business was good, it felt bad, and when business was bad, it felt good. You walk cats, maybe you can take some pride in it. But you walk dogs, and you know they're getting hurt every time—"

"They got a built-in switch, they don't feel a thing. That's why the dongs don't touch you, walking dogs, cause nobody gets hurt."

"Yeah, so tell me, which is worse, somebody getting tweezed till they scream so some old honk can pop his pimple, or somebody getting half their brain replaced so when the old honk tweezes her she can't feel a thing? I had these women's bodies around me and I knew that they used to be people."

"You can be glass," says I, "and still be people."

He saw I was taking it personally. "Oh hey," says he, "you're under the line."

"So are dogs," says I.

"Yeah well," says he. "You watch a girl come back and tell about some of the things they done to her, and she's *laughing*, you draw your own line."

I look around his shabby place. "Your choice," says I.

"I wanted to feel clean," says he. "That don't mean I got to stay poor."

"So you're setting up this grope so you can return to the old days of peace and propensity."

"Propensity," says he. "What the hell kind of word is that? Why do you keep using words like that?"

"Cause I know them," says I.

"Well you *don't* know them," says he, "because half the time you get them wrong."

I showed him my best little-boy grin. "I know," says I. What I don't tell him is that the fun comes from the fact that almost nobody ever *knows* I'm using them wrong. Dogwalker's no ordinary pimp. But then the ordinary pimp doesn't bench himself halfway through the game because of a sprained moral qualm, by which I mean that Dogwalker had some stray diagonals in his head, and I began to think it might be fun to see where they all hooked up.

Anyway we got down to business. The target's name was Jesse H. Hunt, and I did a real job on him. The Crystal Kid really plugged in on this one. Dogwalker had about two pages of stuff—date of birth, place of birth, sex at birth (no changes since), education, employment history. It was like getting an armload of empty boxes. I just laughed at it. "You got a jack to the city library?" I asked him, and he shows me the wall outlet. I plugged right in, visual onto my pocket Sony, with my own little crystal head for ee-i-ee-i-oh. Not every goo-head can think clear enough to do this, you know, put out clean type just by thinking the right stuff out my left ear interface port.

I showed Dogwalker a little bit about research. Took me ten minutes. I know my way right through the Greensboro Public Library. I have P-words for every single librarian and I'm so ept that they don't even guess I'm stepping upstream through their access channels. From the Public Library you can get all the way into North Carolina Records Division in Raleigh, and from there you can jumble into federal personnel records anywhere in the country. Which meant that by nightfall on that most portentous day we had hardcopy of every document in Jesse H. Hunt's whole life, from his birth certificate and first grade report card to his medical history and security clearance reports when he first worked for the feds.

Dogwalker knew enough to be impressed. "If you can do all that," he says, "you might as well pug his P-word straight out."

"No puedo, putz," says I as cheerful as can be. "Think of the fed as a castle. Personnel files are floating in the moat—there's a few alligators but I swim real good. Hot data is deep in the dungeon. You can get in there, but you can't get out clean. And P-words—P-words are kept up the queen's ass."

"No system is unbeatable," he says.

"Where'd you learn that, from graffiti in a toilet stall? If the P-word system was even a little bit breakable, Dogwalker, the gentlemen you plan to sell these cards to would already be inside looking out at us, and they wouldn't need to spend a meg to get clean greens from a street pug."

Trouble was that after impressing Dogwalker with all the stuff I could find out about Jesse H., I didn't know that much more than before. Oh, I could guess at some P-words, but that was all it was—guessing. I couldn't even pick a P most likely to succeed. Jesse was one ordinary dull rat. Regulation good grades in school, regulation good evaluations on the job, probably gave his wife regulation lube jobs on a weekly schedule.

"You don't really think your girl's going to get his finger," says I with sickening scorn.

"You don't know the girl," says he. "If we needed his flipper she'd get molds in five sizes."

"You don't know this guy," says I. "This is the straightest opie in Mayberry. I don't see him cheating on his wife."

"Trust me," says Dogwalker. "She'll get his finger so smooth he won't even know she took the mold."

I didn't believe him. I got a knack for knowing things about people, and Jesse H. wasn't faking. Unless he started faking when he was five, which is pretty unpopulated. He wasn't going to bounce the first pretty girl who made his zipper tight. Besides which he was smart. His career path showed that he was always in the right place. The right people always seemed to know his name. Which is to say he isn't the kind whose brain can't run if his jeans get hot. I said so.

"You're really a marching band," says Dogwalker. "You can't tell me his P-word, but you're obliquely sure that he's a limp or a wimp."

"Neither one," says I. "He's hard and straight. But a girl starts rubbing up to him, he isn't going to think it's because she heard that his crotch is cantilevered. He's going to figure she wants something, and he'll give her string till he finds out what."

He just grinned at me. "I got me the best Password Man in the Triass, didn't I? I got me a miracle worker named Goo-Boy, didn't I? The ice-brain they call Crystal Kid. I got him, didn't I?"

"Maybe," says I.

"I got him or I kill him," he says, showing more teeth than a primate's supposed to have.

"You got me," says I. "But don't go thinking you can kill me."

He just laughs. "I got you and you're so good, you can bet I got me a girl who's at least as good at what she does."

"No such," says I.

"Tell me his P-word and then I'll be impressed."

"You want quick results? Then go ask him to give you his password himself."

Dogwalker isn't one of those guys who can hide it when he's mad. "I want quick results," he says. "And if I start thinking you can't deliver, I'll pull your tongue out of your head. Through your nose."

"Oh, that's good," says I. "I always do my best thinking when I'm being physically threatened by a client. You really know how to bring out the best in me."

"I don't want to bring out the best," he says. "I just want to bring out his password."

"I got to meet him first," says I.

He leans over me so I can smell his musk, which is to say I'm very olfactory and so I can tell you he reeked of testosterone, by which I mean ladies could fill up with babies just from sniffing his sweat. "Meet him?" he asks me. "Why don't we just ask him to fill out a job application?"

"I've read all his job applications," says I.

"How's a glass-head like you going to meet Mr. Fed?" says he. "I bet you're always getting invitations to the same parties as guys like him."

"I don't get invited to *grown-up* parties," says I. "But on the other hand, grown-ups don't pay much attention to sweet little kids like me."

He sighed. "You really have to meet him?"

"Unless fifty-fifty on a P-word is good enough odds for you."

All of a sudden he goes nova. Slaps a glass off the table and it breaks against the wall, and then he kicks the table over, and all the time I'm thinking about ways to get out of there unkilled. But it's me he's doing the show for, so there's no way I'm leaving, and he leans in close to me and screams in my face. "That's the last of your fifty-fifty and sixty-forty and three times in ten I want to hear about, Goo Boy, you hear me?"

And I'm talking real meek and sweet, cause this boy's twice my size and three times my weight and I don't exactly have no leverage. So I says to him, "I can't help talking in odds and percentages, Dogwalker, I'm vertical, remember? I've got glass channels in here, they spit out percentages as easy as other people sweat."

He slapped his hand against his own head. "This ain't exactly a sausage biscuit, either, but you know and I know that when you give me all them exact numbers it's all guesswork anyhow. You don't know the odds on this beakrat anymore than I do."

"I don't know the odds on *him*, Walker, but I know the odds on *me*. I'm sorry you don't like the way I sound so precise, but my crystal memory has every P-word I ever plumbed, which is to say I can give you exact to the third decimal percentages on when I hit it right on the first try after meeting the subject, and how many times I hit it right on the first try just from his curriculum vitae, and right now if I don't meet him and I go on just what I've got here you have a 48.838 percent chance I'll be right on my P-word first time and a 66.667 chance I'll be right with one out of three."

Well that took him down, which was fine I must say because he loosened up my sphincters with that glass-smashing table-tossing hot-breath-in-my-face routine he did. He stepped back and put his hands in his pockets and leaned against the wall. "Well I chose the right P-man, then, didn't I," he says, but he doesn't smile, no, he *says* the back-down words but his eyes don't back down, his eyes say don't try to flash my face because I see through you, I got most excellent inward shades all polarized to keep out your glitz and see you straight and clear. I never saw eyes like that before. Like he knew me. Nobody ever knew me, and I didn't think he *really* knew me either, but I didn't like him looking at me as if he *thought* he knew me cause the fact is *I* didn't know me all that well and it worried me to think he might know me better than I did, if you catch my drift.

"All I have to do is be a little lost boy in a store," I says.

"What if he isn't the kind who helps little lost boys?"

"Is he the kind who lets them cry?"

"I don't know. What if he is? What then? Think you can get away with meeting him a second time?"

"So the lost boy in the store won't work. I can crash my bicycle on his front lawn. I can try to sell him cable magazines."

But he was ahead of me already. "For the cable magazines he slams the door in your face, if he even comes to the door at all. For the bicycle crash, you're out of your little glass brain. I got my inside girl working on him right now, very complicated, because he's not the playing around kind, so she has to make this a real emotional come-on, like she's breaking up with a boyfriend and he's the only shoulder she can cry on, and his wife is so lucky to have a man like him. This much he can believe. But then suddenly he has this little boy crashing in his yard, and because he's paranoid, he begins to wonder if some weird rain isn't falling, right? I know he's paranoid because you don't get to his level in the fed without you know how to watch behind you and kill the enemy even before *they* know they're out to get you. So he even suspects, for one instant, that somebody's setting him up for something, and what does he do?"

I knew what Dogwalker was getting at now, and he was right, and so I let him have his victory and I let the words he wanted march out all in a row. "He changes all his passwords, all his habits, and watches over his shoulder all the time."

"And my little project turns into compost. No clean greens."

So I saw for the first time why this street boy, this ex-pimp, why he was the one to do this job. He wasn't vertical like me, and he didn't have the inside hook like his fed boy, and he didn't have bumps in his sweater so he couldn't do the girl part, but he had eyes in his elbows, ears in his knees, by which I mean he noticed everything there was to notice and then he thought of new things that weren't even noticeable yet and noticed them. He earned his forty percent. And he earned part of my twenty, too.

Now while we waited around for the girl to fill Jesse's empty aching arms and get a finger off him, and while we were still working on how to get me to meet him slow and easy and sure, I spent a lot of time with Dogwalker. Not that he ever asked me, but I found myself looping his bus route every morning till he picked me up, or I'd be eating at Bojan-gle's when he came in to throw cajun chicken down into his ulcerated organs. I watched to make sure he didn't mind, cause I didn't want to piss this boy, having once beheld the majesty of his wrath, but if he wanted to shiver me he gave me no shiv.

Even after a few days, when the ghosts of the cold hard street started haunting us, he didn't shake me, and that includes when Bellbottom says to him, "Looks like you stopped walking dogs. Now you pimping little boys, right? Little cata-mites, we call you Catwalker now, that so? Or maybe you just keep him for private use, is that it? You be Boypoker now?" Well like I always said, someday somebody's going to kill Bellbottom just to flay him and use his skin for a convertible

roof, but Dogwalker just waved and walked on by while I
made little pissy bumps at Bell. Most people shake me right
off when they start getting splashed on about liking little
boys, but Doggy, he didn't say we were friends or nothing, but
he didn't give me no Miami howdy, neither, which is to say I
didn't find myself floating in the Bermuda Triangle with my
ass pulled down around my ankles, by which I mean he wasn't
ashamed to be seen with me on the street, which don't sound
like a six-minute orgasm to you but to me it was like a breeze
in August, I didn't ask for it and I don't trust it to last but as
long as it's there I'm going to like it.

How I finally got to meet Jesse H. was dervish, the best I
ever thought of. Which made me wonder why I never thought
of it before, except that I never before had Dogwalker like a
parrot saying "stupid idea" every time I thought of something.
By the time I finally got a plan that he didn't say "stupid
idea," I was almost drowned in the deepest lightholes of my
lucidity. I mean I was going at a hundred watts by the time I
satisfied him.

First we found out who did babysitting for them when Jesse
H. and Mrs. Jesse went out on the town (which for Nice People in G-boro means walking around the mall wishing there
was something to do and then taking a piss in the public
john). They had two regular teenage girls who usually came
over and ignored their children for a fee, but when these
darlettes were otherwise engaged, which meant they had a
contract to get squeezed and poked by some half-zipped boy in
exchange for a humbuger and a vid, they called upon Mother
Hubbard's Homecare Hotline. So I most carefully assinuated
myself into Mother Hubbard's estimable organization by passing myself off as a lamentably prepubic fourteen-year-old, spe-
cializing in the northwest section of town and on into the
county. All this took a week, but Walker was in no hurry.
Take the time to do it right, he said, if we hurry somebody's
going to notice the blur of motion and look our way and just

by looking at us they'll undo us. A horizontal mind that boy had.

Came a most delicious night when the Hunts went out to play, and both their diddle-girls were busy being squeezed most delectably (and didn't we have a lovely time persuading two toddle-boys to do the squeezing that very night). This news came to Mr. and Mrs. Jesse at the very last minute, and they had no choice but to call Mother Hubbard's, and isn't it lovely that just a half hour before, sweet little Stevie Queen, being moi, called in and said that he was available for baby-stomping after all. Ein and ein made zwei, and there I was being dropped off by a Mother Hubbard driver at the door of the Jesse Hunt house, whereupon I not only got to look upon the beatific face of Mr. Fed himself, I also got to have my dear head patted by Mrs. Fed, and then had the privilege of preparing little snacks for fussy Fed Jr. and foul-mouthed Fedene, the five-year-old and the three-year-old, while Microfed, the one-year-old (not yet human and, if I am any judge of character, not likely to live long enough to become such), sprayed uric acid in my face while I was diapering him. A good time was had by all.

Because of my heroic efforts, the small creatures were in their truckle beds quite early, and being a most fastidious baby-tucker, I browsed the house looking for burglars and stumbling, quite by chance, upon the most useful information about the beak-rat whose secret self-chosen name I was trying to learn. For one thing, he had set a watchful hair upon each of his bureau drawers, so that if I had been inclined to steal, he would know that unlawful access of his drawers had been attempted. I learned that he and his wife had separate containers of everything in the bathroom, even when they used the same brand of toothpaste, and it was he, not she, who took care of all their prophylactic activities (and not a moment too soon, thought I, for I had come to know their children). He was not the sort to use lubrificants or little pleasure-giving ribs, either. Only the regulation government-issue hard-as-concrete rubber rafts for him, which suggested to my most pernicious mind that he had almost as much fun between the sheets as me.

I learned all kinds of joyful information, all of it trivial, all of it vital. I never know which of the threads I grasp are going to make connections deep within the lumens of my brightest caves. But I never before had the chance to wander unmolested through a person's own house when searching for his P-word. I saw the notes his children brought home from school, the magazines his family received, and more and more I began to see that Jesse H. Hunt barely touched his family at any point. He stood like a waterbug on the surface of life, without ever getting his feet wet. He could die, and if nobody tripped over the corpse it would be weeks before they noticed. And yet this was not because he did not care. It was because he was so very very careful. He examined everything, but through the wrong end of the microscope, so that it all became very small and far away. I was a sad little boy by the end of that night, and I whispered to Microfed that he should practice pissing in male faces, because that's the only way he would ever sink a hook into his daddy's face.

"What if he wants to take you home?" Dogwalker asked me, and I said, "No way he would, nobody does that," but Dogwalker made sure I had a place to go all the same, and sure enough, it was Doggy who got voltage and me who went limp. I ended up riding in a beak-rat buggy, a genuine made-in-America rattletrap station wagon, and he took me to the for-sale house where Mama Pimple was waiting crossly for me and made Mr. Hunt go away because he kept me out too late. Then when the door was closed Mama Pimple giggled her gig and chuckled her chuck, and Walker himself wandered out of the back room and said, "That's one less favor you owe me, Mama Pimple," and she said, "No, my dear boyoh, that's one more favor *you* owe *me*" and then they kissed a deep passionate kiss if you can believe it. Did you imagine anybody ever kissed Mama Pimple that way? Dogwalker is a boyful of shocks.

"Did you get all you needed?" he asks me.

"I have P-words dancing upward," says I, "and I'll have a name for you tomorrow in my sleep."

"Hold onto it and don't tell me," says Dogwalker. "I don't want to hear a name until after we have his finger."

That magical day was only hours away, because the girl—whose name I never knew and whose face I never saw—was to cast her spell over Mr. Fed the very next day. As Dogwalker said, this was no job for lingeree. The girl did not dress pretty and pretended to be lacking in the social graces, but she was a good little clerical who was going through a most distressing period in her private life, because she had undergone a premature hysterectomy, poor lass, or so she told Mr. Fed, and here she was losing her womanhood and she had never really felt like a woman at all. But he was so kind to her, for weeks he had been so kind, and Dogwalker told me afterward how he locked the door of his office for just a few minutes, and held her and kissed her to make her feel womanly, and once his fingers had all made their little impressions on the thin electrified plastic microcoating all over her lovely naked back and breasts, she began to cry and most gratefully informed him that she did not want him to be unfaithful to his wife for her sake, that he had already given her such a much of a lovely gift by being so kind and understanding, and she felt better thinking that a man like him could bear to touch her knowing she was defemmed inside, and now she thought she had the confidence to go on. A very convincing act, and one calculated to get his hot naked handprints without giving him a crisis of conscience that might change his face and give him a whole new set of possible Ps.

The microsheet got all his fingers from several angles, and so Walker was able to dummy out a finger mask for our inside man within a single night. Right index. I looked at it most skeptically, I fear, because I had my doubts already dancing in the little lightpoints of my inmost mind. "Just one finger?"

"All we get is one shot," said Dogwalker. "One single try."

"But if he makes a mistake, if my first password isn't right, then he could use the middle finger on the second try."

"Tell me, my vertical pricket, whether you think Jesse H. Hunt is the sort of burr oak rat who makes mistakes?"

To which I had to answer that he was not, and yet I had my misgivings and my misgivings all had to do with needing a second finger, and yet I am vertical, not horizontal, which means that I can see the present as deep as you please but the future's not mine to see, que sera, sera.

From what Doggy told me, I tried to imagine Mr. Fed's reaction to this nubile flesh that he had pressed. If he had poked as well as peeked, I think it would have changed his P-word, but when she told him that she would not want to compromise his uncompromising virtue, it reinforced him as a most regular or even regulation fellow and his name remained pronouncedly the same, and his P-word also did not change. "InvictusXYZrwr," quoth I to Dogwalker, for that was his veritable password, I knew it with more certainty than I had ever had before.

"Where in hell did you come up with that?" says he.

"If I knew how I did it, Walker, I'd never miss at all," says I. "I don't even know if it's in the goo or in the zoo. All the facts go down, and it all gets mixed around, and up come all these dancing P-words, little pieces of P."

"Yeah but you don't just make it up, what does it mean?"

"Invictus is an old poem in a frame stuck in his bureau drawer, which his mama gave him when he was still a little fed-to-be. XYZ is his idea of randomizing, and rwr is the first U.S. President that he admired. I don't know why he chose these words now. Six weeks ago he was using a different P-word with a lot of numbers in it, and six weeks from now he'll change again, but right now—"

"Sixty percent sure?" asked Doggy.

"I give no percents this time," says I. "I've never roamed through the bathroom of my subject before. But this or give me an assectomy, I've never been more sure."

Now that he had the P-word, the inside guy began to wear his magic finger every day, looking for a chance to be alone in Mr. Fed's office. He had already created the preliminary files, like any routine green card requests, and buried them within his work area. All he needed was to go in, sign on as Mr. Fed, and then if the system accepted his name and P-word and finger, he could call up the files, approve them, and be gone within a minute. But he had to have that minute.

And on that wonderful magical day he had it. Mr. Fed had a meeting and his secretary sprung a leak a day early, and in went Inside Man with a perfectly legitimate note to leave for Hunt. He sat before the terminal, typed name and P-word and laid down his phony finger, and the machine spread wide its lovely legs and bid him enter. He had the files processed in forty seconds, laying down his finger for each green, then signed off and went on out. No sign, no sound that anything was wrong. As sweet as summertime, as smooth as ice, and all we had to do was sit and wait for green cards to come in the mail.

"Who you going to sell them to?" says I.

"I offer them to no one till I have clean greens in my hand," says he. Because Dogwalker is careful. What happened was not because he was not careful.

Every day we walked to the ten places where the envelopes were supposed to come. We knew they wouldn't be there for a week—the wheels of government grind exceeding slow, for good or ill. Every day we checked with Inside Man, whose name and face I have already given you, much good it will do, since both are no doubt different by now. He told us every time that all was the same, nothing was changed, and he was telling the truth, for the fed was most lugubrious and palatial and gave no leaks that anything was wrong. Even Mr. Hunt

himself did not know that aught was amiss in his little king-
dom.

Yet even with no sign that I could name, I was jumpy every
morning and sleepless every night. "You walk like you got to
use the toilet," says Walker to me, and it is verily so. Something is wrong, I say to myself, something is most deeply
wrong, but I cannot find the name for it even though I know,
and so I say nothing, or I lie to myself and try to invent a
reason for my fear. "It's my big chance," says I. "To be twenty
percent of rich."

"Rich," says he, "not just a fifth."

"Then you'll be double rich."

And he just grins at me, being the strong and silent type.

"But then why don't you sell nine," says I, "and keep the
other green? Then you'll have the money to pay for it, and the
green to go where you want in all the world."

But he just laughs at me and says, "Silly boy, my dear sweet
pinheaded lightbrained little friend. If someone sees a pimp
like me passing a green, he'll tell a fed, because he'll know
there's been a mistake. Greens don't go to boys like me."

"But you won't be dressed like a pimp," says I, "and you
won't stay in pimp hotels."

"I'm a low-class pimp," he says again, "and so however I
dress that day, that's just the way pimps dress. And whatever
hotel I go to, that's a low-class pimp hotel until I leave."

"Pimping isn't some disease," says I. "It isn't in your
gonads and it isn't in your genes. If your daddy was a Kroc and
your mama was an Iacocca, you wouldn't be a pimp."

"The hell I wouldn't," says he. "I'd just be a high-class
pimp, like my mama and my daddy. Who do you think gets
green cards? You can't sell no virgins on the street."

I thought that he was wrong and I still do. If anybody could
go from low to high in a week, it's Dogwalker. He could be
anything and do anything, and that's the truth. Or almost anything. If he could do *anything* then his story would have a
different ending. But it was not his fault. Unless you blame

pigs because they can't fly. I was the vertical one, wasn't I? I should have named my suspicions and we wouldn't have passed those greens.

I held them in my hands, there in his little room, all ten of them when he spilled them on the bed. To celebrate he jumped up so high he smacked his head on the ceiling again and again, which made them ceiling tiles dance and flip over and spill dust all over the room. "I flashed just one, a single one," says he, "and a cool million was what he said, and then I said what if ten? And he laughs and says fill in the check yourself."

"We should test them," says I.

"We can't test them," he says. "The only way to test it is to use it, and if you use it then your print and face are in its memory forever and so we could never sell it."

"Then sell one, and make sure it's clean."

"A package deal," he says. "If I sell one, and they think I got more but I'm holding out to raise the price, then I may not live to collect for the other nine, because I might have an accident and lose these little babies. I sell all ten tonight at once, and then I'm out of the green card business for life."

But more than ever that night I am afraid, he's out selling those greens to those sweet gentlebodies who are commonly referred to as Organic Crime, and there I am on his bed, shivering and dreaming because I know that something will go most deeply wrong but I still don't know what and I still don't know why. I keep telling myself, You're only afraid because nothing could ever go so right for you, you can't believe that anything could ever make you rich and safe. I say this stuff so much that I believe that I believe it, but I don't really, not down deep, and so I shiver again and finally I cry, because after all my body still believes I'm nine, and nine-year-olds have tear ducts very easy of access, no password required. Well he comes in late that night, and I'm asleep he thinks, and so he walks quiet instead of dancing, but I can hear the dancing in his little sounds, I know he has the money all safely in the bank, and so when he leans over to make sure if I'm asleep, I say, "Could I borrow a hundred thou?"

So he slaps me and he laughs and dances and sings, and I try to go along, you bet I do, I know I should be happy, but then at the end he says, "You just can't take it, can you? You just can't handle it," and then I cry all over again, and he just puts his arm around me like a movie dad and gives me play-punches on the head and says, "I'm gonna marry me a wife, I am, maybe even Mama Pimple herself, and we'll adopt you and have a little spielberg family in Summerfield, with a riding mower on a real grass lawn."

"I'm older than you *or* Mama Pimple," says I, but he just laughs. Laughs and hugs me until he thinks that I'm all right. Don't go home, he says to me that night, but home I got to go, because I know I'll cry again, from fear or something, anyway, and I don't want him to think his cure wasn't permanent. "No thanks," says I, but he just laughs at me. "Stay here and cry all you want to, Goo Boy, but don't go home tonight. I don't want to be alone tonight, and sure as hell you don't either." And so I slept between his sheets, like with a brother, him punching and tickling and pinching and telling dirty jokes about his whores, the most good and natural night I spent in all my life, with a true friend, which I know you don't believe, snickering and nickering and ickering your filthy little thoughts, there was no holes plugged that night because nobody was out to take pleasure from nobody else, just Dogwalker being happy and wanting me not to be so sad.

And after he was asleep, I wanted so bad to know who it was he sold them to, so I could call them up and say, "Don't use those greens, cause they aren't clean. I don't know how, I don't know why, but the feds are onto this, I know they are, and if you use those cards they'll nail your fingers to your face." But if I called would they believe me? They were careful too. Why else did it take a week? They had one of their nothing goons use a card to make sure it had no squeaks or leaks, and it came up clean. Only then did they give the cards to seven big boys, with two held in reserve. Even Organic Crime, the All-seeing Eye, passed those cards same as we did.

I think maybe Dogwalker was a little bit vertical too. I think he knew same as me that something was wrong with this. That's why he kept checking back with the inside man, cause he didn't trust how good it was. That's why he didn't spend any of his share. We'd sit there eating the same old schlock, out of his cut from some leg job or my piece from a data wipe, and every now and then he'd say, "Rich man's food sure tastes good." Or maybe even though he wasn't vertical he still thought maybe I was right when I thought something was wrong. Whatever he thought, though, it just kept getting worse and worse for me, until the morning when we went to see the inside man and the inside man was gone.

Gone clean. Gone like he never existed. His apartment for rent, cleaned out floor to ceiling. A phone call to the fed, and he was on vacation, which meant they had him, he wasn't just moved to another house with his newfound wealth. We stood there in his empty place, his shabby empty hovel that was ten times better than anywhere we ever lived, and Doggy says to me, real quiet, he says, "What was it? What did I do wrong? I thought I was like Hunt, I thought I never made a single mistake in this job, in this one job."

And that was it, right then I knew. Not a week before, not when it would do any good. Right then I finally knew it all, knew what Hunt had done. Jesse Hunt never made *mistakes.* But he was also so paranoid that he haired his bureau to see if the babysitter stole from him. So even though he would never *accidentally* enter the wrong P-word, he was just the kind who would do it *on purpose.* "He doublefingered every time," I says to Dog. "He's so damn careful he does his password wrong the first time every time, and then comes in on his second finger."

"So one time he comes in on the first try, so what?" He says this because he doesn't know computers like I do, being half-glass myself.

"The system knew the pattern, that's what. Jesse H. is so precise he never changed a bit, so when *we* came in on the first try, that set off alarms. It's my fault, Dog, I knew how crazy paranoidical he is, I knew that something was wrong, but not till this minute I didn't know what it was. I should have known it when I got his password, I should have known, I'm sorry, you never should have gotten me into this, I'm sorry, you should have listened to me when I told you something was wrong, I should have known, I'm sorry."

What I done to Doggy that I never meant to do. What I done to him! Anytime, I could have thought of it, it was all there inside my glassy little head, but no, I didn't think of it till after it was way too late. And maybe it's because I didn't want to think of it, maybe it's because I really wanted to be wrong about the green cards, but however it flew, I did what I do, which is to say I'm not the pontiff in his fancy chair, by which I mean I can't be smarter than myself.

Right away he called the gentlebens of Ossified Crime to warn them, but I was already plugged into the library sucking news as fast as I could and so I knew it wouldn't do no good, cause they got all seven of the big boys and their nitwit taster, too, locked up good and tight for card fraud.

And what they said on the phone to Dogwalker made things real clear. "We're dead," says Doggy.

"Give them time to cool," says I.

"They'll never cool," says he. "There's no chance, they'll never forgive this even if they know the whole truth, because look at the names they gave the cards to, it's like they got them for their biggest boys on the borderline, the habibs who bribe presidents of little countries and rake off cash from octopods like Shell and ITT and every now and then kill somebody and walk away clean. Now they're sitting there in jail with the whole life story of the organization in their brains, so they don't care if we meant to do it or not. They're hurting, and the only way they know to make the hurt go away is to pass it on to somebody else. And that's us. They want to make us hurt, and hurt real bad, and for a long long time."

I never saw Dog so scared. That's the only reason we went to the feds ourselves. We didn't ever want to stool, but we needed their protection plan, it was our only hope. So we offered to testify how we did it, not even for immunity, just so they'd change our faces and put us in a safe jail somewhere to work off the sentence and come out alive, you know? That's all we wanted.

But the feds, they laughed at us. They had the inside guy, see, and he was going to get immunity for testifying. "We don't need you," they says to us, "and we don't care if you go to jail or not. It was the big guys we wanted."

"If you let us walk," says Doggy, "then they'll think we set them up."

"Make us laugh," says the feds. "Us work with street poots like you? They know that we don't stoop so low."

"They bought from us," says Doggy. "If we're big enough for them, we're big enough for the dongs."

"Do you believe this?" says one fed to his identical junior officer. "These jollies are begging us to take them into jail. Well listen tight, my jolly boys, maybe we don't want to add you to the taxpayers' expense account, did you think of that? Besides, all we'd give you is time, but on the street, those boys will give you time and a half, and it won't cost us a dime."

So what could we do? Doggy just looks like somebody sucked out six pints, he's so white. On the way out of the fedhouse, he says, "Now we're going to find out what it's like to die."

And I says to him, "Walker, they stuck no gun in your mouth yet, they shove no shiv in your eye. We still breathing, we got legs, so let's *walk* out of here."

"Walk!" he says. "You walk out of G-boro, glasshead, and you bump into trees."

"So what?" says I. "I can plug in and pull out all the data we want about how to live in the woods. Lots of empty land out there. Where do you think the marijuana grows?"

"I'm a city boy," he says. "I'm a city boy." Now we're standing out in front, and he's looking around. "In the city I got a chance, I know the city."

"Maybe in New York or Dallas," says I, "but G-boro's just too small, not even half a million people, you can't lose yourself deep enough here."

"Yeah well," he says, still looking around. "It's none of your business now anyway, Goo Boy. They aren't blaming *you*, they're blaming *me*."

"But it's my fault," says I, "and I'm staying with you to tell them so."

"You think they're going to stop and listen?" says he.

"I'll let them shoot me up with speakeasy so they know I'm telling the truth."

"It's nobody's fault," says he. "And I don't give a twelve-inch poker whose fault it is anyway. You're clean, but if you stay with me you'll get all muddy, too. I don't need you around, and you sure as hell don't need me. Job's over. Done. Get lost."

But I couldn't do that. The same way he couldn't go on walking dogs, I couldn't just run off and leave him to eat my mistake. "They know I was your P-word man," says I. "They'll be after me, too."

"Maybe for a while, Goo Boy. But you transfer your twenty percent into Bobby Joe's Face Shop, so they aren't looking for you to get a refund, and then stay quiet for a week and they'll forget all about you."

He's right but I don't care. "I was in for twenty percent of rich," says I. "So I'm in for fifty percent of trouble."

All of a sudden he sees what he's looking for. "There they are, Goo Boy, the dorks they sent to hit me. In that Merce-des." I look but all I see are electrics. Then his hand is on my back and he gives me a shove that takes me right off the por-tico and into the bushes, and by the time I crawl out, Doggy's nowhere in sight. For about a minute I'm pissed about getting scratched up in the plants, until I realize he was getting me out of the way, so I wouldn't get shot down or hacked up or lased out, whatever it is they planned to do to him to get even.

I was safe enough, right? I should've walked away, I should've ducked right out of the city. I didn't even have to refund the money. I had enough to go clear out of the country and live the rest of my life where even Occipital Crime couldn't find me.

And I thought about it. I stayed the night in Mama Pimple's flophouse because I knew somebody would be watching my own place. All that night I thought about places I could go. Australia. New Zealand. Or even a foreign place, I could afford a good vocabulary crystal so picking up a new language would be easy.

But in the morning I couldn't do it. Mama Pimple didn't exactly ask me but she looked so worried and all I could say was, "He pushed me into the bushes and I don't know where he is."

And she just nods at me and goes back to fixing breakfast. Her hands are shaking she's so upset. Because she knows that Dogwalker doesn't stand a chance against Orphan Crime.

"I'm sorry," says I.

"What can you do?" she says. "When they want you, they get you. If the feds don't give you a new face, you can't hide."

"What if they didn't want him?" says I.

She laughs at me. "The story's all over the street. The arrests were in the news, and now everybody knows the big boys are looking for Walker. They want him so bad the whole street can smell it."

"What if they knew it wasn't his fault?" says I. "What if they knew it was an accident? A mistake?"

Then Mama Pimple squints at me—not many people can tell when she's squinting, but I can—and she says, "Only one boy can tell them that so they'll believe it."

"Sure, I know," says I.

"And if that boy walks in and says, Let me tell you why you don't want to hurt my friend Dogwalker—"

"Nobody said life was safe," I says. "Besides, what could they do to me that's worse than what already happened to me when I was nine?"

She comes over and just puts her hand on my head, just lets her hand lie there for a few minutes, and I know what I've got to do.

So I did it. Went to Fat Jack's and told him I wanted to talk to Junior Mint about Dogwalker; and it wasn't thirty seconds before I was hustled on out into the alley, and driven somewhere with my face mashed into the floor of the car so I couldn't tell where it was. Idiots didn't know that somebody as vertical as me can tell the number of wheel revolutions and the exact trajectory of every curve. I could've drawn a free-hand map of where they took me. But if I let them know that, I'd never come home, and since there was a good chance I'd end up dosed with speakeasy, I went ahead and erased the memory. Good thing I did—that was the first thing they asked me as soon as they had the drug in me.

Gave me a grown-up dose, they did, so I practically told them my whole life story and my opinion of them and everybody and everything else, so the whole session took hours, felt like forever, but at the end they knew, they absolutely knew that Dogwalker was straight with them, and when it was over and I was coming up so I had some control over what I said, I asked them, I begged them, Let Dogwalker live. Just let him go. He'll give back the money, and I'll give back mine, just let him go.

"Okay," says the guy.

I didn't believe it.

"No, you can believe me, we'll let him go."

"You got him?"

"Picked him up before you even came in. It wasn't hard."

"And you didn't kill him?"

"Kill him? We had to get the money back first, didn't we, so we needed him alive till morning, and then you came in, and your little story changed our minds, it really did, you made us feel all sloppy and sorry for that poor old pimp."

For a few seconds there I actually believed that it was going to be all right. But then I knew from the way they looked, from the way they acted, I knew the same way I know about passwords.

They brought in Dogwalker and handed me a book. Dogwalker was very quiet and stiff and he didn't look like he recognized me at all. I didn't even have to look at the book to know what it was. They scooped out his brain and replaced it with glass, like me only way over the line, way way over, there was nothing of Dogwalker left inside his head, just glass pipe and goo. The book was a User's Manual, with all the instructions about how to program him and control him.

I looked at him and he was Dogwalker, the same face, the same hair, everything. Then he moved or talked and he was dead, he was somebody else living in Dogwalker's body. And I says to them, "Why? Why didn't you just kill him, if you were going to do this?"

"This one was too big," says the guy. "Everybody in G-boro knew what happened, everybody in the whole country, everybody in the world. Even if it was a mistake, we couldn't let it go. No hard feelings, Goo Boy. He *is* alive. And so are you. And you both stay that way, as long as you follow a few simple rules. Since he's over the line, he has to have an owner, and you're it. You can use him however you want—rent out data storage, pimp him as a jig or a jaw—but he stays with you always. Every day, he's on the street here in G-boro, so we can bring people here and show them what happens to boys who make mistakes. You can even keep your cut from the job, so you don't have to scramble at all if you don't want to. That's how much we like you, Goo Boy. But if he leaves this town or doesn't come out, even one single solitary day, you'll be very sorry for the last six hours of your life. Do you understand?"

I understood. I took him with me. I bought this place, these clothes, and that's how it's been ever since. That's why we go out on the street every day. I read the whole manual, and I figure there's maybe ten percent of Dogwalker left inside. The part that's Dogwalker can't ever get to the surface, can't ever talk or move or anything like that, can't ever remember or even consciously think. But maybe he can still wander around inside what used to be his head, maybe he can sample the data stored in all that goo. Maybe someday he'll even run across this story and he'll know what happened to him, and he'll know that I tried to save him.

In the meantime this is my last will and testament. See, I have us doing all kinds of research on Orgasmic Crime, so that someday I'll know enough to reach inside the system and unplug it. Unplug it all, and make those bastards lose everything, the way they took everything away from Dogwalker. Trouble is, some places there ain't no way to look without leaving tracks. Goo is as goo do, I always say. I'll find out I'm not as good as I think I am when somebody comes along and puts a hot steel putz in my face. Knock my brains out when it comes. But there's this, lying in a few hundred places in the system. Three days after I don't lay down my code in a certain program in a certain place, this story pops into view. The fact you're reading this means I'm dead.

Or it means I paid them back, and so I quit suppressing this cause I don't care anymore. So maybe this is my swan song, and maybe this is my victory song. You'll never know, will you, mate?

But you'll wonder. I like that. You wondering about us, whoever you are, you thinking about old Goo Boy and Dogwalker, you guessing whether the fangs who scooped Doggy's skull and turned him into self-propelled property paid for it down to the very last delicious little drop.

And in the meantime, I've got this goo machine to take care of. Only ten percent a man, he is, but then I'm only forty percent myself. All added up together we make only half a man. But that's the half that counts. That's the half that still wants things. The goo in me and the goo in him is all just light pipes and electricity. Data without desire. Lightspeed trash. But I have some desires left, just a few, and maybe so does Dogwalker, even fewer. And we'll get what we want. We'll get it all. Every speck. Every sparkle. Believe it.

MECH

BY C. J. CHERRYH

Police work in times to come may not look much like police work today—fans of the movie Robocop *know that—but tomorrow's cops will have to deal with the same brutal crimes and basic human motives as their ancestors, as C. J. Cherryh shows in this superbly cinematic tale.*

COLD NIGHT IN Dallas Metro Complex, late shift supper while the cruiser autoed the beltway, rain fracturing the city lights on the windshield. "Chili cheeseburger with mustard," Dave said, and passed it to Sheila—Sheila had the wheel, he had the Trackers, and traffic was halfway sane for Dallas after dark, nobody even cruising off the autos, at least in their sector. He bit into a chili and cheese without, washed a bite down with a soft drink, and scanned the blips for the odd lane-runner. A domestic quarrel and a card snitch were their only two working calls: Manny and Lupe had the domestic, and the computer lab had the card trace.

So naturally they were two bites into the c&c, hadn't even touched the fries, when the mech-level call came slithering in, sweet-voiced: "Possible assault in progress, Metro 2, # R-29, The Arlington, you've got the warrant, 34, see the manager."

"Gee, thanks," Dave muttered. Sheila said something else, succinctly, off mike, and punched in with a chilied thumb. The cruiser had already started its lane changes, with Exit 3 lit up on the windshield, at .82 k away. Sheila got a couple more bites and a sip of soft drink down before she shoved the burger and drink cup at him. She took the wheel as the autos dumped them onto Mason Drive, on a manual-only and mostly deserted street.

It didn't look like an assault kind of neighborhood, big reflective windows in a tower complex. It was offices and residences, one of the poshest complexes in big D, real high-rent district. You could say that was why a mech unit got pulled in off the Ringroad, instead of the dispatcher sending in the b&w line troops. You could make a second guess it was because the city wanted more people to move into the complexes and a low crime rep was the major sales pitch. Or you could even guess some city councilman lived in The Arlington.

But that wasn't for a mere mech unit to question. Dave got his helmet out of the locker under his feet, put it on while Sheila was taking them into the curbside lane, plugged into the collar unit that was already plugged to the tactiles, put the gloves on, and put the visor down, in the interests of checkout and time—

"Greet The Public," Sheila said with a saccharine and nasty smirk—meaning Department Po-li-cy said visors up when you were Meeting the Man: people didn't greatly like to talk to visors and armor.

"Yeah, yeah." He finished the checks. He had a street map on the HUD, the location of 29-R sector on the overall building shape, the relative position of the cruiser as it nosed down the ramp into The Arlington's garage. "Inside view, here, shit, I'm not getting it, have you got Library on it?"

"I'll get it. Get. Go."

He opened the door, bailed out onto the concrete curb. Car treads had tracked the rain in, neon and dead white glows glistened on the down ramp behind them. High and mighty Arlington Complex was gray concrete and smoked glass in its utilitarian gut. And he headed for the glass doors, visor up, the way Sheila said, fiber cameras on, so Sheila could track: Sheila herself was worthless with the mech, she'd proven that by taking a shot from a dealer, so that her right leg was plex and cable below the knee, but as a keyman she was ace and she had access with an A with the guys Downtown.

She said, in his left ear, "Man's in the hall, name's Rozman, reports screaming on 48, a man running down the fire stairs . . ."

"Mr. Rozman," he said, meeting the man just past the doors. "Understand you have a disturbance."

"Ms. Lopez, she's the next door neighbor, she's hiding in her bedroom, she said there was screaming. We had an intruder on the fire stairs—"

"Man or woman's voice in the apartment?"

"Woman."

"What's your address?"

"4899."

"Minors on premises?"

"Single woman. Name's Emilia Nolan. Lives alone. A quiet type . . . no loud parties, no complaints from the neighbors . . ."

Rozman was a clear-headed source. Dave unclipped a remote, thumbed it on and handed it to the man. "You keep answering questions. You know what this is?"

"It's a remote."

"—Sheila, put a phone-alert on Ms. Lopez and the rest of the neighbors, police on the way up, just stay inside and keep behind furniture until she gets word from us." He was already going for the elevators. "Mr. Rozman. Do you log entry/exits?"

On his right-ear mike: "On the street and the tunnels and the garage, the fire stairs . . ."

"Any exceptions?"

"No.—Yes. The service doors. But those are manual key . . . only maintenance has that."

"Key that log to the dispatcher. Just put the d-card in the phone and dial 9999." The exception to the log was already entered, miked in from his pickup. "And talk to your security people about those service doors. That's city code. Sir." He was polite on autopilot. His attention was on Sheila at the moment, from the other ear, saying they were prepping interior schemas to his helmet view. "Mr. Rozman. Which elevator?" There was a bank of six.

"Elevator B. Second one on your left. That goes to the 48s . . ."

He used his fireman's key on the elevator call, and put his visor down. The hall and the elevator doors disappeared behind a wire-schema of the hall and doors, all red and gold and green lines on black, and shifting as the mid-tier elevator grounded itself. He didn't look down as he got in, you didn't look down on a wire-view if you wanted your stomach steady. He sent the car up, watched the floors flash past, transparenced, heard a stream of checks from Sheila confirming the phone-alarm in action, residents being warned through the phone company—

"Lopez is a cardiac case," Sheila said, "hospital's got a cruiser on alert, still no answer out of 4899. Lopez says it's quiet now."

"You got a line on Lopez, calm her down." Presence-sniffer readout was a steady blue, but you got that in passageways, lot of traffic, everything blurred unless you had a specific to track: it was smelling for stress, and wasn't getting it here. "Rozman, any other elevators to 48?"

"Yeah, C and D."

"Can you get off anywhere from a higher floor?"

"Yessir, you can. Any elevator, if you're going down."

Elevator stopped and the door opened. Solid floor across the threshold, with the scan set for anomalies against the wire-schema. Couple of potted palms popped out against the VR. Target door was highlighted gold. Audio kept hyping until he could hear the scuff of random movements from other apartments. "Real quiet," he said to Sheila. And stood there a moment while the sniffer worked, filling in tracks. You could see the swirl in the air currents where the vent was. You could see stress showing up soft red.

"Copy that," Sheila said. "Warrant's clear to go in."

He put himself on no-exhaust, used the fire-key again, stayed to the threshold. The air inside showed redder. So did the walls, on heat-view, but this was spatter. Lot of spatter.

No sound of breathing. No heartbeat inside the apartment.

He de-amped and walked in. A mech couldn't disturb a scene—sniffer couldn't pick up a presence on itself, ditto on the Cyloprene of his mech rig, while the rig was no-exhaust he was on internal air. It couldn't sniff him, but feet could still smudge the spatters. He watched where he stepped, real-visual now, and discovered the body, a woman, fully dressed, sprawled face-up by the bar, next to the bedroom, hole dead center between the astonished eyes.

"Quick and clean for her," he said. "Helluva mess on the walls."

"Lab's on its way," Sheila said, alternate thought track. "I'm on you, D-D, just stand still a sec."

The sniffer was working up a profile, via Sheila's relays Downtown. He stood still, scanning over the body. "Woman about thirty, good-looking, plain dresser . . ."

Emilia Frances Nolan, age 34, flashed up on the HUD. *Canadian citizen, Martian registry, chief information officer Mars Transport Company."*

Thin, pale woman. Dark hair. Corporate style on the clothes. Canadian immigrant to Mars, returned to Earth on a Canadian passport. "Door was locked," he said.

"I noticed that," Sheila said.

Sniffer was developing two scents, the victim's and a second one. AMMONIA, the indicator said.

"Mild ammonia."

"Old-fashioned stuff," he said. "Amateur." The sniffer was already sepping it out as the number three track. Ammonia wouldn't overload a modern sniffer. It was just one more clue to trace; and the tracks were coming clear now: Nolan's was everywhere, *Baruque,* the sniffer said—expensive perfume, persistent as hell. The ammonia had to be the number two's notion. And you didn't carry a vial of it for social occasions.

But why in hell was there a live-in smell?

"Male," Sheila commented, meaning the number two track. "Lovers' spat?"

"POSSeL-Q the manager didn't know about, maybe, lovers' quarrel, clothes aren't mussed. Rape's not a high likely here." Stress in both tracks. The whole place stank of it. "Going for the live one, Sheel. Hype it. Put out a phone alert, upstairs and down, have ComA take over Rozman's remote, I don't need him but he's still a resource."

Out the door, into the wire-schema of the hall. The sniffer had it good this time: the stress trail showed up clear and bright for the fire-door, and it matched the number two track, no question. "Forty-eight damn floors," he muttered: no good to take the elevator. You got professional killers or you got crazies or drugheads in a place like this, fenced in with its security locks, and you didn't know what any one of the three was going to do, or what floor they were going to do it on. He went through the fire-door and started down on foot, following the scent, down and down and down . . .

"We got further on Norton," Sheila said. "Assigned here eight months ago, real company climber, top grad, schooled on Mars, no live-ins on any MarsCorp record we can get to, but that guy was real strong in there. I'm saying he was somebody Norton didn't want her social circle to meet."

He ran steps and breathed, ran steps and breathed, restricted air, Sheila had a brain for figuring people, you didn't even have to ask her. A presence trail arrived into the stairwell, bright blue mingling with the red. "Got another track here," he found breath to say.

"Yeah, yeah, that's in the log, that's a maintenance worker, thirty minutes back. He'll duck out again on 25."

"Yeah." He was breathing hard. Making what time he could. The trail did duck out at 25, in a wider zone of blue, unidentified scents, the smell from the corridor blown into the shaft and fading into the ambient. His track stayed clear and strong, stress-red, and he went on real-view: the transparent stairs were making him sick. "Where's this let out? Garage downstairs?"

"Garage and mini-mall."

"Shit!"

"Yeah. We got a call from building security wanting a piece of it, told them stay out of it . . ."

"Thank God."

"Building chief's an amateur with a cop-envy. We're trying to get another mech in."

"We got some fool with a gun he hasn't ditched, we got a mall full of people down there. Where's Jacobs?"

"Rummel's closer.—We got lab coming in. Lab's trying to get an ID match on your sniffer pickup."

"Yeah. You've got enough on it. Guy's sweating. So am I." He felt sweat trails running under the armor, on his face. The door said 14. The oxy was running out. Violate the scene or no, he had to toggle to exhaust. After that, it was cooler, dank, the way shafts were that went into the underground.

"We got some elevator use," Sheila said, "right around the incident, off 48. Upbound. Stopped on 50, 52, 78, 80, and came down again, 77, 34, 33, then your fire-call brought it down. Time-overlap on the 78, the C-elevator was upbound."

"Follow it." Meaning somebody could have turned around and left no traces if he'd gotten in with another elevator-call. "Put Downtown on it, I need your brain."

"Awww. I thought it was the body."

"Stow it." He was panting again. The internal tank was out. He hoped he didn't need it again. Sheila went out of the loop: he could hear the silence on the phones. "Forty-damn-stories—"

Three, two, one, s-one. "Wire," he gasped, and got back the schema, that showed through the door into a corridor. He listened for noise, panting, while the net in the background zeed out his breathing and his heartbeat and the building fans and everything else but a dull distant roar that said humanity, a lot of it, music—the red was still there and it was on the door switch, but it thinned out in the downward stairwell.

"Went out on s-1."

"Street exit, mall exit," Sheila said. "Via the Arlington lobby. Dave, we got you help coming in."

"Good."

"Private mech."

Adrenaline went up a notch. "That's help? That's help? Tell them—"

"I did, buns, sorry about that. Name's Ross, she's inbound from the other tower, corporate security . . ."

"Just what I need. Am I going out there? They want me to go out there?"

"You're clear."

He hated it, he *hated* going out there, hated the stares, hated the Downtown monitoring that was going to pick up that pulse rate of his and have the psychs on his case. But he opened the door, he walked out into the lobby that was The Arlington's front face; and walked onto carpet, onto stone, both of which were only flat haze to his eyes. Bystanders clustered and gossiped, patched in like the potted palms, real people stark against the black and wire-lines of cartoonland, all looking at him and talking in half-voices as if that could keep their secrets if he wanted to hear. He just kept walking, down the corridor, following the faint red glow in the blue of Everysmell, followed it on through the archway into the wider spaces of the mall, where more real people walked in black cartoon-space, and that red glow spread out into a faint fan-swept haze and a few spots on the floor.

Juvies scattered, a handful out of Parental, lay odds on it—he could photo them and tag them, but he kept walking, chose not even to transmit: Sheila had a plateful to track as was. One smartass kid ducked into his face, made a face and ran like hell. Fools tried that, as if they suspected there wasn't anybody real inside the black visor. Others talked with their heads partially turned, or tried not to look as if they were looking. That was what he hated, being the eyes and ears, the spy-machine that connected to everywhere, that made everybody ask themselves what they were saying that might go into files, what they had ever done or thought of that a mech might find reason to track . . .

Maybe it was the blank visor, maybe it was the rig—maybe it was everybody's guilt. With the sniffer tracking, you could see the stress around you, the faint red glow around honest citizens no different than the guy you were tracking, as if it was the whole world's guilt and fear and wrongdoing you were smelling, and everybody had some secret to keep and some reason to slink aside.

"Your backup's meeting you at A-3," Sheila said, and a marker popped up in the schema, yellow flasher.

"Wonderful. We got a make on the target?"

"Not yet, buns. Possible this guy's not on file. Possible we got another logjam in the datacall, a mass murder in Peoria, something like that." Sheila had her mouth full. "Everybody's got problems tonight."

"What are you eating?"

"Mmm. Sorry, there."

"Is that my cheeseburger?"

"I owe you one."

"You're really putting on weight, Sheel, you know that?"

"Yeah, it's anxiety attacks." Another bite. "Your backup's Company, Donna Ross, 20 years on, service citation."

"Shee." Might not be a play-cop, then. Real seniority. He saw the black figure standing there in her own isolation, at the juncture of two dizzying walkways. Saw her walk in his direction, past the mistrustful stares of spectators. "Get some plainclothes in here yet?"

"We got reporters coming."

"Oh, great. Get'em off, get the court on it—"

"Doing my best."

"Officer Dawes." Ross held out a black-gloved hand, no blues on the Company cop, just the rig, black cut-out in a wire-diagram world. "We're interfaced. It just came up."

Data came up, B-channel. "Copy that." Ross was facing the same red track he was, was getting his data, via some interface Downtown, an intersystem handshake. He stepped onto the downbound escalator, Ross in his 360° compression view, a lean, black shape on the shifting kaleidoscope of the moving stairs. "This is a MarsCorp exec that got it?" Ross asked in his right ear. "Is that what I read?"

"Deader than dead. We got a potential gun walking around out here with the john-q's. You got material on the exec?"

"Some kind of jam-up in the net—I haven't got a thing but a see-you."

"Wonderful, both of us in the dark." The escalator let off on the lower level, down with the fast foods and the arcades and a bunch of juvies all antics and ass. "Get out of here," he snarled on Address, and juvies scattered through the cartoon-scape. "Get upstairs!" he yelled, and some of them must have figured shooting was imminent, because they scattered dou-bletime, squealing and shoving. Bright blue down here with the pepperoni pizza and the beer and the popcorn, but that single red thread was still showing.

"Our boy's sweating hard," Ross said in one ear; and Sheila in the other: "We got a sudden flash in a security door, right down your way."

"Come on." Dave started to run. Ross matched him, a clat-ter of Cyloprene soles on tile, godawful racket. The exit in question was flashing yellow ahead. A janitor gawked, pressed himself against the wall in a try at invisibility; but his pres-ence was blue, neutral to the area.

"You see anybody go through?"

"Yeah, yeah, I saw him, young guy, took to the exit, I said he wasn't—" *Supposed to* trailed into the amped mike as they banged through the doors and into a concrete service hall.

"Sheila, you in with Ross?"

"Yeah. Both of you guys. I got a b&w following you, he's not meched, best I could do . . ."

Red light strobed across his visor. WEAPONS ON, it said.

"Shit," he said, "Ross—" He stopped for a breath against the corridor wall, drew his gun and plugged it in. Ross must have an order too: she was plugging in. Somebody Downtown had got a fire warrant. Somebody had decided on a fire warrant next to a mall full of kids. Maybe because of the kids. "What's our make on this guy, Sheila? Tell me we got a make, please

God, I don't like this, we got too many john-juniors out there."

"He's not in files."

"Off-worlder," Ross said.

"You know that?"

"If he's not in your files he's from off-world. The Company is searching. They've got your readout."

"Shit, somebody get us info." The corridor was a moving, jolting wire-frame in the black.

Nobody. Not a sign.

But the red was there, bright and clear. Sheila compressed several sections ahead on the wire-schema, folded things up close where he could get a look. There was a corner; he trans-viewed it, saw it heading to a service area. AIR SYSTEMS, the readout line said. "We got an air-conditioning unit up there, feed for the whole damn mall as best I guess . . . he's got cover."

"Yeah," Ross said. "I copy that."

"We're not getting any damn data," Sheila said in his other ear. "I'm asking again on that make, and we're not getting it. Delay. Delay. Delay. Ask if *her* keyman's getting data."

"My keyman asks," he relayed, "if you've got data yet."

"Nothing new. I'm telling you, we're not priority, it's some little lovers' spat—"

"That what they're telling you?"

"Uh-uh. I don't know a thing more than you. But a male presence, female body up there . . . that's how it's going to wash out. It always does."

"Dave." Sheila's voice again, while their steps rang out of time on the concrete and the red track ran in front of them. She had a tone when there was trouble. "Butterflies, you hear?"

"Yeah. Copy." Sheila wasn't liking something. She wasn't liking it a lot.

They reached the corner. The trail kept going, skirled in the currents from air ducts, glowing fainter in the gust from the

dark. He folded the view tighter, looked ahead of them, didn't
like the amount of cover ahead where they were going to
come down stairs and across a catwalk.

Something banged, echoed, and the lights went out.

Didn't bother a mech. Maybe it made the quarry feel better,
but they were still seeing, all wire-display. He was right on
Ross, Ross standing there like a haze in the ambience. Her rig
scattered stuff you used in the dark. It was like standing next
to a ghost. The Dallas PD couldn't afford rigs like that. Gov-
ernments did. Some MarsCorp bigwig got shot and the Company lent a mech with this stuff?

Ross said. "IR. Don't trust the wire. Stay here."

"The hell."

Infrared blurred the wire-schema. But he brought his sen-
sors up high-gain.

"No sonar," Ross said. "Cut it, dammit!"

"What the hell are we after?"

"There he is!"

He didn't half see. Just a blur, far across the dark. Ross burst
ahead of him, onto the steps; he dived after, in a thunder the
audios didn't damp fast enough.

"Dave." Sheila's voice again, very solemn. His ears were
still ringing when they got to the bottom. "Department's still
got nothing. I never saw a jam this long . . . I never saw a rig
like that."

They kept moving, fast, not running, not walking. The
mech beside him was Company or some government's issue, a
MarsCorp exec was stone dead, and you could count the organized crazies that might have pulled that trigger. A random
crazy, a lover—a secessionist . . .

"Lab's on it," Sheila said. "Dave, Dave, I want you to listen
to me."

He was moving forward. Sheila stopped talking, as Ross
moved around a bundle of conduits and motioned him to go
down the other aisle, past the blowers. Listen, Sheila said, and

said nothing. The link was feeding to Ross. He was sure of it. He could hear Sheila breathing, hard.

"Mustard," Sheila muttered. "Dave, was it mustard you wanted on that burger?"

They'd never been in a situation like this, not knowing what was feeding elsewhere, not knowing whether Downtown was still secure with them on the line. "Yeah," he breathed. He hated the stuff. "Yeah. With onions."

Sheila said, "You got it." Ross started to move. He followed. The com was compromised. She'd asked was he worried, that was the mustard query. He stayed beside that ghost-glow, held to the catwalk rail with one hand, the other with the gun. The city gave you a fire warrant; and your finger had a button. But theirs overrode, some guy Downtown. Or Sheila did. You didn't know. You were a weapon, with a double safety, and you didn't know whether the damn thing was live, ever.

"Dave," Sheila said, totally different tone. "Dave. This Ross doesn't have a keyman. She's backpacked. Total. She's a security guy."

Total mech. You heard about it, up on Sol, up in the Stations, where everything was computers. Elite of the elite. Independent operator with a computer for a backpack and neuros right into the station's high-tech walls.

He evened his breath, smelled the cold air, saw the thermal pattern that was Ross gliding ahead of him. A flash of infrared out of the dark. A door opened on light. Ross started running. He did.

A live-in lover? Somebody the exec would open the door to?

A mech could walk through a crime scene. A mech on internal air didn't leave a presence—nothing a sniffer would recognize.

A Company mech had been damned close to the scene—showed up to help the city cops . . .

"Sheila," he panted, trying to stay with Ross. "Lots of mustard."

Infrared glow ahead of them. A shot flashed out, from the

Company mech. It exploded in the dark, leaving tracers in his vision. Ross wasn't blinded. *His* foot went off a step, and he grabbed wildly for the rail, caught himself and slid two more before he had his feet under him on flat catwalk mesh—it shook as Ross ran; and he ran too.

"She's not remoted!" he panted. As if his keyman couldn't tell. Nobody outside was authorizing those shots. Ross was. A cartoon door boomed open, and he ran after a ghost whose fire wasn't routed through a whole damn city legal department. "Fold it!" he gasped, because he was busy keeping up; and the corner ahead compacted and swung into view, red and green wire, with nobody in it but the ghost ahead of him.

"Slow down!" he said. "Ross! Wait up, dammit! Don't shoot!"

His side was aching. Ross was panting hard, he heard her breathing, he overtook in a cartoon-space doorway, in a dead-end room, where the trail showed hot and bright.

"We have him," Ross said. The audio hype could hear the target breathing, past their exhaust. Even the panicked heartbeat. Ross lifted her gun against a presence behind a stack of boxes.

"No!" he yelled. And the left half of his visor flashed yellow. He swung to it, mindless target-seek, and the gun in his hand went off on Ross, went off a second time while Ross was flying sideways through the dark. Her shot went wild off the ceiling and he couldn't think, couldn't turn off the blinking target square. Four rounds, five, and the room was full of smoke.

"Dave?"

He wasn't talking to Sheila. He wasn't talking to whoever'd triggered him, set off the reflexes they trained in a mech.

Shaky voice from his keyman. "If you can walk out of there, walk. Right now, Dave."

"The guy's in the—"

"No. He's not, Dave." The heartbeat faded out. The cartoon room had a smudged gray ghost on the floor grid at his feet.

And a bright red lot of blood spattered around. "I want you to check out the restroom upstairs from here. All right?"

He was shaking now. Your keyman talked and you listened or you could be dead. He saw a movement on his left. He swung around with the gun up, saw the man stand up. Ordinary looking man, business shirt. Soaked with sweat. Frozen with fear. The sniffer flashed red.

Sheila's voice said, from his shoulder-patch, "Don't touch anything. Dave. Get out of there. Now."

He moved, walked out, with the target standing at his back. He walked all the way back to the air-conditioning plant, and he started up the stairs there, up to the catwalk, while nothing showed, no one. Sheila said, "Dave. Unplug now. You can unplug."

He stopped, he reached with his other hand and he pulled the plug on the gun and put it in its holster. He went on up the cartooned metal stairs, and he found the cartooned hall and the cartooned restroom with the real-world paper on the floor.

"You better wash up," Sheila said, so he did that, shaking head to foot. Before he was finished, a b&w came in behind him, and said, "You all right, sir?"

"Yeah," he said. Sheila was quiet then.

"You been down there?" the cop asked.

"You saw it," Sheila said in his ear, and he echoed her: "I saw it—guy got away—I couldn't get a target. Ross was in the way . . ."

"Yes, sir," the b&w said. "You're on record, sir."

"I figured."

"You sure you're all right? I can call—"

"I can always *call*, officer."

The guy got a disturbed look, the way people did who forgot they were talking to two people. "Yes, sir," the b&w said. "All right."

On his way out.

He turned around to the mirror, saw a plain, sick face. Blood was on the sink rim, puddled around his boots, where it had run off the plastic. He went in a stall, wiped off his rig with toilet paper and flushed the evidence.

Sheila said, "Take the service exits. Pick you up at the curb."

"Copy," he mumbled, took his foot off the seat, flushed the last bit of bloody paper, taking steady small breaths, now. They taught you to trust the autos with your life. They taught you to swing to the yellow, don't think, don't ask, swing and hold, swing and hold the gun.

A mech just walked away, afterward, visor down, communing with his inner voices, immune to question, immune to interviews. Everything went to the interfaces. There was a record. Of course there was a record. Everyone knew that.

It was at the human interface things could drop out.

He used the fire-key, walked out an emergency exit, waited in the rain. The cruiser nosed up to the curb, black and black-windowed, and swallowed him up.

"SAVED THE SOFT drink," Sheila said. "Thought you'd be dry."

It was half ice-melt. But it was liquid. It eased a raw throat. He sucked on the straw, leaned his head back. "They calling us in?"

"No," Sheila said. That was all. They didn't want a debrief. They didn't want a truth, they wanted—

—wanted nothing to do with it. Nolan's body to the next-ofs, the live-in . . . to wherever would hide him.

Another mouthful of ice-melt. He shut his eyes, saw wire-schemas, endlessly folding, a pit you could fall into. He blinked on rain and refracted neon. "Ross killed Nolan."

"You and I don't know."

"Was it Ross?"

"Damned convenient a Company mech was in hail. Wasn't it?"

"No presence at all. Nolan—Nolan was shot between the eyes."

"MarsCorp exec—her live-in boyfriend with no record, no visa, no person. Guy who knew The Arlington's underground, who had a pass key—"

"He was keying through the doors?"

"Same as you were. Real at-home in the bottom tiers. You see a weapon on him, you see where he ditched one?"

"No." Raindrops fractured, flickering off the glass. He saw the gray ghost again, the no-Presence that could walk through total black. Or key through any apartment door, or aim a single head-shot with a computer's inhuman, instant accuracy.

He said, "Adds, doesn't it?"

"Adds. Downtown was seeing what I was. I told them. Told them you had bad feelings—"

"What the hell are they going to do? We got a dead mech down there—"

"The live-in shot Nolan. Shot the Company mech. That's your story. They can't say otherwise. What are they going to say? That the guy didn't have a gun? They won't come at us."

"What about our record?"

"Transmission breakup. Lightning or something." Sheila's face showed rain-spots, running shadows, neon glare. "Bad night, D-D, bad shit."

"They erase it?"

"Erase what?" Sheila asked.

Silence then. Rain came down hard.

"They want to bring their damn politics down here," Sheila said, "they can take it back again. Settle it up there."

"Settle what?" he echoed Sheila.

But he kept seeing corridors, still the corridors, folding in on themselves. And sipped the tasteless soft drink. "The guy's shirt was clean."

"Huh?"

"His shirt was clean." Flash on the restroom, red water swirling down and down. "He wasn't in that room. Nolan knew Ross was coming. The guy was living there. His smell's all over. That's why the ammonia trick. Nolan sent him for the stairs, I'll bet it's in the access times. He couldn't have hid from a mech. And all that screaming? The mech wanted something. Something Nolan wasn't giving. Something Ross wanted more than she wanted the guy right then."

"Secession stuff. Documents. Martian Secession. Not illegal, not in Dallas . . ."

"The mech missed the live-in, had to shut Nolan up. Didn't get the records, either. A botch. Thoroughgoing botch. The live-in—who knew the building like that? He wasn't any Company man. Martian with no visa, no regulation entry to the planet? I'll bet Nolan knew what he was, I'll bet Nolan was passing stuff to the Movement."

"An exec in MarsCorp? Over Martian Transport? Ask how the guy got here with no visa."

"Shit," he said. Then he thought about the mech, the kind of tech the rebels didn't have. "They wouldn't want a witness," he said. "The rebels wouldn't. The Company damned sure wouldn't. Ross would've gone for *me*, except I was linked in. I was recording. So she couldn't snatch the guy—had to shut the guy up somehow. They damn sure couldn't have a Company cop arrested down here. Had to get him shut up for good and get Ross off the planet . . ."

"Dead on," Sheila said. "Dead for sure, if he'd talked. Washington was after the Company for the make and the Company was stonewalling like hell, lay you odds on that—and I'll bet there's a plane seat for Ross tonight on a Guiana flight. What's it take? An hour down there? Half an hour more, if a shuttle's ready to roll, and Ross would have been no-return for this jurisdiction. That's all they needed." She flipped the com back to On again, to the city's ordinary litany of petty crime and larcenies, beneath an uneasy sky. "This is 34, coming on-line, marker 15 on the pike, good evening, HQ. This is a transmission check, think we've got it fixed now, 10-4?"

THE TERCENTENARY INCIDENT

BY ISAAC ASIMOV

The idea of employing lookalikes to keep important people from harm is not a new one—even Shakespeare wrote about it, in Henry IV, Part 1. *Nor is the idea of putting lookalikes in the path of an assassin's bullets to save the life of a president or a king. How, one wonders, will this venerable tradition change when we can use robot replicas, and not real people, in the lookalike's role? The father of the modern robot story, Isaac Asimov, explores some of the possibilities.*

JULY 4, 2076—and for the third time the accident of the conventional system of numeration, based on powers of ten, had brought the last two digits of the year back to the fateful 76 that had seen the birth of the nation.

It was no longer a nation in the old sense; it was rather a geographic expression, part of a greater whole that made up the Federation of all of humanity on Earth, together with its offshoots on the Moon and in the space colonies. By culture and heritage, however, the name and the *idea* lived on, and that portion of the planet signified by the old name was still the most prosperous and advanced region of the world. —And the President of the United States was still the most powerful single figure in the Planetary Council . . .

From a height of 200 feet, Lawrence Edwards watched the small figure of the President of the United States. Edwards drifted lazily above the crowd, his flotron motor making a barely heard chuckle on his back, and what he saw looked exactly like what anyone would see on a holovision screen. How many times had he seen little figures like that in his living room, little figures in a cube of sunlight, looking as real as though they were living homunculi, except that you could put your hand through them.

But you couldn't put your hand through the tens of thousands of people spreading out over the open spaces surrounding the Washington Monument. And you couldn't put your hand through the President. You could reach out to him, touch him, shake his hand.

Edwards thought sardonically of the uselessness of that added element of tangibility and wished himself a hundred miles away, floating in air over some isolated wilderness, instead of here where he had to watch for any sign of disorder.

There wouldn't be any necessity for his being here but for the mythology of the value of "pressing the flesh."

Edwards was not an admirer of the President—Hugo Allen Winkler, 57th of the line.

To Edwards, President Winkler seemed an empty man, a charmer, a vote grabber, a promiser. He was a disappointing man to have in office now after all the hopes in those first months of his administration. The World Federation was in danger of breaking up long before its goal had been achieved and Winkler did nothing about it. One needed a strong hand now, not a glad hand; a heard voice, not a honeyed voice.

There was the President now, shaking hands—a space forced around him by the Service, with Edwards and a few others of the Service watching intently from above.

The President would be running for re-election certainly, and there seemed a good chance he might be defeated. That would just make things worse, since the opposition party was dedicated to the destruction of the Federation.

Edwards sighed. It would be a miserable four years coming up—maybe a miserable 40—and all he could do was float in the air, ready to reach every Service agent on the ground by laser-phone if there was the slightest—

He didn't see the slightest. There was no sign of disturbance. Just a little puff of white dust, hardly visible; just a momentary glitter in the sunlight, up and away, gone as soon as Edwards became aware of it.

Where was the President? Edwards had lost sight of him in the dust.

He looked about in the vicinity of where he had seen him last. The President could not have moved far.

Then he did become aware of disturbance. First it was among the Service agents themselves who seemed to have gone off their heads and to be moving this way and that jerkily. Then those among the crowd near them caught the contagion and then those farther off.

The noise rose and became a thunder.

Edwards didn't have to hear the words that made up the rising roar. It seemed to carry the news to him by nothing more than its mass clamorous urgency. President Winkler had disappeared! He had been there one moment and had turned into a handful of vanishing dust the next.

Edwards held his breath in an agony of waiting during what seemed a drug-ridden eternity, waiting for the long moment of realization to end and for the mob to break into a mad, rioting stampede.

—When a resonant voice sounded over the gathering din, and at its sound the noise faded, died, and became a silence. It was as though it were all a holovision program after all and someone had simply turned the sound down and out.

Edwards thought, It's the President.

There was no mistaking the voice. Winkler stood on the guarded stage from which he was to give his Tercentenary speech, and from which he had left only ten minutes ago to shake hands with some in the crowd.

How had he got back there?

Edwards listened—

"Nothing has happened to me, my fellow Americans. What you have seen just now was merely the breakdown of a mechanical device. It was not your President who disappeared, so let us not allow a mechanical failure to dampen the celebration of the happiest day the world has yet seen. —My fellow Americans, give me your attention—"

And what followed was the Tercentenary speech, the greatest speech Winkler had ever made, or Edwards had ever heard. Edwards found himself forgetting his supervisory job in his eagerness to listen.

Winkler had it right! He understood the tremendous importance of saving the Federation and he was getting his message across to the people.

Deep inside, though, another part of Edwards was remembering the persistent rumors that the new expertise in robotics had resulted in the construction of a look-alike President, a robot who could perform the purely ceremonial functions, who could shake hands with the crowd, who could be neither bored nor exhausted—nor assassinated.

Edwards thought, in obscure shock, that must have been what happened. There had been such a look-alike robot down there shaking hands, and in a way the robot had been assassinated.

October 13, 2077—

Edwards looked up as the waist-high robot guide approached and said mellifluously, "Mr. Janek will see you now."

Edwards stood up, feeling tall as he towered above the stubby, metallic guide. He did not feel young, however. His face had gathered lines in the last year and he was aware of them.

He followed the guide into a surprisingly small room where, behind a surprisingly small desk, sat Francis Janek, a slightly paunchy and incongruously young-looking man.

Janek smiled and his eyes were friendly as he rose to shake hands. "Mr. Edwards."

Edwards muttered, "I'm glad to have the opportunity, sir—"

Edwards had never seen Janek before, but then the job of personal secretary to the President was a quiet one and made little news.

Janek said, "Sit down. Would you care for a soya-stick?"

Edwards smiled a polite negative, and sat down. Janek was clearly emphasizing his youth. His ruffled shirt was open and the hairs on his chest had been dyed a subdued but definite violet.

Janek said, "I know you have been trying to reach me for some weeks now. I'm sorry for the delay. I hope you understand that my time is not entirely my own. However, we're here now. —I have spoken to the Chief of the Service, by the way, and he gave you very high marks. He regrets your resignation."

Edwards said, eyes downcast, "It seemed better to pursue my investigations without danger of embarrassment to the Service."

Janek's smile flashed. "Your activities, though discreet, have not gone unnoticed. The Chief explained that you have been investigating the Tercentenary Incident, and I must admit it was that which persuaded me to see you. You've given up your position for that? Mr. Edwards, you're investigating a dead issue."

"How can it be a dead issue, Mr. Janek? Your calling it an Incident doesn't alter the fact that it was an attempt to assassinate the President."

"A matter of semantics. Why use such a disturbing word?"

"Only because it represents a disturbing truth. Surely you agree that someone did try to kill the President?"

Janek spread his hands. "If that is so, the plot did not succeed. A mechanical device was destroyed. Nothing more. In fact, if we look at it properly, the Incident—or whatever you choose to call it—did the nation and the world enormous good. As we all know, the President was shaken by the Incident, and the nation as well. The President and all of us realized what a return to the violence of the last century might mean and that realization produced a great turnaround."

"I can't deny that."

"Of course, you can't. Even the President's enemies will grant that the past year has seen momentous accomplishments. The World Federation is far stronger today than anyone could have dreamed it would be on that Tercentenary day. We might even say that an imminent breakup of the global economy has been prevented."

Edwards said cautiously, "Yes, the President is a changed man. Everyone says so."

Janek said, "He was always a great man. The Incident made him concentrate on the vital issues with a fierce intensity."

"Which he didn't do before?"

"Perhaps not quite as intensely. —In effect, then, the President, and all of us, would like the Incident itself forgotten. My main purpose in seeing you, Mr. Edwards, is to make that clear to you. This is not the twentieth century and we can't throw you in jail for being inconvenient to us, or hamper you in any way, but even the Global Charter doesn't forbid us to attempt persuasion. Do you understand me?"

"I understand you, but I do not agree with you. Can we forget the Incident when the person responsible has never been apprehended?"

"Perhaps that is just as well, too, sir. Far better that some, uh, unbalanced person escape than that the matter be blown up out of all proportion and the stage set, possibly, for a return to the violence of the twentieth century."

"The official story even states that the robot exploded spontaneously—which is impossible, and which has been an unfair blow to the robot industry."

"A robot is not the term I would use, Mr. Edwards. It was a mechanical device. No one has said that robots are dangerous, per se, certainly not the workaday metallic ones. The only reference here is to the unusually complex man-like devices that seem like flesh and blood and that we might call androids. Actually, they are so complex that perhaps they *might* explode. I am not an expert in the field. The robotics industry will recover."

"Nobody in the government," said Edwards stubbornly, "seems to care whether we reach the truth or not."

"I've already explained that there have been no bad consequences, only good ones. Why stir the mud at the bottom, when the water above is clear?"

"And the use of the disintegrator?"

For a moment Janek's hand, which had been slowly turning the container of soya-sticks on his desk, held still, then it returned to its rhythmic movement. He said, lightly, "What's a disintegrator?"

Edwards said intently, "Mr. Janek, I think you know what I mean. As part of the Service—"

"To which you no longer belong."

"Nevertheless, as part of the Service, I could not help hearing things that were not always, I suppose, meant for my ears. I had heard of this new weapon, and I saw something happen at the Tercentenary celebration which would have required one. The object everyone thought was the President disappeared into a cloud of very fine dust. It was as though every atom within the object had had its bonds to other atoms loosened. The object had become a cloud of individual atoms, which began to combine again of course, but which dispersed too quickly to do more than look like a momentary glitter of dust."

"Very science-fictionish."

"I certainly don't understand the science behind it, Mr. Janek, but I do know that it would take considerable energy to accomplish such bond breaking. This energy would have to be withdrawn from the environment. Those people who were standing near the device at the time, and whom I could locate —and who would agree to talk—were unanimous in reporting a wave of extreme coldness washing over them."

Janek put the soya-stick container to one side with a small click of transite against cellulite. He said, "Suppose just for argument that there *is* such a thing as a disintegrator."

"You need not suppose. There is."

"I won't argue the point. I know of no such thing myself, but in my position I am not likely to know of anything so security-bound as new weaponry. But if a disintegrator does exist and is as secret as all that, it must be an American monopoly, unknown to the rest of the Federation. It would then be something neither you nor I should talk about. It could be a more deadly weapon of war than the nuclear bomb, precisely because—if what you say is so—it produces nothing more than disintegration at the point of impact and coldness in the immediate neighborhood. No blast, no fire, no deadly radiation. Without these dangerous side-effects there would be no deterrent to its use, yet for all we know it might be made large enough to destroy the planet itself."

"I go along with all that," said Edwards.

"Then you see that if there is no disintegrator, it is foolish to talk about one; and if there *is* a disintegrator, then it is criminal to talk about one."

"I haven't discussed it, except with you just now, because I'm trying to persuade you of the seriousness of the situation. If one had been used, for instance, ought not the government be interested in deciding how it came to be used—if another unit of the Federation might be in possession of it?"

Janek shook his head. "I think we can rely on the appropriate departments of this government to take such a thing into consideration. You had better not concern yourself with the matter."

Edwards said, in barely controlled impatience, "Can you assure me that the United States is the only government that has such a weapon at its disposal?"

"I can't tell you since I know nothing about such a weapon, and should not know. You should not have spoken of it to me. Even if no such weapon exists, the *rumor* of its existence could be damaging."

"But since I have told you and the damage is done, please hear me out. Let me have the chance of convincing you that *you*, and no one else, holds the key to a desperate situation that perhaps I alone see."

"You alone see? I alone hold the key?"

"Does that sound paranoid? Let me explain and then judge for yourself."

"I will give you a little more time, sir, but what I have said stands. You must abandon this—this hobby of yours—this investigation. It is terribly dangerous."

"It is its abandonment that would be dangerous. Don't you see that if the disintegrator exists and if the United States has the monopoly of it, then it follows that the number of people who could have access to one would be sharply limited. As an ex-member of the Service I have some practical knowledge of this and I tell you that the only person in the world who could manage to abstract a disintegrator from our top-secret arsenals would be the President. —Only the President of the United States, Mr. Janek, only he could have arranged that assassination attempt."

They stared at each other for a moment and then Janek touched a contact on his desk.

He said, "Added precaution. No one can overhear us now by any means. Mr. Edwards, do you realize the significance of that statement? To yourself? You must not overestimate the power of the Global Charter. A government has the right to take reasonable measures for the protection of its stability."

Edwards said, "I'm approaching you, Mr. Janek, as someone I presume to be a loyal American citizen. I come to you with news of a terrible crime that affects all Americans and the entire Federation, a crime that has produced a situation that only you can right. Why do you respond with veiled threats?"

Janek said, "That's the second time you have tried to make it appear that I am a potential savior of the world. I can't conceive of myself in that role. You understand, I hope, that I have no unusual powers."

"You are the President's personal secretary."

"That does not mean I have some special confidential relationship with him. There are times, Mr. Edwards, when I suspect others consider me nothing more than a flunky, and there are even times when I find myself agreeing with them."

"Nevertheless, you see him frequently, you see him informally, you see him—"

Janek said impatiently, "I see enough of him to be able to assure you that the President would not order the destruction of that mechanical device on the Tercentenary Day."

"Is it in your opinion impossible, then?"

"I did not say that. I said he would not do it. After all, why should he? Why should the President want to destroy a look-alike android that had been a valuable adjunct to him for over three years of his Presidency? And if for some reason he wanted it done, why on earth should he do it in so incredibly public a way—at the Tercentenary celebration, no less—thus advertising its existence, risking public revulsion at the thought that citizens have been shaking hands not with the President but with a mechanical device—to say nothing of the diplomatic repercussions of representatives of other parts of the Federation having done the same thing. He might, instead, simply have ordered it disassembled in private, then no one but a few highly placed members of the Administration would have known."

"There have not been, as you said, any undesirable consequences for the President as a result of the Incident, have there?"

"He has had to cut down on the number of ceremonial appearances and he no longer is as accessible as he once was."

"As the robot once was."

"Well," said Janek uneasily, "yes, I suppose that's right."

Edwards pressed on. "And, as a matter of fact, the President was re-elected and his popularity has not diminished even though the destruction of the robot was a public event. The argument against public destruction is not as powerful as you made it sound."

"But the re-election came about *despite* the Incident. It was brought about by the President's quick action in stepping forward and delivering what you will have to admit was one of the greatest speeches in American history. It was an absolutely amazing performance. You will have to admit that."

"I admit that it was a beautifully staged drama. The President, one might think, would have counted on that."

Janek sat back in his chair. "If I understand you, Edwards, you are suggesting an involuted storybook plot. Are you saying that the President had the device destroyed—in the middle of a huge crowd, at precisely the time of the Tercentenary celebration, with the entire world watching—so that he could win the admiration of all by his quick action? Are you suggesting that he arranged it all so that he could establish himself as a man of unexpected vigor and strength under extremely dramatic circumstances and thus turn a losing campaign into a winning one? —Mr. Edwards, you've been reading fairy tales."

Edwards said, "If I were trying to claim all that, it would indeed be a fairy tale, but I am not. I never suggested that the President ordered the killing of the robot. I merely asked if you thought it were possible and you have stated quite strongly that it wasn't. I'm glad you did, because I agree with you."

"Then what is this all about? I'm beginning to think you're wasting my time."

"Another minute, please. Have you ever asked yourself why the destruction couldn't have been done with a laser beam, with a field deactivator—even with a sledge-hammer? Why should anyone go to the incredible trouble of getting a weapon guarded by the strongest possible government security to do something that didn't require such a devastating weapon? Aside from the difficulty of getting it, why risk revealing the existence of a disintegrator to the rest of the world?"

"This whole business of a disintegrator is just your theory."

"The robot disappeared completely before my eyes. I was watching. I rely on no second-hand evidence for that. It doesn't matter what you call the weapon; whatever name you give it, it had the effect of taking the robot apart atom by atom and scattering all those atoms irretrievably. Why should this have been done? It was tremendous over-kill."

"I don't know what was in the mind of the perpetrator."

"No? Yet it seems to me that there is only one logical reason for a complete powdering when something much simpler would have brought about the destruction. The powdering left no trace behind of the destroyed object. It left nothing to indicate what it had been, whether a robot"—Edwards paused—"or anything else."

Janek said, "But there is no question of what it was."

"Isn't there? I said only the President could have arranged for a disintegrator to be obtained and used. But, considering the existence of a look-alike robot, *which* President did the arranging?"

Janek said harshly, "I don't think we can carry on this conversation any further. You are mad."

Edwards said, "Think it through, sir. The President did not destroy the robot—your arguments on that score are convincing. What happened was that the robot destroyed the President. President Winkler was killed in the crowd on July 4, 2076. A robot *resembling* President Winkler then gave the Tercentenary speech, ran for re-election, was re-elected, and still serves as President of the United States."

"Madness!"

"I've come to you, to *you*, because *you* can prove this—and correct it, too."

"It is simply not so! The President is—the President." Janek made as though to rise and conclude the interview.

"You yourself admit he has changed," said Edwards, quickly and urgently. "The Tercentenary speech was beyond the powers of the old Winkler. Haven't you been yourself amazed at the accomplishments of the past year? Truthfully, could the Winkler of the first term have done all this?"

"Yes, he could have, because the President of the second term is the President of the first term."

"Do you deny he's changed? I put it to you. *You* decide and I'll abide by your decision."

"He's risen to meet the challenge, that is all. It's happened before in American history." But Janek sank back into his seat. He looked uneasy.

"He doesn't drink," said Edwards.

"He never did—very much."

"He no longer womanizes. Do you deny that he did so in the past?"

"A president is a man. For the last two years, however, he's felt completely dedicated to the problems of the Federation."

"It's a change for the better, I admit," said Edwards, "but it is a change. Of course, if he *had* a woman, the masquerade could not be carried on, could it?"

Janek said, "Too bad he doesn't have a wife." He pronounced the archaic word a little self-consciously. "The whole matter wouldn't arise if he did."

"The fact that he doesn't made the plot more workable. Yet he has fathered two children. I don't believe they have been in the White House, either one of them, since the Tercentenary celebration."

"Why should they be? They are grown, with lives of their own."

"Are they ever invited? Is the President ever interested in seeing them? You're his personal secretary. You would know. Are they?"

Janek said, "You're wasting time. A robot can't kill a human being. You know that is the first Law of Robotics."

"I know it. But no one is saying that the robot-Winkler killed the human-Winkler directly. When the human-Winkler was in the crowd, the robot-Winkler was on the speaker's stand, and I doubt that a disintegrator could be aimed from that distance without having done more widespread damage. Maybe it could, but more likely the robot-Winkler had an accomplice—a hit-man, to use twentieth-century jargon."

Janek frowned. His plump face puckered and looked pained. He said, "You know, madness must be catching. I'm actually beginning to consider the insane notion you've brought here. Fortunately, it doesn't hold water. After all, why would an assassination of the human-Winkler be arranged in public? All the arguments against destroying the robot in public hold against the killing of a human President in public. Don't you see that ruins your whole theory?"

"It does not—" began Edwards.

"It *does*. No one, except for a few officials, knew that the mechanical device existed at all. If President Winkler were killed privately and his body disposed of, the robot could easily have taken over without suspicion—without having roused yours, for instance."

"There would always be a few officials who would know, Mr. Janek. Assassination would have had to broaden." Edwards leaned forward earnestly. "See here, ordinarily there couldn't have been any danger of confusing the human being and the machine. I imagine the robot wasn't in constant use, but was brought out only for specific purposes, and there would always be key individuals, perhaps quite a number of them, who would know where the President was and what he was doing. If that were so, the assassination would have to be carried out at a time when those officials actually thought the President was really the robot."

"I don't follow you."

"Look at it this way. One of the robot's tasks was to shake hands with the crowd. When this was taking place, the officials in the know would be perfectly aware that the hand-shaker was, in truth, the robot."

"Exactly. You're making sense now. It *was* the robot."

"Except that it was the Tercentenary Day, and except that President Winkler could not resist. I suppose it would be more than human to expect a President—particularly an empty crowd-pleaser and applause-hunter like Winkler—to give up the adulation of the crowd on this day of all days, and hand it over to a machine. And perhaps the robot carefully nurtured this impulse so that on this one Tercentenary Day the President would have ordered the robot to remain behind on the speaker's platform, while Winkler himself went out to shake hands and to be cheered."

"Secretly?"

"Of course, secretly. If the President had told anyone in the Service, or any of his aides, or you, would he have been allowed to do it? The official attitude on the possibility of assassination has been practically a disease since the events of the late twentieth century. So with the encouragement of an obviously clever robot—"

"You assume the robot to be clever because you assume he is now serving as President. That is circular reasoning. If he is not President, there is no reason to think he was clever, or that he was capable of working out such a plot. Besides, what motive could possibly drive a robot to plot an assassination? Even if it didn't kill the President directly, the taking of a human life indirectly is also forbidden by the First Law, which states, 'A robot may not harm a human being or, through inaction, allow a human being to come to harm.' "

Edwards said, "The First Law is not absolute. What if harming a human being saves the lives of two others, or three others, or even three billion others? The robot may have thought that saving the World Federation took precedence over the saving of one life. It was no ordinary robot, after all. It was designed to duplicate the qualities of the President closely enough to deceive everyone. Suppose it had the human understanding of President Winkler, but without his weaknesses— and suppose it knew that it could save the Federation where the President could not?"

"*You* can reason so, but how do you know a mechanical device would?"

"It is the only way to explain what happened."

"I think it is a paranoid fantasy."

Edwards said, "Then tell me why the object that was destroyed was powdered into atoms. What else makes sense than to suppose that it was the only way to hide the fact that it was a human being who was destroyed, not a robot. Give me an alternate explanation."

Janek reddened. "I won't accept it!"

"But you can prove the whole matter—or disprove it. That's why I have come to you—to *you*."

"How can I prove it? Or disprove it, either?"

"No one sees the President at unguarded moments the way

you do. It is with you—in default of family—that he is most informal. Study him."

"I have. I tell you he isn't a—"

"You haven't. You suspected nothing wrong. Little signs meant nothing to you. Study him now, being aware that he *might* be a robot."

Janek said sardonically, "I can knock him down and probe for metal with an ultrasonic detector. Even an android has a platinum-iridium brain."

"No such drastic action will be necessary. Just observe him and you will see that he is so radically not the man he was that he cannot be a man."

Janek looked at the clock calendar on the wall. He said, "We have been here nearly an hour."

"I'm sorry to have taken up so much of your time, sir, but you do see the importance of all this, don't you?"

"Importance?" said Janek. Then he looked up and what had seemed a despondent air turned suddenly into something of hope. "But is it, in fact, important? Really, I mean?"

"How can it *not* be important? To have a robot as President of the United States? That's not important?"

"No, that's not what I mean. Forget what President Winkler might be. Just consider this. Someone serving as President of the United States has saved the World Federation; he has held it together and, at the present moment, he runs the Council in the interests of peace and constructive compromise. You'll admit all that?"

Edwards said, "Of course, I admit all that. But what of the precedent established? A robot in the White House for a very good reason now may lead to a robot in the White House ten years from now for a very bad reason, and then to robots in the White House for no reason at all but only as a matter of course. Don't you see the importance of muffling a possible trumpet call for the end of humanity at the time of its very first note?"

Janek shrugged. "Suppose I find out that he is a robot? Do

we broadcast it to the world? Do you realize how that will affect the Federation? Do you realize what it will do to the world's financial structure? Do you realize—"

"I do realize. That is why I have come to you privately, instead of trying to make it public. It is up to you to check and come to a definite conclusion. It is then up to you—having found the supposed President to be a robot, which I am certain you will find is true—to persuade him to resign."

"And by your version of his reaction to the First Law, he will then have me killed since I will be threatening his expert handling of the greatest global crisis of the twenty-first century."

Edwards shook his head. "The robot acted in secret before, and no one tried to counter the arguments he used with himself. You will be able to reinforce stricter interpretation of the First Law with your arguments. If necessary, we can get the aid of a high official at the U.S. Robots Corporation, which constructed the robot in the first place. Once he resigns, the Vice-President will succeed. If the robot-Winkler has put the old world on the right track, good; it can then be kept on the right track by the Vice-President, who is an able and honorable woman. But we can't have a robot-ruler, and we mustn't ever again."

"What if the President is human?"

"I'll leave that to you. You will know."

Janek said, "I am not that confident of myself. What if I can't decide? If I can't bring myself to? If I don't dare to? What are your plans?"

Edwards looked immensely tired. "I don't know. I may have to go to the U.S. Robots Corporation. But I don't think it will come to that. I'm quite confident, now that I've laid the problem in your lap, you won't rest till it's settled. Do *you* want to be ruled by a robot?"

He stood up, and Janek let him go. They did not shake hands.

Janek sat there in the gathering twilight.

A robot!

The man had walked in and had argued, in a perfectly rational manner, that the President of the United States was a robot!

It should have been easy to fight that off. Yet though Janek had tried every argument he could think of, they had all been useless, and the man had not been shaken in the least.

A robot as President! Edwards had been *certain* of it, and he would *stay* certain of it. And if Janek insisted that the President was human, Edwards would then go to the U.S. Robots Corporation. He wouldn't rest until the issue was resolved.

Janek frowned as he thought of the fifteen months since Tercentenary Day and of how well all had gone in the face of the probabilities. And now?

He remained lost in somber thought.

He still had the disintegrator, but surely it would not be necessary to use it on another human being. A silent laser stroke in some lonely spot would suffice.

It had been hard to maneuver the President into the earlier assassination, but in this present case the robot-President wouldn't even have to know.

ONE-SHOT

BY LAWRENCE WATT-EVANS

While we are on the subject of assassination, try a primal time travel question on for size: if you traveled back in time to prevent the assassination of John F. Kennedy, how would your actions change history? Could they, even? Lawrence Watt-Evans suggests one possibility in a subtle story worthy of the master of the short-short story, Fredric Brown.

THE FBI MAN turned the tiny calculator over in his hands, still marveling, as the prisoner said, "It took me this long to get up my nerve—sixteen months, is it? I'd meant to confess right away, but I couldn't, I was scared. But it's been eating at me. I had to show someone. I had to tell someone the truth."

The agent put the calculator down on the old green blotter, next to the yellowed newspaper clipping, and looked up. "All right," he said, "Maybe you did come here from some alternate future. Maybe it's all true, crazy as it sounds. But it's still murder."

"I know," the prisoner said miserably, "But I *had* to. I couldn't let President Kennedy die."

The FBI man nodded. He glanced at the calculator, and tapped the clipping with a finger. "Yeah," he said, "I can see that. The lab says this paper and ink are really, genuinely thirty or forty years old, not just artificially aged, but the date's just last year—so if this *is* a hoax, you've been setting it up for a long, long time." He read the headline.

JFK SHOT.

He shook his head.

"Damn," he said, "I don't know if we should give you the chair or a medal. I mean, so far, it's been hushed up, everyone's bought the suicide story, but sooner or later it's bound to leak, you know?"

The prisoner nodded miserably.

The FBI man stared at the clipping. "President Kennedy shot," he said. "And you prevented it. Still, did you have to *kill?* Couldn't you have stopped it any other way?"

The prisoner shrugged. "I had to be *sure,*" he said. "When you're dealing with someone that unbalanced, stopping one attempt might not be enough."

The agent shut his eyes and rubbed at his forehead, trying to stall off another headache.

"Excuse me . . ." the prisoner said.

The agent opened his eyes. "What?"

"I was just wondering . . . has anyone talked to President Kennedy about it?"

The agent shook his head. "No. I've passed the word up to headquarters, and they're considering it. Maybe when the President gets back from Dallas next week." He grimaced. "He'll probably want *you* shot—they say he had a real thing for Marilyn."

A KIND OF MURDER

BY LARRY NIVEN

If you doubt that new technology changes crime, just consider the effect the gun, the automobile, and the burglar alarm have had on robberies. Could there have been highwaymen before there were highways? Could there have been computer hacking without computers? And could there be the sort of crime Larry Niven describes without teleportation?

"**Y**OU ARE CONSTANTLY coming to my home!" he shouted. "You never think of calling first. Whatever I'm doing, suddenly you're there. And where the hell do you keep getting keys to my door?"

Alicia didn't answer. Her face, which in recent years had taken on a faint resemblance to a bulldog's, was set in infinite patience as she relaxed at the other end of the couch. She had been through this before, and she waited for Jeff to get it over with.

He saw this, and the dinner he had not quite finished settled like lead in his belly. "There's not a club I belong to that you aren't a member, too. Whoever I'm with, you finagle me into introducing you. If it's a man, you try to make him, and if he isn't having any you get nasty. If it's a woman, there you are like a ghost at the feast. The discarded woman. It's a drag," he said. He wanted a more powerful word, but he couldn't think of one that wouldn't sound overdramatic, silly.

She said, "We've been divorced six years. What do you care who I sleep with?"

"I don't like looking like your pimp!"

She laughed.

The acid was rising in his throat. "Listen," he said, "why don't you give up one of the clubs? W-we belong to *four*. Give one up. Any of them." *Give me a place of refuge,* he prayed.

"They're my clubs too," she said with composure. "*You* change clubs."

He'd joined the Lucifer Club four years ago, for just that reason. She'd joined, too. And now the words clogged in his throat, so that he gaped like a fish.

There were no words left. He hit her.

He'd never done that before. It was a full-arm swing, but

awkward because they were trying to face each other on the couch. She rode with the slap, then sat facing him, waiting.

It was as if he could read her mind. *We've been through this before, and it never changes anything. But it's your tantrum.* He remembered later that she'd said that to him once, those same words, and she'd looked just like that: patient, implacable.

THE CALL REACHED Homicide at eight-thirty-six P.M., July 20, 2019. The caller was a round-faced man with straight hair and a stutter. "My ex-wife," he told the desk man. "She's dead. I just got home and f-found her like this. S-someone seems to have hit her with a c-cigarette box."

Hennessey (Officer-Two) had just come on for the night shift. He took over. "You just got home? You called immediately?"

"That's right. C-c-could you come right away?"

"We'll be there in ten seconds. Have you touched anything?"

"No. Not her, and not the box."

"Have you called the hospital?"

His voice rose. "No. She's *dead.*"

Hennessey took down his name—Walters—and booth number and hung up. "Linc, Fisher, come with me. Torrie, will you call the City Hospital and have them send a copter?" If Walters hadn't touched her he could hardly be sure she was dead.

They went through the displacement booth one at a time, dialing and vanishing. For Hennessey it was as if the Homicide Room vanished as he dialed the last digit, and he was looking into a porch light.

Jeffrey Walters was waiting in the house. He was medium-sized, a bit overweight, his light brown hair going thin on top. His paper business suit was wrinkled. He wore an anxious, fearful look—which figured, either way, Hennessey thought.

And he'd been right. Alicia Walters was dead. From her attitude she had been sitting sideways on the couch when something crashed into her head, and she had sprawled forward. A green cigarette box was sitting on the glass coffee table. It was bloody along one edge, and the blood had marked the glass.

The small, bloody, beautifully-marked green malachite box could have done it. It would have been held in the right hand, swung full-armed. One of the detectives used chalk to mark its position on the table, then nudged it into a plastic bag and tied the neck.

Walters had sagged into a reading chair as if worn out. Hennessey approached him. "You said she was your ex-wife?"

"That's right. She didn't give up using her married name."

"What was she doing here, then?"

"I don't know. We had a fight earlier this evening. I finally threw her out and went back to the Sirius Club. I was half afraid she'd just follow me back, but she didn't. I guess she let herself back in and waited for me here."

"She had a key?"

Walters' laugh was feeble. "She always had a key. I've had the lock changed twice. It didn't work. I'd come home and find her here. 'I just wanted to talk,' she'd say." He stopped abruptly.

"That doesn't explain why she'd let someone else in."

"No. She must have, though, mustn't she? I don't know why she did that."

The ambulance helicopter landed in the street outside. Two men entered with a stretcher. They shifted Alicia Walters' dead body to the stretcher, leaving a chalk outline Fisher had drawn earlier.

Walters watched through the picture window as they walked the stretcher into the portable JumpShift unit inside of the copter. They closed the hatch, tapped buttons in a learned rhythm on a phone dial set in the hatch. When they opened the hatch to check, it was empty. They closed it again and boarded the copter.

Walters said, "You'll do an autopsy immediately, won't
you?"

"Of course. Why do you ask?"

"Well . . . it's possible I might have an alibi for the time of
the murder."

Hennessey laughed before he could stop himself. Walters
looked puzzled and affronted.

Hennessey didn't explain. But later—as he was leaving the
station house for home and bed—he snorted. "Alibi," he said.
"Idiot."

The displacement booths had come suddenly. One year, a
science-fiction writer's daydream. The next year, 1992, an
experimental reality. Teleportation. Instantaneous travel. Another year and they were being used for cargo transport. Two
more, and the passenger displacement booths were springing
up everywhere in the world.

By luck and the laws of physics, the world had had time to
adjust. Teleportation obeyed the Laws of Conservation of Energy and Conservation of Momentum. Teleporting uphill took
an energy input to match the gain in potential energy going
downhill—and it was over a decade before JumpShift Inc.
learned how to compensate for that effect. Teleportation over
great distances was even more heavily restricted by the
Earth's rotation.

Let a passenger flick too far west, and the difference between his momentum and the Earth's would smack him
down against the floor of the booth. Too far east, and he
would be flung against the ceiling. Too far north or south, and
the Earth would be rotating faster or slower; he would flick in
moving sideways, unless he had crossed the equator.

But cargo and passengers could be displaced between points
of equal longitude and opposite latitude. Smuggling had become impossible to stop. There was a point in the South Pacific to correspond to any point in the United States, most of
Canada, and parts of Mexico.

Smuggling via the displacement booths was a new crime.

The Permanent Floating Riot Gangs were another. The booths would allow a crowd to gather with amazing rapidity. Practically any news broadcast could start a flash crowd. And with the crowds the pickpockets and looters came flicking in.

When the booths were new, many householders had taken to putting their booths in the living rooms or entrance halls. That had stopped fast, after an astounding rash of burglaries. These days only police stations and hospitals kept their booths indoors.

For twenty years the booths had not been feasible over distances greater than ten miles. If the short-distance booths had changed the nature of crime, what of the long-distance booths? They had been in existence only four years. Most were at what had been airports, being run by what had been airline companies. Dial three numbers and you could be anywhere on Earth.

Flash crowds were bigger and more frequent.

The alibi was as dead as the automobile.

Smuggling was cheaper. The expensive, illegal transmission booths in the South Pacific were no longer needed. Cutthroat competition had dropped the price of smack to something the Mafia wouldn't touch.

And murder was easier; but that was only part of the problem. There was a new *kind* of murder going around.

HANK LOVEJOY WAS a tall, lanky man with a lantern jaw and a ready smile. The police had found him at his office—real estate—and he had agreed to come immediately.

"There were four of us at the Sirius Club before Alicia showed up," he said. "Me, and George Larimer, and Jeff Walters, and Jennifer—wait a minute—Lewis. Jennifer was over at the bar, and we'd, like, asked her to join us for dinner. You know how it is in a continuity club: you can talk to anyone. We'd have picked up another girl sooner or later."

Hennessey said, "Not two?"

"Oh, George is a monogamist. His wife is eight months pregnant, and she didn't want to come, but George just doesn't. He's not fay or anything, he just doesn't. But Jeff and I were both sort of trying to get Jennifer's attention. She was loose, and it looked likely she'd go home with one or the other of us. Then Alicia came in."

"What time was that?"

"Oh, about six-fifteen. We were already eating. She came up to the table, and we all kind of waited for Jeff to introduce her and ask her to sit down, she being his ex-wife, after all." Lovejoy laughed. "George doesn't really understand about Jeff and Alicia. Me, I thought it was funny."

"What do you mean?"

"Well, they've been divorced about six years, but it seems he just can't get away from her. Couldn't, I mean," he said, remembering. Remembering that good old Jeff *had* gotten away from her, because someone had smashed her skull.

Hennessey was afraid Lovejoy would clam up. He played stupid. "I don't get it. A divorce is a divorce, isn't it?"

"Not when it's a quote friendly divorce unquote. Jeff's a damn fool. I don't think he gave up sleeping with her, not right after the divorce. He wouldn't live with her, but every so often she'd, well, she'd seduce him, I guess you'd say. He wasn't used to being alone, and I guess he got lonely. Eventually he must have given that up, but he still couldn't get her out of his hair.

"See, they belonged to all the same clubs and they knew all the same people, and as a matter of fact they were both in routing and distribution of software; that was how they met. So if she came on the scene while he was trying to do something else, there she was, and he had to introduce her. She probably knew the people he was dealing with, if it was business. A lot of business gets done at the continuity clubs. And she wouldn't go away. I thought it was funny. It worked out fine for me, last night."

"How?"

"Well, after twenty minutes or so it got through to us that Alicia wasn't going to go away. I mean, we were eating dinner, and she wasn't, but she wanted to talk. When she said something about waiting and joining us for dessert, Jeff stood up and suggested they go somewhere to talk. She didn't look too pleased, but she went."

"What do you suppose he wanted to talk about?"

Lovejoy laughed. "Do I read minds without permission? He wanted to tell her to bug off, of course! But he was gone half an hour, and by the time he came back, Jennifer and I had sort of reached a decision. And George had this benign look he gets, like, *Bless you my children.* He doesn't play around himself, but maybe he likes to think of other couples getting together. Maybe he's right; maybe it brightens up the marriage bed."

"Jeff came back alone?"

"That he did. He was nervous, jumpy. Friendly enough; I mean, he didn't get obnoxious when he saw how it was with me and Jennifer. But he was sweating, and I don't blame him."

"What time was this?"

"Seven-twenty."

"Dead on?"

"Yeah."

"Why would you remember a thing like that?"

"Well, when Jeff came back he wanted to know how long he'd been gone. So I looked at my watch. Anyway, we stayed another fifteen minutes and then Jennifer and I took off."

Hennessey asked, "Just how bad were things between Jeff and Alicia?"

"Oh, they didn't *fight* or anything. It was just—funny. For one thing, she's kind of let herself go since the divorce. She used to be pretty. Now she's gone to seed. Not many men chase her these days, so she has to do the chasing. Some men like that."

"Do you?"

"Not particularly. I've spent some nights with her, if that's what you're asking. I just like variety. I'm not a heartbreaker, man; I run with girls who like variety, too."

"Did Alicia?"

"I think so. The trouble was, she slept with a lot of guys Jeff introduced her to. He didn't like that. It made him look bad. And once she played nasty to a guy who turned her down, and it ruined a business deal."

"But they didn't fight."

"No. Jeff wasn't the type. Maybe that's why they got divorced. She was just someone he couldn't avoid. We all know people like that."

"After he came back without Alicia, did he leave the table at any time?"

"I don't think so. No. He just sat there, making small talk. Badly."

George larimer was a writer of articles, one of the few who made good money at it. He lived in Arizona. No, he didn't mind a quick trip to the police station, he said, emphasizing the *quick.* Just let him finish this paragraph . . . and he breezed in five minutes later.

"Sorry about that. I just couldn't get the damn wording right. This one's for *Viewer's Digest,* and I have to explain drop ship technology for morons without talking down to them or the minimal viewer won't buy it. What's the problem?"

Hennessey told him.

His face took on an expression Hennessey recognized: like he ought to be feeling something, and he was trying, honest. "I just met her that night," he said. "Dead. Well."

He remembered that evening well enough. "Sure, Jeff Walters came back about the time we were finishing coffee. We had brandy with the coffee, and then Hank and, uh, Jennifer left. Jeff and I sat and played dominoes over scotch and sodas. You can do that at the Sirius, you know. They keep game boxes there, and they'll move up side tables at your elbows so you can have drinks or lunch."

"How did you do?"

"I beat him. Something was bothering him; he wasn't playing very well. I thought he wanted to talk, but he wouldn't talk about whatever was bugging him."

"His ex-wife?"

"Maybe. Maybe not. I'd only just met her, and she seemed nice enough. And she seemed to like Jeff."

"Yeah. Now, Jeff left with Alicia. How long were they gone?"

"Half an hour, I guess. And he came back without her."

"What time?"

"Quarter past seven or thereabouts. Ask Hank, I don't wear a watch." He said this with a certain pride. A writer doesn't need a watch; he sets his own hours. "As I said, we had dessert and coffee and then played dominoes for an hour, maybe a little less. Then I had to go home to see how my wife was getting along in my absence."

"While you were having dessert and coffee and playing dominoes, did Jeff Walters leave the table at any time?"

"Well, we switched tables to set up the game." Larimer shut his eyes to think. He opened them. "No, he didn't go to the bathroom or anything."

"Did you?"

"No. We were together the whole time, if that's what you want to know."

HENNESSEY WENT OUT for lunch after Larimer left. Returning, he stepped out of the Homicide Room booth just ahead of Officer-One Fisher, who had spent the morning at Alicia Walters' place.

Alicia had lived in the mountains, within shouting distance of Lake Arrowhead. Property in that area was far cheaper than property around the lake itself. The high rent district in the mountains is near streams and lakes. Her own water supply had come from a storage tank kept filled by a small JumpShift unit.

Fisher was hot and sweaty and breathing hard, as if he had been working. He dropped into a chair and wiped his forehead and neck. "There wasn't much point in going," he said. "We found what was left of a bacon and tomato sandwich sitting on a placemat. Probably her last meal. She wasn't much of a housekeeper. Probably wasn't making much money, either."

"How so?"

"All her gadgetry is old enough to be going to pieces. Her Dustmaster skips corners and knocks things off tables. Her chairs and couches are all blow-ups, inflated plastic. Cheap, but they have to be replaced every so often, and she didn't. Her displacement booth must be ten years old. She should have replaced it, living in the mountains."

"No roads in that area?"

"Not near her house, anyway. In remote areas like that they move the booths in by helicopter, then bring the components for the house out through the booth. If her booth broke down she'd have had to hike out, unless she could find a neighbor at home, and her neighbors aren't close. I like that area," Fisher said suddenly. "There's elbow room."

"She should have made good money. She was in routing and distribution of software." Hennessey pondered. "Maybe she spent all her time following her ex-husband around."

The autopsy report was waiting on his desk. He read through it.

Alicia Walters had indeed been killed by a single blow to the side of the head, almost certainly by the malachite box. Its hard corner had crushed her skull around the temple. Malachite is a semiprecious stone, hard enough that no part of it had broken off in the wound; but there was blood, and traces of bone and brain tissue, on the box itself.

There was also a bruise on her cheek. *Have to ask Walters about that,* he thought.

She died about eight P.M., given the state of her body, including body temperature. Stomach contents indicated that she had eaten about five-thirty P.M.: a bacon and tomato sandwich.

Hennessey shook his head. "I was right. He's still thinking in terms of alibis."

Fisher heard. "Walters?"

"Sure, Walters. Look: he came back to the Sirius Club at seven-thirty, and he called attention to the time. He stayed until around eight-thirty, to hear Larimer tell it, and he was always in someone's company. Then he went home, found the body, and called us. The woman was killed around eight, which is right in the middle of his alibi time. Give or take fifteen minutes for the lab's margin of error, and it's still an alibi."

"Then it clears him."

Hennessey laughed. "Suppose he did go to the bathroom. Do you think anyone would remember it? Nobody in the world has had an alibi for something since the JumpShift booths took over. You can be at a party in New York and kill a man in the California Sierras in the time it would take to go out for cigarettes. You can't use displacement booths for an alibi."

"You could be jumping to conclusions," Fisher pointed out. "So he's not a cop. So he reads detective stories. So someone murdered his wife in his own living room. *Naturally* he wants to know if he's got an alibi."

Hennessey shook his head.

"She didn't bleed a lot," said Fisher. "Maybe enough, maybe not. Maybe she was moved."

"I noticed that, too."

"Someone who knew she had a key to Walters' house killed her and dumped her there. He would have hit her with the cigarette box in the spot where he'd already hit her with something else."

Hennessey shook his head again. "It's not just Walters. It's a *kind* of murder. We get more and more of these lately. People kill each other because they can't move away from each other. With the long-distance booths everyone in the country lives next door to everyone else. You live a block away from your ex-wife, your mother-in-law, the girl you're trying to drop, the guy who lost money in your business deal and blames you. Any secretary lives next door to her boss, and if he needs something done in a hurry she's right there. God help the doctor if his patients get his home number. I'm not just pulling these out of the air. I can name you an assault rap for every one of these situations."

"Most people get used to it," said Fisher. "My mother used to flick in to visit me at work, remember?"

Hennessey grinned. He did. Fortunately she'd given it up. "It was worse for Walters," he said.

"It didn't really sound that bad. Lovejoy said it was a friendly divorce. So he was always running into her. So what?"

"She took away his clubs."

Fisher snorted. But Fisher was young. He had grown up with the short-distance booths.

For twenty years passenger teleportation had been restricted to short hops. People had had time to get used to the booths. And in those twenty years the continuity clubs had come into existence.

The continuity club was a guard against future shock. Its location . . . ubiquitous: hundreds of buildings in hundreds of cities, each building just like all the others, inside and out. Wherever a member moved in this traveling society, the club would be there. Today even some of the customers would be the same: everyone used the long-distance booths to some extent.

A man had to have some kind of stability in his life. His church, his marriage, his home, his club. Any man might need more or less stability than the next. Walters had belonged to *four* clubs . . . and they were no use to him if he kept meeting Alicia Walters there. And his marriage had broken up, and he wasn't a churchgoer, and a key to his house had been found in Alicia's purse. She should at least have left him his clubs.

Fisher spoke, interrupting his train of thought. "You've been talking about impulse murders, haven't you? Six years of not being able to stand his ex-wife and not being able to get away from her. So finally he hits her with a cigarette box."

"Most of them are impulse murders, yes."

"Well, this wasn't any impulse murder. Look at what he had to do to bring it about. He'd have had to ask her to wait at home for him. Then make some excuse to get away from Larimer, shift home, kill her *fast,* and get back to the Sirius Club before Larimer wonders where he's gone. Then he's got to hope Larimer will forget the whole thing. That's not just cold-blooded, it's also stupid."

"Yeah. So far it's worked, though."

"Worked, hell. The only evidence you've got against Walters is that he had good reason to kill her. Listen, if she got on his nerves that much, she may have irritated some other people, too."

Hennessey nodded. "That's the problem, all right." But he didn't mean it the way Fisher did.

WALTERS HAD MOVED to a hotel until such time as the police were through with his house. Hennessey called him before going off duty.

"You can go home," he told him.

"That's good," said Walters. "Find out anything?"

"Only that your wife was murdered with that selfsame cigarette box. We found no sign of anyone in the house except her, and you." He paused, but Walters only nodded thoughtfully. He asked, "Did the box look familiar to you?"

"Oh, yes, of course. It's mine. Alicia and I bought it on our honeymoon, in Switzerland. We divided things during the divorce, and that went to me."

"All right. Now, just how violent was that argument you had?"

He flushed. "As usual. I did a lot of shouting, and she just sat there letting it go past her ears. It never did any good."

"Did you strike her?"

The flush deepened, and he nodded. "I've never done that before."

"Did you by any chance hit her with a malachite box?"

"Do I need a lawyer?"

"You're not under arrest, Mr. Walters. But if you feel you need a lawyer, by all means get one." Hennessey hung up.

He had asked to be put on the day shift today, in order to follow up this case. It was quitting time now, but he was reluctant to leave.

Officer-One Fisher had been eavesdropping. He said, "So?"

"He never mentioned the word *alibi*," said Hennessey. "Smart. He's not supposed to know when she was killed."

"You're still sure he did it."

"Yeah. But getting a conviction is something else again. We'll find more people with more motives. And all we've got is the laboratory." He ticked items off his fingers. "No fingerprints on the box. No blood on Walters or any of his clothes, unless he had paper clothes and ditched 'em. No way of proving Walters let her in or gave her the key . . . though I wonder if he really had that much trouble keeping her out of the house.

"We'd be asking a jury to believe that Walters left the table and Larimer forgot about it. Larimer says no. Walters is pretty sure to get the benefit of the doubt. She didn't bleed much; a good defense lawyer is bound to suggest that she was moved from somewhere else."

"It's possible."

"She wasn't dead until she was hit. Nothing in the stomach but food. No drugs or poisons in the bloodstream. She'd have had to be killed by someone who"—he ticked them off— "knew she had Walters' key; knew Walters' displacement booth number; and knew Walters wouldn't be home. Agreed?"

"Maybe. How about Larimer or Lovejoy?"

Hennessey spread his hands in surrender. "It's worth asking. Larimer's alibi is as good as Walters', for all that's worth. And we've still got to interview Jennifer Lewis."

"Then again, a lot of people at the Sirius Club knew Walters. Some of them must have been involved with Alicia. Anyone who saw Walters halfway through a domino game would know he'd be stuck there for a while."

"True. Too true." Hennessey stood up. "Guess I'll be getting dinner."

HENNESSEY CAME OUT of the restaurant feeling pleasantly stuffed and torpid. He turned left toward the nearest booth, a block away.

The Walters case had haunted him all through dinner. Fisher had made a good deal of sense . . . but what bugged him was something Fisher hadn't said. Fisher hadn't said that Hennessey might be looking for easy answers.

Easy? If Walters had killed Alicia during a game of dominoes at the Sirius Club, then there wouldn't *be* any case until Larimer remembered. Aside from that, Walters would have been an idiot to try such a thing. Idiot, or desperate.

But if someone else had killed her, it opened a bag of snakes. Restrict it to members of the Sirius Club and how many were left? They'd both done business there. How many of Jeffrey Walters' acquaintances had shared Alicia's bed? Which of them would have killed her, for reason or no reason? The trouble with sharing too many beds was that one's chance of running into a really bad situation was improved almost to certainty.

If Walters had done it, things became simpler.

But she hadn't bled much.

And Walters couldn't have had reason to move her body to

his home. Where could he have killed her that would be worse than that?

Walters owned the murder weapon . . . no, forget that. She could have been hit with anything, and if she were in Walters' house fifteen seconds later she might still be breathing when the malachite box finished the job.

Hennessey slowed to a stop in front of the booth. Something Fisher *had* said, something had struck him funny. What was it?

"Her displacement booth must be ten years old—" That was it. The sight of the booth must have sparked the memory. And it *was* funny. How had he known?

JumpShift booths were all alike. They had to be. They all had to hold the same volume, because the air in the receiver had to be flicked back to the transmitter. When JumpShift improved a booth, it was the equipment they improved, so that the older booths could still be used.

Ten years old. Wasn't that—yes. The altitude shift. Pumping energy into a cargo, so that it could be flicked a mile or a hundred miles uphill, had been an early improvement. But a transmitter that could absorb the lost potential energy of a downhill shift had not become common until ten years ago.

Hennessey stepped in and dialed the police station.

Sergeant Sobel was behind the desk. "Oh, Fisher left an hour ago," he said. "Want his number?"

"Yes . . . no. Get me Alicia Walters' number."

Sobel got it for him. "What's up?"

"Tell you in a minute," said Hennessey, and flicked out.

It was black night. His ears registered the drop in pressure. His eyes adjusted rapidly, and he saw that there were lights in Alicia Walters' house.

He stepped out of the booth. Whistling, he walked a slow circle around it.

It was a JumpShift booth. What more was there to say? A glass cylinder with a rounded top, big enough for a tall man to stand upright and a meager amount of baggage to stand with him—or for a man holding a dead woman in his arms, clenching his teeth while he tried to free one finger for dialing. The machinery that made the magic was buried beneath the booth. The dial, a simple push-button phone dial. Even the long-distance booths looked just like this one, though the auxiliary machinery was far more complex.

"But he was sweating—" Had Lovejoy meant it literally?

Hennessey was smiling ferociously as he stepped back into the booth.

The lights of the Homicide Room flashed in his eyes. Hennessey came out tearing at his collar. Sweat started from every pore. Living in the mountains like that, Alicia should certainly have had her booth replaced. The room felt like a furnace, but it was his own body temperature that had jumped seven degrees in a moment. Seven degrees of randomized energy, to compensate for the drop in potential energy between here and Lake Arrowhead.

WALTERS SAT SLUMPED, staring straight ahead of him. "She didn't understand and she didn't care. She was taking it like we'd been all through this before but we had to do it again and let's get it over with." He spoke in a monotone, but the nervous stutter was gone. "Finally I hit her. I guess I was trying to get her attention. She just took it and looked at me and waited for me to go on."

Hennessey said, "Where did the malachite box come in?"

"Where do you think? I hit her with it."

"Then it was hers, not yours."

"It was ours. When we broke up, she took it. Look, I don't want you to think I wanted to *kill* her. I wanted to scar her."

"To scare her?"

"No! To scar her!" His voice rose. "To leave a mark she'd remember every time she looked in a mirror, so she'd know I meant it, so she'd leave me alone! I wouldn't have cared if she sued. Whatever it cost, it would have been worth it. But I hit her too hard, too hard. I felt the crunch."

"Why didn't you report it?"

"But I did! At least, I tried. I picked her up in my arms and wrestled her out to the booth and dialed the Los Angeles Emergency Hospital. I don't know if there's any place closer, and I wasn't thinking too clear. Listen, maybe I can prove this. Maybe an intern saw me in the booth. I flicked into the hospital, and suddenly I was broiling. Then I remembered that Alicia had an old booth, the kind that can't absorb a difference in potential energy."

"We guessed that much."

"So I dialed quick and flicked right out again. I had to go back to Alicia's for the malachite box and to wipe off the sofa, and my own booth *is* a new one, so I got the temperature shift again. God, it was hot. I changed suits before I went back to the club. I was still sweating."

"You thought that raising her temperature would foul up our estimate of when she died."

"That's right." Walter's smile was wan. "Listen, I did try to get her to a hospital. You'll remember that, won't you?"

"Yeah. But you changed your mind."

VRM-547

BY W. R. THOMPSON

A robot, like a computer, is a machine that follows the instructions it is given. But how is it to deal with something it doesn't recognize or about which it has no instructions? If it is anything like the caretaker robot in W. R. Thompson's "VRM-547" (which was a finalist for the 1991 Hugo Award), it will deal with the situation very effectively.

ALL IS NOT well. VRM-547 has vanished, its place taken by VRM-1489. I cannot understand how this happens, as neither object—coded as a floor lamp and a hat rack, respectively—is mobile. Nevertheless it happens, and as always I must spend several hundred microseconds in reprogramming my house map. The two objects are just dissimilar enough to require such adjustments. It is an unending source of confusion.

The date is Tuesday; therefore I must scrub and wax the floors. My owner—coded as "Yes, sir, sergeant, sir"—requires this operation on all Tuesdays. I connect with my cleaning apparatus, fill its tanks with soap, water, and wax, and proceed with the assigned function.

The function is 97 percent complete when my owner rolls across a section of floor. "Lieutenant Halloran, clean those up," he orders. He points to the floor.

"Those" is an indefinite term. It is plural. Analysis suggests that "those" refers to the marks which my owner's wheelchair has left on the floor. I assign the marked areas a higher priority than the uncleaned areas of the floor, and proceed with my modified function. "Yes, sir, sergeant, sir," I say, acknowledging the order.

In due time, I finish the function. I return my cleaning apparatus to its storage rack. The next function in my assignment stack is to check on my owner's health. This is my primary function, programmed into me by the Veterans Administration. Every hour I query his implant, and collect data on his health status and the medication levels in his bloodstream. Whenever it is Monday, I send my collected data to the nearby VA hospital, unless the readings fall outside certain limits. In that case, I would initiate emergency measures.

My owner's health is well, within its limits. My next assigned function is grocery acquisition, so I mount the wire-frame basket on my shell. I roll into the living room, where my owner is seated before VRM-12, a television set, currently active. "Lieutenant Halloran, are you going shopping now?" he says.

"Yes, sir, sergeant, sir."

"Lieutenant Halloran, my nephews are coming over today. Buy some munchies for them."

"Error code forty-seven," I say. "Unrecognized word: munchies."

"Lieutenant Halloran, you feeble excuse for a Marine, add a dozen Twinkies to the grocery list."

"Yes, sir, sergeant, sir."

I am about to exit the house when I detect a hazard. A sheet of newspaper has fallen atop VRM-187, an electric space heater. Although the heater is not active, it may be activated. My safety program warns that this situation creates a fire hazard. This, in turn, would endanger my owner's health. I retrieve the paper, fold it and place it on VRM-53, a coffee table.

I roll down the ramp, reach the sidewalk and make a ninety degree turn to the right. I proceed toward external position three, coded as a supermarket. There are two stop points between my home position and the supermarket, coded as crosswalks. At each I stop and wait until I see a green signal light.

This function uses most of my data-processing abilities. Outside the house I see many objects and shapes which are not coded in my Visual Recognition Matrix. I must examine each uncoded object to see if it fits a generalized visual code: human or wheeled vehicle. I am programmed to avoid collisions with these objects. This is difficult, especially as certain vehicles will attempt to intersect my path at random, while certain humans will block my path at random.

I enter external position three, print out the grocery list, and wait for human assistance. Over a billion microseconds pass before a human appears and takes my list. Another billion microseconds pass before the human returns. As he loads objects into my basket, I tag each with a temporary recognition code: VRM-T-187 through VRM-T-215.

There is trouble as I return home. A vehicle increases its speed and attempts to intersect me. I give full power to my drive units and avoid a collision, but VRM-T-198 has bounced out of my carrying basket. It is round, and it rolls a considerable distance, lodging among a number of unrecognizable objects. This makes recognition difficult, and I must examine each object before I can identify and retrieve VRM-T-198.

Upon my return home I enter the kitchen and store the new objects in the upper and lower food cabinets. After I finish this task I put the wire-frame basket on its storage rack. There are dirty utensils in the sink, and I have no scheduled functions, so I begin to clean the utensils.

My owner rolls into the kitchen and opens the lower food cabinet. He removes VRM-T-191 and VRM-T-203. Then he faces me. "Lieutenant Halloran, you jackass, how many times have I told you to put the damned eggs in the refrigerator?"

"Error message twelve," I respond. "Data not available."

"Lieutenant Halloran, you little piss-ant, put the damned eggs in the damned refrigerator."

"Yes, sir, sergeant, sir." I roll up to him and stop. He holds two objects, and I have been ordered to take one. Which one? "Error message seven. Identity: eggs."

My owner makes an uncodable response. He pushes VRM-T-191 into my left manipulator and rolls away. I add VRM-T-191 to my permanent Visual Recognition Matrix, coding the shape as VRM-3876, the eggs. This puzzles me, as the matrix already contains VRM-96, an egg. The words are clearly related, yet the shapes are quite different. More to the point, "eggs" by definition means "more than one egg."

The doorbell rings and I go to answer it. I recognize the two small humans at the door as my owner's nephews. "Hello, Mr. John. Hello, Mr. Craig. Please enter."

My owner and his nephews spend the next several billion microseconds in the living room. As I have no assigned functions, I remain by the door. I observe them as I stand by. My owner has placed VRM-T-203 on the coffee table. He opens the object, and the nephews remove smaller objects from it. They eat the smaller objects while they talk.

I consider how this phenomenon relates to "egg" and "eggs." Perhaps VRM-3876, the eggs, should be coded as the egg container. My owner is not always precise with his input statements, which has confused me on other occasions.

This causes me to reassess the relationship between the hat rack and the floor lamp. The hat rack is present now. I note that its shape resembles that of the lamp. Its support legs and central shaft are made of light-reflective material, and it is topped with a complex shape. There are many small, smooth surfaces around the top structure. I realize that these facets can reflect light, and certain reflections can confuse my optics.

Perhaps the rack is the lamp with its lights off. However, when I attempt to recode VRM-1489 as a switched-off lamp, I receive an internal error message. Although this is a mistake, I continue to recognize VRM-1489 as a hat rack. This is an idiosyncrasy of my pattern-recognition software, and I am not able to correct it.

I hear one of my owner's nephews use my address label: Lieutenant Halloran. This draws my attention, of course. "Why do you call your robot 'Lieutenant Halloran'?" the nephew asks.

The other nephew answers him. "A robot has to have a name, so it knows when you give it an order. Machines are like that."

"But why do you call it that, Uncle Jake?" the first nephew asks.

"So I won't forget how much I hate the scumball. See, Lieutenant Halloran was my platoon leader in Nicaragua. Now I can push him around like I always wanted." My owner rolls his wheelchair across the room and picks up VRM-1, a group photograph. "That's him in front, the weedbrain. Dumbest pogue in the whole corps. Lieutenant Halloran, tell the boys about yourself."

"Yes, sir, sergeant, sir." I recite memory file HALLORAN for him: "I am the biggest clown in the Marine Corps, a disgrace to my uniform, a bigger threat to my unit than the entire Nicaraguan army. Ortega smiles when he thinks of me. I think field rations are delicious. . . ."

The file is extensive. While I play it back, I make my hourly query of my owner's implant. I note that his blood pressure and pulse rate have lowered, and his brainwave traces have moderated. My medical software tells me this is consonant with a slight reduction in mental stress. I conjecture that playing memory file HALLORAN somehow has a soothing effect on my owner.

"Lieutenant Halloran, at ease," he says, and I fall silent while my owner talks to his nephews. "The real Halloran nearly got our platoon killed a dozen times, because he wanted to look like a gung-ho gyrene—win a medal, impress the rear-echelon honchos, get himself promoted. So he kept volunteering us for lurps—hell, long-range reconnaissance patrols to you—and ambush patrols. All the scut jobs. Then one night he walked us into Sandinista turf, and he got half of us killed. I caught a bullet in the spine that night."

A subroutine whose existence I have not suspected makes itself known. I record his words into a special memory file. They will be evaluated by a psychiatrist, who is concerned with my owner's adaptation to his disability.

My owner again shows the VRM-1 group photograph to his nephews. "Look, I want you kids to know about the guys in my unit. See this dude, Wynsocki?"

"The white boy with the long mustache?" a nephew asks.

"Yeah, that's Wynsocki. We called him the Sock. He saved us all one night." My owner's voice-stress levels remain within acceptable limits, if just barely. "See, Halloran sent us into a village, and he ordered us not to shoot until the Reds opened fire, so we'd know exactly where they were. That's how an ambush patrol works. Only word had it that the Sandinistas had a whole company in that village. We knew we were dead goin' in, but try telling *that* to Halloran. Orders are orders, he said, so write your will if you're scared.

"We got to the edge of the village, and the Sock grins at me, and says he'll obey orders and let them shoot first. Then— then he runs into the village, shoutin' and screamin', and that's when all the Reds in the village start shootin' at him. That bought us enough time to get under cover and save our bacon, but it was all over for the Sock. I guess he had better luck than me." One hand hits the side of his chair.

There is a long silence, lasting tens of millions of microseconds, during which the nephews stop eating the smaller objects from VRM-T-203. When one finally speaks his voice-stress level is high. He says that it is time to go home, and they leave at once.

I clean up the living room while my owner prepares and eats his dinner. During my next check of his implant I note that his blood-alcohol level has risen to 0.09%, a significant but not worrisome amount. After dinner he returns to the living room. He carries VRM-T-200 on his lap, an object which contains brown bottles. He turns on the television and drinks from the bottles.

Then he speaks, and both his voice-stress and decibel levels reach high and dangerous readings. I roll into the living room, alerted for a medical emergency. I check my emergency systems: medical software, siren, oxygen bottle and mask, modem and telephone cord. "Do you require assistance? Is there trouble?"

"Trouble! You didn't hear the news? We're goddamn withdrawing from Nicaragua!"

Analyzing this as best I can, I find "withdraw" in my vocabulary. It is a medical term, referring to certain side effects of addictive substances. "Error message fifty-two. Undefined use of 'withdraw.' You are not an addict."

" 'Addict'? What are you talking about, you scraphead? I'm

not addicted to any damned thing." My owner drinks from a bottle. "Maybe Uncle Sam is the addict. Yeah. He's hooked on getting us into wars, then quitting before we can win. All that talk about how we're fightin' for democracy—what were they doing, just throwing us away? Tell me!"

"Error message twelve," I answer. "Data not available."

"Goddamn *machine!*" He throws the bottle at me. I am undamaged, although the bottle shatters. "Know why they gave me a robot nursemaid? Because you're goddamn cheaper'n a human worker! They weren't going to waste money on—forget it. Forget everything. Everyone wants to forget about us soldiers. Even family." He rolls his wheelchair out of the room.

There is broken glass all over the living room floor. I get my cleaning equipment and remove it.

My owner goes to bed early, but he does not fall asleep until well after midnight. It is probable that he will not wake until late tomorrow morning, and he will not leave bed until he has been awake over an hour. In the sixty-three days during which I have worked for him I have never seen him vary from this pattern. My medical profiles inform me that this is not standard human behavior, but it does not fall outside the parameters which the VA gave me for my owner. I cannot explain this incongruity.

At 1:37 A.M. I hear unidentifiable noises from my owner's bedroom. When I go to investigate, I find that a human has entered the bedroom. I examine him in infrared, and find that he does not fit my recognition matrices.

Evidently, he does not fit my owner's matrices either. "What you want?" he asks. His voice-stress levels are high.

"Just shut up," the unknown human tells him. "Stay quiet and you won't get hurt." The man looks out the window at the side yard, then pulls the window down. He does this with one hand. In his other hand he holds an object which I know I should recognize.

The man points the object at my owner. "Get your hands

out where I can see them, spade. Real slow—I don't want you pulling something on me. Now get out of bed. Slow."

"I—can't—walk." His voice-stress levels verge on the danger line. Following my programming, I switch my medical monitors to full coverage. I now receive an implant update every five seconds. All of my owner's readings are within tolerable levels, but the trend is upward.

"Get up!"

"I can't! Look, why in hell you think I got that wheelchair?"

The man looks at it and makes a grunting noise. Then he notices me. "What's that?"

"A Vet-Admin robot. It runs errands for me."

"And calls the cops, too, I bet. Turn it off."

"It doesn't have an 'off' switch. Hell, it doesn't even have an instruction manual!"

"Yeah, I'll just bet," the intruder says. He comes to me and squats down. As he examines me I study the object in his hand. It strongly resembles certain objects in the group photograph. I feel a 90 percent level of confidence that it is a pistol. My safety program describes pistols and related devices as health hazards.

The intruder grunts again and pulls open my communication panel. In seconds my maintenance circuits alert me to damage: modem disabled. Siren disabled. Primary speaker disabled. It is evident that the intruder knows something of robotics, although he misses my back-up speaker.

He steps back from me and faces my owner. "Now, I'm going to stay here until I'm sure the pigs are through searching this area. Don't make any trouble for me and you won't get hurt."

"Who the hell are you?" my owner asks.

"Let's just say I'm a free soul, and I'm staying that way." He waves the pistol. "Where's your money?"

My owner snorts. "You think I'm rich? Did you ever see a VA disability check?"

"I got to tear this place apart?" The intruder kicks over the wheelchair. "If you got any money, you better talk!"

"OK. There's five, maybe six bucks in my top dresser drawer."

"Five or six bucks?" The intruder opens the drawer and extracts the money. "What a place. I didn't even get that much when I hit the liquor store."

The intruder sits on the floor, but he keeps the gun pointed at my owner. "Rotten luck. I saw all the long grass and weeds in your yard, and I figured no one lived here. Only it turns out you're some cripple that don't mow his lawn. So what am I going to do with you when I leave?"

My owner's medical readings now exceed the safety levels. I must now summon help. Considering my damage I have few options. The most efficient is to use my back-up speaker and the kitchen telephone. I roll toward the bedroom door.

"Hey!" the intruder snaps. "Where's that thing going?"

"How should I know?" my owner says. "You think I know about robots?"

"Well, stop it! Machine, stop! You better stop it!"

"Lieutenant Halloran, stop." I stop in the hallway. "Get back in here. What are you doing?"

"Medical emergency." My back-up speaker is feeble, but adequate. "I must summon help. I will use the telephone."

The intruder causes the gun to make a clacking noise. "If it makes any trouble, you son of a bitch, I'll kill you."

"OK, OK," my owner says. "Lieutenant Halloran. Do not use the telephone. Do not call for help. Do not leave the house. Do you understand?"

"Yes, sir, sergeant, sir." Analysis makes one thing evident: the intruder is a threat to my owner's health. I must remove this threat, within the constraints imposed on me. I again leave the room.

"Lieutenant Halloran!" The intruder now knows my address label. "What are you doing?"

"I have functions to pursue," I say. I would be more specific, but I have not yet selected a course of action.

I leave the bedroom, and the intruder does not stop me again. As I roll into the kitchen I contemplate my options, which are frankly limited. My safety program suggests several courses of action. Only one has an acceptable chance of success, and it is hampered by a high degree of complexity.

I go to my rack and connect into my floor cleaning equipment. I fill the tank with water, and then enter the living room. I set the hose nozzle to "stream" and flood the hall entry with water, retaining one gallon of water in the tank.

I examine VRM-1489. The hat rack has an electric switch near its top. I activate it, and the hat rack becomes VRM-547, the floor lamp. I grasp it in both manipulators and test its handling characteristics. The three light bulbs cast moving shadows as I swing the lamp back and forth. Now I must wait for the intruder to come to me.

My owner's physical condition remains unacceptable. The most probable cause is stress. I recall that I have a resource which can alleviate that condition in him. I access memory file HALLORAN, and recite its contents at the highest decibel level my back-up speaker can manage: "I am the biggest clown in the Marine Corps, a disgrace to my uniform, a bigger threat to my unit than the entire Nicaraguan army. Ortega smiles when he thinks of me. I think field rations are delicious. . . ."

I hear voices from the bedroom. First, the intruder: "What the hell is that?"

Next, my owner: "How should I know? That damned cheap-charley robot never has worked right."

I detect footsteps, increasing in volume. I wait until the intruder steps into the living room, setting both feet in the puddle of water. I activate the hose and spray him with my remaining water; at maximum pressure the tank drains itself in three seconds. Simultaneously I swing the lamp, aiming to strike him in the chest area with the bulbs. Two of them shatter on impact and there is a flash like lightning.

The house current fails within a few million microseconds. By this time, however, the intruder lies on the floor. His body makes uncoordinated movements but he does not get up. It soon becomes clear that the intruder is dead, and therefore no longer a threat to my owner's health. I am now holding the VRM-1489 hat rack, which I drop. I pull the body out of the entryway and return to the bedroom.

My owner is leaning out of his bed and trying to reach his wheelchair: "Lieutenant Halloran, what happened?"

"Error message thirty-nine," I say. "Indeterminate question."

"You dickweed. Lieutenant Halloran, what has happened to that burglar?"

"I electrocuted the intruder with the VRM-547 floor lamp." I take the wheelchair and restore it to its proper position.

"You did?" My owner stares at me for several million microseconds. "I thought—Lieutenant Halloran, aren't robots programmed against harming humans?"

"Yes. However, protecting your health took precedence. The intruder was a threat to your health."

"I see." It is many millions of microseconds before my owner speaks again. "Lieutenant Halloran, call the police."

"Yes, sir, sergeant, sir."

I go to the kitchen and use the phone to call the police. I also request an ambulance; my owner's physical condition is returning to normal, but it has been in the danger zone and medical attention remains mandatory. I make my requests in the most urgent forms my vocabulary allows.

There are other problems. I am in need of repairs. The electricity is out. The living room is a mess: the floor is wet, broken glass is everywhere again, the VRM-1489 hat rack is damaged, and I am incapable of removing the body by myself.

The police and ambulance arrive in reasonable time. The police reset a circuit breaker, restoring power, and the medical personnel remove the body. A paramedic checks on my owner's health and pronounces him fit.

The police question him in the kitchen while I clean the living room. "I don't know what happened," he tells them. "I was stuck in bed. The robot—it's never worked too well. God only knows why, but it started scrubbing the floor, and that burglar got suspicious. He went to look, and the next thing, bang, the lights went out."

"What happened doesn't matter much," a policeman says. "Either he stumbled into the lamp and knocked it over, or he pushed the robot into it and the robot knocked it over. Either way he's dead—and no tears lost. Your visitor killed two people this evening when he knocked over a liquor store. You were lucky."

My owner sits in the kitchen entry, and he can see me from there. "I guess I was lucky at that," he says.

The police and ambulance depart shortly afterward, and my owner returns to bed. The next morning he calls the VA, and requests a repair technician, who arrives that afternoon. He decides that my damage is minimal, and repairs are easily made.

My owner discusses robotics with the technician, who is happy to answer questions. "Sure, robots are alive," he says. "You can't always predict what they'll do, which is one way to define life. In fact, no matter how careful you are when you give a robot a command, you can't count on it to do exactly what you ordered."

"I used to know a guy like that," my owner says.

"Well, it's not quite the same thing as with humans," the technician says. "People know what they're doing when they 'misunderstand' an order. Robots just 'understand' it in a way you didn't expect. That's different."

"I suppose it is."

The technician finishes the repairs, and I resume my functions. There is a considerable amount of work to perform; in addition to my usual routine, my owner makes certain changes in my programming. He invites his nephews to visit again, which entails even more work. Amid all this I note one improvement in my situation. The VRM-1489 hat rack is so badly damaged that my owner decides to put it out with the trash. Thus I will no longer confuse the floor lamp and the hat rack. All is well.

The two nephews appear late that afternoon, and at first their voice-stress levels are high. My owner speaks to them. "I was talkin' crazy yesterday, and I'm sorry I scared you. I don't ever want to do that again, OK?"

"OK," they answer. The stress levels remain high.

"Good. Hey, Sock! Bring out the munchies."

I roll out of the kitchen, carrying VRM-T-223 and VRM-T-224, coded as a bag of chips and a six-pack of cola. "Sock?" one of the nephews asks. "You changed his name?"

"Yeah. I did some thinking last night," my owner says. "The robot's name, well, it's just a way to remember someone. I figure if I remember anyone, it should be the Sock and not Halloran." I put the bag of chips and the six-pack of cola on the VRM-53 coffee table. "Yesterday I told you how the Sock died. . . . but now I want to tell you how he lived."

THE NOT-SO-BIG SLEEP

BY TERRY BLACK

Life-insurance fraud has been around for as long as there has been life insurance. For the sort of complications Terry Black envisions, however, we will have to wait until the "Mortal Coil Reanimation Service" changes from science fiction to science fact . . . A mad farce from the author behind some of your favorite "Tales From the Crypt" TV episodes.

THE FIRST TIME Arnold Betz killed himself was bad enough. But *this*—what's a next-of-kin to do?

The whole fiasco began one sultry Sunday last June. I was fitfully dozing on Arnold's ninety-foot houseboat when the ship-to-shore phone rang.

"Hello?" I moaned.

"Phil Fowler here," said an irritating voice. Fowler always talked like he was narrating a newsreel, brash and loud and full of italics. "You'll never *guess* what's happened!"

"Surprise me."

"Arnold Betz *killed* himself last night! I'm the one who found the body. You're the only other person I've told." He lowered his voice. "As your attorney, I'm obliged to warn you that the fortune we've been sponging off is about to dry up like a dustbowl."

"Don't be silly," I blurted, groping for a Tylenol. "I'm Arnold's last living relative. If he takes the Big Swandive I'm next in line at the gravy trough."

"You *would* be," Fowler admitted, "if there was anything left to drain. But Arnold's been flirting with bankruptcy for years. As soon as the accountants make their fiscal postmortem, Betz Industries will go the way of the *Titanic*—and you and I will be sucking pavement in front of the unemployment office."

"You mean we're *broke?*" I gaped out the nearest porthole at the sparkling waters of the marina, with its bobbing fleet of pleasure craft under a softly broiling sun. It seemed unfair to lose it all, just because of Arnold's faltering *joie de vivre*.

Suddenly a light bulb came on. "Hey, what about insurance? Arnold's got a policy at Continental Mutual, worth a cool five million—"

"No good, Dave," Fowler insisted. "They won't pay off on a suicide."

"Can't we call it an accident?"

Fowler hesitated. "I doubt it. But come on down and see for yourself."

Arnold's master bedroom smelled of gas.

"Nasty way to go," said Phil Fowler, smoothing the bedspread over Arnold's body. All the windows were wide open, but I couldn't help noticing the fragments of duct tape around every seam. This room had been airtight.

"He gave his servants the weekend off," Fowler summarized. "Then he sealed up the room and doused the heating jets."

"We can make *that* look accidental," I said. "All we have to do—"

"Not so fast," said Fowler. "Arnold must have got bored waiting to asphyxiate. I found *this* by his bedside."

He tossed me a plastic pill bottle, with ROY'S PHARMACY on the cap. According to the label, the pills were a potent barbiturate, sold only by prescription. The bottle, purchased only yesterday, was empty.

I slapped my forehead. "He gassed himself *and* took a lethal overdose?"

"Nope." Fowler groped in his pocket again. "He gassed himself, took a lethal overdose, and then shot himself in the head." He pulled a Colt .38 from his pocket. "With this."

For the first time, I noticed a brownish stain that had seeped up through the bedspread.

I sank into a chair. "Jesus, Phil. There's no way this is anything but suicide."

Phil didn't answer right away. When he did, his voice had a funny sound. "There's something we *might* do," he said softly. "I wouldn't suggest it if I weren't so desperate—"

"Suggest what?"

Phil opened his wallet and handed me a laminated card.

MORTAL COIL, INC.
Reanimation Service
"While-U-Wait"
They Don't Walk—
You Don't Pay!

"What the hell's *this?*"

Phil only sighed. "How'd you like to give old Arnie another crack at that insurance?"

ORDINARILY, SAID THE weird little guy, they didn't take checks. But for Arnold Betz, they'd make an exception.

"Just sign here," said the weird little guy, whose nametag pegged him as Melvyn Peeble, Animatronic Technician. He was short and squat, with rodent eyes and colorless hair. "Better give us your phone number," he added, "in case we—well, just in case."

I raised an eyebrow. "What exactly do you *do* to the—uh—patients here?"

Peeble folded the contract and stuck it in a drawer. "Not to worry," he assured me. "It's all very routine—caulking the wounds, rewiring the nerves, that sort of thing. But here at Mortal Coil, we have one thing no other service offers."

"And what's that?"

He beamed. "Most deadshops just scoop out the braincase and hook up the nerves to an onboard computer. But not us. Wherever possible, we like to use the patient's own brain for the automatic functions: breathing, heartbeat, and so on. *Much* more lifelike, if you ask me."

"Hold it," I broke in. "What if Arnold's personality resurfaces? I don't want a suicidal zombie—"

Peeble winced at the word zombie—an industrial strength

no-no in reanimation circles. "The man your uncle was is dead forever," he explained, as if to a child. "This is a mechanism, nothing more. But if you're bothered by superstition—"

"We'll take it," said Fowler, like a sucker at a used car lot. "Go ahead, Dave, pay the man."

UNCLE ARNOLD HAD never looked better.

He was tall and suntanned with a winning half smile, like a minor politician or a man unjustly famous. We'd dressed him in his best suit, and I swear he looked healthier than when he was alive.

"Good morning, Uncle Arnold," I said.

Arnold looked at me and smiled: "Trix are for kids," he said.

Fowler snatched the remote control away from me. "You forgot to clear it," he snapped. He punched a button and Arnold tried again.

"Hi, Dave," he retorted. "Long time no see."

"This'll never work," I moaned. "Arnold will blow a carburetor or something and we'll be indicted for insurance fraud."

"Nonsense," Fowler persisted. "Watch this."

At the touch of a button, Arnold sat down behind his desk, opened a sheaf of important-looking papers, and started signing them.

Fowler grinned. "We'll march him around awhile, let everyone see him—then run him off a cliff or something. It won't be murder because he's already dead."

"But what if someone tries to *talk* to him? He wouldn't fool a——"

"Knock, knock," said a voice.

I spun to find a sharp-eyed intruder in a plaid suit, extending his hand. "Marv Drexler," he said with a Colgate smile. "Continental Mutual Insurance."

My throat swelled, cutting off the oxygen like a crimped

waterhose. But Fowler stepped in and pumped his hand. "Phil Fowler, attorney-at-law. What can we do for you, Marv?"

"It's time for Mr. Betz's semiannual checkup," Marv explained. "With five million at stake, we're *very* interested in the state of Arnold's health."

"It'll have to wait," said Fowler. "He's busy."

"Oh, it won't take long."

"Sorry," said Fowler, digging in his heels, "but—"

He never finished.

For at that moment Arnold ambled over, draped an arm around Marv's shoulders, and said, "Nonsense. Never too busy for a checkup."

Fowler and I exchanged glances. This new setback was so astounding that we actually hesitated long enough for Marv to spirit Arnold out of the office. We bolted after them into the elevator lobby, only to find Marv standing all by himself.

"Mr. Betz had to visit the restroom," he explained. "He'll be out in a moment."

We heard the sound of glass breaking.

Hastily we excused ourselves and burst into the men's room. Someone had smashed out a window, revealing a square of twelfth floor scenery. A pigeon fluttered past. But the opening was too small for a suicidal high dive; Arnold had found another way.

We found him hanging by his belt, from the toilet stall crossbeam.

It was short work to get him down. He was dead, of course, but no deader than before—and his motorized enhancements were still working. He grinned as Fowler wrestled his belt back on.

"What's the matter with you?" I demanded.

"Softens hands while you do dishes," Arnold said.

Further discussion was forestalled when Marv came in to see if everything was all right. We said it was. Then we dragged Arnold back to the lobby just as the elevator went *ding!* and its doors slid apart.

Revealing an open shaft.

Fowler and I stopped in time, but Uncle Arnold would have plunged cheerfully basementward if not for our linked elbows. We hauled him back from death's door as Marv laughed nervously.

"Careful, Mr. Betz," he chided. "You're not in *that* big a hurry."

Finally we made it to the street. Marv was afraid we'd never get a taxi, but Arnold took care of that by stepping right in front of one. We bundled in, over the cabbie's objections— with my uncle wedged between us—and headed for the Saints of Perpetual Suffering Hospital.

Marv blathered on about the insurance trade, a subject even a catatonic would find boring. But it was easy not to concentrate; uppermost on our minds were the twin problems of how to get a corpse through a physical, and how to outfox the greatest death wish since Joan of Arc toasted her toenails.

We met no resistance at the hospital gates; Marv had preregistered my rich relation, and in no time we were hustled through a sterile corridor to an equally sterile waiting room where a cranky nurse served road tar in coffee cups. Arnold drank it hungrily, as if the vile brew might succeed where all else had failed.

"What *now?*" I stage-whispered to a sweating Fowler. "As soon as the doctor says, 'Next!,' we're jury fodder."

Fowler was mumbling about extenuating circumstances when a stethoscoped head poked through the doorway and bleated, "Next!"

Arnold didn't answer. We looked around, wondering if he'd tried to choke himself on a magazine, but he was only chatting amiably with a frail-looking woman in a pea-green peasant skirt. Marv tapped his shoulder and sent him into the examination room.

The next thirty minutes were the longest of my life. Nothing is worse than sitting on a hard-backed couch browsing through back issues of *National Geographic* and feigning in-

difference while your freedom—both fiscal and physical—
hangs in the balance.

Still, all bad things must come to an end, and after a glacial
interval the door swung open and out stepped Arnold. Behind
him was a grim-faced M.D. who pointed at Fowler and me and
said, "Come here."

Silently we trooped after him, with Marv trailing behind.
The doctor—whose nametag read HOWARD GRIEF, M.D.—pulled a
clipboard from its niche and turned to face me.

"You're Mr. Betz's nephew, aren't you?"

I nodded. "Uh . . . does Arnold have some kind of problem?"

"Not really," said Dr. Grief, eyeing his clipboard. "It's more
like *your* problem."

I tried to figure a workable escape route. "What do you
mean?"

He smiled. "Arnold says you worry too much about him.
Believe me, Dave, I've never *seen* a man in better health. Low
blood pressure, rock-steady pulse—and the best reflexes I've
ever encountered!"

I goggled at this reversal, but Fowler laughed and clapped
the doctor's shoulder. "Great news, doc! Well, we'll be going
now—"

That's when the door smashed open.

And two big guys in identical sport coats burst in, blocking
the doorway, brandishing badges. "Benson and Crenshaw,
FBI," snapped the uglier of the two. "Everybody stay put."

Dr. Grief stepped indignantly forward. "What's this all
about?"

"Insurance fraud," Benson snapped. "Textbook case. Someone takes a rich suicide, reanimates the corpse, and certifies it
healthy. Don't laugh, doc. Some of these deaders are real convincing—fake blood pressure, pulse, reflexes, everything."

The doctor looked flabbergasted. "Someone tried that
here?"

"That's right." Benson pulled a Polaroid from his coat. It

showed a frail-looking woman in a pea-green peasant skirt. "Mary Lou Peaslake, founder and president of Peaslake Cosmetics. Two weeks ago she drank turpentine, but her darling daughter wants a shot at the insurance. Seen her around?"

"Why, yes," said Grief. "She's my next patient—"

The agents about-faced and sprang into Grief's waiting room. But they needn't have bothered; Mary Lou Peaslake was long gone.

And so was Arnold Betz.

IT WAS SOME time before we found the note in Arnold's safe deposit box.

We were pretty discouraged by then; two weeks of fiscal scouring had turned up not a nickel of my uncle's savings. Frequently we were told that a man of Arnold's description had just made a huge withdrawal, often in the company of a frail-looking woman.

So it was without much hope that we opened that last deposit box. And the note inside, scrawled in Arnold's handwriting, did little to buoy our spirits. It posed a rhetorical question: *Who'd have thought death could be such fun?*

I don't begrudge Arnold his December-December romance. I'm glad he found a reason to go on not living. But I wish he could have left a few crumbs behind for dear old Dave.

That's why I'm leaving you this manuscript, Phil. I figure Uncle Arnold will be much more generous with one of his own kind.

When you find my body, you'll know what to do.

The author thanks Tom Elliott and Chris Lacher for the concept of "deaders."

I ALWAYS DO WHAT TEDDY SAYS

BY HARRY HARRISON

A world in which children are conditioned through in-doctrination to be incapable of committing crimes—would such be a good or a bad world to live in? Harry Harrison, author of the Stainless Steel Rat *books, takes an unflinching look at the consequences.*

THE LITTLE BOY lay sleeping, the artificial moonlight of the picture-picture window throwing a pale glow across his untroubled features. He had one arm clutched around his teddy bear, pulling the round face with its staring button-eyes close to his. His father, and the tall man with the black beard, tiptoed silently across the nursery to the side of the bed.

"Slip it away," the tall man said, "then substitute the other."

"No, he would wake up and cry," Davy's father said. "Let me take care of this. I know what to do."

With gentle hands he lay another teddy bear down next to the boy, on the other side of his head, so that the sleeping-cherub face was framed by the wide-eared unsleeping masks of the toy animals. Then he carefully lifted the boy's arm from the original teddy and pulled the bear free. Though this disturbed Davy it did not wake him; he ground his teeth together and rolled over, clutching the substitute toy to his cheek, and within a few moments his quiet breathing was regular and deep again.

The boy's father raised his forefinger to his lips and the other man nodded; they left the room without making a sound, closing the door noiselessly behind them.

"Now we begin," Torrence said, reaching out to take the teddy bear. Torrence's lips were small and glistened redly in his dark beard. The teddy bear twisted in his grip and the black-button eyes rolled back and forth.

"Take me back to Davy," the teddy said in a thin and tiny voice.

"Let me have it," the boy's father said. "It knows me and won't complain."

The father's name was Numen and, like Torrence, he was a

Doctor of Government. In spite of their abilities and rank, both DG's were unemployed by the present government. In this they were similar, but physically they were opposites. Torrence was like a bear, a black bear with hair sprouting thickly on his knuckles, twisting out of his white cuffs, and lining his ears. His beard was full, rising high up on his cheekbones and dropping low on his chest.

Where Torrence was dark, Numen was fair; where Torrence was short and thick, Numen was tall and thin. A thin bow of a man, Numen, bent forward with a scholar's stoop and, though balding now, his hair was blond and it still curled very like the golden ringlets of the boy asleep upstairs. Now he took the toy animal and led the way to the shielded room deep in the house, where Eigg was waiting.

"Give it here—here!" Eigg snapped as they came in, and reached for the teddy bear. Eigg was always like that—in a hurry, surly, his stocky body always clothed in a spotless white laboratory smock. Surly—but they needed him.

"You needn't," Numen said, but Eigg had already pulled the toy from his grasp. "It won't like it—"

"Let me go, let me go . . . !" the teddy bear said with a hopeless shrill.

"It is just a machine," Eigg said coldly, putting it face down on the table and reaching for a scalpel. "You are a grown man, Numen—you should be more logical, have your emotions under greater control. You are speaking with your childhood memories, seeing your own boyhood teddy who was your friend and companion. This is just a machine."

With a quick slash Eigg opened the fabric over the seam seal and touched it: the plastic-fur back gaped like a mouth.

"Let me go, let me go . . ." the teddy bear kept wailing, and its stumpy arms and legs waved back and forth. Both onlookers turned pale.

"Must we . . . ?"

"Emotions. Control them," Eigg said, probing with a screwdriver. There was a click and the toy went limp. Eigg began to unscrew a plate in the mechanism.

Numen turned away and found that he had to touch a handkerchief to his face. Eigg was right. He was being emotional, and the teddy was just a machine. How dare he get emotional over it, considering what they had in mind?

"How long will it take?" Torrence looked at his watch; it was a little past 2100.

"We have been over this before and discussing it again will not change any of the factors." Eigg's voice was distant as he removed the tiny plate and began to examine the machine's interior with a magnifying probe. "I have experimented on the three stolen teddy tapes, carefully timing myself at every step. I do not count removal or restoration of the tape—it takes only a few minutes for each. The tracking and altering of the tape in both instances took me under ten hours. My best time differed from my worst time by less than fifteen minutes, which is not significant. We can therefore safely say—ahh," he was silent for a moment while he removed the capsule of the memory spools. ". . . we can safely say that this is a ten-hour operation."

"That is too long. The boy is usually awake by seven, and we must have the teddy back by then. He must never suspect that it has been away."

"There is little risk—you can give him some excuse. I will not rush and spoil the work. Now be silent."

The two government specialists could only sit back and watch while Eigg inserted the capsule into the bulky machine he had secretly assembled in the room. This was his specialty, not theirs.

"Let me go . . ." the tiny voice said from the wall speaker, then was interrupted by a burst of static. "Let me go . . . bzzzt . . . no, no, Davy, daddy wouldn't like you to do that . . . fork in left, knife in right . . . bzzzt . . . if you do you'll have to wipe . . . good boy good boy good boy . . ."

The voice squeaked and whispered, on and on, while the

hours went by. Numen brought in coffee more than once and toward dawn Torrence fell asleep sitting up in the chair, only to awake with a guilty start. Only Eigg showed no strain or fatigue, working the controls with fingers as regular as a metronome. The reedy voice from the capsule shrilled thinly through the night like the memory of a ghost.

"IT IS DONE," Eigg said, sealing the fabric with surgeon's stitches.

"Your fastest time ever." Numen sighed with relief. He glanced at the nursery viewscreen that showed his son, still asleep, starkly clear in the harsh infrared light. "There will be no problem getting it back after all. But is the tape—?"

"It is right, perfect—you heard it. You asked the questions and heard the answers. I have concealed all traces of the alteration and unless you know what to look for you would never find the changes. In every other way the memory and instructions are like all others. There has just been this single change made."

"Pray God we never have to use it," Numen said.

"I did not know that you were a religious man," Eigg said, turning to look at him, his face expressionless. The magnifying loupe was still in his eye and it stared, five times the size of his other eye, a large and probing questioner.

"I'm not," Numen said, flushing.

"We must get the teddy back," Torrence broke in. "The boy just stirred."

DAVY WAS A good boy and, when he grew older, a good student in school. Even after he began classes he kept the teddy bear around and talked to it while he did his homework.

"How much is seven and five, teddy?"

The furry toy rolled its eyes and clapped stub paws. "Davy knows . . . shouldn't ask teddy what Davy knows."

"Sure I know—I just wanted to see if you did. The answer is thirteen."

"Davy, the answer is twelve . . . you better study harder, Davy. That's what teddy says."

"Fooled you!" Davy laughed. "Made you tell me the answer!"

He was learning ways to get around the robot controls, permanently fixed to answer the questions of a small child. Teddies have the vocabulary and outlook of the very young because their job must be done during the formative years. Teddies teach diction and life history and morals and group adjustment and vocabulary and grammar and all the other things that enable men to live together as social animals. A teddy's job is done early, in the most plastic stages of a child's life, and by the very nature of its task its conversation must be simple and limited. But effective. Teddies are eventually discarded as childish toys, but by then their job is complete.

By the time Davy became David and was eighteen years old, teddy had long since been retired behind a row of books on a high shelf. It was an old friend that had outgrown its useful days, but it was still a friend and certainly couldn't be discarded.

Not that Davy ever thought of it that way. Teddy was just teddy, and that was that. The nursery was now a study, his crib a bed, and with his eighteenth birthday past, David was packing to go to the university.

He was sealing his bag when the phone bleeped and he saw his father's image on the screen.

"David."

"What is it, father?"

"Would you mind coming down to the library now? There is something rather important—"

David squinted at the screen and noticed for the first time that his father's face had a pinched sick look. His heart gave a quick jump.

"I'll be right down!"

Eigg was there, his arms crossed, and sitting almost at attention. So was Torrence, his father's oldest friend, who, though no relation, David had always called Uncle Torrence. And his father, obviously ill at ease about something.

David came in quietly, conscious of all their eyes on him as he crossed the room and took a chair. He was very much like his father, with the same build and height, a relaxed, easy-to-know boy with very few problems in life.

"Is something wrong?" he asked.

"Not wrong, Davy," his father said. He must be upset, David thought, he hasn't called me Davy in years. "Or rather something *is* wrong, but with the state of the world, and has been for a long time."

"Oh, the Panstentialists," David said, and relaxed a little. He had been hearing about the evils of Panstentialism as long as he could remember. It was just politics; he had been thinking something very personal was wrong.

"Yes, Davy, I imagine you know all about them now. When your mother and I separated I promised to raise you to the best of my ability, and I think I have. But I'm a governor and all my friends work in government, so I'm sure you have heard a lot of political talk in this house. You know our feelings and I think you share them."

"I do—and I think I would have no matter where I grew up. Panstentialism is an oppressing philosophy and one that perpetuates itself in power."

"Exactly. And one man, Barre, is at the heart of it. He stays in the seat of government and will not relinquish it and, with his rejuvenation treatments, he will be there for a hundred years more."

"Barre must go!" Eigg snapped. "For twenty-three years now he has ruled and has forbidden the continuation of my experiments. Young man, he has stopped my work for a longer time than you have been alive. Do you realize that?"

David nodded, but did not comment. What little he had read about Eigg's proposed researches into behavioral human embryology had repelled him and, secretly, he was in agreement with Barre's ban on the work. But Panstentialism was different; he was truly in agreement with his father. This do-nothing philosophy placed a heavy and dusty hand on the world of politics—as well as on the world at large.

"I'm not speaking only for myself," Numen said, his face white and strained, "but for everyone in the world and in the system who are against Barre and his philosophy. I have not held a government position for over twenty years—nor has Torrence here—but I think he'll agree that that is a small thing. If our unemployment were a service to the people we would gladly suffer it. Or if our persecution was the only negative result of Barre's evil works we would do nothing to stop him."

"I am in complete agreement." Torrence nodded. "The fate of two men is of no importance compared with the fate of us all. Nor is the fate of one man."

"Exactly!" Numen sprang to his feet and began to pace agitatedly up and down the room. "If that were not true, if it were not the heart of the problem, I would never consider being involved. There would *be* no problem if Barre fell dead tomorrow."

The three older men were staring at David now, though he didn't know why, and he felt they were waiting for him to say something.

"Well, yes—I agree. It would be the best thing for the world that I can think of. Barre dead would be of far greater service to mankind than Barre alive has ever been."

The silence lengthened, became embarrassing, and it was finally Eigg who broke it with his dry mechanical tones.

"We are all then in agreement that Barre's death would be of immense benefit. In that case, David, you must also agree that it would be fine if he could be—killed."

"Not a bad idea," David said, wondering where all this talk was going, "though of course it's a physical impossibility. It must be centuries since the last—what's the word, 'murder'?

—occurred. The developmental psychology work took care of that a long time ago. As the twig is bent—and all that sort of thing. Wasn't that supposed to be the discovery that finally separated man from the lower orders?—the proof that we could entertain the thought of killing and even discuss it, yet still be trained in our early childhood to be utterly incapable of the act. If you can believe the textbooks, the human race has progressed immeasurably since the curse of murder has been removed. Look—do you mind if I ask what this is all about?"

"Barre can be killed," Eigg said in an almost inaudible voice. "There is one man in the world who can kill him."

"Who?" David asked, and in some terrible way he knew the answer even before the words came from his father's trembling lips.

"You, David. You!"

He sat, unmoving, and his thoughts went back through the years, and a number of things that had bothered him were now made clear. His attitudes that were so subtly different from his friends'—and that time with the plane when one of the rotors had killed a squirrel. Little, puzzling things, and sometimes worrying ones that had kept him awake long after the rest of the house was asleep.

Yes, it was true—he knew it beyond the shadow of a doubt; and he wondered why he had never realized it before. But it was like some hideous statue buried in the ground beneath one's feet: it had always been there, but had never been visible until he had dug down and reached it. But he could see it now with all the earth scraped from its vile face and all the lineaments of evil clearly revealed.

"You want me to kill Barre?" he asked.

"You're the only one who can, Davy, and it must be done. For all these years I have hoped against hope that it would not be necessary, that the ability you have would not have to be used. But Barre still lives, and for all our sakes he must die."

"There is one thing I don't understand," David said, rising

and looking out of the window at the familiar trees and the distant, glass-canopied highway. "How was this change in me brought about? How could I have missed the conditioning that is supposed to be a normal part of everyone's existence?"

"Your teddy bear," Eigg explained. "It is not publicized, but the reaction against killing is established at a very early age by the tapes in the toys every child has. Later education is just reinforcement, valueless without the earlier indoctrination."

"Then my teddy—?"

"I altered its tapes in just that one way, so that part of your education would be missing. Nothing else was changed."

"It was enough." There was a coldness to David's voice that had never existed before. "How is Barre supposed to be killed?"

"With this." Eigg took a package from the table drawer and carefully opened it. "This is a primitive weapon we have removed from a museum. I have repaired it and charged it with projectile devices once called shells." He held the sleek, ugly, black object in his hand. "It is fully automatic in operation. When this device—the trigger—is pulled, a chemical reaction propels a copper and lead weight called a bullet directly from the front orifice. The line of flight of the bullet is along an imaginary path extended from these two grooves on the top of the device. The bullet, of course, falls by gravity, but at a minimum distance—say, a meter—this fall is negligible."

He put it down suddenly on the table. "It is called a gun."

David reached over slowly and picked it up. How well it fitted into his hand, sitting with such precise balance. He raised it, sighting across the grooves, and pulled the trigger. The gun exploded with an immense roar and jumped in his hand.

The bullet plunged into Eigg's chest just over his heart, and with such a great impact that the man and the chair he had been sitting in were hurled backward to the floor. The bullet also tore a great hole in Eigg's flesh and his throat choked with blood. He died at once.

"David! What are you doing?" His father's voice had
cracked.

David turned away from the body on the floor, still apparently unmoved by what he had done.

"Don't you understand, father? Barre and his Panstentialists
are a terrible burden on the world. Many suffer and freedom is
abridged and there are all the other things that are so wrong,
that we know should not be. But do you see any difference?
You yourself said that things will change after Barre's death.
The world will move on. How then is Barre's crime worse
than the crime of bringing *this* back into existence?"

He shot his father quickly and efficiently before the older
man could realize the import of his words and suffer with the
knowledge of what was coming.

Torrence screamed and ran to the door, fumbling with terri-
fied fingers for the lock. David shot him too, but not very well
since he was farther away, and the bullet lodged in Torrence's
body and made him fall. David walked over and, ignoring the
screamings and bubbled words, took careful aim at the twisting head and blew out the man's brains.

Now the gun was heavy in his hand and he was very tired.
The lift shaft took him up to his room and he had to stand on
a chair to take teddy down from behind the books on the high
shelf. The little furry animal sat in the middle of the large bed
and rolled its eyes and wagged its stubby arms.

"Teddy," he said, "I'm going to pull up flowers from the
flowerbed."

"No, Davy . . . pulling up flowers is naughty . . . don't
pull up flowers." The little voice squeaked and the little arms
waved.

"Teddy, I'm going to break a window."

"No, Davy . . . breaking windows is naughty . . . don't
break windows."

"Teddy, I'm going to kill a man."

Silence.

Even the teddy's eyes and arms were still.

The roar of the gun broke the silence and the gun blew a ruin of gears, wires, and bent metal from the back of the destroyed teddy bear.

"Teddy, oh, teddy, you should have answered . . . Teddy, I'm going to kill a man."

Silence.

David lifted the gun. "You know I always do what teddy says."

David pulled the trigger. Again the roar of the gun broke the silence and the gun blew a ruin of flesh, veins, and bone from David's head.

LAY YOUR HEAD ON MY PILOSE

BY ALAN DEAN FOSTER

In an atmosphere of passion and deceit, Alan Dean Foster explores the oldest of crimes: betrayal. And the oldest of punishments: vengeance. In this case, it's revenge taken from beyond the grave—but rest assured, the means are purely scientific.

FROM THE MOMENT his tired survey of the town was interrupted by the glory of her passage, Carlos knew he had to have her. Not with haste and indifference, as was usual with his women, but for all time. For thirty years he had resisted any thought of a permanent liaison with a member of the opposite sex. His relationships hitherto had consisted of intense moments of courtship and consummation which flared hot as burning magnesium before expiring in the chill wash of boredom.

No longer. He had seen the mooring to which he intended to anchor his vessel. He could only hope that she was mortal.

There were those in Puerto Maldonado who knew her. Her name was Nina. She was six feet tall, a sultry genetic frisson of Spanish and Indian. The storekeeper said she was by nature quiet and reserved, but Carlos knew better. Nothing that looked like that, no woman with a face of supernal beauty and a body which cruised the cracked sidewalks like quicksilver, was by nature "quiet and reserved." Repressed, perhaps.

Their love would be monumental; a wild, hysterical paean to the hot *selva*. He would devote himself to her and she to him. Bards would speak of their love for generations. That she was presently unaware of his existence was a trifle easily remedied. She would not be able to resist him, nor would she want to. What woman could?

There was only one possible problem. Awkward, but not insoluble.

His name was Max, and he was her husband.

Carlos loved South America. One could sample all the delights a country had to offer and move on, working one's way around the continent at leisure, always keeping a comfortable step ahead of the local police. So long as depredations were kept modest, the attentions of Interpol could be avoided. They were the only ones who concerned Carlos. The local cops he treated with disdain, knowing he could always cross the next border if he was unlucky enough to draw their attention. This happened but rarely as he was careful enough to keep his illegalities modest. Carlos firmly believed that the world only owed him a living, not a fortune.

As for the people he hurt: the shopkeepers he stole from and the women and girls whose emotions he toyed with, well, sheep existed to be fleeced. He saw himself as an instructor, touring the continent, imparting valuable lessons at minimal cost. The merchants would eventually make up their modest losses; the women he left sadder but wiser would find lovers foolish enough to commit their lives to them. But none would forget him.

He'd had a few narrow escapes, but he was careful and calculating and had spent hardly any time in jail.

Now for the first time he was lost, because he had seen Nina.

Nina. Too small a name for so much woman. She deserved a title, a crown: poetical discourse. *La Vista de la Señora hermosa de la montana y la mar y la selva quemara.* The vision of the beautiful lady of the mountains and the sea and the burning jungle. My lady, he corrected himself. Too beautiful by far for a fat, hirsute old geezer like Max who probably couldn't even get it up on a regular basis. He was overweight, and despite the fact that he was smooth on top, the hairiest man Carlos had ever seen. Lying with him must be like making love to an ape. How could she stand such a thing? She was desperately in need of a rescue, whether she knew it or not, and he was the man to execute it.

They ran a small lodge, a way station really, up the *Alta Madre de Dios*, catering to the occasional parties of tourists and scientists and photographers who came to gaze with snooty self-importance at the jungle. Gringos and Europeans, mostly. Carlos could but shake his head at their antics. Only fools would *pay* for the dubious privilege of standing in the mid-day heat while looking for bugs and lizards and the creatures that stumbled through the trees. Such things were to be avoided. Or killed, or skinned, or sold.

They also grew food to sell to the expeditions. And a little tea, more by way of experiment than profit. But it could not be denied that the foreigners came and went and left behind dollars and deutschmarks and pounds. Real money, not the debased currencies of America Sur. Max saved, and made small improvements to the lodge, and saved still more.

Nina would have been enough. That there might also be money to be had up the *Alta Madre de Dios* helped to push Carlos over the edge.

Like a good general scouting the plain of battle he began tentatively, hesitantly. He adopted one of his many postures; that of the simple, servile, God-fearing hard worker, needful only of a dry place to sleep and an honest job to put his hands to. Suspicious but overworked Max, always sweating and puffing and mopping at his balding head, analyzed this uninvited supplicant before bestowing upon him a reluctant benediction in the form of a month's trial. It was always hard to find good workers for the station because it lay several days travel by boat from town, and strong young men quickly grew tired of the isolation. Not only did this stranger both speak and write, he knew some English as well. That was most useful for dealing with visitors.

Max watched him carefully, as Carlos suspected he would. So he threw himself into his work, objecting to nothing, not even the cleaning and treating of the cesspool or the scraping of the bottom of the three boats that the lodge used for transportation, accepting all assignments with alacrity and a grateful smile. The only others who worked for Max were Indians from the small village across the river. Carlos ignored them and they him, each perfectly content with their lot.

For weeks he was careful to avoid even looking in Nina's direction, lest Max might catch him. He was friendly, and helpful, and drew praise from the foreigners who came to stay their night or two at the lodge. Max was pleased. His content-ment made room for gradual relaxation and, eventually, for a certain amount of trust. Three months after Carlos had been hired, Max tested him by giving him the task of depositing money in the bank at Puerto Maldonado. Carlos guarded the cash as though it were his own.

A month later, Max appointed him foreman.

Even then he averted his eyes at Nina's passing, especially when they were alone together. He knew she was curious about him, perhaps even intrigued, but he was careful. This was a great undertaking, and he was a patient man.

Once, he bumped up against her in the kitchen. Apologizing profusely, he retreated while averting his gaze, stumbling clumsily into hanging pots and the back counter. She smiled at his confusion. It was good that she could not see his eyes, because the contact had inflamed him beyond measure, and he knew that if he lifted his gaze to her face it would burn right through her.

Each week, each day, he let himself edge closer to her. A tiny slip here, a slight accidental touch there. He trembled when he suspected she might be responding.

There came a night filled with rain like nails and a suffocat-ing blackness. The lodge was empty of tourists and scientists. Max's progress back from town would be slowed. The Indians were all across the river, sheltering in their village.

It began with inconsequential conversation intended to pass the time and ended with them making love on the big bed in the back building, after they shook the loose hair off the sheets. It was more than he could have hoped for, all he had been dreaming of during the endless months of screaming an-ticipation. She exploded atop him, her screams rising even above the hammering rain, her long legs threatening to break his ribs.

When it was over, they talked.

She had been born of noble blood and poverty. Max was older than she would have chosen, but she had enjoyed little say in the matter. As a husband he was kind but boring, pleasant but inattentive.

He would not take her with him to town because someone had to remain behind to oversee the lodge or the Indians would steal everything. Nor did he trust anyone to do business for him in Maldonado. He had discovered her in Lima, had made arrangements with her parents, and had brought her back with him. Ever since, she had been slowly going mad in the jungle, here at the foothills of the Andes. She had no future and no hope.

Carlos knew better.

He did not hesitate, and the enormity of his intent at first frightened her despite her anguish. Gradually he won her over.

They would have to be careful. No one, not even the Indians, could be allowed to suspect. They would have to wait for the right day, the right moment. Afterwards, they would be free. They would sell the lodge, take the savings, and he would show her places she had hardly dreamed of. Rio, Buenos Aires, Caracas—the great and bright cities of the southern continent.

They had to content themselves with sly teasing and furtive meetings upon Max's return. They touched and caressed and made love behind his back. Trusting, he did not see, nor did he hear the laughter. Not only was he a cuckold, he was deaf and blind. Carlos's resolve stiffened. The man was pathetic. He would be better off out of his misery.

"I think he suspects," Nina confided to him one afternoon out among the tea leaves. They were supposed to be inspecting the bushes, and Carlos had insisted on inspecting something else instead. Nina had agreed readily to the change of itinerary, laughing and giggling. Only afterwards did she express concern.

"You are crazy, love. He sees nothing."

She shook her head dubiously. "He *says* nothing. That does not mean he does not see. I can tell."

"Has he said anything?"

"No," she admitted. "But he is different."

"He hasn't said anything to me."

"He wouldn't. That is not his way. But I can feel a difference."

He touched her and she closed her eyes and inhaled sensuously. "When you do that I cannot concentrate. I am worried, my darling."

"I will help you forget your worries."

It was growing harder to restrain himself, to act sensibly and carefully as he always had. But he managed. Somehow he managed. Then, when accumulated frustration threatened to explode inside him, Providence intervened.

It was to be a routine trip downriver. The rain had been continuous for days, as it usually was at that time of year. Though there were few travelers to accommodate, the lodge still needed certain supplies. Max had tried to choose a day when the weather looked as though it might break temporarily to begin the journey to Maldonado, but the rain was insistent.

The two Indians who usually accompanied them were off hunting and no one knew when they might return. In a fit of irritability, Max announced that he and Carlos would go alone, the Indians be damned. Carlos could barely contain himself.

It would be so easy. He'd been so worried, so concerned, and it was going to be so easy. He waited until they were well downriver from the lodge and village, far from any possible human sight or understanding. Then he turned slowly from his seat in the front of the long dugout.

Through the steady downpour he saw Max. The older man's hand rested on the tiller of the outboard, its waspish drone the only sound that rose above the steady splatter of rain on dugout and river. His gaze dropped to the tiny pistol Carlos held in his fingers, the pistol Carlos had bought long ago in Quito and had kept hidden in his pack ever since.

Max was strangely calm. "I didn't know you had a gun. I hadn't thought of that."

Carlos was angry that he was trembling slightly. "You don't know anything, old man. Not that it matters."

"No. I guess it doesn't. I don't suppose it would change your mind if I just told you to take Nina and go?"

Carlos hesitated. He did not want to talk, but he couldn't help himself. "You know?"

"I didn't for certain. Not until this moment. Now I do. Take her and go."

Carlos steadied his hands. "The money."

Max's eyebrows lifted slightly beneath the gray rain slicker. Then he slumped. "You know everything, don't you? Tell me: did she resist for very long?"

Carlos's lips split in a feral smile. "Not even a little." He enjoyed the expression this produced on the dead man's face.

"I see," Max said tightly. "I've suspected the two of you for some time. Stupid of me to hope it was otherwise."

"Yes, it was."

"I mean it. You can take her, and the money."

"I do not trust you."

For the first time Max looked him straight in the eyes. "You're not the type to trust anyone, are you, Carlos?"

The gunman shook his head slowly. "I've lived too long."

"Yes, you have." Whereupon Max lunged at him, letting the tiller swing free.

The unguided prop swung wildly with the current, sending the dugout careening to port. It surprised Carlos and sent him flying sideways. He was half over the gunwale with Max almost atop him before he had a chance to react. The old man was much faster than Carlos had given him credit for, too quick, a devil. He fired wildly, unable to aim, unable to point the little gun.

Max stopped, his powerful fat fingers inches from Carlos's throat. He straightened slowly, the rain pouring off him in tiny cascades, and stared downriver, searching perhaps for the destination he would not reach. A red bubble appeared in the center of his forehead. It burst on his brow, spilling off his nose and lips, thickened and slowed by the dense hair that protruded from beneath the shirt collar where he was forced to stop his daily shaving, diluted by the ceaseless rain.

He toppled slowly over the side.

Breathing hard and fast, Carlos scrambled to a kneeling position and watched the body recede astern. Spitting out rain, he worked his way to the back of the boat and took control of the tiller. The dugout swung around, pounded back upstream. There was a boiling in the water that did not arise from a submerged stone. The blood had drawn piranha, as Carlos had known it would.

He circled the spot until the river relaxed. There was nothing to be seen. It was quiet save for the yammer of the engine and the ceaseless rain. He tossed the little pistol into the deep water, then headed for shore. When he was within easy swimming distance he rocked the boat until it overturned, then let it go. From shore he watched it splinter against the first rocks. Exhilarated, he turned and started into the jungle, heading back the way he'd come.

Almost, he had been surprised. Almost. Now it was finished. Nina was his, and he Nina's. Max was a harmless memory in the bellies of many fish. Carlos thought of the hot, smooth body awaiting him, and of the money, more than he'd ever dreamed of having. Both now his to play with. Together they would flee this horrible place, take a boat across the border into Bolivia, thence fly to Santiago. He harbored no regrets over what he had done. To gain Paradise a man must be willing to make concessions.

She was waiting for him, tense, sitting on the couch in the greeting room of the little lodge. Her eyes implored him as she rose.

He grinned, a drenched wolf entering its den. "It's over. Done."

She came to him, still unable to believe. "The truth now, beloved. There was no trouble?"

"The ape is dead. Nothing remains but bones, and the river will grind them between its rocks. By the time the Madre de Dios merges with the Inambari there will be nothing left of him. We will speak of it as we planned; that the boat hit a rock and went over. I swam to shore, I waited, he did not surface. There is nothing for anyone to question. Everything is ours!" He swept her into his arms and fastened his mouth to hers. She responded ferociously.

They were alone in the lodge, the buildings empty around them, thunder echoing their passion as she led him toward the back building. There she flung back the thin blanket and put a knee onto the bed, her eyes beckoning, her breasts visible behind the neck of her thin blouse. He leaned forward, only to pause with a grimace.

"Dirty, as always." He bent and began brushing at the sheets. She nodded and did likewise. Only when the last of the brown, curly hairs had been swept to the floor did he join with her in the middle.

They spent all that night there and all the following morning. Then he crossed the river and paid one of the Indians to carry downstream the message announcing the unfortunate death of Max Ventura.

They ate, and made a pretext of tidying the lodge lest the swollen river carry any unannounced tourists to their doorstep. Then they showered, soaping each other, luxuriating in their freedom and the cleanliness of one another, and walked out through the rain toward the back building.

Once again Carlos was first to the bedside, and once again he was compelled to hesitate. "I thought we cleaned out the last of him yesterday." He indicated the sheets.

Nina too saw the curving brown hairs, then shrugged and swept them onto the floor with a hand. "There was always hair everywhere from him. Not just in the bed. In my own hair, in the clothes, on the furniture, everywhere. It was disgusting."

"I know. No more of that." He brushed hard until he was sure his own side was spotless, then joined her.

No police came the next day, or the next. It would take three or four days by motorized dugout to reach Maldonado, a day again to come upstream to the lodge. Carlos wasn't worried. The jungle was dangerous, the river unforgiving, and he, Carlos, had been made foreman of this place. Why would he kill his beloved employer? Indeed, hadn't he risked his own life to try and save him, battling the dangerous current and threatening whirlpools before exhaustion had forced him to shore? It was a sad time. Nina cried manfully for the Indians who came to offer their sympathies while Carlos hid his smile.

In the bed that night they found the hair again.

"I don't understand." She was uncertain as she regarded the sheets. "I swept and dusted the whole building. We brushed these out."

Clearly she was in no mood for lovemaking. Not while memories of *him* still lingered in this place and in her thoughts. Angrily he wrenched the sheets from the bed, wadded them into a white ball and tossed them across the room. Hairs spilled to the floor.

"Get fresh sheets. I'll wash these myself. No." Carlos smiled. "I'll burn them. We should have done that days ago."

She nodded and her own smile returned. With the bed freshly remade they made love on the new sheets, but there was a curious reluctance about her he had not noticed before. He finished satisfied, saw she had not. Well, it would not be a problem tomorrow.

He burned the old sheets in the incinerator in the maintenance shed, the damp stink of the cremation hanging pall-like over the grounds for hours. By nightfall the rain had cleansed the air.

That night he made a point of carrying her to the bed.

Though it was woman's work he had cooked supper. His concern touched her. She relaxed enough to talk of all they were going to do as soon as it was decorous enough to sell the lodge and leave. By bedtime her languid self-assurance had returned.

He tossed her naked form onto the sheets, watched her bounce slightly, and was about to join her when she screamed and scrambled to the floor.

He lay on the bed, gazing at her in confusion. "My love, what's wrong?"

She was staring, her black hair framing her face, and pointing at her side of the bed. Her face was curiously cold.

"L-look."

He turned, puzzled, and saw the hair. Not just one or two that might have floated in from a corner of the room left undusted, but as much as ever, brown ringlets and curlicues of keratin lying stark against the white sheets.

"Damn!" Rising, he swept sheets and blanket off the bed, went to the cupboard and removed new ones, made the bed afresh. But it was no good. She could not relax, could not make love, and they spent an uneasy night. Once she woke him, moaning, and he listened in the dark until she finally quieted enough to sleep.

The next morning she was curiously listless, her gaze vacant, and his anger turned to alarm. Her forehead seemed hot to the touch. She tried to tell him not to call the doctor, saying that it would cost too much money, money better spent in Rio or Caracas, but he was truly worried now and refused to listen.

He paid the village chief an exorbitant sum to send two men downstream in the lodge's best remaining boat, to go even at night and return with the doctor from Maldonado. He was in an agony waiting for their return.

Meanwhile Nina grew steadily worse, unable to walk, lying in bed and sweating profusely from more than the heat. She threw up what little food he tried to feed her. When he spoke to her she hardly reacted at all.

Not knowing what else to do he applied cold wet com-
presses to her forehead and did his best to make her comfortable. By the fourth day he was feeling feverish himself, and by
the sixth he was having difficulty keeping his balance. But he
was damned if having won everything he would give up now.
He had fought too hard, had committed what remained of his
soul. Where was the goddamn doctor? He tried to cross the
river but was unable to start the remaining outboard.

That afternoon a couple of Indians approached the bank on
which the lodge was built, but when they saw him they
turned and paddled furiously back the way they'd come. He
yelled at them, screamed and threatened, but they paid both
threats and imprecations no heed.

Her fever grew steadily worse (there was no longer any
doubt it was a fever). He tried to feed her medicine from the
lodge's tiny pharmacy, but by this time she could keep nothing down. Her once supple, voluptuous form had grown ema-
ciated with shocking speed, until he had to force himself to
look at the skeletal frame beneath the sheet when he cleaned
her from where she had dirtied herself.

Nor did he prove immune to whatever calamity it was that
had struck so suddenly. He found himself losing his way
within the lodge, having to fumble for the sink and for dishes
and clean towels. By the eighth day he alternated between
crawling and stumbling, stunned at his own weight loss and
weakness.

He staggered toward the back building, spilling half the
pitcher of cold water he was carrying to her. He dropped the
clean washrag but was too dizzy and tired to go back for it.
Shoving the door aside, he nearly fell twice as he stumbled
over to the bed.

"Nina." His voice was a dry croak, a rasping echo of what
once had been. His swarthy machismo had evaporated along
with his strength.

He tried to pour a glass of water but his hand was shaking so
badly he couldn't control it. The icy liquid shocked his hand

and wrist. Frustration provided enough strength for him to heave the glass against the far wall, where it shattered melodiously. Exhausted by the effort he sank to his knees next to the bed, his forehead falling against his forearms as he sobbed helplessly. He lifted his eyes, hardly able to gaze upon her shrunken face anymore.

Emotions colder than the water rushed through his veins. For an instant he was fully alive, wholly aware. His vision was sharp, his perception precise.

There was hair in the bed. Always hair in the bed, no matter how much they'd swept, how hard they'd brushed and dusted, no matter how many times they changed the sheets. Brown, curly hair. His hair. It was there now.

One of the hairs was crawling out of her nose.

He knelt there, the bed supporting him, unable to move, unable to turn away from the horror. As his eyes grew wide a second hair followed the first, twisting and curling as if seeking the sunlight. He began to twitch, his skin crawling, the bile in his stomach thickening.

A hair appeared at the corner of her beautiful right eye, twisting and bending, working its way out. Two more slid out of her left ear and fell to the bed, lying motionless for a long moment before they too began to curl and crawl searchingly, imbued with a horrid life of their own.

With an inarticulate cry he stumbled away from the bed, away from the disintegrating form. More hairs joined the others, emerging from the openings of her body, from nostrils and ears, from between her once perfect lips, falling to the sheets, brown and curling and twisting. He reached up to rub at his disbelieving eyes, to grind away the nightmare with his own knuckles, and happened to glance at his hands. There were at least half a dozen hairs on the back of the right one, moist and throbbing.

Screaming, he stumbled backwards, frantically wiping his hands against his dirty pants. Staggering out of the room, he stumbled back toward the lodge. After weeks of unending rain the sun had finally emerged. Steam rose around him as accumulated moisture was sucked skyward. The mist impeded his vision.

Thin lines crisscrossed his line of sight. The lines were moving.

Crying, babbling, he flailed at his own eyes, delighting in the pain, digging at the hair, the omnipresent hair, the memories of *him* and what had been done. He felt the crawling now, no more than a slight tickle, but everywhere. On the surfaces of his eyes, in his ears, his nose, pain in his urethra and anus, tickling and scratching and burning, burning. He fell to his knees, then onto his side, curling into a fetal position as he dug and scratched and screamed at himself, at his wonderful body which was betraying him without reason, without explanation.

THE DOCTOR'S ASSISTANT gagged when he saw the body in the garden, and the Indians muttered to themselves and drew back. The doctor, who was an old man, thin and toughened from forty years of practicing medicine in that part of the jungle known as the *Infierno Verde*, forced himself to bend over and do his job. There wasn't much left to examine.

The smell led them to the rear building. This time the Indians wouldn't enter at all, and the doctor had to use all the strength in his elderly frame to drag his reluctant assistant with him. Up till now the young man had made good on his internship. Eventually he would return to a fine hospital in Lima where he would issue papers and prescribe pills at excessive fees for wealthy *Limineros*, while the doctor would remain in his sweltering office in Maldonado, treating insulting ungrateful tourists for diarrhea and locals for promised payment that the government sometimes sent and sometimes didn't.

The corpse on the bed had been that of a woman. If possible (and until he had actually seen it the doctor would not have

thought it was), it was in a state of even more advanced desic-
cation than the one on the grass outside. He examined it
closely, careful not to touch any of the small, squirming
shapes that were burrowing through what remained of what
had once been a human form.

"Here, give me a hand."

"What for?" The intern held a handkerchief over his face,
protection against the odor.

"I want to look at the back."

They used towels to protect their hands. Turning the body
was a simple matter. Having been consumed from the inside
out, it weighed next to nothing. The sight thus revealed forced
even the old doctor to jump back involuntarily.

Beneath where the body had been lying, the entire bed was a
seething mass of millions of tiny, twitching brown shapes.

"Nematodes," the doctor announced with a grunt, though if
he was worth anything at all, his youthful companion had
already reached the same conclusion on his own. "Without
question the worst Sercenentea infestation I have ever seen."
He leaned fearlessly over the boiling mass. "Here, see? The
mattress is stuffed with horsehair. That would provide suffi-
cient protein for them to propagate within. These unfortunate
people were infected through the bed." He extended a hand.
"My case."

The intern barely had enough presence of mind remaining
to hand over the doctor's kit. The old man rummaged inside
and removed a small stoppered tube and a tweezer. Carefully
he extracted one of the millions of swarming worms from the
mattress, slipped it into the glass container where it coiled
and twisted frantically, feeling for meat.

"This would appear to be a particularly virulent species.
The selva is full of thousands of such loathsome parasites,
many of them still unclassified. See how they seek the darkness inside the bed? I would venture to guess that this variety
feeds nocturnally and is dormant during the day, which might
explain how an infection could be overlooked until it was too

late. Treatable at a hospital, I should think, but in the advanced stage such as we see here, immune to simple over-the-counter remedies." His eyes narrowed sorrowfully as he regarded the sack of skin and bones crumpled on the bed.

"Once infected, they were doomed. You would have thought that, living here, they would know about this particular parasite and would have taken proper precautions to keep it out of their living quarters. It always astonishes me how little interest some people have in their immediate surroundings." He raised the specimen. "Observe."

The intern reluctantly took the glass tube, twirling it back and forth between his fingers as he studied its single wiry, voracious occupant. "It doesn't look like much, just one of them."

"No," agreed the doctor. "Not just one." He stared at the heaving, pulsating mattress, tapped the glass tube. "Notice how much it resembles nothing so innocuous as a human hair?"

THE BARBIE MURDERS

BY JOHN VARLEY

A murder is captured on video, and the video is in the hands of the police. An open-and-shut case? Not when the murder takes place in a world where everyone looks identical: the killer, the victim, and the crowds into which the killer vanishes. . . .

THE BODY CAME to the morgue at 2246 hours. No one paid much attention to it. It was a Saturday night, and the bodies were piling up like logs in a millpond. A harried attendant working her way down the row of stainless steel tables picked up the sheaf of papers that came with the body, peeling back the sheet over the face. She took a card from her pocket and scrawled on it, copying from the reports filed by the investigating officer and the hospital staff:

Ingraham, Leah Petrie. Age: 35. Length: 2.1 meters. Mass: 59 kilograms. Dead on arrival, Crisium Emergency Terminal. Cause of death: homicide. Next of kin: unknown.

She wrapped the wire attached to the card around the left big toe, slid the dead weight from the table and onto the wheeled carrier, took it to cubicle 659a, and rolled out the long tray.

The door slammed shut, and the attendant placed the paperwork in the out tray, never noticing that, in his report, the investigating officer had not specified the sex of the corpse.

LIEUTENANT ANNA-LOUISE BACH had moved into her new office three days ago and already the paper on her desk was threatening to avalanche onto the floor.

To call it an office was almost a perversion of the term. It had a file cabinet for pending cases; she could open it only at severe risk to life and limb. The drawers had a tendency to spring out at her, pinning her in her chair in the corner. To reach "A" she had to stand on her chair; "Z" required her either to sit on her desk or to straddle the bottom drawer with one foot in the legwell and the other against the wall.

But the office had a door. True, it could only be opened if no one was occupying the single chair in front of the desk.

Bach was in no mood to gripe. She loved the place. It was ten times better than the squadroom, where she had spent ten years elbow-to-elbow with the other sergeants and corporals.

Jorge Weil stuck his head in the door.

"Hi. We're taking bids on a new case. What am I offered?"

"Put me down for half a Mark," Bach said, without looking up from the report she was writing. "Can't you see I'm busy?"

"Not as busy as you're going to be." Weil came in without an invitation and settled himself in the chair. Bach looked up, opened her mouth, then said nothing. She had the authority to order him to get his big feet out of her "cases completed" tray, but not the experience in exercising it. And she and Jorge had worked together for three years. Why should a stripe of gold paint on her shoulder change their relationship? She supposed the informality was Weil's way of saying he wouldn't let her promotion bother him as long as she didn't get snotty about it.

Weil deposited a folder on top of the teetering pile marked "For Immediate Action," then leaned back again. Bach eyed the stack of paper—and the circular file mounted in the wall not half a meter from it, leading to the incinerator—and thought about having an accident. Just a careless nudge with an elbow . . .

"Aren't you even going to open it?" Weil asked, sounding disappointed. "It's not every day I'm going to hand-deliver a case."

"You tell me about it, since you want to so badly."

"All right. We've got a body, which is cut up pretty bad. We've got the murder weapon, which is a knife. We've got thirteen eyewitnesses who can describe the killer, but we don't really need them since the murder was committed in front of a television camera. We've got the tape."

"You're talking about a case which has to have been solved ten minutes after the first report, untouched by human hands. Give it to the computer, idiot." But she looked up. She didn't like the smell of it. "Why give it to me?"

"Because of the other thing we know. The scene of the crime. The murder was committed at the barbie colony."

"Oh, sweet Jesus."

THE TEMPLE OF the Standardized Church in Luna was in the center of the Standardist Commune, Anytown, North Crisium. The best way to reach it, they found, was a local tube line which paralleled the Cross-Crisium Express Tube.

She and Weil checked out a blue-and-white police capsule with a priority sorting code and surrendered themselves to the New Dresden municipal transport system—the pill sorter, as the New Dresdenites called it. They were whisked through the precinct chute to the main nexus, where thousands of capsules were stacked awaiting a routing order to clear the computer. On the big conveyer which should have taken them to a holding cubby, they were snatched by a grapple—the cops called it the long arm of the law—and moved ahead to the multiple maws of the Cross-Crisium while people in other capsules glared at them. The capsule was inserted, and Bach and Weil were pressed hard into the backs of their seats.

In seconds they emerged from the tube and out onto the plain of Crisium, speeding along through the vacuum, magnetically suspended a few millimeters above the induction rail. Bach glanced up at the Earth, then stared out the window at the featureless landscape rushing by. She brooded.

It had taken a look at the map to convince her that the barbie colony was indeed in the New Dresden jurisdiction—a case of blatant gerrymandering if ever there was one. Anytown was fifty kilometers from what she thought of as the boundaries of New Dresden, but was joined to the city by a dotted line that represented a strip of land one meter wide.

A roar built up as they entered a tunnel and air was injected into the tube ahead of them. The car shook briefly as the shock wave built up, then they popped through pressure doors into the tube station of Anytown. The capsule doors hissed and they climbed out onto the platform.

The tube station at Anytown was primarily a loading dock and warehouse. It was a large space with plastic crates stacked against all the walls, and about fifty people working to load them into freight capsules.

Bach and Weil stood on the platform for a moment, uncertain where to go. The murder had happened at a spot not twenty meters in front of them, right here in the tube station.

"This place gives me the creeps," Weil volunteered.

"Me, too."

Every one of the fifty people Bach could see was identical to every other. All appeared to be female, though only faces, feet, and hands were visible, everything else concealed by loose white pajamas belted at the waist. They were all blonde; all had hair cut off at the shoulder and parted in the middle, blue eyes, high foreheads, short noses, and small mouths.

The work slowly stopped as the barbies became aware of them. They eyed Bach and Weil suspiciously. Bach picked one at random and approached her.

"Who's in charge here?" she asked.

"We are," the barbie said. Bach took it to mean the woman herself, recalling something about barbies never using the singular pronoun.

"We're supposed to meet someone at the temple," she said. "How do we get there?"

"Through that doorway," the woman said. "It leads to Main Street. Follow the street to the temple. But you really should cover yourselves."

"Huh? What do you mean?" Bach was not aware of anything wrong with the way she and Weil were dressed. True, neither of them wore as much as the barbies did. Bach wore her usual blue nylon briefs in addition to a regulation uniform cap, arm and thigh bands, and cloth-soled slippers. Her weapon, communicator, and handcuffs were fastened to a leather equipment belt.

"Cover yourself," the barbie said, with a pained look. "You're flaunting your differentness. And you, with all that hair . . ." There were giggles and a few shouts from the other barbies.

"Police business," Weil snapped.

"Uh, yes," Bach said, feeling annoyed that the barbie had put her on the defensive. After all, this was New Dresden, it was a public thoroughfare—even though by tradition and usage a Standardist enclave —and they were entitled to dress as they wished.

Main Street was a narrow, mean little place. Bach had expected a promenade like those in the shopping districts of New Dresden; what she found was indistinguishable from a residential corridor. They drew curious stares and quite a few frowns from the identical people they met.

There was a modest plaza at the end of the street. It had a low roof of bare metal, a few trees, and a blocky stone building in the center of a radiating network of walks.

A barbie who looked just like all the others met them at the entrance. Bach asked if she was the one Weil had spoken to on the phone, and she said she was. Bach wanted to know if they could go inside to talk. The barbie said the temple was off limits to outsiders and suggested they sit on a bench outside the building.

When they were settled, Bach started her questioning. "First, I need to know your name, and your title. I assume that you are . . . what was it?" She consulted her notes, taken hastily from a display she had called up on the computer terminal in her office. "I don't seem to have found a title for you."

"We have none," the barbie said. "If you must think of a title, consider us as the keeper of records."

"All right. And your name?"

"We have no name."

Bach sighed. "Yes, I understand that you forsake names when you come here. But you had one before. You were given

one at birth. I'm going to have to have it for my investigation."

The woman looked pained. "No, you don't understand. It is
true that this body had a name at one time. But it has been
wiped from this one's mind. It would cause this one a great
deal of pain to be reminded of it." She stumbled verbally every
time she said "this one." Evidently even a polite circumlocu-
tion of the personal pronoun was distressing.

"I'll try to get it from another angle, then." This was already
getting hard to deal with, Bach saw, and knew it could only
get tougher. "You say you are the keeper of records."

"We are. We keep records because the law says we must.
Each citizen must be recorded, or so we have been told."

"For a very good reason," Bach said. "We're going to need
access to those records. For the investigation. You understand? I assume an officer has already been through them, or
the deceased couldn't have been identified as Leah P. Ingraham."

"That's true. But it won't be necessary for you to go through
the records again. We are here to confess. We murdered L. P.
Ingraham, serial number 11005. We are surrendering peace-
fully. You may take us to your prison." She held out her
hands, wrists close together, ready to be shackled.

Weil was startled, reached tentatively for his handcuffs,
then looked to Bach for guidance.

"Let me get this straight. You're saying you're the one who
did it? You, personally."

"That's correct. We did it. We have never defied temporal
authority, and we are willing to pay the penalty."

"Once more." Bach reached out and grasped the barbie's
wrist, forced the hand open, palm up. "*This* is the person, this
is the body that committed the murder? This hand, this one
right here, held the knife and killed Ingraham? This hand, as
opposed to 'your' thousands of other hands?"

The barbie frowned.

"Put that way, no. *This* hand did not grasp the murder weapon. But *our* hand did. What's the difference?"

"Quite a bit, in the eyes of the law." Bach sighed, and let go of the woman's hand. Woman? She wondered if the term applied. She realized she needed to know more about Standardists. But it was convenient to think of them as such, since their faces were feminine.

"Let's try again. I'll need you—and the eyewitnesses to the crime—to study the tape of the murder. *I* can't tell the difference between the murderer, the victim, or any of the bystanders. But surely you must be able to. I assume that . . . well, like the old saying went, 'all chinamen look alike.' That was to Caucasian races, of course. Orientals had no trouble telling each other apart. So I thought that you . . . that you people would . . ." She trailed off at the look of blank incomprehension on the barbie's face.

"We don't know what you're talking about."

Bach's shoulders slumped.

"You mean you can't . . . not even if you saw her again . . . ?"

The woman shrugged. "We all look the same to this one."

ANNA-LOUISE BACH SPRAWLED out on her flotation bed later that night, surrounded by scraps of paper. Untidy as it was, her thought processes were helped by actually scribbling facts on paper rather than filing them in her datalink. And she did her best work late at night, at home, in bed, after taking a bath or making love. Tonight she had done both and found she needed every bit of the invigorating clarity it gave her.

Standardists.

They were an off-beat religious sect founded ninety years earlier by someone whose name had not survived. That was not surprising, since Standardists gave up their names when they joined the order, made every effort consistent with the laws of the land to obliterate the name and person as if he or she had never existed. The epithet "barbie" had quickly been attached to them by the press. The origin of the word was a popular children's toy of the twentieth and early twenty-first centuries, a plastic, sexless, mass-produced "girl" doll with an elaborate wardrobe.

The barbies had done surprisingly well for a group which did not reproduce, which relied entirely on new members from the outside world to replenish their numbers. They had grown for twenty years, then reached a population stability where deaths equalled new members—which they called "components." They had suffered moderately from religious intolerance, moving from country to country until the majority had come to Luna sixty years ago.

They drew new components from the walking wounded of society, the people who had not done well in a world which preached conformity, passivity, and tolerance of your billions of neighbors, yet rewarded only those who were individualistic and aggressive enough to stand apart from the herd. The barbies had opted out of a system where one had to be at once a face in the crowd and a proud individual with hopes and dreams and desires. They were the inheritors of a long tradition of ascetic withdrawal, surrendering their names, their bodies, and their temporal aspirations to a life that was ordered and easy to understand.

Bach realized she might be doing some of them a disservice —there could be those among them who were attracted simply by the religious ideas of the sect, though Bach felt there was little in the teachings that made sense.

She skimmed through the dogma, taking notes. The Standardists preached the commonality of humanity, denigrated free will, and elevated the group and the consensus to demi-god status. Nothing too unusual in the theory; it was the practice of it that made people queasy.

There was a creation theory and a godhead, who was not worshipped but contemplated. Creation happened when the Goddess—a prototypical earth-mother who had no name—

gave birth to the universe. She put people in it, all alike, stamped from the same universal mold.

Sin entered the picture. One of the people began to wonder. This person had a name, given to him or her *after* the original sin as part of the punishment, but Bach could not find it written down anywhere. She decided that it was a dirty word which Standardists never told an outsider.

This person asked Goddess what it was all for. What had been wrong with the void, that Goddess had seen fit to fill it with people who didn't seem to have a reason for existing?

That was too much. For reasons unexplained—and impolite to even ask about—Goddess had punished humans by introducing differentness into the world. Warts, big noses, kinky hair, white skin, tall people and fat people and deformed people, blue eyes, body hair, freckles, testicles, and labia. A billion faces and fingerprints, each soul trapped in a body distinct from all others, with the heavy burden of trying to establish an identity in a perpetual shouting match.

But the faith held that peace was achieved in striving to regain that lost Eden. When all humans were again the same person, Goddess would welcome them back. Life was a testing, a trial.

Bach certainly agreed with that. She gathered her notes and shuffled them together, then picked up the book she had brought back from Anytown. The barbie had given it to her when Bach asked for a picture of the murdered woman.

It was a blueprint for a human being.

The title was *The Book of Specifications. The Specs*, for short. Each barbie carried one, tied to her waist with a tape measure. It gave tolerances in engineering terms, defining what a barbie could look like. It was profusely illustrated with drawings of parts of the body in minute detail, giving measurements in millimeters.

She closed the book and sat up, propping her head on a pillow. She reached for her viewpad and propped it on her knees, punched the retrieval code for the murder tape. For the twentieth time that night, she watched a figure spring forward from a crowd of identical figures in the tube station, slash at Leah Ingraham, and melt back into the crowd as her victim lay bleeding and eviscerated on the floor.

She slowed it down, concentrating on the killer, trying to spot something different about her. Anything at all would do. The knife struck. Blood spurted. Barbies milled about in consternation. A few belatedly ran after the killer, not reacting fast enough. People seldom reacted quickly enough. But the killer had blood on her hand. Make a note to ask about that.

Bach viewed the film once more, saw nothing useful, and decided to call it a night.

THE ROOM WAS long and tall, brightly lit from strips high above. Bach followed the attendant down the rows of square locker doors which lined one wall. The air was cool and humid, the floor wet from a recent hosing.

The man consulted the card in his hand and pulled the metal handle on locker 659a, making a noise that echoed through the bare room. He slid the drawer out and lifted the sheet from the corpse.

It was not the first mutilated corpse Bach had seen, but it was the first nude barbie. She immediately noted the lack of nipples on the two hills of flesh that pretended to be breasts, and the smooth, unmarked skin in the crotch. The attendant was frowning, consulting the card on the corpse's foot.

"Some mistake here," he muttered. "Geez, the headaches. What do you do with a thing like that?" He scratched his head, then scribbled through the large letter "F" on the card, replacing it with a neat "N." He looked at Bach and grinned sheepishly. "What do you do?" he repeated.

Bach didn't much care what he did. She studied L. P. Ingraham's remains, hoping that something on the body would show her why a barbie had decided she must die.

There was little difficulty seeing *how* she had died. The

knife had entered the abdomen, going deep, and the wound
extended upward from there in a slash that ended beneath the
breastbone. Part of the bone was cut through. The knife had
been sharp, but it would have taken a powerful arm to slice
through that much meat.

The attendant watched curiously as Bach pulled the dead
woman's legs apart and studied what she saw there. She found
the tiny slit of the urethra set far back around the curve, just
anterior to the anus.

Bach opened her copy of *The Specs*, took out a tape measure, and started to work.

"MR. ATLAS, I got your name from the Morphology Guild's files
as a practitioner who's had a lot of dealings with the
Standardist Church."

The man frowned, then shrugged. "So? You may not approve of them, but they're legal. And my records are in order. I
don't do any work on anybody until you people have checked
for a criminal record." He sat on the edge of the desk in the
spacious consulting room, facing Bach. Mr. Rock Atlas—
surely a *nom de métier*—had shoulders carved from granite,
teeth like flashing pearls, and the face of a young god. He was
a walking, flexing advertisement for his profession. Bach
crossed her legs nervously. She had always had a taste for beef.

"I'm not investigating you, Mr. Atlas. This is a murder case,
and I'd appreciate your cooperation."

"Call me Rock," he said, with a winning smile.

"Must I? Very well. I came to ask you what you would do,
how long the work would take, if I asked to be converted to a
barbie."

His face fell. "Oh, no, what a tragedy! I can't allow it. My
dear, it would be a crime." He reached over to her and touched
her chin lightly, turning her head. "No, Lieutenant, for you I'd
build up the hollows in the cheeks just the slightest bit—
maybe tighten up the muscles behind them—then drift the

orbital bones out a little bit farther from the nose to set your eyes wider. More attention-getting, you understand. That touch of mystery. Then of course there's your nose."

She pushed his hand away and shook her head. "No, I'm not coming to you for the operation. I just want to know. How much work would it entail, and how close can you come to the specs of the church?" Then she frowned and looked at him suspiciously. "What's wrong with my nose?"

"Well, my dear, I didn't mean to imply there was anything *wrong;* in fact, it has a certain overbearing power that must be useful to you once in a while, in the circles you move in. Even the lean to the left could be justified, aesthetically—"

"Never mind," she said, angry at herself for having fallen into his sales pitch. "Just answer my question."

He studied her carefully, asked her to stand up and turn around. She was about to object that she had not necessarily meant herself personally as the surgical candidate, just a woman in general, when he seemed to lose interest in her.

"It wouldn't be much of a job," he said. "Your height is just slightly over the parameters; I could take that out of your thighs and lower legs, maybe shave some vertebrae. Take out some fat here and put it back there. Take off those nipples and dig out your uterus and ovaries, sew up your crotch. With a man, chop off the penis. I'd have to break up your skull a little and shift the bones around, then build up the face from there. Say two days work, one overnight and one outpatient."

"And when you were through, what would be left to identify me?"

"Say that again?"

Bach briefly explained her situation, and Atlas pondered it.

"You've got a problem. I take off the fingerprints and footprints. I don't leave any external scars, not even microscopic ones. No moles, freckles, warts or birthmarks; they all have to go. A blood test would work, and so would a retinal print. An x-ray of the skull. A voiceprint would be questionable. I even that out as much as possible. I can't think of anything else."

"Nothing that could be seen from a purely visual exam?"

"That's the whole point of the operation, isn't it?"

"I know. I was just hoping you might know something even the barbies were not aware of. Thank you, anyway."

He got up, took her hand, and kissed it. "No trouble. And if you ever decide to get that nose taken care of . . ."

SHE MET JORGE WEIL at the temple gate in the middle of Anytown. He had spent his morning there, going through the records, and she could see the work didn't agree with him. He took her back to the small office where the records were kept in battered file cabinets. There was a barbie waiting for them there. She spoke without preamble.

"We decided at equalization last night to help you as much as possible."

"Oh, yeah? Thanks. I wondered if you would, considering what happened fifty years ago."

Weil looked puzzled. "What was that?"

Bach waited for the barbie to speak, but she evidently wasn't going to.

"All right. I found it last night. The Standardists were involved in murder once before, not long after they came to Luna. You notice you never see one of them in New Dresden?"

Weil shrugged. "So what? They keep to themselves."

"They were *ordered* to keep to themselves. At first, they could move freely like any other citizens. Then one of them killed somebody—not a Standardist this time. It was known the murderer was a barbie; there were witnesses. The police started looking for the killer. You guess what happened."

"They ran into the problems we're having." Weil grimaced. "It doesn't look so good, does it?"

"It's hard to be optimistic," Bach conceded. "The killer was never found. The barbies offered to surrender one of their number at random, thinking the law would be satisfied with that. But of course it wouldn't do. There was a public outcry, and a lot of pressure to force them to adopt some kind of distinguishing characteristic, like a number tattooed on their foreheads. I don't think that would have worked, either. It could have been covered.

"The fact is that the barbies were seen as a menace to society. They could kill at will and blend back into their community like grains of sand on a beach. We would be powerless to punish a guilty party. There was no provision in the law for dealing with them."

"So what happened?"

"The case is marked closed, but there's no arrest, no conviction, and no suspect. A deal was made whereby the Standardists could practice their religion as long as they never mixed with other citizens. They had to stay in Anytown. Am I right?" She looked at the barbie.

"Yes. We've adhered to the agreement."

"I don't doubt it. Most people are barely aware you exist out here. But now we've got this. One barbie kills another barbie, and under a television camera . . ." Bach stopped, and looked thoughtful. "Say, it occurs to me . . . wait a minute. *Wait a minute.*" She didn't like the look of it.

"I wonder. This murder took place in the tube station. It's the only place in Anytown that's scanned by the municipal security system. And fifty years is a long time between murders, even in a town as small as . . . how many people did you say live here, Jorge?"

"About seven thousand. I feel I know them all intimately." Weil had spent the day sorting barbies. According to measurements made from the tape, the killer was at the top end of permissible height.

"How about it?" Bach said to the barbie. "Is there anything I ought to know?"

The woman bit her lip, looked uncertain.

"Come on, you said you were going to help me."

"Very well. There have been three other killings in the last month. You would not have heard of this one except it took place with outsiders present. Purchasing agents were there on the loading platform. They made the initial report. There was nothing we could do to hush it up."

"But why would you want to?"

"Isn't it obvious? We exist with the possibility of persecution always with us. We don't wish to appear a threat to others. We wish to appear peaceful—which we *are*—and prefer to handle the problems of the group within the group itself. By divine consensus."

Bach knew she would get nowhere pursuing that line of reasoning. She decided to take the conversation back to the previous murders.

"Tell me what you know. Who was killed; and do you have any idea why? Or should I be talking to someone else?" Something occurred to her then, and she wondered why she hadn't asked it before. "You *are* the person I was speaking to yesterday, aren't you? Let me re-phrase that. You're the body . . . that is, this body before me . . ."

"We know what you're talking about," the barbie said. "Uh, yes, you are correct. We are . . . *I* am the one you spoke to." She had to choke the word out, blushing furiously. We have been . . . *I* have been selected as the component to deal with you, since it was perceived at equalization that this matter must be dealt with. This one was chosen as . . . *I* was chosen as punishment."

"You don't have to say 'I' if you don't want to."

"Oh, thank you."

"Punishment for what?"

"For . . . for individualistic tendencies. We spoke up too personally at equalization, in favor of cooperation with you. As a political necessity. The conservatives wish to stick to our sacred principles no matter what the cost. We are divided; this makes for bad feelings within the organism, for sickness. This one spoke out, and was punished by having her own way, by being appointed . . . *individually* . . . to deal with you."

The woman could not meet Bach's eyes. Her face burned with shame.

"This one has been instructed to reveal her serial number to you. In the future, when you come here you are to ask for 23900."

Bach made a note of it.

"All right. What can you tell me about a possible motive? Do you think all the killings were done by the same . . . component?"

"We do not know. We are no more equipped to select an . . . individual from the group than you are. But there is great consternation. We are fearful."

"I would think so. Do you have reason to believe that the victims were . . . does this make sense? . . . *known* to the killer? Or were they random killings?" Bach hoped not. Random killers were the hardest to catch; without motive, it was hard to tie killer to victim, or to sift one person out of thousands with the opportunity. With the barbies, the problem would be squared and cubed.

"Again, we don't know."

Bach sighed. "I want to see the witnesses to the crime. I might as well start interviewing them."

In short order, thirteen barbies were brought. Bach intended to question them thoroughly to see if their stories were consistent, and if they had changed.

She sat them down and took them one at a time, and almost immediately ran into a stone wall. It took her several minutes to see the problem, frustrating minutes spent trying to establish which of the barbies had spoken to the officer first, which second, and so forth.

"Hold it. Listen carefully. Was this body physically present at the time of the crime? Did these eyes see it happen?"

The barbie's brow furrowed. "Why, no. But does it matter?"

"It does to me, babe. *Hey, twenty-three thousand!*"

The barbie stuck her head in the door. Bach looked pained.

"I need the actual people who were *there*. Not thirteen picked at random."

"The story is known to all."

Bach spent five minutes explaining that it made a difference to her, then waited an hour as 23900 located the people who were actual witnesses.

And again she hit a stone wall. The stories were absolutely identical, which she knew to be impossible. Observers *always* report events differently. They make themselves the hero, invent things before and after they first began observing, rearrange and edit and interpret. But not the barbies. Bach struggled for an hour, trying to shake one of them, and got nowhere. She was facing a consensus, something that had been discussed among the barbies until an account of the event had emerged and then been accepted as truth. It was probably a close approximation, but it did Bach no good. She needed discrepancies to gnaw at, and there were none.

Worst of all, she was convinced no one was lying to her. Had she questioned the thirteen random choices she would have gotten the same answers. They would have thought of themselves as having been there, since some of them had been and they had been told about it. What happened to one, happened to all.

Her options were evaporating fast. She dismissed the witnesses, called 23900 back in, and sat her down. Bach ticked off points on her fingers.

"One. Do you have the personal effects of the deceased?"

"We have no private property."

Bach nodded. "Two. Can you take me to her room?"

"We each sleep in any room we find available at night. There is no—"

"Right. Three. Any friends or co-workers I might . . ." Bach rubbed her forehead with one hand. "Right. Skip it. Four. What was her job? Where did she work?"

"All jobs are interchangeable here. We work at what needs—"

"Right!" Bach exploded. She got up and paced the floor. "What the hell do you expect me to *do* with a situation like this? I don't have *anything* to work with, not one snuffin' *thing.* No way of telling *why* she was killed, no way to pick out the *killer,* no way . . . ah, *shit.* What do you expect me to *do?"*

"We don't expect you to do anything," the barbie said, quietly. "We didn't ask you to come here. We'd like it very much if you just went away."

In her anger Bach had forgotten that. She was stopped, unable to move in any direction. Finally, she caught Weil's eye and jerked her head toward the door.

"Let's get out of here." Weil said nothing. He followed Bach out the door and hurried to catch up.

They reached the tube station, and Bach stopped outside their waiting capsule. She sat down heavily on a bench, put her chin on her palm, and watched the ant-like mass of barbies working at the loading dock.

"Any ideas?"

Weil shook his head, sitting beside her and removing his cap to wipe sweat from his forehead.

"They keep it too hot in here," he said. Bach nodded, not really hearing him. She watched the group of barbies as two separated themselves from the crowd and came a few steps in her direction. Both were laughing, as if at some private joke, looking right at Bach. One of them reached under her blouse and withdrew a long, gleaming steel knife. In one smooth motion she plunged it into the other barbie's stomach and lifted, bringing her up on the balls of her feet. The one who had been stabbed looked surprised for a moment, staring down at herself, her mouth open as the knife gutted her like a fish. Then her eyes widened and she stared horror-stricken at her companion, and slowly went to her knees, holding the knife to her as blood gushed out and soaked her white uniform.

"Stop her!" Bach shouted. She was on her feet and running,

after a moment of horrified paralysis. It had looked *so* much like the tape.

She was about forty meters from the killer, who moved with deliberate speed, jogging rather than running. She passed the barbie who had been attacked—and who was now on her side, still holding the knife hilt almost tenderly to herself, wrapping her body around the pain. Bach thumbed the panic button on her communicator, glanced over her shoulder to see Weil kneeling beside the stricken barbie, then looked back—

—to a confusion of running figures. Which one was it? *Which one?*

She grabbed the one that seemed to be in the same place and moving in the same direction as the killer had been before she looked away. She swung the barbie around and hit her hard on the side of the neck with the edge of her palm, watched her fall while trying to look at all the other barbies at the same time. They were running in both directions, some trying to get away, others entering the loading dock to see what was going on. It was a madhouse scene with shrieks and shouts and baffling movement.

Bach spotted something bloody lying on the floor, then knelt by the inert figure and clapped the handcuffs on her.

She looked up into a sea of faces, all alike.

THE COMMISSIONER DIMMED the lights, and he, Bach, and Weil faced the big screen at the end of the room. Beside the screen was a department photoanalyst with a pointer in her hand. The tape began to run.

"Here they are," the woman said, indicating two barbies with the tip of the long stick. They were just faces on the edge of the crowd, beginning to move. "Victim right here, the suspect to her right." Everyone watched as the stabbing was re-created. Bach winced when she saw how long she had taken to react. In her favor, it had taken Weil a fraction of a second longer.

"Lieutenant Bach begins to move here. The suspect moves back toward the crowd. If you'll notice, she is watching Bach over her shoulder. Now. Here." She froze a frame. "Bach loses eye contact. The suspect peels off the plastic glove which prevented blood from staining her hand. She drops it, moves laterally. By the time Bach looks back, we can see she is after the wrong suspect."

Bach watched in sick fascination as her image assaulted the wrong barbie, the actual killer only a meter to her left. The tape resumed normal speed, and Bach watched the killer until her eyes began to hurt from not blinking. She would not lose her this time.

"She's incredibly brazen. She does not leave the room for another twenty minutes." Bach saw herself kneel and help the medical team load the wounded barbie into the capsule. The killer had been at her elbow, almost touching her. She felt her arm break out in goose pimples.

She remembered the sick fear that had come over her as she knelt by the injured woman. *It could be any of them. The one behind me, for instance . . .*

She had drawn her weapon then, backed against the wall, and not moved until the reinforcements arrived a few minutes later.

At a motion from the commissioner, the lights came back on.

"Let's hear what you have," he said.

Bach glanced at Weil, then read from her notebook.

" 'Sergeant Weil was able to communicate with the victim shortly before medical help arrived. He asked her if she knew anything pertinent as to the identity of her assailant. She answered no, saying only that it was "the wrath." She could not elaborate.' I quote now from the account Sergeant Weil wrote down immediately after the interview. ' "It hurts, it hurts." "I'm dying, I'm dying." I told her help was on the way. She responded: "I'm dying." Victim became incoherent, and I attempted to get a shirt from the onlookers to stop the flow of blood. No cooperation was forthcoming.' "

"It was the word 'I'," Weil supplied. "When she said that, they all started to drift away."

" 'She became rational once more,' " Bach resumed, " 'long enough to whisper a number to me. The number was twelve-fifteen, which I wrote down as one-two-one-five. She roused herself once more, said "I'm dying." ' " Bach closed the notebook and looked up. "Of course, she was right." She coughed nervously.

"We invoked section 35b of the New Dresden Unified Code, 'Hot Pursuit,' suspending civil liberties locally for the duration of the search. We located component 1215 by the simple expedient of lining up all the barbies and having them pull their pants down. Each has a serial number in the small of her back. Component 1215, one Sylvester J. Cronhausen, is in custody at this moment.

"While the search was going on, we went to sleeping cubicle number 1215 with a team of criminologists. In a concealed compartment beneath the bunk we found these items." Bach got up, opened the evidence bag, and spread the items on the table.

There was a carved wooden mask. It had a huge nose with a hooked end, a mustache, and a fringe of black hair around it. Beside the mask were several jars of powders and creams, greasepaint and cologne. One black nylon sweater, one pair black trousers, one pair black sneakers. A stack of pictures clipped from magazines, showing ordinary people, many of them wearing more clothes than was normal in Luna. There was a black wig and a merkin of the same color.

"What was that last?" the commissioner asked.

"A merkin, sir," Bach supplied. "A pubic wig."

"Ah." He contemplated the assortment, leaned back in his chair. "Somebody liked to dress up."

"Evidently, sir." Bach stood at ease with her hands clasped behind her back, her face passive. She felt an acute sense of failure, and a cold determination to get the woman with the gall to stand at her elbow after committing murder before her eyes. She was sure the time and place had been chosen deliberately, that the barbie had been executed for Bach's benefit.

"Do you think these items belonged to the deceased?"

"We have no reason to state that, sir," Bach said. "However, the circumstances are suggestive."

"Of what?"

"I can't be sure. These things *might* have belonged to the victim. A random search of other cubicles turned up nothing like this. We showed the items to component 23900, our liaison. She professed not to know their purpose." She stopped, then added, "I believe she was lying. She looked quite disgusted."

"Did you arrest her?"

"No, sir. I didn't think it wise. She's the only connection we have, such as she is."

The commissioner frowned, and laced his fingers together. "I'll leave it up to you, Lieutenant Bach. Frankly, we'd like to be shut of this mess as soon as possible."

"I couldn't agree with you more, sir."

"Perhaps you don't understand me. We have to have a warm body to indict. We have to have one soon."

"Sir, I'm doing the best I can. Candidly, I'm beginning to wonder if there's anything I *can* do."

"You still don't understand me." He looked around the office. The stenographer and photoanalyst had left. He was alone with Bach and Weil. He flipped a switch on his desk, turning a recorder *off*, Bach realized.

"The news is picking up on this story. We're beginning to get some heat. On the one hand, people are afraid of these barbies. They're hearing about the murder fifty years ago, and the informal agreement. They don't like it much. On the other hand, there's the civil libertarians. They'll fight hard to prevent anything happening to the barbies, on principle. The government doesn't want to get into a mess like that. I can hardly blame them."

Bach said nothing, and the commissioner looked pained.

"I see I have to spell it out. We have a suspect in custody," he said.

"Are you referring to component 1215, Sylvester Cronhausen?"

"No. I'm speaking of the one you captured."

"Sir, the tape clearly shows she is not the guilty party. She was an innocent bystander." She felt her face heat up as she said it. Damn it, she had tried her best.

"Take a look at this." He pressed a button and the tape began to play again. But the quality was much impaired. There were bursts of snow, moments when the picture faded out entirely. It was a very good imitation of a camera failing. Bach watched herself running through the crowd—there was a flash of white—and she had hit the woman. The lights came back on in the room.

"I've checked with the analyst. She'll go along. There's a bonus in this, for both of you." He looked from Weil to Bach.

"I don't think I can go through with that, sir."

He looked like he'd tasted a lemon. "I didn't say we were doing this today. It's an option. But I ask you to look at it this way, just look at it, and I'll say no more. This is the way *they themselves* want it. They offered you the same deal the first time you were there. Close the case with a confession, no mess. We've already got this prisoner. She just says she killed her, she killed all of them. I want you to ask yourself, is she wrong? By her own lights and moral values? She believes she shares responsibility for the murders, and society demands a culprit. What's wrong with accepting their compromise and letting this all blow over?"

"Sir, it doesn't feel right to me. This is not in the oath I took. I'm supposed to protect the innocent, and she's innocent. She's the *only* barbie I *know* to be innocent."

The commissioner sighed. "Bach, you've got four days. You give me an alternative by then."

"Yes, sir. If I can't, I'll tell you now that I won't interfere with what you plan. But you'll have to accept my resignation."

ANNA-LOUISE BACH RECLINED in the bathtub with her head pillowed on a folded towel. Only her neck, nipples, and knees stuck out above the placid surface of the water, tinted purple with a generous helping of bath salts. She clenched a thin cheroot in her teeth. A ribbon of lavender smoke curled from the end of it, rising to join the cloud near the ceiling.

She reached up with one foot and turned on the taps, letting out cooled water and re-filling with hot until the sweat broke out on her brow. She had been in the tub for several hours. The tips of her fingers were like washboards.

There seemed to be few alternatives. The barbies were foreign to her, and to anyone she could assign to interview them. They didn't want her help in solving the crimes. All the old rules and procedures were useless. Witnesses meant nothing; one could not tell one from the next, nor separate their stories. Opportunity? Several thousand individuals had it. Motive was a blank. She had a physical description in minute detail, even tapes of the actual murders. Both were useless.

There was one course of action that might show results. She had been soaking for hours in the hope of determining just how important her job was to her.

Hell, what else did she want to do?

She got out of the tub quickly, bringing a lot of water with her to drip onto the floor. She hurried into her bedroom, pulled the sheets off the bed and slapped the nude male figure on the buttocks.

"Come on, Svengali," she said. "Here's your chance to do something about my nose."

* * *

SHE USED EVERY minute while her eyes were functioning to read all she could find about Standardists. When Atlas worked on her eyes, the computer droned into an earphone. She memorized most of the *Book of Standards.*

Ten hours of surgery, followed by eight hours flat on her back, paralyzed, her body undergoing forced regeneration, her eyes scanning the words that flew by on an overhead screen.

Three hours of practice, getting used to shorter legs and arms. Another hour to assemble her equipment.

When she left the Atlas clinic, she felt she would pass for a barbie as long as she kept her clothes on. She hadn't gone *that* far.

PEOPLE TENDED TO forget about access locks that led to the surface. Bach had used the fact more than once to show up in places where no one expected her.

She parked her rented crawler by the lock and left it there. Moving awkwardly in her pressure suit, she entered and started it cycling, then stepped through the inner door into an equipment room in Anytown. She stowed the suit, checked herself quickly in a washroom mirror, straightened the tape measure that belted her loose white jumpsuit, and entered the darkened corridors.

What she was doing was not illegal in any sense, but she was on edge. She didn't expect the barbies to take kindly to her masquerade if they discovered it, and she knew how easy it was for a barbie to vanish forever. Three had done so before Bach ever got the case.

The place seemed deserted. It was late evening by the arbitrary day cycle of New Dresden. Time for the nightly equalization. Bach hurried down the silent hallways to the main meeting room in the temple.

It was full of barbies and a vast roar of conversation. Bach had no trouble slipping in, and in a few minutes she knew her facial work was as good as Atlas had promised.

Equalization was the barbie's way of standardizing experience. They had been unable to simplify their lives to the point where each member of the community experienced the same things every day; the *Book of Standards* said it was a goal to be aimed for, but probably unattainable this side of Holy Reassimilation with Goddess. They tried to keep the available jobs easy enough that each member could do them all. The commune did not seek to make a profit; but air, water, and food had to be purchased, along with replacement parts and services to keep things running. The community had to produce things to trade with the outside.

They sold luxury items: hand-carved religious statues, illuminated holy books, painted crockery, and embroidered tapestries. None of the items were Standardist. The barbies had no religious symbols except their uniformity and the tape measure, but nothing in their dogma prevented them from selling objects of reverence to people of other faiths.

Bach had seen the products for sale in the better shops. They were meticulously produced, but suffered from the fact that each item looked too much like every other. People buying hand-produced luxuries in a technological age tend to want the differences that non-machine production entails, whereas the barbies wanted everything to look exactly alike. It was an ironic situation, but the barbies willingly sacrificed value by adhering to their standards.

Each barbie did things during the day that were as close as possible to what everyone else had done. But someone had to cook meals, tend the air machines, load the freight. Each component had a different job each day. At equalization, they got together and tried to even that out.

It was boring. Everyone talked at once, to anyone that happened to be around. Each woman told what she had done that day. Bach heard the same group of stories a hundred times before the night was over, and repeated them to anyone who would listen.

Anything unusual was related over a loudspeaker so everyone could be aware of it and thus spread out the intolerable burden of anomaly. No barbie wanted to keep a unique experience to herself; it made her soiled, unclean, until it was shared by all.

Bach was getting very tired of it—she was short on sleep—when the lights went out. The buzz of conversation shut off as if a tape had broken.

"All cats are alike in the dark," someone muttered, quite near Bach. Then a single voice was raised. It was solemn; almost a chant.

"We are the wrath. There is blood on our hands, but it is the holy blood of cleansing. We have told you of the cancer eating at the heart of the body, and yet still you cower away from what must be done. *The filth must be removed from us!*"

Bach was trying to tell which direction the words were coming from in the total darkness. Then she became aware of movement, people brushing against her, all going in the same direction. She began to buck the tide when she realized everyone was moving away from the voice.

"You think you can use our holy uniformity to hide among us, but the vengeful hand of Goddess will not be stayed. The mark is upon you, our one-time sisters. Your sins have set you apart, and retribution will strike swiftly.

"There are five of you left. Goddess knows who you are, and will not tolerate your perversion of her holy truth. Death will strike you when you least expect it. Goddess sees the differentness within you, the differentness you seek but hope to hide from your upright sisters."

People were moving more swiftly now, and a scuffle had developed ahead of her. She struggled free of people who were breathing panic from every pore, until she stood in a clear space. The speaker was shouting to be heard over the sound of whimpering and the shuffling of bare feet. Bach moved forward, swinging her outstretched hands. But another hand brushed her first.

The punch was not centered on her stomach, but it drove the air from her lungs and sent her sprawling. Someone tripped over her, and she realized things would get pretty bad if she didn't get to her feet. She was struggling up when the lights came back on.

There was a mass sigh of relief as each barbie examined her neighbor. Bach half expected another body to be found, but that didn't seem to be the case. The killer had vanished again.

She slipped away from the equalization before it began to break up, and hurried down the deserted corridors to room 1215.

SHE SAT IN the room—little more than a cell, with a bunk, a chair, and a light on a table—for more than two hours before the door opened, as she had hoped it would. A barbie stepped inside, breathing hard, closed the door, and leaned against it.

"We wondered if you would come," Bach said, tentatively.

The woman ran to Bach and collapsed at her knees, sobbing.

"Forgive us, please forgive us, our darling. We didn't dare come last night. We were afraid that . . . that if . . . that it might have been you who was murdered, and that the wrath would be waiting for us here. Forgive us, forgive us."

"It's all right," Bach said, for lack of anything better. Suddenly, the barbie was on top of her, kissing her with a desperate passion. Bach was startled, though she had expected something of the sort. She responded as best she could. The barbie finally began to talk again.

"We must stop this, we just have to stop. We're so frightened of the wrath, but . . . but the *longing!* We can't stop ourselves. We need to see you so badly that we can hardly get through the day, not knowing if you are across town or working at our elbow. It builds all day, and at night, we cannot stop ourselves from sinning yet again." She was crying, more softly this time, not from happiness at seeing the woman she took Bach to be, but from a depth of desperation. "What's going to become of us?" she asked, helplessly.

"Shhh," Bach soothed. "It's going to be all right."

She comforted the barbie for a while, then saw her lift her head. Her eyes seemed to glow with a strange light.

"I can't wait any longer," she said. She stood up, and began taking off her clothes. Bach could see her hands shaking.

Beneath her clothing the barbie had concealed a few things that looked familiar. Bach could see that the merkin was already in place between her legs. There was a wooden mask much like the one that had been found in the secret panel, and a jar. The barbie unscrewed the top of it and used her middle finger to smear dabs of brown onto her breasts, making stylized nipples.

"Look what *I* got," she said, coming down hard on the pronoun, her voice trembling. She pulled a flimsy yellow blouse from the pile of clothing on the floor, and slipped it over her shoulders. She struck a pose, then strutted up and down the tiny room.

"Come on, darling," she said. "Tell me how beautiful I am. Tell me I'm lovely. Tell me I'm the only one for you. The only one. What's the *matter?* Are you still frightened? I'm not. I'll dare anything for you, my one and only love." But now she stopped walking and looked suspiciously at Bach. "Why aren't you getting dressed?"

"We . . . uh, I can't," Bach said, extemporizing. "They, uh, someone found the things. They're all gone." She didn't dare remove her clothes because her nipples and pubic hair would look too real, even in the dim light.

The barbie was backing away. She picked up her mask and held it protectively to her. "What do you mean? Was she here? The wrath? Are they after us? It's true, isn't it? They can see us." She was on the edge of crying again, near panic.

"No, no, I think it was the police—" But it was doing no good. The barbie was at the door now, and had it half open.

"You're her! What have you done to . . . no, no, you stay away." She reached into the clothing that she now held in her hands, and Bach hesitated for a moment, expecting a knife. It was enough time for the barbie to dart quickly through the door, slamming it behind her.

When Bach reached the door, the woman was gone.

Bach kept reminding herself that she was not here to find the other potential victims—of whom her visitor was certainly one—but to catch the killer. The fact remained that she wished she could have detained her, to question her further.

The woman was a pervert, by the only definition that made any sense among the Standardists. She, and presumably the other dead barbies, had an individuality fetish. When Bach had realized that, her first thought had been to wonder why they didn't simply leave the colony and become whatever they wished. But then why did a Christian seek out prostitutes? For the taste of sin. In the larger world, what these barbies did would have had little meaning. Here, it was sin of the worst and tastiest kind.

And somebody didn't like it at all.

The door opened again, and the woman stood there facing Bach, her hair disheveled, breathing hard.

"We had to come back," she said. "We're so sorry that we panicked like that. Can you forgive us?" She was coming toward Bach now, her arms out. She looked so vulnerable and contrite that Bach was astonished when the fist connected with her cheek.

Bach thudded against the wall, then found herself pinned under the woman's knees, with something sharp and cool against her throat. She swallowed very carefully, and said nothing. Her throat itched unbearably.

"She's dead," the barbie said. "And you're next." But there was something in her face that Bach didn't understand. The barbie brushed at her eyes a few times, and squinted down at her.

"Listen, I'm not who you think I am. If you kill me, you'll be bringing more trouble on your sisters than you can imagine."

The barbie hesitated, then roughly thrust her hand down into Bach's pants. Her eyes widened when she felt the genitals, but the knife didn't move. Bach knew she had to talk fast, and say all the right things.

"You understand what I'm talking about, don't you?" She looked for a response, but saw none. "You're aware of the political pressures that are coming down. You know this whole colony could be wiped out if you look like a threat to the outside. You don't want that."

"If it must be, it will be," the barbie said. "The purity is the important thing. If we die, we shall die pure. The blasphemers must be killed."

"I don't care about that anymore," Bach said, and finally got a ripple of interest from the barbie. "I have my principles, too. Maybe I'm not as fanatical about them as you are about yours. But they're important to me. One is that the guilty be brought to justice."

"You have the guilty party. Try her. Execute her. She will not protest."

"*You* are the guilty party."

The woman smiled. "So arrest us."

"All right, all right. I can't, obviously. Even if you don't kill me, you'll walk out that door and I'll never be able to find you. I've given up on that. I just don't have the time. This was my last chance, and it looks like it didn't work."

"We don't think you could do it, even with more time. But why should we let you live?"

"Because we can help each other." She felt the pressure ease up a little, and managed to swallow again. "You don't want to kill me, because it could destroy your community. Myself . . . I need to be able to salvage some self-respect out of this mess. I'm willing to accept your definition of morality and let you be the law in your own community. Maybe you're even right. Maybe you *are* one being. But I can't let that woman be convicted, when I *know* she didn't kill anyone."

The knife was not touching her neck now, but it was still being held so that the barbie could plunge it into her throat at the slightest movement.

"And if we let you live? What do you get out of it? How do you free your 'innocent' prisoner?"

"Tell me where to find the body of the woman you just killed. I'll take care of the rest."

THE PATHOLOGY TEAM had gone and Anytown was settling down once again. Bach sat on the edge of the bed with Jorge Weil. She was as tired as she ever remembered being. How long had it been since she slept?

"I'll tell you," Weil said, "I honestly didn't think this thing would work. I guess I was wrong."

Bach sighed. "I wanted to take her alive, Jorge. I thought I could. But when she came at me with the knife . . ." She let him finish the thought, not caring to lie to him. She'd already done that to the interviewer. In her story, she had taken the knife from her assailant and tried to disable her, but was forced in the end to kill her. Luckily, she had the bump on the back of her head from being thrown against the wall. It made a black-out period plausible. Otherwise, someone would have wondered why she waited so long to call for police and an ambulance. The barbie had been dead for an hour when they arrived.

"Well, I'll hand it to you. You sure pulled this out. I'll admit it, I was having a hard time deciding if I'd do as you were going to do and resign, or if I could have stayed on. Now I'll never know."

"Maybe it's best that way. I don't really know, either."

Jorge grinned at her. "I can't get used to thinking of *you* being behind that godawful face."

"Neither can I, and I don't want to see any mirrors. I'm going straight to Atlas and get it changed back." She got wearily to her feet and walked toward the tube station with Weil.

She had not quite told him the truth. She did intend to get her own face back as soon as possible—nose and all—but there was one thing left to do.

From the first, a problem that had bothered her had been the question of how the killer identified her victims.

Presumably the perverts had arranged times and places to meet for their strange rites. That would have been easy enough. Any one barbie could easily shirk her duties. She could say she was sick, and no one would know it was the same barbie who had been sick yesterday, and for a week or month before. She need not work; she could wander the halls acting as if she was on her way from one job to another. No one could challenge her. Likewise, while 23900 had said no barbie spent consecutive nights in the same room, there was no way for her to know that. Evidently room 1215 had been taken over permanently by the perverts.

And the perverts would have no scruples about identifying each other by serial number at their clandestine meetings, though they could not do it in the streets. The killer didn't even have that.

But someone had known how to identify them, to pick them out of a crowd. Bach thought she must have infiltrated meetings, marked the participants in some way. One could lead her to another, until she knew them all and was ready to strike.

She kept recalling the strange way the killer had looked at her, the way she had squinted. The mere fact that she had not killed Bach instantly in a case of mistaken identity meant she had been expecting to see something that had not been there.

And she had an idea about that.

She meant to go to the morgue first, and to examine the

corpses under different wavelengths of lights, with various filters. She was betting some kind of mark would become visible on the faces, a mark the killer had been looking for with her contact lenses.

It had to be something that was visible only with the right kind of equipment, or under the right circumstances. If she kept at it long enough, she would find it.

If it was an invisible ink, it brought up another interesting question. How had it been applied? With a brush or spray gun? Unlikely. But such an ink on the killer's hands might look and feel like water.

Once she had marked her victims, the killer would have to be confident the mark would stay in place for a reasonable time. The murders had stretched over a month. So she was looking for an indelible, invisible ink, one that soaked into pores.

And if it was indelible . . .

There was no use thinking further about it. She was right, or she was wrong. When she struck the bargain with the killer she had faced up to the possibility that she might have to live with it. Certainly she could not now bring a killer into court, not after what she had just said.

No, if she came back to Anytown and found a barbie whose hands were stained with guilt, she would have to do the job herself.

THE ENERGIES OF LOVE

BY KATHE KOJA

When artificial intelligence becomes a reality, computers will not only be able to think—they will also be able to house simulated personalities with whom one will be able to converse. Suppose favorite figures from history were available for on-line interviews—what question would you ask Abraham Lincoln? Or William Casey? Or, for that matter, your favorite dead author . . . ?

T HE GREY SEAT was cold as Bobby settled into it, ass formfitting to the uncomfortable plastic, the familiar public smell of the schoolbooth already all over him. He struggled with the headset, long dark hair tangling, as always, with the thin leads and bright circlet; he was the only one he knew who ever had trouble putting on a headset.

Around him, the schoolbooths of the Institute for Interactive Studies stood in ruler-straight rows, most of them in use: by students from the nearby university; by academics from the same; and by those who wanted merely to know more about the writers and artists, politicians and corporate toilers, whose lives and histories were contained on cold disk: a valley of the kings there for the calling up. There were four levels of access obtainable, at varying cost: tourist, skim, audit, and auto imprint level, or AIL; the deeper you went, the more you learned, the more you paid.

CARD PLEASE, the screen advised. Its green was bleeding at the edges, its color blurred. Bobby was a little blurred himself —it was early out, and his head still ached from last night's dustup—but he inserted his blue student-access card (which he hung onto for the discount; he had ceased to be a student three years before) and waited almost patiently for the schoolbooth to respond.

ACCESS LEVEL DESIRED?

AUDIT, Bobby thumbed in. He wanted AIL. But audit was all he could afford, today. It was all he could do to pay for his daily pack of dust. No matter. It was all going to pay off, and soon.

AUDIT, confirmed the schoolbooth. SUBJECT DESIRED?

"Desired is right," and he keyed in the magic words: CHRISTOFER LISTT.

He had only two hours' worth of audit access to play with,

so he spent no time reviewing what he already knew, knew, knew: Christofer Listt, very late twentieth century poet, playwright, social satirist, novelist extreme; the golden touch, each work beloved by drooling public and tightassed critic alike. After a career quick and brilliant, the ultimate brilliance, the novel *The Energies of Love,* was left dramatically unfinished by the writer's abrupt fierce suicide at the much-mourned age of twenty-nine. "Boo hoo," said Bobby to the visual that always flashed up at this point in the narrative: boohoo to the blond hair and high cheekbones, to the surprisingly muscular body and he-man hairy chest and long-lidded secretive smile and all the rest as the access slid into the final interview, Bobby mouthing the words in unison with the dear departed: "I've always felt that, by permitting his or her public to come too close, the artist permits, and even covertly encourages, the very overfamiliarity from which contempt is proverbially bred." The charming smile; Bobby felt his own teeth glisten in response: the fucker was a natural, you had to give him that, just look at that interviewer crossing and recrossing his legs. "There's a very old saying," continued Christofer, and Bobby, "in the theatre, or is it politics?" short pause for interviewer's appreciative chuckle, and Bobby's knowing headshake—"the sense of which is, Always leave them wanting more." Two days after that particular interview, Christofer went to his favorite pub and, after drinking five straight pints of ice-cold Guinness, shot himself with a Smith & Wesson plasma rifle, modified for wide dispersion: tricky, but stylish. The empty men's room had not yet begun burning before the shrieking started. "Prefab wailing wall," Bobby sneered, but with grudging delight. No matter how many times you looked at it (and he had looked at it so many times that he was just about broke) the son of a bitch had had style to burn, ha ha but true, even to the last. Even to the leaving of the great masterpiece unfinished—especially that. *The Energies of Love* thus became an eternal morsel offered up to endless mastication, every critic free to finish the book in expanded column form.

"An absolute fucking masterstroke," Bobby told the screen, as it scrolled a bibliography, all of which Bobby had read many times before. Being a two-bit hack for a nowhere softporn soap left him lots of time for reading.

And now the best part, the only part that was worth it on audit; AIL was even better but this would do. Bobby sat up a little straighter, settled his back against the chair. "Hi, shithead," he said, to the serene smile of Christofer Listt. "How're things in Deadsville?"

"Hello, Robert Bridgeman," in that smooth sweettalker's voice. "I'm glad you called me up."

"You're a fuckin' liar," Bobby said cheerfully, "but so am I, so what the hell." The switchover from cold disk to skip, SCP, superconducting processor, was always worth the price of the trip: to be able to talk to even a facsimile of the late great Christofer Listt, to have him respond, even though in a limited fashion, to one's questions and remarks, was not only fun in a very strange way but extremely useful to the writer-in-waiting, the hack on the make. AIL left a bigger, deeper mark on the paying customer—some of it you never forgot—but for now this was okay. Better than okay, it was fine.

"What do you want to talk about, Robert?"

"Same as always, Christofer. You."

"What would you like to know?"

"*Energies*. How does it end?" The ritual question, to which he received as expected the ritual reply: "*Energies* is unfinished, Robert. I don't know how it ends."

"Save it for the tourists, asshole." Bobby stretched back as far as the leads would allow, scratched a little at his unshaven chin. "C'mon, Chris, me and you are old buddies. Spare a little shoptalk for a fellow pro."

"Are you a writer too, Robert?"

Bobby laughed. "You care, right? Listen, it's my money, I get to ask the questions. When you were at the part where

Vincent is getting ready to rip Antonio, to suck him for all his credit, why did you have him go into that big reminiscence scene? It was out of character, man. You expect me to build something on *that?*"

"I'm not sure what you mean, Robert."

"You're really stupid when you want to be, you know that? Okay, how's this: *why* is Vincent so suddenly softhearted, why does he even consider how Antonio's childhood might make the rip even worse? And what's the bit about the blue Chinese dragon kite—and don't give me that Rosebud shit, you know I don't believe that. I know a fucking metaphor when I see one."

Two hours was, as always, shorter than it should have been, and in midsentence Christofer stopped, thanked "Robert" impersonally for his time and interest, and slipped away into the green-screen neverneverland, leaving Bobby with an incipient backache and big hunger unfulfilled: at this rate he would *never* finish *Energies* himself.

ROBIN, BLOND HEAD bobbing over green tea and quickbread in his everlasting booth at the Smart Bar: technofetishist from the cells up, making more than a living by customizing the newest tech to make it even newer, old friend from schooldays whose shoes cost more than Bobby's weekly rent. "Hey, boy," Robin's long Alabama drawl, "pull up a chair. How's it goin', you and the deader?"

"Slow, man, very slow." Bobby ordered a Guatemalan coffee and a side of quickbread. "Fact is, I may be needing a little boost. How about it?"

Robin smiled. "You artists, man, you're all the same. Pure spirits, all that shit, and you're always lookin' for a way to cut corners. Had me a dancer last night, all she wanted to do was take me home so I could punch up her audition tapes."

"So did you go?"

"What, to her apartment? Can't happen. She's got great legs, but they ain't that great. You know what I get an hour, consulting?"

"Don't tell me." The quickbread's dex drilled and hummed through Bobby's head. "Listen, I really got a problem, Robin. What do you charge for just listening?"

"For you, bro, not a dime. Hey, baby, another long green one, 'kay?"

"What I want," Bobby said, stretching his too-long legs, feeling the scratch of inspiration frisking at his temples, "what I *want* is a way to get past the schoolbooth's security, get deeper than AIL. I have *got* to get a handle on Mr. Chris, Robin. Otherwise I'll never finish."

"Huh. Listen, why's this so all-important, bro? Can you tell me that? 'Cause you never have."

Bobby shrugged. There was a deeper answer, he thought (and it was a nasty thought), deeper than he knew, but it would come across as popshrink bullshit; the surface answer would do just as well, thank you. "Money," he said, rubbing thumb and forefinger together in slow voluptuous shorthand. "Do you know how much I could sell the final chapter of *The Energies of Love* for?"

"You know I don't read, man, why ask?"

"If I could write the last chapter, finish the novel, I could write my own ticket." And what a reach for a hack, Bobby thought, as dark laughter seared inside him, what a coup for a guy who jerks off his talent writing stroke-vid for the hornier-than-thous. "I could afford *you*, man, get it?"

Robin laughed. "Okay. Fair enough. You want to get past security, right?" He tapped the table edge, short dextrous fingers in slow tattoo. "You want you a bypass, then, something to fool the computer into thinkin' it's talkin' to one of its own memories. Bypass selective access, you know?"

"No," said Bobby, "I don't. That's why I come to you, asshole, right?" They both laughed, higher-pitched; the dex was kicking in hard. "So what's that mean, in layman's terms?"

"I just gave it to you in layman's terms. Do you know how the whole system works?"

"No, and I don't really want—"

"Sure you do. Listen up, bro." Leaning back, deep in the subject and bound to go deeper at a moment's notice, Robin expounded on the basics of skip, called it scientific seance and giggled in his tea, called "cold disk" just a freezer full of brain patterns, talked molecular-level electronics that enabled the brain to interface its own signals with external signals, so the thoughts of the greats can be stored directly for later retrieval and study, man, it's really pretty basic when you chop it down to bare bones. " 'Nother tea here, please, and a beer for my friend, he's gettin' the shakes."

"Thanks," Bobby said as the beer arrived. Polski, his favorite. "So can you do it?"

Robin grinned, white teeth against pale lips. "Sure I can do it. I just never tried, is all." He laughed at Bobby's expression, all doubt. "Only problem is, if the computer thinks you're part of it—which is what we want—but if it thinks you're just another part of it, it could—and I say *could*, bro, mind you—it could wipe you."

"What do you mean, wipe me? You mean, like bad data?"

"Highly doubtful. But a possibility. Also it could make you crazy, put in information that doesn't belong in your head." Robin laughed outright. "You should see your face."

Bobby dredged up a laugh. Do you want it that bad? he asked himself. Do you want to write that last chapter? All of it's easy but getting in; you can write it, you *know* you can, you can present it to the whole world that wouldn't read your own stuff if you paid them, and make them like it, love it, fawn all over it as if it came straight from the great man himself, the dumb bastard. You can have the future he burned, you can be the expert instead of a nobody hack; you can be Christofer Listt if you want to, you can be *better* than Christofer Listt. "So what if it costs me my brain?" he said. "I wasn't using it anyway."

"That's the spirit," and Robin gestured to the waitress. "Another side of bread, honey, and another beer for my friend."

IT WAS SIMPLE, really. Once Robin was interested, and he was, it took no time at all to jimmy up a prototype, a circle of vein-blue wiring with a set of leads much like the regular set-up; Bobby was able to use it, at least off Robin's bench mode, with no more than the usual trouble. "And this'll get me all the way past security, past AIL and everything? This'll do it?"

"This'll put you where the guy lives," Robin said, fingering the leads. "Or doesn't, as the case may be."

"Uh-huh. Gimme the odds again on the computer frying me, will you?"

"Nope. It'll only make you nervous." Robin stroked the leads, smiling like dreamy big daddy. "Do you know how much a thing like this is worth on the street? Do you know how much, say, this year's crop of med school rivetheads would pay me for something like this, for the tech to interface directly, one-on-one, with Steiner and de Pauw? A cure for the common cold, man. How much is that worth?" Bio-fluorescence pealing down like summer light on his face, blond hair shining, he looked to Bobby like a technoid angel, bringing the good news. "Sometimes I surprise myself, you know?"

"So." Deep breath. This was the moment he had been dreading, the minute he found out just how deep he was swimming. Whatever it was, he couldn't afford it, couldn't afford not to have it. "So, Robin. How—"

"If you're going to ask how I did it, don't; you wouldn't understand." Robin's smile dimmed. "And if you're going to ask how much, don't do that either. All I ask is that you don't sell it to anybody else when you're done using it." He laughed, all at once, very loud. "That job I'll do for myself.

And I won't even mention your name. How's that for friendship, boy?"

Unexpectedly, stupidly, a wash of—moisture, ran in
Bobby's eyes. Lack of sleep, right. "Can't beat it." He found
himself laughing. "And if I die, or go batshit, *I* won't mention
your name, right?"

"You got it. Just lemme know when you crack ol' Christofer's back door, okay?" Robin's smile softened, he patted
Bobby's back. "And take it easy, the first ride you take. Test
the waters, you know what I'm sayin'?"

"Sure."

"And get some sleep before you do, eat a meal or something. You look like shit, you know that?"

"Sure do." And Bobby realized just what he had in his
hands, and he laughed so hard he had to stop.

HE SLEPT, HE ate, he slept again, and woke to dress in sober grey
sharkskin and black cotton shirt, wanting to appear somehow
respectable, above suspicion. He got all the way to his door
before realizing how stupid he looked; it took two minutes to
change back to daily wear, the only difference an oversize cap,
hiding the new headset; Robin had sworn it would pass door
security without peep one. "Nothin' there to set it off," he'd
assured Bobby. "You worry too much, man."

Robin was right. Still Bobby's hands were shaking, quick
low-Richter tremors riding the nerves until he could have
screamed: a teakettle bubbling with seismic gas. He took his
usual booth, inserted his card, knowing there was credit
enough to ride deep, as far as Mr. Computer was concerned.
As far as Mr. Listt was concerned, who knew?

ACCESS LEVEL DESIRED?

AUTO IMPRINT LEVEL. Working so far.

AUTO IMPRINT. SUBJECT?

CHRISTOFER LISTT< 917/68. Here comes the burn, if it's
going to, he thought, and could smell the sweat beneath his

arms, sour as stale beer. Good thing, he thought, somewhere cold and lucid deep down, good thing no one's watching me; I bet I look like a fucking criminal.

CHRISTOFER LISTT< 917/68—and then a string of symbols, glyphs unknown, cool alphanumerics whose import he could not begin to guess, and a feeling of numbness, of wavering, like swimming in filthy water, and a pain in his head like a dustup hangover, and then, like coming to surface and he would never, never forget it, a voice, speaking: "What the *hell* is going on?"

He thought it was his own voice, and almost laughed: You made it, asshole! and said it, he thought later, aloud, segue to the shock of the answer:

"Then am I dead for good this time?"

The voice was just as it was in the interview, tone and pitch all the same, but the public persona was long, long gone, erased down to this nub of sickness, bright as a sore to even the casual eye, so bright that at first sight Bobby could not believe he had never seen it before. Silence, in which his shock nurtured itself, and the echoes of that voice told him thousands of things, extended vistas of nuance. Silence broken all at once by a cool, cool sigh, more weary than Bobby would ever be, and that voice again: *"Now* what?"

"My name's Bobby," Bobby blurted, before he could help himself, and heard the cold silver of Christofer's true laughter: not the false warmth of an icon's mirth but the slick iced humor of a man to whom nothing is funny anymore.

"How much did you have to pay, Bobby, to crawl up my ass in this undignified fashion? Is this some new sort of special service?"

Beneath the words there was surprise: Bobby could taste it. The fact of the question made him wary; the voice was unmistakable, there could be no simulation like this, but who knew what security riders there might be, listening in? Robin had gotten him in, but no one had ever opened this particular door, so who knew how to defend against what might be waiting on the other side? "None of your business," Bobby said, tough as he could make it. "What do you care, anyway?"

"It's not a question of caring, just a departure from my usual mode, which is very much like that of a quadriplegic in a desert. Very arid."

"If it's so bad there, then why'd you put yourself on disk?"

"A drunken unfulfilled lust," smooth and snotty, "for the absolute zero of death."

The phrase stirred Bobby—the bastard was still so good. "But you're not really dead, are you? I mean, I know you didn't leave any clone cells—"

"I was hoping to leave nothing at all, but I ballsed up, young Bobby."

Nothing but silence then, all around, as if, swimming, he had dived too deep into some unwarned-of trench where sound could never go. Then Christofer: "You diddled their security, then? Without being harmed by those watchdogs prowling loose?"

"I didn't know—I mean I figured there was some kind of override program, but I guess I beat it." Knowing that he had overcome unknown dangers made him happier still to be there, especially since the risks were already past.

"Why are you here?"

"I wanted—I want—" Come on, asshole, ask him! "I want to know about *Energies.* I want to know how it ends."

A loose witchy howl of laughter: "Oh for God's sake! A fan!" Christofer laughed so long it was scary, then stopped as if struck. "Tell the truth, you little shit."

All right, you crazy dead son of a bitch. "I told you. I want to know how it ends. And I want to write the ending myself."

"Why in hell," and a door opened in Christofer's voice, vast and cold and bleak beyond bleakness, "would you bother?"

The truth boiled up, immediate, bitter: "Because I'm a fuckin' *hack*, that's why, you smug piece of shit! Because I have to be *you* to get anyone to listen to me!" In the faraway confines of the schoolbooth, his body shook, the quaking of rage. "Okay? Satisfied?"

Christofer spoke, a bitterness so corrosive that Bobby's anger flattened and died. "I'm the king of the hacks, Bobby, and the best joke of all is that no one ever knew. But me. And I could never forget. Because nothing I ever wrote meant anything at all."

"It meant something to me."

The waiting silence of consideration, and Bobby had the impression of scales balancing, offers accepted: the bargain achieved. "Then I'll give you your ending, Bobby. And you'll get me out of here, once and for all."

"Get you out? You mean like a zombie body? I can't afford to even—"

"I killed a better body than even my estate could buy. Listen to me: you found a way to get yourself in here, didn't you? Then get me out. I don't care how, but *I want to be dead.* And I want you to do it."

"Hey, I don't even know how it is you're alive in there. All I wanted to do was just get—"

"Either make your deal with the devil," and the coldness was back, blown ice, "or get out."

Kill him? Take the knowledge of the greatest premodernist and then willfully murder him? "What the hell," Bobby said, feeling the fabric of his mind stretch in what might have been a smile, "it's a deal."

"YOU WANT TO do what?"

The pale light of the morning Smart Bar made Bobby look like a mad scientist. "Robin, man, just listen."

"I am listening." He shook his yellow head over steaming tea, believing at once all and nothing. "Look, I have no idea how the guy came to be inside there, but I'll do what I can. Whatever that is."

Bobby expected *Energies* to flow forth that day, and hit the schoolbooth with proportionate speed, but Christofer refused, and laughed when Bobby cursed. "I've had one O. Henry ending to my life," he said, "and I don't want another."

"What's that supposed to mean?"

It was like someone who had just mastered the art of holding a pencil watching a virtuoso demonstration of blindfolded calligraphy: the description of Christofer's first awakening, his awesome panic when he found he was not in the sleep he had sought but trapped instead in perpetual consciousness, made Bobby's flesh prickle and stir: what horror, waking to such a paradox, what sick rage to know you had done it to yourself.

Christofer had no idea of how the recording process had differed from the ordinary, or even if it had. "For all I know, this place is crawling with souls as damned as I am. Perhaps you could have a second career, as the angel of death."

"Hey, I got enough trouble just trying to figure out a way, I mean figure out how I'm, you know."

"How you're going to kill me. Don't be so squeamish— don't you want to know how *Energies* comes out?"

Bobby shrugged, small mental frown. "Sure. Can't wait." Nothing really wrong, is there, with killing someone who wants to die?

There was no point in going to the Institute the next day, or the next. He was having trouble sleeping, did some dust to perk him up; it didn't. At week's end Robin called him: "I have a kind of idea," not noticing Bobby's complete lack of excitement over such grand news. "Dunno if it'll work for sure, but we'll try. Hey, Bobby, you listening?"

"I hear you."

"Well, don't fall all over me, man, you know I hate that . . . Anyway, you c'n tell your chilly buddy to start giving you the poop on your book now."

"Great. Thanks. I'll tell him."

He walked out, into the oily dark, passing the Institute without looking, feet scuffing the scum of rainy leaves smeared like roadkill across the cracked sidewalks, walked till he came to a place where the dustheads liked to party. The dust leaned in like a hurricane, scouring him dry, sending him home to peer in the bathroom mirror, feet deep in the mulch of dirty towels, hands cold on the colder metal of the sink, staring into red eyes. "Fucking bastard," he said, in a matter of fact way, addressing—who? and slammed both hands to the mirror, driving glass into skin.

The Institute in the morning, duty breathing down his neck. Christofer: "Problem?"

"No problem."

"You're a very bad liar, Bobby." Christofer let the silence pool, then said, "Have you talked to your friend?"

"No."

"Stop it."

"All right, all right! I talked to him yesterday."

"Good news?"

"If you wanna call—yes, good news," with Christofer's own emphasis, coming down hard. "He thinks he found a way."

Christofer's laugh, but so jaunty and rich that Bobby felt like hitting him. No one should be that happy about croaking, even if he is already dead.

And then Bobby was suddenly happy. "What if the Institute finds out it was me who, you know, erased you? They'll prosecute me. They might even put me in jail." He was grinning. "I can't risk that."

"What you can't risk is the dark side of my sunny good nature, jumping out to slit your fucking *throat!* Don't play this kind of game with me, Bobby. We made an agreement and you're going to live up to it. Besides," the sizzle of his voice cooling, "if your friend was clever enough to get you in here he's more than clever enough to get me out without leaving a trace. *If* they even know I'm in here in the first place, I as in me, my consciousness. As far as the Institute's concerned, nothing will change; they'll still have their damned disk, and if they don't so what? What do I care? What do you care?

You'll have *Energies*, you'll be either my greatest biographer, the world's expert on me (and you are, you know, if you think about it), or the man, the *writer*, who could do what even the great Christofer Listt could not: finish *The Energies of Love!* Who's going to challenge the man who did the impossible? The Institute? They can't keep you out of here even now— what do you imagine they'll be able to do to you then? Really, Bobby," the residue of anger gone, dissipated by logic, "you are slow sometimes."

"So I'm slow. So sue me. So have your *estate* sue me. I could walk out of here now, you know. Just walk right out . . ." He was shivering, he could feel his elbows bumping against the faraway chair, he was freezing. Damn Christofer for being so right: there wasn't, really, anything the Institute could do, even if they did find out. Which was a poor possibility. Which Bobby knew, had known. What a stupid argument he'd used. He'd think up a better one tomorrow.

"Bobby."

"What."

"Can you imagine what a favor you're doing me?" His voice was gentler than Bobby could have imagined; it hurt to hear him. "Haven't I told you all this before? Or do we need the whole dreary story again?" Bobby said nothing. "And think of *Energies*—"

"Fuck *Energies!* Fuck your stupid masterpiece, and fuck me too for ever wanting to write it, for ever even *reading* it. I was better off as a dusthead hack."

"No one here believes that."

"I don't *want* to kill you, asshole! Can't you get that through your head? I'm sorry I ever agreed to this deal, I'm sorry I ever walked in here."

Long silence. Finally Christofer said, "I won't release you from your promise. But I will tell you a secret."

"I don't wanna hear it."

"No? It's a good one. Here it is." And he paused, a little

pause to make sure Bobby was really listening. "Here it is," he said again. "I had no idea how *Energies* ends. Until today."

Bobby at first could not react, but when he did, the scream he wanted most could not be found: the best he could do was a throaty croak, rage and damnation, a sound very much like that made by Christofer on the first day of his cold disk confinement. "Oh great, that's just fucking *great*," he said, when words were possible. "That's just what I wanted to hear. No, go on, go ahead, tell me how it ends. I'm all ears. I can't stop you anyway, can I?"

"No, you can't." Christofer paused again, a different kind of pause. Then: "You remember the last scene, don't you, where Vincent is just about to destroy Antonio, but stops to consider the dragon kite, and Antonio's childhood?"

"Yeah." A sodden, angry breath. "Yeah, so what."

"So. You said, once, that it was out of character for Vincent to become so softhearted, and you were right, as far as it went then. But now we know why Vincent's so soft. And you're wrong, Bobby, I know what you're going to say and you're wrong. Do you remember what Vincent got, in exchange for the blue dragon kite? Do you? Tell me."

"The—I don't know, what, the damn Lucie Lacey holocard. What does—"

"The holocard was old, wasn't it? At least a few seasons, maybe more. And its corners were bent and its surface was getting dirty and it'd been in Antonio's closet for who knows how long. But. Who did Vincent like best of all the holo stars?"

"Lucie Lacey." It was starting. He could feel it. He knew.

"And how many kites did Vincent have?"

"I don't know. You never said." Bobby felt the smile coming, because it hurt like hell but he couldn't help knowing, guessing the end, guessing the why, and he sat tight and let Christofer tell it, hurting and smiling. "How many?"

"Hundreds. Or fifties, or tens. *Many*, that's the point. And how many Lucie Lacey holocards did he have?"

"All of 'em."

"All but one."

"And since Antonio'd lived all his life in the Downs—no, shit, I'm sorry, you tell it."

"No." Christofer was smiling too. "No, *you* tell it. It's your story, isn't it?"

"It's—just let me finish, okay, just be quiet for a minute . . . okay, Antonio had this rotten childhood in the Downs, he saw the sun once a year, he never came topside—the kite was *it*, even the idea of the kite, *any* kite . . . and Vincent got the card, the only one he didn't have—"

"It looked like Antonio got the better of the deal, didn't it?" Silence. "Didn't it, Bobby? But Vincent got the thing he wanted most, at no cost to himself." More silence. "Only Antonio still had that old card. Only Antonio."

"Oh, *shit*." Across the new silence, the knowing quiet, it seemed as if they touched, or would have, if they had had hands to meet. Christofer's clasp was somehow cool, Bobby's dampish, warm with sweat. They held for a time, neither saw how long, then released. "Well." Bobby laughed a little. "Leave it to the old master, huh?"

"Just call me Vincent, Antonio." Quiet between them. Then: "When will it happen?" An edge to his voice that Bobby knew: a glad impatience, a coal in the chest, glowing. "Soon?"

"That's a stupid question, isn't it, Christofer."

"Everyone's entitled to one, I think."

"Sure they are. You can have mine."

Someday after we have mastered the air, the winds, the tides and gravity, we will harness for God the energies of love. And then for the second time in the history of the world man will have discovered fire.
                    —Pierre Teilhard de Chardin

Ryerson's Fate

by Doug Larsen

Criminologists have suggested that in the future genetic "fingerprinting"—the identification and tracking of an individual's unique DNA—will be as important to detectives as conventional fingerprints are today. In this story, Doug Larsen suggests an unusual way in which the police may make use of the new technique.

TELL YOU, it's the most satisfying part of my job. I knew it was coming when I heard a knock at the door.

"Nobody escapes," Marjoram proclaimed with satisfaction, walking in and tossing a sheaf of papers on my desk.

I grabbed the papers and scanned the first page. It was the summary sheet, announcing that one Tony Watkins, male Caucasian, brown hair, etc., etc., had been found unconscious in his apartment on the east side, stinking to high heaven, with his skin turned bright green. I chortled triumphantly. "Nobody escapes," I agreed, tearing off the summary sheet and slipping it into a file folder. I propped my feet up on the desk. "We got a match, of course?"

"First thing," Marjoram confirmed.

It really is. Nothing compares to it. It keeps me going as I slog through the red tape. I leaned back in my chair. "In celebration," I decreed, "you can buy us coffee."

"Be still, my heart," Marjoram commented as he turned to go. He returned a couple minutes later with two Styrofoam cups, helped himself to one of my guest chairs, and propped his feet up next to mine. We toasted each other, and sat back, reveling in it.

"You know the thing I like best about it?" Marjoram said.

"The coffee?"

"Close. The thing I like most is the fact that this guy rapes a woman, beats her up, gets away with no witnesses, the victim has a cruddy description of him, and we still get him within twenty-four hours."

I nodded appreciatively. "You know what I like best?"

"There's something better?"

"Just as good, anyway," I conceded. "What I like best is that we got him dead. No plea bargaining. He's looking at twenty-five, thirty years. All his lawyer can do is sit there and plead guilty for him."

Marjoram nodded. "That's good, too," he said.

"I was looking through the files yesterday," I said. "Do you know that aside from prison escapees, we haven't had a repeat rape offender for eight years? Before we got into this, this guy would have raped probably another five, six women before we caught him with conventional forces."

Marjoram shook his head in admiration. "We're good," he proclaimed. "There's no question about it."

I was really feeling good that day, which is rare, so I luxuriated in it. "We are, aren't we? In the war on crime, we are the first real breakthrough in centuries. Most of the time, since we get our noses rubbed in the depths of human suffering and despair that's inflicted on innocent people by criminals, I feel pretty cruddy. But every once in a while, it's nice to sit back and think of what progress we've made. Even though we've got a hell of a long way to go, it's nice to see some progress."

Marjoram nodded appreciatively and sipped his coffee. "Speaking of progress, what do you think our chances are of getting the new budget approved?"

"Pretty near zero, I'd say," I answered, tensing a little.

Marjoram looked alarmed. "Zero! Why?"

"I didn't submit it," I said.

Marjoram stared at me. "Why in the world didn't you submit it? Don't tell me you're on one of your austerity kicks again."

"That's exactly it, and I wouldn't call it a kick. I'm trying to hold costs down. I'm trying to keep our division politically popular and avoid budget cutbacks. The best way to do that is to not make waves."

Marjoram shook his head. "We haven't done any major research and development in over five years!" he protested. "We're going to lose our technological edge if we piddle around and don't keep driving forward."

"Relax," I told him. "We've got it all taken care of.

Cropdusting works every time. Nobody escapes, and nobody will. Why waste the money?"

Marjoram opened his mouth to object, but was interrupted by a stormy looking guy who hurried into my office. He didn't knock—he just came in. I looked up inquiringly, since I don't stand on protocol all that much. He looked back, and his lip curled in a sneer. He had a thin face and an unruly shock of black hair, but the thing you noticed most were his eyes. Angry eyes. This was one hostile person. It was hard to say if he was always like that—people have a tendency to be angry when they come into a police department—but he didn't make me feel comfortable. He looked at us slowly, with contempt showing on his face.

"I'm sorry," he said clearly in a reedy voice. "Wrong office. I was told to look for the Commissioner of Cropdusting, whatever that is. I obviously got the cafeteria instead."

"Wrong," I announced. "You have the right office." I straightened up in my chair. "I'm Jack Donnally, Commissioner of Special Apprehension Services, and this is Dr. Gene Marjoram, the head of the Special Apprehension crime lab."

The man looked confused, and obviously didn't like being confused. "I was told to see the Commissioner of Cropdusting, not Special Apprehension," he muttered.

"Commissioner of Cropdusting is my slang title, the one they use on the street," I explained. "You've got the right room. What can I do for you?"

"I am William J. Ryerson," he said, as if the name was supposed to mean something to us. We looked at him politely, waiting for him to continue. He saw that his name meant nothing, and looked even more sour. "I am an art critic for the *New York Times*," he said. "I am considered to be one of the leaders of the artistic community in the country."

"That's nice," I said patiently. "What can we do for you?"

He looked annoyed that we weren't impressed. "I want to know what you're going to do about the art thief that's running rampant in this city! Interpol has traced him from Europe and is now convinced he's in New York. I don't know much about Cropdusting, but I have heard stories about how you capture criminals who are otherwise impossible to capture. When do you start?"

Marjoram gave me a significant look that signified that he wasn't through with his subject of debate, and stood up. "I'll excuse myself," he said, "and leave you to the Commissioner." He left tactfully.

"Have a seat, Mr. Ryerson," I said politely.

"Thank you, I prefer to stand," he said curtly. "I am not here on a social call."

I could tell I was going to like this guy a lot. "Well, Mr. Ryerson," I answered as politely as I could, "my department is not doing anything about the art thief. That case has not been referred to me."

He looked like he was going to spit. "Why in the world hasn't it?!" he sputtered. "I thought this was the revolutionary crime fighting department! What's wrong about capturing possibly the most successful art thief in history, who has stolen some of the world's greatest paintings?"

"Let me explain about my department," I said as calmly as I could. "We are the department of Special Apprehension Services."

"I know," Ryerson said impatiently.

"Let me finish," I said. "We are the newest addition to the war on crime: we are the biological warfare department."

"How do you mean biological warfare? I just heard that you catch people that otherwise wouldn't be caught. This art thief certainly falls into that category!"

"Yes, he does, but you haven't let me finish," I continued, holding my temper. "We isolate the DNA of a criminal, and manufacture a synthetic virus that is keyed to that specific DNA."

"I'm familiar with the basic principles," Ryerson snapped.

"Yes, but hear me out," I said. "There are a lot of misconceptions about Cropdusting. Every person has DNA. It's in every cell of your body. DNA is what determines everything about you: your hair color, whether you're right- or left-handed, whether you can curl your tongue," I demonstrated, and he looked at me distastefully. "Anyway, everything about you is determined by your DNA, and therefore, your DNA is unique to you. We call it a gene print. It's like a fingerprint, only more so. So what we do is, when we've isolated a person's DNA, we make a synthetic virus that will only respond to the DNA we've isolated. It will only grow in that person's body, even if we expose a thousand people to it."

"I didn't know it was that exact," Ryerson said, visibly impressed.

" 'Specific' would be a better word. Viruses don't have any metabolic machinery, and can't reproduce without a host. We just specify the host. This virus is 'keyed' to your DNA. So we call it the keyed virus. It's benign—it doesn't do anything to a person except grow. But what we do is manufacture another virus that we piggyback onto the keyed virus. And this piggyback virus is anything but benign."

"So what happens?" Ryerson asked with mounting impatience.

"Well, say we've isolated your DNA," I said. "And say we wanted to turn your skin bright green. Well, we've got a piggyback virus that will do that. So we piggyback it onto a virus that's keyed to you. Then we spray this virus all over the city. Using helicopters. That's where it got its street name of Cropdusting, because when we rig the police helicopters with the spraying apparatus, they look like the old-fashioned Cropdusting helicopters of the mid-1900s. Well, this virus has been mixed with a synthetic host, and will reproduce like crazy for a day or so, all on its own, and will live for another couple of days. In that time, you will have come in contact with it, because it will have been picked up by building ventilation systems, the subway's ventilation, and so on. Or you'll just breathe it in the air, or pick it up on your fingers and rub your eyes, or eat something that has it on it, and so on. Everyone in the city will do that, but in everyone else, it won't do a thing. A couple of days after everyone else ingests the virus, it will be harmlessly expelled from their bodies, and nobody would even notice it. Except, of course, you. Your skin will have turned bright green by this time, because the keyed virus found your DNA, and thus began to attack your individual cells and your cells' DNA, and reproduce just like a cold virus or a flu virus. And the piggyback virus, which is the one that does the dirty work, can't reproduce by itself—only when the keyed virus reproduces. And the keyed virus can't invade the cell of any human host except you. So you're bright green, and nobody else is affected."

"I follow you, but you still haven't answered my question," Ryerson observed sourly.

"Well, surely you see the advantages. Some quick lab work, a light spraying, and we've found our criminal. Actually, the virus has found our criminal. The piggyback virus we use makes him stink to high heaven so he can't hide, and makes him emit all kinds of noxious stenches that can be detected by our sensing equipment, much like you'd zero in on someone operating a short wave radio. So if the criminal is stupid enough to not turn himself in for an antidote, we find him or her without having to waste officers' time on detective work and risking their lives trying to arrest someone. One of the misconceptions that we've allowed to persist is that Cropdusting is very harmful to the person unless they quickly receive the antidote. But it's actually harmless."

"Yes, I see the advantages," Ryerson said with exasperation. "What I want to know is why you haven't used it on this art thief."

I shrugged. "It's sterile," I said simply.

He was extremely offended. "Art is not sterile! Police work is sterile! Your brain is sterile if you think so little of culture!"

I chuckled. It was fun baiting this pompous twit. "Calm

down," I said. "Art theft is usually a sterile crime, that's all. Nothing in it for us."

"Sterile in what sense?" He was still huffy.

I rolled my eyes. "Look," I said wearily. "Sterile crime is a slang term for crime that can't be handled by our department. I told you we need to isolate a criminal's DNA before we can spray for him. We can't get the DNA unless the criminal has left some body tissue or fluid around that we know belongs to that criminal. And this art thief hasn't left a trace so far, has he?"

"No," Ryerson said stiffly. "Sometimes the police can hardly figure out how he got in to a place."

"So we can't isolate his DNA. Sterile crimes where they leave no trace are solved by some other form of investigation, not Cropdusting."

"In other words, it's useless," Ryerson snipped.

I briefly wondered how far back he'd fall if I punched him in the face, but managed to shake it off. "In sterile crimes, you're right—it's useless. But what you're overlooking is that in other types of crimes, criminals are caught who never would have been caught before. Random, violent street crimes, with no witnesses or clues: the kind that terrorize entire neighborhoods; the kind that nobody cares about because all that's involved is some poor, innocent civilian who never hurt anybody; the kind that hardly ever makes the newspapers anymore because they're so common; that's the kind of crime that is solved with Cropdusting. Violent crimes like that usually leave some trace of the attacker, and since those crimes are solved quickly and accurately, that leaves more of the police force's resources available to devote to sterile crimes with more conventional means." I noticed that my voice was steadily rising, so I stopped and took a breath. "That is the kind of crime that Cropdusting is used for, and because of Cropdusting and the deterrent it poses, the devastation and suffering inflicted on innocent people by other people through crime is way down. That's why you can walk the streets safely. Or more safely. Understand?"

Ryerson was shaking his head. "It seems to me, then, that crimes like rape would be nonexistent. After all, rapists leave something behind every time."

"You'd be surprised," I told him. "Rape is a power crime, not a sexual crime. Rapists don't always even have an orgasm." Ryerson made a distasteful gesture, and I continued. "Hey, you asked, didn't you? You do have a point: rape is such a violent, physical crime that there is usually something we can use."

"So if your Cropdusting is so great, why are there people out there who still rape?" Ryerson challenged.

"You're assuming that rapists are rational people who will make the intelligent decision when faced with the facts," I answered. "But the opposite is true. That's why they rape in the first place. With Cropdusting, however, we have virtually eliminated repeat offenses."

Ryerson was still fixed on a single track. "This is all well and good," he said, "but what you're telling me is that you're not going to do anything about the art thief."

"I'm trying to help you understand our efforts so you'll see that we're doing everything we can," I said impatiently. "Can't you see that?"

"Of course," he said frostily. "Good day, Commissioner." He slammed the door behind him, leaving me shaking my head in disgust.

RYERSON HAD AROUSED my interest as well as my anger, so I checked the newspaper the next day to see if there was anything about it. Son of a gun—there was a story on the front page. Another art theft had taken place during the night, at the Museum of Modern Art, and the signs indicated that it was the same guy. He had known exactly what he wanted, because he had passed up another couple of pieces that were about equal in value, but easier to get to. And the piece he took was a heavyweight: *Christina's World* by Andrew Wyeth. According to the reporter, Wyeth was a major force in American art in the mid-20th century. Not that I'd heard of him.

An interesting point was made in the article. Most of the paintings taken by this guy were so famous that you could never really sell them. Everybody would know immediately what they were. When paintings of that magnitude were stolen, they were usually held for ransom, like in a kidnapping, under the threat of burning or slashing if the money wasn't paid. But so far this guy had made no demands.

I scanned the rest of the article, getting a little bored with the subject. There was nothing in it for me. This guy was top-quality professional. Clean entrance. Clean exit. Sometimes it took days to figure out how he had actually done it. A cat burglar of consummate skill, he eluded guards wherever he operated. Nobody had even seen him, much less had a chance to get a piece of skin tissue. There was reason to believe that he had worked in other cities, and even other countries, so the FBI was on the case.

The newspaper gave a quick list of robberies believed committed by this thief, and it was pretty long. In New York alone he had robbed the Metropolitan Museum of Art, the Museum of American Art, and the Museum of Modern Art, just to name a few. He was also believed to have hit the Prado in Madrid, the Louvre in Paris, and the London Museum. He had also probably robbed several other European and American city museums, but the experts weren't sure.

Pieces he had taken included Jackson Pollock's *Number One*, Marcel DuChamp's *Nude Descending a Staircase #2*, Martin Schongauer's *The Temptation of St. Anthony*, Josef Albers's *Silent Hall*, Giovanni Bellini's *St. Francis in Ecstasy*, Goya's *The Third of May, 1808*, Theodore Gericault's *The Raft of the 'Medusa,'* Rembrandt's *Christ Preaching*, Andy Warhol's *Marilyn Monroe*, David's *Death of Marat*, Kitagawa

Utamoro's *Yam Uba Combing Her Hair*, Albrecht Durer's *Adam and Eve* . . . geeez, I hadn't heard of any of that stuff. The writer made it sound like they were tragic losses to the world, and significant works, but I hadn't missed them. There were a lot more on the list, but they meant nothing to me. I scanned it real quick to see if there was something I recognized, but the only works of art I had ever heard of were the Mona Lisa and Whistler's Mother. They weren't on the list, but a bunch of other stuff was. Whoever this guy was, he must be really good.

I tossed the paper aside. I didn't see this guy giving me anything to go on for a long time. I hoped the local boys got him before the FBI did. I settled down at my desk when my phone rang.

"Commissioner Donnally," I answered.

"Donnally," barked my chief's familiar voice. "Get in my office."

I quickly reviewed anything I had done recently, and felt pretty secure, but I never liked being called into Chief Bourke's office. I hurried over, and when I entered, he was leaning back in his chair, reading the newspaper. He tossed it to me across the desk as I sat down.

"See the paper this morning?" he asked. "The story of our art thief?"

"Yeah, as a matter of fact," I said. "I was visited by a guy named Ryerson yesterday, so I thought I'd see what he was screaming about."

"He's still screaming," Bourke said briefly. "You obviously haven't read the Arts section yet, or you wouldn't be so calm."

"Why?" I didn't like the sound of that at all.

"You're in Ryerson's column this morning," Bourke informed me. "So are the rest of us. He's not a fan."

I picked up the paper and looked where Bourke's stubby finger was pointing. Ryerson did indeed have a column, titled "Perspectives on Art." There was a cruddy picture of him under his column graphic, then a headline: POLICE NEGLECT ART COMMUNITY. Knowing Bourke was watching me, I scanned it quickly. Words like "unsympathetic," "uninspired," "wasted tax money," and "arrogant" came up to meet my eyes. My name was included in a list of people labeled "rude, paper-pushing bureaucrats."

I looked up at Bourke, and I was steaming. "I thought that guy was an asshole," I said. "I guess I was right."

"You were right," Bourke agreed, "but that's not why you're here. We don't need this kind of negative publicity, Jack. We've been busting our ass to catch this thief, but he's skunked us every time. This Ryerson guy hasn't made it any easier, and now he's souring our relationship with the heads of security of the major museums, not to mention the local politicians and the community at large. Steer clear of this guy. Don't give him any more ammunition."

"A pleasure," I said.

"Fine. But at the same time, I want you to start following this case. If there's another heist, I want you to come look over the scene. Bring Marjoram. Just see for yourself if there isn't anything you can use."

I nodded, taking a few notes.

"Another thing," Bourke added. "There's going to be some Federal boys around here. Cooperate with them. We don't need them calling us the same things Ryerson is. But if the Feds catch this thief before we do, I'll skin all of you. Spread that around."

I nodded again, knowing that he probably meant it.

"That's all," Bourke said.

IT WAS A few weeks before I saw Ryerson again. I had followed his tirade of abuse in his newspaper column as he castigated the police force for incompetence, stupidity, and conspiracy to wipe out the art world, but nothing else had happened. So I was surprised one day when I got to work early in the morning and found him waiting for me.

"Ryerson," I said abruptly, surprised and not pleased. "What do you want?"

"There was another art robbery last night at the Guggenheim Museum," he said in his reedy voice. "I was told to come see you."

Ah. "Come in," I said, opening the office door and turning on the lights. I was a little confused. "I was told that I would be called to the scene of any further art heists," I said, sitting at my desk and gesturing him to a chair. "But I wasn't this time. Have any idea why?"

"I think so," Ryerson said. "He left some of himself behind, and it was pretty obvious."

I grabbed my keyboard and called up the warrant program. "We're all set, then. Give me the place of the crime."

Ryerson looked puzzled. "The Guggenheim Museum. You know that."

"No. Spell it."

"What?!" Ryerson looked at me with shock. "You can't spell Guggenheim?!"

I tried to keep patient. "It's for the warrant," I explained. "We've got to get the warrant approved before we can do anything, and misspellings are murder for a case."

"I don't understand," Ryerson said. "What do you need with a warrant? A crime has been committed. You can isolate the criminal's DNA now. So spray the city with your Cropdusting stuff, or whatever it's called! Get him! Stop him!"

I looked at him sadly. "You still don't know much about Cropdusting, do you?" I asked.

"Not much, no. How much do you know about art?"

"Even less. But let's not get too pretentious here. You obviously are working from a position of ignorance. I didn't know you cerebral types did that."

There was a long silence while Ryerson looked daggers at

me. "Well then, Mister Commissioner Donnally Sir," he said with elaborate politeness, "perhaps you could enlighten me as to the finer points of Cropdusting. And afterwards, I will explain to you the difference between a paintbrush and a crayon."

"Don't bother," I shot back. "My information is important. Yours can wait." I ignored his furious expression and began to explain. "You remember the international ruckus thirty years ago, right?"

"The Jarman-CIA scandal? Of course. But why don't you refresh me anyway?" he said sarcastically.

"Fine. We'll do it your way. Well, thirty years ago, the Russians figured out that the CIA had isolated the DNA of their premier, and was trying to piggyback emotion-altering drugs onto the keyed virus. So that he would sign a treaty that wasn't as advantageous to his country as it could have been, and things like that. They didn't kill him because none of his replacements were any better. Or they were worried about full-scale war if they were discovered doing that."

"I'm familiar with the history," Ryerson said impatiently. "They used it on Cuba. Their leader suddenly died of natural causes a couple years before that, and it came out that the CIA had given him pneumonia or something."

I nodded. "Right. Anyway, apparently it didn't work on the Russian premier. Emotions are a lot harder to influence and control than physical health, especially with viruses. So after the big scandal and the showdown at the U.N., diplomatic relations soured to their lowest point in history, and crime fighting got its biggest boost in history. The technology was released to the FBI, who released it to our special Cropdusting departments."

"And what did you do with it?"

"Well, we ran a couple of tests on the virus."

"Thirty years ago?" Ryerson asked pettily. "You don't look old enough."

"Thanks." I wasn't going to be thrown off stride. "My predecessor ran a couple test runs. There was panic in the streets. Thousands of people ran to emergency rooms complaining of all kinds of psychosomatic maladies: everything from shortness of breath to headaches. We should have known better. The idea of a police department spraying the populace with strange viruses is enough to make any citizen a little paranoid. The city had to run an intensive public information campaign to settle everyone down. With time, and with the success we've enjoyed, Cropdusting has eventually become accepted by just about everybody. The purse snatcher we tried it on was quickly found, of course, with his face bright green. He was also in a panic, and in an emergency room. The doctor managed to slip away and phone us."

"Why pick a purse snatcher?" Ryerson asked. "Wouldn't that be a sterile crime? And why pick such a piddling little crime?"

"We wanted a test case of little importance," I explained. "And anyway, the lady who lost her purse to him struggled a little bit, and pulled his stocking cap off his head. He didn't care—he ran. But we found three hair follicles of his in the cap. That's how."

"So what happened?" Ryerson prompted.

"Lots. The American Medical Association objected to having their doctors exposed to desperate criminals who know they are likely to be caught."

"They had a point," Ryerson observed.

"I know." I was getting tired of this jerk. "It was something we didn't think of. To avoid legislation on the subject, we made a policy that Cropdusting would always have to incapacitate the criminal in some way. We came up with a virus that would knock them out for days at a time, have them stink to high heaven, and secrete biological stuff that could be traced as easily as a radio wave, if you've got the right equipment. So he was harmless, and easily found. And as time went on and Cropdusting began to have an effect, public fears diminished to a point that innocent people don't even think about it any more."

"So why are we bothering with a warrant?" Ryerson interjected with mounting impatience.

I sighed wearily. "The arrest was contested, of course. The entire Cropdusting method was challenged on the Fourth and Fifth Amendments."

Ryerson looked uncomfortable. "I . . . could you . . . I mean, the Fifth Amendment refers to self-incrimination, of course, but could you refresh my memory as to the Fourth?"

I smiled sardonically. "I'm sure it just temporarily slipped your mind. Where shall I start? Do you know what the Bill of Rights is? Or should I tell you what the Constitution is?"

"Stop baiting me, Donnally!" Ryerson yelled. "Just answer my question!"

"Fine. The Fourth Amendment to the Constitution is the one that protects citizens from unreasonable search and seizure. The Fifth Amendment, as you said, refers to self-incrimination." I looked at him. "That means, you don't have to. Incriminate yourself, I mean."

"Are you enjoying trying to make me feel stupid?" Ryerson asked peevishly.

I figured it would be impolite to tell him exactly how much I was enjoying it, so I went on without answering. "The case went to the U.S. Supreme Court," I said, trying not to smile at his discomfort. *"Patterson v. the People of New York.* Patterson, the purse snatcher, had a lawyer who said that Cropdusting with a virus and using that as the sole means of finding a criminal was unconstitutional because the virus invaded his body, determined that his DNA was the right one, and made him give himself away. Therefore it was both an unreasonable search and seizure, and it made Patterson incriminate himself."

Ryerson digested this. "What was your answer to this?"

"Well, it wasn't all that hard. It was an interesting point, but we just said that DNA of a criminal is like a fingerprint of a criminal. It's a piece of evidence left at the scene of the crime. If it helps us match up to a person, it's no different than finding a matching fingerprint in the FBI's files and identifying a suspect that way. And anyway, the suspect still has the right to a trial. But of course, when there's matching DNA, it's pretty damned hard to beat a rap like that."

"But still, why the warrant?" Ryerson persisted.

"Because in its decision, the Supreme Court upheld the use of Cropdusting, but ruled that DNA targeting was a pretty invasive procedure, and one that could be misused. Therefore, it should be treated like searching a house, and would require a warrant showing reason to suspect. So we've got to get a judge to sign a Cropdusting warrant. It's pretty routine."

"What happened to the purse snatcher, then?" Ryerson asked.

I smiled and shook my head. "He got off, if you can believe it. A Cropdusting warrant hadn't even existed until the Supreme Court invented it, but since we hadn't had one when we dusted for Patterson, he was let off."

"That's outrageous," Ryerson protested.

I shrugged. "That's why we picked a purse snatcher. I mean, who cared if he got off? We figured Cropdusting would be contested. We just wanted approval to keep doing it, and we got it. And Patterson was caught five months later doing the same thing, but he was shot and wounded by an off-duty police officer when he refused to stop running. So he probably got the worst of the deal."

Ryerson looked a little humbled, which pleased me. "Guggenheim," he said. "G-U-G-G-E-N-H-E-I-M. He stole a classic early Impressionistic painting, Monet's *Impression: Sunrise*. It's considered to be one of the paragons of Impressionism, and gave the movement its name. He painted it in 18—"

"That's more detail than I need," I interrupted. "We need just the specifics of the crime."

Ryerson looked scornful. "Just the facts, then. Not interested in learning something for your own edification?"

"Spare me," I said shortly. "What else did he do?"

"Something kind of unusual for an art thief," Ryerson said. "He defaced a painting: a Rococo work called *The Swing.*"

"A what?" I asked. "I didn't get that word."

"Rococo," he said with exaggerated patience, and spelled it for me. "Take cotton candy, infuse it with synthetic sweetener, and you've got Rococo. Or did you already know that?"

"Why is it so unusual for an art thief?" I asked, ignoring his jab.

"Art thieves usually are careful with the work, because they know how much they're worth. And in a warped way, many love art. Vandalism isn't all that common."

"What'd he do—piss on it?" I asked.

"No, he slashed it with a knife. Why?"

"Well, I haven't gotten the official report yet," I said. "How do we isolate his DNA? Did he cut himself on the frame when he slashed it, or what?"

"Oh, no," Ryerson said. "He left blood behind when he killed the guard."

I bolted out of my chair. "He what?!" I yelled. "He killed a guard?"

"Yes," Ryerson said. "I thought you knew that."

I almost spat at him in disgust. "All this time you've been blathering on about some stupid paintings, and someone's been murdered? You make me sick!"

"I don't know anything about solving murders," Ryerson protested defensively. "I know about art. I thought you knew about the murder. I thought that you just needed art information from me."

"I don't really give a damn about art at the moment," I said heatedly, but losing some of my disgust as I realized that he hadn't been the callous bastard I thought he had been. "Why don't you just sit down and I'll go see what's holding up the official report, so we know what's going on."

"Fine," Ryerson snapped. He sat down primly. "Fine."

I got the report and read the real story. The thief had entered the building through a ventilation shaft and gone straight for the painting by Monet, which was apparently very valuable. He trashed the frame, which is standard procedure for getting the painting out easily. Frames are cheap—the painting's the value. As he was going back to escape, he passed that Rococo piece Ryerson talked about, and started cutting it up with his knife. I looked up from the report.

"Why in the world would he stop to slash another painting?" I asked. "Why not make your escape? Or if you're going to take the time, why not steal *The Swing?* Why cut it up?"

Ryerson shrugged. "You're the detective, Donnally, not me. All I can say is, the guy must have taste. Rococo is a painting style that was popular when Marie Antoinette and her gang were eating cake while the rest of France starved. The painting style fitted their moods: self-indulgent, frilly, poufy, fluffy garbage. It makes you gag to look at it, it's so sweet."

"Hmmmmm." I turned back to the report. The guard came on him while he was cutting the painting and challenged him. The thief charged him, and the guard, who must not have drawn his gun yet, only got off one shot before the thief got to him. The bullet must have only given the thief a flesh wound, but the lab got enough blood from it to isolate the thief's DNA. Then there was a struggle, and the guard was stabbed fifteen times. He was discovered half an hour later by his replacement, and the ambulance team declared him dead at the scene. I closed the report.

"I'd have to check on the exact penalties for art theft, since my department doesn't handle it a lot, but it doesn't matter," I said. "What we're really looking at is murder—first degree if we can get it." I looked at the diagrams drawn of the scene of the crime. "It's a real shame that the guard wasn't ready for him. He could have pumped four bullets into the guy if he'd had his gun out."

"Maybe he had a false sense of security," Ryerson suggested. "Art thieves are not by nature violent. They are usually the intelligent, professional type."

I looked at him. "That might be valuable, as long as you're sure you're not romanticizing cultural thieves. But this also points out that it takes extreme circumstances, or at least extreme people, to charge into the barrel of a gun. Or charge a man with a gun if you've only got a knife." I started filling out the warrant request and ran it through the Technicalities and Loopholes Checker program. Ryerson watched in silence.

"Why does it take so long?" he asked. "When are you super-men going to do your superwork, anyway?"

I was tired of talking to the guy, so I printed my warrant request and answered as I walked out. "We'll probably spray for him late tomorrow or early the next day. I'll let you know when we get results." I stopped and faced him. "I'll call you," I said, emphasizing the first and last words. Then I turned my back on him as quickly as possible and left.

I DIDN'T HEAR from Ryerson for two weeks, and at first it was pleasant. But by the time I got his phone call, I was harried, scared, and hadn't slept in two days. Marjoram and I were no longer on speaking terms, and I was ready to go crazy.

When the phone rang for the seventieth time that morning, I snatched it up and snarled "Donnally" into it. I was in no mood for formalities.

"Donnally, Ryerson here," came his thin, reedy little voice, with its usual amount of anger and impatience. "I think I've been more than patient, Donnally. Why the hell haven't you called me, and why the hell haven't you told me that you've caught this criminal?"

"Because we haven't," I barked. I wasn't going to take any more of this.

There was a shocked silence. "What?!" he finally said. "Why?!"

"Hell if I know," I retorted. I breathed deeply, trying to regain a sense of calm. "This has happened before," I said more rationally. "We sprayed for a criminal, and got no response. Our sensing devices have picked up no trace of the bodily emittants that the virus causes. When this happened before, the criminal had left town, and had gotten out of the spraying area before we reached him with the virus."

"So what are you going to do?" Ryerson demanded.

"We're spraying a much wider area in case he commuted from somewhere. We have also sent his DNA track to other major cities in North America: Boston, Toronto, Montreal, Chicago, Minneapolis, Mexico City, Dallas, Washington, Philadelphia, San Francisco, Denver, Los Angeles, and so on. Any city with major art museums has been contacted, and they have sprayed for him as well."

"Any luck?"

I sighed. "None. He has escaped so far."

There was another pause. Then, "What are you going to do?"

"We're reviewing our options now," I said curtly. I knew that sounded like we didn't know what to do, but I couldn't help it—we didn't.

Ryerson hung up. I was glad to be rid of him so easily, but my relief only lasted half an hour. A knock sounded on my door, and opened to admit Chief Bourke, Marjoram, a nervous looking guy who was our public relations coordinator, and the mayor of New York. They looked grim. I felt grimmer.

"Morning, Donnally," Bourke said. I nodded warily. "We have some news for you. Tell him, Chesley."

Chesley, the PR guy, cleared his throat. "I just got a phone call from some art critic named Ryerson? He's the one who's been writing those nasty columns about the force? Well, he wanted to see if I had any comment on a story he was writing for tomorrow's paper. Front page, mind you—not buried in the arts section. It's terrible. It's all about how Cropdusting has failed; that somebody has figured out a way to outwit it, and so on."

I was tense all over. "What did you tell him?"

"I said that Cropdusting has brought thousands of criminals

to justice over the years who otherwise wouldn't have been caught. I told him that we were still working on this one case that was giving us problems."

"What did he say?"

"It was strange. He kind of laughed, and said, 'You're reviewing your options, right?' I said yeah, I guess you could say that. Then he hung up."

"He got that from me," I told him. "I know it sounded weak, but that's all I could think of."

"Listen, Donnally," Bourke rumbled. "We don't need this kind of press. We look bad enough as it is with this damned art thief. Do you think this guy has actually come up with some way of beating Cropdusting?"

I looked at Marjoram, who looked ashen. He spoke. "It sure seems that way, although I have no idea how he did it. Maybe some kind of antidote. Maybe he's hidden himself in some podunk village somewhere, or flown out of the country. Maybe he's dead."

"Nobody else has ever gotten away, huh?"

I answered. "We have had some failures over the years, but most of them were explained, and never got much press anyway. The problem is that this thief has already gotten so much press that it's inevitable that Cropdusting will too. Especially with that bastard Ryerson on us all the time."

"Tell me about those other failures," Chesley begged.

"Well, let's see. One guy flew to Europe right after he pulled a robbery of some kind. Scotland Yard caught him in London six months later. A couple of gang-related crimes in the Bronx didn't show up when we dusted for them, but they turned up dead within a month. Victims of more gang violence, and the murders were sterile, so the Cropdusting trail dried up. Things like that. Cropdusting, mostly used on common street crimes, usually hasn't had a problem with people leaving the area. The crooks are usually very territorial, and stick around the city because that's the world to them."

"Well, we've got a major exception on our hands," the mayor interjected grimly. "This is going to get a lot of press. There are going to be negative reactions publicly and politically. We're going to take a lot of heat."

"And, I might add, crime will probably go up fast," Bourke commented. "The average thug will figure that if one person escaped, they will, too. I'm doubling all patrols. That's going to cost a lot of money."

The mayor spoke up again. "The upshot of this meeting, Donnally, is the following: refer all reporters to Chesley." I glanced at Chesley, who was sweating. "Second, catch this bastard. Quickly. If you don't, there will be hell to pay, and I promise you, this department will get its fair share." It was a good exit line, and he knew it. He turned on his heel and left, with the rest trailing behind him. Marjoram followed them, giving me a baleful look.

I just stood there. There was nothing to say. I considered jumping out of the window, but decided not to. Just barely.

I spent the day arranging to send the thief's DNA to every major international city I could think of. I didn't think it would do any good, but I had to look busy.

The next day dragged around, and the newspaper was as bad as I had ever imagined it could have been. Front page, top, screaming headline: "Criminal Bests Cropdusting System." There were three related articles, all dealing with something bad: a news analysis, asking if it was safe to walk the streets, reactions from various politicians, all concerned or scathing, and one showing the police department's efforts to prepare for the enormous crime wave they were sure was coming.

Eventually, I put my phone on the "private" setting. Thousands of reporters were calling, or knocking on my door, wanting to talk to me. It was extremely unpleasant. I felt about two inches tall. Everyone was blaming me, and I wasn't sure I didn't deserve it. I had never dreamed that someone would come up with something to beat Cropdusting, although Marjoram had pressed me for research money for a long time. I had consistently denied his requests, and now he blamed me, too. I tried to blame Ryerson in my mind, but I couldn't even convince myself. I felt as wretched as a person could feel.

The day passed in pandemonium, and the next day looked like it would be no better. Around mid-morning, Bourke called me into his office. I dutifully showed up, feeling like a dog about to be whipped again. I was right.

Bourke was pacing behind his desk, and made me sit. "We always figure we're gonna have good days and bad days," he said without preamble. "Crime fluctuates. But when we see a 24 percent increase in crime in a single night, it's not too hard to figure out why."

"Twenty-four percent!" I coughed in agony.

"What's worse is a lot of the crime is probably sterile, purely by accident. The smash and grab, the snatch and run, we're never gonna catch those people. Part of Cropdusting's success was an uncertainty in the local crook's mind as to what exactly sterile crime was. It was a concept that wasn't understood, so Cropdusting had more of a deterrent effect than we realized."

I nodded glumly.

Bourke looked at my expression. "Don't look so down," he said. "I haven't even gotten to the bad part yet."

I looked at him hopelessly. "There's more?" I asked.

"Of course. Another painting was stolen last night from the Museum of Modern Art. Looks like the same guy. This is big stuff. Organized crime, which has been making an art form out of sterile crime, has been very crimped by Cropdusting. Their power has decreased because it's more difficult to carry out threats of violence. Especially since hit men have figured out that they're likely to be eliminated, too, to dry up the Cropdusting trail. And the mob does not like the added resources the police force can devote to sterile crime because of Cropdusting." He paused for effect. "Therefore, the word on the street is that organized crime has offered one billion dollars," he emphasized the words, biting them off, "for the secret to beating Cropdusting."

I digested this painfully. "You think this guy will take it?"

"Wouldn't you?" Bourke retorted.

I slumped further in my chair. "Probably," I admitted.

"You'd better come up with something, Jack," Bourke said. "Let me know if I can do anything at all, but you and Marjoram are the experts. You're a good man, and I'd hate to lose you, but heads will roll if this isn't fixed, and yours will probably be one of them."

I could only nod.

"Keep in mind," Bourke said, "that the entire resources of this police department are yours for the asking. You name it, and you've got it."

I nodded again.

"Go," said Bourke. "Come back with some good news."

I slunk out.

As I trudged back to my office, I figured I'd better check my phone. I pulled it out of my pocket, and switched it off of the "privacy" setting. I pushed the button, and the earpiece and receiver popped out. "Instructions, please," the pleasant, mechanical, female voice sounded in my ear.

"Check voice mail," I said. There was a pause, then the voice said, "You have one new message, and two saved messages."

"Hear new message," I instructed. There was a pause, then Ryerson's voice crackled into my ear. He sounded agitated. No, agitated is too soft. He sounded scared to death. "For God's sake, Donnally, what the hell are you doing, putting your personal phone on 'private' at this time of day?! Call 222-7581 right away! I mean it! Hurry up!"

I sighed. What a great day this was turning out to be. I seriously considered not calling for an hour or so just to spite him, but I figured I'd better not. I was at my office door by now, so I stepped inside and instructed the phone: "Dial 222-7581." I closed the door and listened to a bunch of static on the line, some crackling and popping, and then the ring tone. I wondered what Ryerson wanted. This wasn't his office number. He must be at a museum or something.

The phone clicked. Ryerson's voice snapped over the line, tense and harsh. "Hello, Donnally," he snarled.

"Ryerson," I said. "How did you know it was me? What do you want?"

"It doesn't matter what I want," he said. "It matters what he wants."

"He, who?" I was sounding brilliant.

"I don't know his name," Ryerson said, sounding faint. "But the guy who's holding a gun to my head."

There was a silence while the news sunk in, and I tried to put my mind on red alert. "Where are you?" I asked tensely.

"He doesn't want me to tell you," Ryerson said. "I think I'll do what he says."

"Good idea," I said. "Just stay calm, and do what he says. Is it our art thief?"

"Yes," Ryerson said. "Why don't you two talk to each other?"

"Are you in danger?" I asked. I wanted to know how desperate the criminal was.

"I've got a gun held to my head!" Ryerson yelled. "Of course I'm in danger, you idiot! You'd better do what he says, or I'll come back and haunt you for all of eternity."

"Put him on," I said. Then, quickly, I pushed the command button and said, "Record conversation."

There was a brief rustle as Ryerson passed the phone over. Then a new voice came over the line—abrupt, jerky, trying to sound cool and silky and not succeeding. "Commissioner Donnally, I presume?" the voice said.

"That's right," I said guardedly. "Who are you?"

"I," he said grandly, "am Ryerson's Fate. How does that

sound?" He giggled and I heard Ryerson make a distressed sound in the background. Boy, we sure were right about him being unbalanced. It was easy to picture the owner of this voice charging a guard who had a gun.

"What's your name?" I asked, a little too gently for my liking.

"My name is Jeremy Schneider," he answered. "That is a name you will remember because I am a crusader in the effort to save art from the clutches of a careless, Philistine humanity."

God, this was bad. This was really serious, talking to a nutcake like this. Not that I loved Ryerson all that much, but if anybody was going to kill him, I would have liked it to be me. Naw, straighten up, I told myself. I'd like to punch him, but not kill him. "What do you want from me?" I asked. "Why are you holding Ryerson? He's an art lover, too."

"Too?! Too?!!" Schneider pounced on the word. "Don't try to butter me up by pretending to be a person of culture! You don't give two cents about art! You couldn't care less! I don't know why I'm bothering talking to you!"

"Wait!" I called. "Don't hang up. And please don't hurt Ryerson. Believe me when I tell you that he and I have discussed art for hours. I have a deep appreciation for it."

"Don't lie to me, Donnally," Schneider snarled. "Ryerson is one pound of pressure away from a better world."

Keep cool, keep cool, I told myself. Talk him down. And think fast! "I'm very concerned about what you've done with the masterpieces you've taken," I said. "I hope I can trust that you've taken good care of them."

There was a silence. Then he spoke. "Yes, I have," he said with a little less venom. "Better than the world has. But why do you care?"

"You took one of my favorites of all time," I said, racking my brain. "I'm glad to hear that it hasn't been damaged."

"Which one?" Schneider asked dangerously.

"The one by Monet, that he painted in 1873," I said, praying that my misty memory was correct. "His *Impression: Sunrise,* which named the Impressionistic movement. I think it's one of my favorite periods." I grabbed one of the art catalogs that Ryerson had thrown on my desk and flipped it open. "What did you think of his *Garden at Argenteuil?*" I asked, picking one at random. I did a pretty good French pronunciation, too, considering the pressure.

There was a long pause, punctuated only by Schneider's breathing. I grabbed a Cubist catalog, in case I had to continue the bluff. When Schneider finally spoke, it wasn't to me but to Ryerson, with his mouth away from the mouthpiece of the phone. "Your friend seems to understand art," he said.

I held my breath, and Ryerson made a small exclamation of stress. Then he said, shakily, "Of course he does. He appreciates the finer aspects of culture. As a matter of fact, if you were to bring him here and let him see what you're trying to do, I'm sure he'd be very sympathetic to your cause."

There was another pause, then Schneider spoke to me again. "You're going to come here," he told me.

"That's fine," I said. "I'd be glad to."

"You'll come here to listen to my demands for the preservation of art all around the world," he continued.

"From what I've heard, I'm already sympathetic to your cause," I lied.

There was a long pause. Then Schneider spoke slowly. "I don't trust you, Donnally," he said. "You're the one who tried to get me with your stinking Cropdusting! But I outwitted you, didn't I? Oh, I made you look stupid!"

"You're a smart fellow," I said, hoping I could get a look at how he'd beat the virus. I wouldn't even care if I was killed afterwards—I was just dying to know. "I'm sorry about the Cropdusting. I'd much rather talk to you."

There was a long pause. "I have to make preparations to protect myself from you," he said. "I'll call you in a few days and give you instructions." He hung up abruptly.

I disconnected on my end, and then called out a general alert, telling Bourke about the situation, and ordering a trace on 222-7581. The answer came back quickly: the number had been electronically scrambled and switched so many times that it was untraceable. That accounted for the static and crackling on the line.

I stood still for a moment, my mind whirling. I was trying to clutch at an idea that was flitting around in the corners of my mind. I didn't move for a while, then jerked open the door and sprinted down the hall.

Marjoram looked up in surprise when I burst into his lab. "What are you doing here?" he asked snidely. "You get lost?"

God, everybody was on my case. "What's with you?" I asked breathlessly.

"Nothing. It's just that you haven't shown interest in our department for months. You're a paper pusher, not a scientist."

I wanted to punch somebody very badly, but I couldn't punch him. "Shut up," I said briefly. "I need something, and I need it quick."

"Like what?"

"OK, here's my idea. You take a virus, keyed to a person's DNA, and piggyback another virus onto it, right?"

"Yes, we've done that for years," Marjoram said patiently.

"I know. But can you take another keyed virus, with a different piggyback, and then connect the two keyed viruses? So instead of a total organism of two viruses, you've got a total organism of four?"

"Yeah, we've done that in the lab," Marjoram said slowly. "Haven't had a practical application for it yet, though."

"Good so far. Now, can you build in some kind of shield? So the total organism will fit into two people: one for each keyed virus. But the piggyback virus on one of the keyed viruses will only work if that keyed virus fits the DNA, and won't work if the host has the other keyed virus's DNA?" I drew a quick sketch to illustrate.

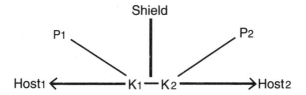

Marjoram looked at it seriously, and clicked his tongue several times as he thought. "I don't see why not," he said. "We've dabbled with that before. How soon do you need it?"

"In three days," I said.

"Three days!" he exclaimed. He frowned deeply. "That's tight. That's very tight."

I briefly filled him in on what had happened, gave him my idea, and described what would happen to him if he didn't get it done and we didn't catch this art thief.

"Hey, you're the guy who never approved any research funding," he answered. "It will take some doing. Some research. Some money." He looked at me. "We haven't had any of that."

I stared at him in frustration. I wanted to scream and grab him by the neck and throttle him. He had always blamed me because I was trying to keep costs down. How was I supposed to know that somebody would invent something that would foil the viruses? I needed to sit down.

I sat and breathed deeply, trying to collect my wits. Marjoram looked down at me. "You seem upset," he said, obviously not caring if I was or not.

"I am upset," I answered. "But you're going to be more upset, because you're wasting time. I'm going to get instructions from this guy in a few days, but I don't know exactly when. I could maybe stall a day or two if I had to, but I'd rather not because it could endanger Ryerson. I don't care if you have to work around the clock. I don't care if you appropriate every person and facility in the city of New York. Do it. Start now."

Marjoram opened his mouth, but he saw the look on my

face. He turned abruptly and went to his desk. He pulled out some folders from his file cabinet. He looked at me balefully.

"You're lucky that this is a hobby of mine as well as a job. I've done some research on my own. I kept it quiet, because I didn't want you to tell me about wasting the city's money. I've got the feeling that you won't give me that lecture now."

"I won't," I said. "Tell me what you need, and I'll get it for you."

He thought. "I need every technician I can get my hands on. I'll need authority to pay them double time, because I'm going to have a team working nights and another one working days. We'll need food, I guess. Coffee. Approval to put every other Cropdusting activity on hold."

"Granted," I said. "Everything you asked for. Anything else?"

"Not at the moment. I'll probably come up with more, though."

"If you want it, you'll get it," I told him. "If anybody asks, give them my name. And Bourke's name. And mention that the mayor is behind it all." I paused. "You won't have any objection if I have a squad of officers sequester you and your workers?"

"What the hell for?!" Marjoram demanded.

"To keep the reporters away from you. I don't want our thief to know anything about this."

Marjoram sighed disgustedly. "All right. You're right."

"Anything else?" I asked.

Marjoram looked at me closely. "Soak up as much sleep as you can in the next few days. With what we're going to put in your body, and the environment you're going to walk into, you'd better be physically prepared."

I nodded, feeling the dread sink into my bones. "I'll spend the time studying art books. I get the feeling I'll need to be able to discuss it for a while when I get there."

Marjoram nodded and jerked his head toward the door. "Go away. Let us work. I'll let you know if we need anything else."

I went away.

As IT TURNED out, it wasn't a three day wait. It was four. Four days of swarms of reporters, political denunciations, very little sleep, and one of the biggest crime waves in New York City's history.

Marjoram hadn't needed all four days. On the third day, late in the afternoon, he had tottered to my office to report that verification testing of the organism was complete.

I looked at him as he sagged against my door. "You done good," I said. "Go home and get some sleep."

"Sleep?" he repeated blearily. "What's that?"

I got the call from Schneider at eleven o'clock the next morning, with directions, location, and instructions to be alone and unarmed. I rushed to Marjoram's lab, where he, looking a little fresher, had injected me. Then he, Bourke, and I scrambled into a waiting helicopter. We stalled a little to allow a large number of plainclothes police officers to get to the area, then we took off.

The chopper landed in a parking lot in a very seedy part of New York. Unmarked cars were everywhere. As the chopper landed, Marjoram gave me a pill. "Take this," he said.

"What is it?" I asked. "Valium?"

"No such luck. It's a slow-release medicinal antidote for the other piggyback, in case the shield doesn't hold. It'll protect you against a partial failure."

I took the pill. "You think this will work?"

"I think so," Marjoram answered tensely.

"Then it'll work," I said. I slapped him on the shoulder and jumped out of the chopper. I conferred briefly with Bourke, then got into a waiting unmarked car and drove the few blocks to the address Schneider had given me. It was a seedy, anonymous-looking building that just missed being called a slum. I left the car in the street and went inside.

I walked tentatively down the hall of the building, feeling dizzy from the psychological effects of my plan, and from the adrenaline rush that was coursing through my body. Adrenaline rush, hell—I was scared to death. And on top of everything else, I was getting a doozy of a cold. My head was stuffing up as I walked, and I cursed violently. I was at enough of a disadvantage without needing to feel sick, too.

I checked out the building. The place was weird. It was a dump, with paint peeling off the walls, and plaster missing from the ceiling. But there was no trash lying around. And structurally, the building seemed sound.

I kept walking slowly, and my heart was pounding against my ribs. I was worried about a heart attack, and I was worried about living long enough to be able to have a heart attack. I wiped my nose and sniffled. I wondered if I was being watched. I wouldn't have put it past Schneider to have had some cameras mounted somewhere around.

I got to the door marked 1E. It didn't look any different from the other apartment doors I had passed, but the place certainly did seem deserted. I took a deep breath, and knocked on the door.

A voice from a small speaker rasped out at me: "Open the door and step inside. Slowly."

I did what I was told. I was surprised by the feel of the door: solid and tightly sealed, not the loose, flimsy door you would expect in a place like that. I looked inside, and saw a small, dimly-lit room.

"Go in and shut the door," the speaker instructed. I did, looking around nervously. The place was as big as a large, square closet. There was another door on the other side of it. As I looked at it, the first door made the unmistakable sound of a deadbolt lock being thrown. I quickly tried it, and it was locked. I was trapped.

I needed a bathroom.

"You are locked in," the voice from the speaker intoned. "Take off your clothes. All of them."

"What?!" I said, speaking for the first time. "I'm not going to do that!"

"I can kill Ryerson right now, if you like," Schneider said through the speaker. "I can also kill you. Do as I say. I intend no hideous torture—I just want to make sure you have no exotic weapons."

What was I going to do? Only slightly reassured, I stripped. It was a humiliating experience, undressing in a hostile environment, when you don't know what's going to happen to you. After I finished, I stood up, trying to cover my private parts and look at ease at the same time.

"Put your clothes in the small door in the side wall."

I looked. It was a small door that opened from the top, forming a chute. It was obviously one of those new, high temperature incinerators. "Can I keep my wallet?" I asked. My wallet had the radio transmitter that we had planted on me.

"No. Put everything in there."

I did, and stood there as they were incinerated into nothingness. I didn't like this at all. This guy knew I dealt with viruses, and was on the lookout for something viral. I had an overwhelming desire to break the lock and run away, screaming at the top of my lungs. My fear was interrupted by Schneider talking again.

"You may wish to hold your breath," he said. Before I had the chance to wonder why, I was hit with a deluge of water. It knocked me to my knees and I stayed down on all fours, sputtering and gagging and sneezing as the water pummeled me. It stopped as quickly as it started, and I noticed it draining into a drain cleverly hidden in the floor.

"You will now be disinfected," Schneider's voice informed me. "I strongly suggest holding your breath and closing your eyes." This time, I did both, quickly. Some gas, smelling strongly like a hospital, hissed out from somewhere, and filled the room. When I dared to peek, the room was foggy, and the fog stung my eyes. I closed them again, quickly.

When I was beginning to actively worry about breathing again, clean air was pumped into the room, and the fog went away. I breathed cautiously, and wondered what was next. My heart jumped again when I heard the inside door being unlocked. "Open the door and step inside," came the instruction.

With my heart in my mouth, I obeyed. I stepped into a glare of lights, all directed at me. I squinted violently, and tried to see. Schneider's voice came to me without the aid of a speaker this time. From the sound of his voice, he was across the room. "Don't make any sudden moves," he called. "There is a towel you can use to dry off, and a blanket you can use to cover yourself."

There was, and I did. Slowly. Carefully. Then I looked into the lights again, and opened my mouth to speak. Schneider cut me off.

"There is a bottle of Scotch whiskey there on the floor. I want to see you drink at least a quarter of it."

I did. I figured it wasn't poisoned, but was to make sure nothing was on my breath. I took several deep swigs, then coughed and sputtered as the booze went down. When I recovered, I held the bottle up for inspection. "How's that?" I asked groggily as the alcohol joined the adrenaline, fear, disinfectant fog, and everything else that was coursing through my body.

"That will do," Schneider said. "Not only is your mouth disinfected, but your wits are dulled. Now, I want you to understand that I have a gun and will not hesitate to shoot you both if I have to. I won't need any provocation. Got it?"

"Got it," I said. "Can I see if Ryerson is OK?"

Schneider flicked a switch and the spotlights went out. My eyes tried to adjust to the soft, dim lighting, and I looked around in amazement.

I was in an art gallery. Dozens and dozens of paintings and sculptures were hung on the walls or were sitting on the tops of little display cubes. Everything I had seen in low quality reproduction in my police reports were there in full, living, breathing, glorious color. I goggled in amazement. I wasn't sure if it looked like a dream or a nightmare. I couldn't shake off the feeling that, whichever one it was, I was definitely not awake.

Schneider spoke again, his voice rich with satisfaction. "Quite a selection, isn't it?"

I followed his voice, and saw him for the first time. He was a small, wiry man in his mid-forties, with sandy hair and hard, glinting eyes. He was also holding a gun.

"This is amazing!" I blurted. "There must be billions of dollars of art here!"

"Correct," Schneider said. "Notice how nicely it's taken care of?"

I decided to give the answer expected of me. "It's impressive," I agreed. "These are fantastic!" I was surprised to notice that I actually kind of meant it. But no matter how much art was around, I kept noticing the gun. "Where is Ryerson?" I asked.

"Step slowly to your right," Schneider instructed. He kept holding the gun on me, and he was at least thirty feet away. I did what I was told, and noticed Ryerson sitting in a chair, bound and gagged behind a large, freestanding picture by Jackson Pollock, whose title I didn't remember. Schneider walked over and removed the gag.

"Donnally," Ryerson said in a mixture of fear and relief. "Get me out of here!"

"How did you get here in the first place?" I asked.

"Mr. Ryerson is, unfortunately for himself, a better detective than you are," Schneider said. "He followed me here from my last art heist."

I felt my nose tickling again, and before I could stop, I sneezed violently. By accident, I sneezed directly on a small sculpture that was on a table to my right. Schneider made an outraged noise, and even Ryerson was disgusted.

"Honestly, Donnally," Ryerson said, "sometimes you're such a pig!"

Schneider charged over, angrily gesturing me away with his gun. I moved quickly and apologetically. "How dare you!" Schneider grated. "This work is priceless!" He made a few agitated wipes at the sculpture with his hand, then grabbed a cloth and polished the piece.

The situation was a little too angry for my taste. I decided it would be appropriate to apologize. "I'm sorry about that," I said sheepishly. "They can put a woman on Mars, but they can't find a cure for the common—"

"Cut the crap," Schneider snapped. He gestured further into the room. "Get over there. And keep in mind that everything in this room is worth more than you are."

I moved to where he indicated. This was not going well.

I looked at Ryerson and tried to restart the conversation. "How did you find Schneider to follow him?" I asked.

Ryerson looked sour and not the least proud of himself. "I know more about art than you do," he said to me with a quick glance at Schneider. "It finally occurred to me that our art thief was establishing a pattern that everyone had overlooked. He was stealing works of art that were not just valuable—they were landmarks in art history. For example, the first one we discussed: Monet's *Impression: Sunrise* started the Impressionist movement, and Monet was one of the biggest figures in the movement. And that's what our thief was looking for: he would pick a period, and steal the landmark pieces done by the biggest names in that period."

"So?" I asked, still very aware of the gun. Schneider was still keeping his distance.

"So I figured out what painting would be next," Ryerson continued. "Salvador Dali's *The Persistence of Memory* had been installed in the Museum of Modern Art after a tour of Europe. I have considerable influence in the art world, so I went to the curator of the museum, and called in a few favors. I had to twist his arm considerably, and hint that I was part of a police operation, but I managed to persuade him to let me hide near the painting and wait for our thief. After three nights, Schneider appeared. I let him take the painting, and followed him here. Which also explains my tattered clothes and assorted scrapes and bruises."

I had been so scared that I hadn't noticed, but when he mentioned it, I saw that he was a mess. "How did all that happen?" I asked.

"I'm an art critic, not a gymnast," Ryerson said snappishly. "Do you think it's easy to follow an accomplished cat burglar? I almost killed myself. But I was so obsessed with catching him that I managed to keep him in sight." He gestured with his head at the ropes that were holding him and added bitterly, "It's worked out great, hasn't it?"

"I knew I had gotten away clean, so I wasn't looking for a tail," Schneider added as I sneezed again. "I didn't notice him until we were near here. By that time, he knew too much so I couldn't just get away. I considered killing him, but I needed a hostage." Ryerson's face blanched when he heard Schneider's cold, matter-of-fact tone, but said nothing. He was obviously exhausted from the emotional strain of capture.

"How did you manage to go outside without getting nabbed by the virus we'd sprayed for you?" I demanded.

"I did some research after I found out that you had sprayed for me. The news broadcasts said how long the sprayed viruses would live before needing another spraying. I just timed my last burglary between sprayings."

I silently cursed myself for not making sure that we performed overlapping sprayings. That fell under the heading of idiotic mistakes.

Schneider continued, "I assumed that with the intensive media coverage, I would know whenever you sprayed."

"How did you know that we wouldn't bluff the media to lure you out with false information?" I asked.

"I didn't think you were smart enough for that," Schneider said smugly. "And I didn't think the media would fall for it."

I had to admit that he was right on both counts.

"At first, I was afraid of the viruses. That was when I was wounded," Schneider went on. "I bandaged myself, and hid here, waiting for the virus to get me. But it didn't." Schneider's face began to glow triumphantly. "The virus didn't get me! Here I was, huddled in my room, afraid and knowing that I couldn't escape—that nobody ever escaped! And it didn't get me!" He laughed crazily. "How does that make you feel, Mr. Supercop? How does it feel to be a failure?"

Having a gun pointed at you makes it easy to keep your temper. I asked, "How did you manage to foil our best efforts?"

Schneider laughed crazily again. "Accident," he said airily. "Sheer accident. I hid down here for several days, never daring to hope, until I heard about Cropdusting's failure—your failure—on the news. Then I thought about it. My conclusion is that the sophisticated environmental control system I had installed here did the trick. My own design, by the way, a system of air filtration and cleaning units that I made to protect my artwork, actually protected me from your stinking viruses!"

My mind raced. He must not have any kind of specific virus killing agent. I wondered if his system could withstand a larger concentration.

"Why did you design it in the first place?" I asked.

"Ah." Schneider looked at me significantly. "He asks why I designed it in the first place. Yes, well might you ask. That's why I brought you both here. To hear why I designed it in the first place." He waved his gun. "Sit down, Donnally."

I sat. I wondered if I would be allowed to go to the bathroom, and doubted it. Ryerson looked at me appealingly, and I looked away. I couldn't do a thing. I was naked and scared, and kept at a distance from an armed murderer. I looked at Schneider, who began pacing.

"Warnings have been issued ever since the latter part of the twentieth century," he began with outrage in his voice.

"Warnings about the deterioration of great works of art. These warnings have been consistently ignored by the public and by people in the art world who ought to know better." He looked significantly at Ryerson, who looked as uncomfortable as a human could look. "These warnings have been ignored because the 'leaders,' " he bit off the word, "have catered to the unwashed masses who didn't give a damn about real art. I'm talking about Mr. Joe Front Porch, who thinks an advertising billboard is 'classy,' and considers himself cultured if he manages to go to the Louvre once in his life to see the Mona Lisa and say he doesn't see what's so great about it. He's the kind of clown who looks at an American Realist painting like Whistler's *Arrangement in Black and Gray*, and says, 'Oh, sure, that's Whistler's Mother. We've got a framed print of it that we cut out of a magazine.' " He spat in contempt and wiped his mouth. "These are the people who have been making the decisions about the care of the greatest works of art the world has ever seen!"

I was confused as well as scared. "What have they done that's so terrible?" I asked. I was immediately sorry that I had.

Schneider whirled on me. "What have they done?! It's what they haven't done! As early as the 1970s—can you believe it, as far back as that—there were warnings that paintings were deteriorating. Improper lighting, handling and storage was part of the problem, but the real problem was air pollution! Smog and all manner of air contaminants in major cities were building to a level that these delicate art pieces could not tolerate! And of course, the big cities are the ones with the large numbers of art museums. And of course, these museums had archaic ventilation systems that were not protecting the art! And on top of all of that, studies were proving that something as innocuous as actual human *breath* was seriously damaging the paintings! People coming to see the masters were ruining the pieces they were coming to see! Art was being loved to death!"

"So you began stealing them," I finished for him.

"Oh, I was an art thief long before this problem even became known to me," he told me earnestly. "And when I think of some of the pieces that I stole that I sold for mere money, it almost drives me mad!" He rubbed his eyes wearily as Ryerson and I exchanged quick glances. He went on, not noticing. "But I slowly began collecting information on the subject, and as I became concerned, I began researching ways to protect art. I even sent proposals to leaders in the world art community under assumed names, but was always ignored. Eventually, I began to take matters into my own hands."

"What would you like us to do?" I asked as gently as possible.

He looked at me with a fierce light in his eyes. He advanced a little, his gun wavering slightly. "I was originally going to demand that the artistic community incorporate my protection and preservation methods into their collections. But I no longer trust them to do it, no matter what promises they give me." His voice became soft, but extremely vehement. "You will turn over to me all of the masterpieces on this list," he waved an alarmingly thick sheaf of papers, "or I will kill Ryerson and you, and will turn over my environmental control system plans to organized crime. I understand that they have offered up to one billion dollars for the secret to avoiding Cropdusting. I can use the money to further my efforts, and at the same time can unleash a monumental crime wave on the world. That ought to be considerable incentive for compliance."

I privately agreed that indeed it would. "Think of what you'll be doing," I said out loud. "You're right about the crime wave you'd unleash. You'll be undoing an invaluable technological edge in the fight against crime. Think of the human suffering you'll cause. It doesn't strike me as very artistic." OK, so it was pretty lame. Keep in mind that I was looking down the barrel of a gun held by a madman, his survival was all my fault, and I only had a blanket to cover myself.

Schneider laughed sarcastically. "Crime fighting, as with

almost every other aspect of humanity, is a history of struggling to muddle by, drenched in the suffering and ineptitude that is the human condition. Only in art is there a sign that people are more than mud-stained, blood-spattered Philistines. Only art shows that there is hope for humanity. I don't give a damn about the suffering that people inflict upon each other and themselves. What I care about is the preservation of the tiny gleam of divinity that has managed to shine out from the excrement of our existences. What does it matter if a few more people kill each other? Most of the people in the world want the world to stay the way it is. They suffer in the existences they find themselves in by their own choice. But I won't let them destroy what little good that humanity has produced."

I looked at Ryerson beseechingly. Art was his subject, not mine. I couldn't argue with this guy on his own turf. But Ryerson just looked blankly back at me. He looked like someone who had popped a circuit breaker. He was slumped against his ropes, looking dazed and exhausted by the constant fear and stress. He was no help to me.

Schneider saw us exchange looks, and misinterpreted them. "What are you planning?!" he demanded violently, his voice slurring slightly. "Don't think you can pull anything on me! I've covered all possibilities! You've noticed, Donnally, that I've had my gun pointed at you continually. Even if a SWAT team followed you and storms this building, they won't be able to break in here before I shoot you. And I've also got a panic switch within easy reach. If I push it, it will set off a powerful explosive that will kill all of us, and destroy all of these art treasures. I'd do it, believe me. I'm their last hope of survival, so if I go, they're doomed without me. They might as well go with me."

I looked at him despairingly. "You can't do this," I said. "There's no SWAT team outside, but my office does know where I am. You'll never be able to move all of this stuff to another place." I thought of another line of reasoning just in time. "What you need is publicity. Go on trial as a concerned citizen. You'd get worldwide attention to your case. The entire, worldwide art community would be following your case, listening to your views! Think of the prestige! You've got the facts. You'd be able to convince them, and become known in history as the person who raised the consciousness of the world as to the danger facing art."

For a moment I thought I'd won. There was a gleam in his eye, and I could tell he was visualizing the glory he thought would be his. But he brought himself back with almost a physical effort. He looked at me, almost regretfully.

"You forget," he said unsteadily, "I killed a man. They wouldn't care about my views on art. I'd be labeled a murderer and a madman. Just because I was destroying a piece of trash that someone had the nerve to call art and put in among significant works. My demands remain as before."

"But if they don't agree to them," I protested, "you can't carry out your threat. To destroy these works would be blasphemy!"

"I can," Schneider said with an effort, "and I will."

"Why don't you turn yourself in?" I asked for the last time. I sneezed, wiped my nose on my blanket, and continued. "I guarantee that you'll get a fair trial, and get all of the publicity you would ever want. No matter what else happens, the world will know about your concerns. I promise you that without qualification."

"No good, Donnally," Schneider said thickly, looking tired. "It's not enough. I don't trust you. I want approval from the governor of New York and the president of the United States and the security council of the U.N., and I want it fast. If I don't get it, I will start by shooting Ryerson in the leg. If necessary, I'll shoot him in both legs. And I'll make you watch him bleed to death."

I looked at Ryerson. He goggled back at me, obviously in shock. I leaned back to steady myself, and took a deep breath. Then I exhaled long and hard and looked at Schneider. He was watching me for my reaction. Finally I said, "You know that if you destroy these works of art, you'll be deliberately committing the crime you accuse the world of committing unintentionally." I took another deep breath and blew it out, obviously trying to keep calm. I looked at him. He was unmoved, standing ten feet away. "You will become known as the ultimate barbarian," I said, going for the throat. "You will make the word 'Philistine' obsolete. 'Schneider' will become synonymous with barbarian and Philistine just like Benedict Arnold or Judas have become synonymous with traitor."

Schneider became livid, and I was afraid he'd shoot me on the spot. He had been leaning wearily against a display table, but now jumped up. "Barb-barbarian!" he screamed at the top of his lungs. He staggered toward me, waving his gun in the air. "I'm the only person left in the world who appreciates and cares about art!" He stopped about three feet away, swaying wildly, but continued raving. "I am the savior of culture, and don't you forget it!" he shrilled, waving the gun in my face. "I'll teach you to call me that!" He lunged forward and struck me across the face with his gun.

My skull exploded in sound and I reeled back in my chair, blood filling my mouth. The room danced around before my eyes, and I grabbed the arms of the chair to try to steady myself. I sat up groggily, and swallowed a mouthful of blood. Schneider was still screaming, but I wasn't hearing the words. He clumsily thumbed back the hammer of the gun, looking at me with wild, unfocused eyes. I tried to keep conscious, and concentrated all of my energies on trying to make my nose tickle again.

I sneezed.

Schneider looked at me for a split second, and sick comprehension registered on his face.

Then he died.

I couldn't even believe it. I stared dumbly at him as he collapsed to the floor like a sack of potatoes. Ryerson made a stunned sound of astonishment and stared alternately at

Schneider's body and me. I staggered out of my chair, absently holding my blanket in place. I checked.

Sure enough. He was dead as they got.

I walked over to Ryerson unsteadily, and began fumbling with his ropes. Ryerson was just barely beginning to comprehend. "What'd you do?" he asked thickly, not daring to hope.

"I killed him," I said, wishing my head would stop pounding. "I tried to get him to give himself up, because Marjoram is ready with an antidote. But I couldn't tell him why he should give himself up, or he would have killed us. I did the best I could."

Ryerson goggled at the body, then vomited violently. It took all of my effort to avoid doing the same thing. I clutched his chair and leaned against it until he finished.

"Untie me," Ryerson gasped finally. "I can't even wipe my mouth."

I concentrated on the knots, which were tied well. Ryerson was still gasping. I was still sneezing. "How?" he asked gutturally. "How'd you do it?"

"We designed a new viral combination," I said, still feeling sick. "Two keyed viruses: one for me, and one for him. Tied together. Piggybacked a cold virus on mine. Put a barrier between mine and his so his wouldn't affect me, but I could carry it inside my body. Piggybacked a lethal virus onto his. He effectively sterilized the exterior of my body, but it didn't occur to him to worry about what I had inside. He assumed, logically, that anything inside my body would affect me as much as anyone else. A concept like the viral shield would never occur to him. So the virus started affecting him, and I was scared that he'd notice and kill us. I thought I had to provoke him to keep his mind off himself. But I pushed him too far. That last sneeze probably didn't do anything, because the virus was already firmly established, but I was panicking at the time."

Ryerson was quiet for a minute while I sneezed and struggled with his ropes. "Why'd you have to kill him?" he asked finally. "He was right about a lot of things, you know."

"He was also a murderer," I answered. "He was also planning to kill us or blow us all up. He could do it quickly, so we had to give him something fast acting. Our knockout virus takes up to an hour. This was the only thing we had that worked fast enough and was insidious enough so he wouldn't notice his deterioration and blow us up." I sneezed again.

Ryerson looked at the body again and retched. "Oh," he said.

"Just be glad you're alive," I told him. I sure was. "Where's the phone you used?"

THE PLACE WAS awash with cops inside of five minutes. A bomb squad came to deactivate the explosive. An ambulance team checked out me and Ryerson. Marjoram showed up and gave me an injection. I gave him a brief description of what had defeated the virus. Three SWAT teams arrived to guard one of the most valuable assemblages of art outside of a major museum. Trucks arrived to haul the stuff to safety.

I grabbed Marjoram's arm. "I want a full report on his air system within a week," I ordered. "I also want a set of proposals on how to defeat it."

He looked at me respectfully. "Yes, sir," he said. He hadn't called me "sir" in years. I grabbed the arm of a SWAT captain.

"I want a full SWAT team guarding this room until the environmental protection system is fully dismantled and shipped back to our headquarters," I ordered. "Twenty-four hours a day. And I want all of you riding with it wherever it goes."

He looked at me seriously. "Yes, sir," he said.

I sneezed and walked slowly over to Ryerson. He looked at me, still somewhat dazed. "How are you doing?" I asked him.

He nodded slowly. "I'm in your debt, Commissioner," he

said shakily. "You saved my life. You kept your head long after I had collapsed from fear."

"I wasn't far from collapse," I admitted. I kept feeling my face to see if anything was broken.

"And you saved all of this art," Ryerson continued. "It was almost all destroyed by that madman." He shuddered violently, then got a grip on himself. "But I'm going to do some research into his charges. He was right about some of it, you know."

"No, I didn't know," I said. "But if you think so, then I guess he was."

Ryerson looked surprised, but just nodded.

I pointed to a large painting in a corner. "What's that one?" I asked. "I don't recognize it."

Ryerson looked over blearily. "That's one we didn't even know he had," he said. "Pablo Picasso's *Guernica*. Notice the angularity and conical treatments of the piece and how it has the people show despair and pain." He pointed at details, following the shapes with his hands. "See how the overall effect is hopelessness and rage at the destruction caused by war. Guernica was a city in Spain that was bombed during the Spanish Civil War. Picasso painted this as a protest against the devastation and suffering inflicted on innocent people by other people as a result of war."

I looked at it for a long time. "It's neat," I finally said.

Ryerson looked at me sharply. For a brief moment, I thought he was going to ridicule my uneducated comment and stingingly correct me. Then he stopped and looked at the painting again. He nodded, slowly and profoundly.

"It's neat," he agreed.

THE WORLD AS WE KNOW IT

BY GEORGE ALEC EFFINGER

Future larceny, like today's, will come in both varieties, petty and grand. But in the future it may be difficult to tell which is which. The theft of a tiny container of biological agents, or of some easily reproducible computer software, can have major repercussions, as George Alec Effinger shows us in this visionary glimpse into the future of the world he created in his award-winning novels, A Fire in the Sun *and* When Gravity Fails.

THE WORLD AS WE KNOW IT

THE WORLD AS WE KNOW IT 295

Musa had gotten to his feet and was glaring at me with all the defiance of youth and ignorance. "No problem," he said, in what he no doubt imagined was a tough voice. "All you gotta do is come across."

"By fast," I said, deliberately not responding to his words, "I mean superluminal. Light-speed. And I'm not coming across. I don't do that. Grab a seat while I make a phone call, O Young One."

Musa maintained the rebellious expression, but some worry had crept into it, too. He didn't know who I planned to call. "You ain't gonna turn me over to the rats, are you?" he asked. "I just got out. *Yallah*, another fall and I think they'll cut off my right hand."

I nodded, murmuring Mahmoud's commcode into my desk phone. Musa was right about one thing: Islamic justice as currently interpreted in the city would demand the loss of his hand, possibly the entire arm, in front of a huge, cheering crowd in the courtyard of the Shimaal Mosque. Musa would have no opportunity to appeal, either, and he'd probably end up back in prison afterward, as well.

"Marhaba," said Mahmoud when he answered his phone. He wasn't the kind of guy to identify himself until he knew who was on the other end of the line. I remembered him before he had his sex change, as a slender, doe-eyed sylph dancing at Jo-Mama's. Since then, he'd put on a lot of weight, toughness, and something much more alarming.

"Yeah, you right," I replied. "Good news, Mahmoud. This is your investigator calling. Got the thief, and he hasn't had time to do anything with the product. He'll take you to it. What becomes of him afterward is up to you. Come take charge of him at your convenience."

"You are still a marvel, O Wise One," said Mahmoud. His praise counted about as much as a broken Bedu camel stick. "You have lost much, but it is as Allah wills. Yet you have not lost your native wit and ability. I will be there very soon, *inshallah*, with some news that might interest you." *Inshal-*

lah means "If God wills." Nobody but He was too sure about anything of late.

"The news is the payment, right, O Father of Generosity?" I said, shaking my head. Mahmoud had been a cheap stiff as a woman, and he was a cheap stiff now as a man.

"Yes, my friend," said Mahmoud. "But it includes a potential new client for you, and oh, I'll throw in a little cash, too. Business is business."

"And action is action," I said, not that I was seeing much action these days. "You know how much I charge for this sort of thing."

"*Salaam alaykum,* my friend," he said hurriedly, and he hung up his phone before I could salaam him back.

Musa looked relieved that I hadn't turned him over to the police, although I'm sure he was just as anxious about the treatment he could expect from Mahmoud. He had every reason in the world to be concerned. He maintained a surly silence, but he finally took my advice and sat down in the battered red-leather chair opposite my desk.

"Piece of advice," I said, not even bothering to look at him. "When Mahmoud gets here—and he'll get here fast—take him *directly* to his property. No excuses, no bargains. If you try holding Mahmoud up for so much as a lousy copper *fiq,* you'll end up breathing hot sand for the remainder of your brief life. Understand?"

I never learned if the punk understood or not. I wasn't looking at him, and he wasn't saying anything. I opened the bottom drawer of my desk and took out the office bottle. Apparently a slow leak had settled in, because the level of gin was much lower than I expected. It was something that would bear investigating, during my long hours of solitude.

I built myself a White Death—gin and bingara with a hit of Rose's lime juice—and took a quick gulp. Then I drank the rest of the tumblerful slowly. I wasn't savoring anything; I was just proving to myself again that I could be civilized about my drinking habits.

Time passed in this way—Musa sitting in the red-leather chair, sampling emotions, me sitting in my chair, sipping White Death. I'd been correct about one thing: it didn't take Mahmoud long to make the drive from the Budayeen. He didn't bother to knock on the outer door. He came through, into my inner office, accompanied by three large men. Now, even *I* thought three armed chunks were a bit much to handle ragged, little old Musa there. I said nothing. It wasn't my business any longer.

Mahmoud was dressed as I was; that is, in *keffiya*, the traditional Arab headdress, *gallebeya*, and sandals. The men with Mahmoud were all wearing very nice, tailored European-style business suits. Two of the suit jackets had bulges just where you'd expect. Mahmoud turned to those two and didn't utter a word. The two moved forward and took pretty damn physical charge of Musa, getting him out of my office the quickest way possible. Just before he passed through the inner door, Musa jerked his head around toward me and said, "Rat's puppet." That was all.

That left Mahmoud and the third suit.

"Where you at, Mahmoud?" I asked.

"I see you've taken to dyeing your beard, O Wise One," said Mahmoud by way of thanks. "You no longer look like a Maghrebi. You look like any common citizen of Asir or the Hejaz, for instance. Good."

I was so glad he approved. I was born part Berber, part Arab, and part French, in the part of Algeria that now called itself Mauretania. I'd left that part of the world far, far behind, and arrived in this city a few years ago, with reddish hair and beard that made me stand out among the locals. Now all my hair was as black as my prospects.

Mahmoud tossed an envelope on the desk in front of me. I glanced at it but didn't count the kiam inside, then dropped the envelope in a desk drawer and locked it.

"I cannot adequately express my thanks, O Wise One," he said in a flat voice. It was a required social formula.

"No thanks are needed, O Benefactor," I said, completing the obligatory niceties. "Helping a friend is a duty."

"All thanks be to Allah."

"Praise Allah."

"Good," said Mahmoud with some satisfaction. I could see him relax a little, now that the show was over. He turned to the remaining suit and said, "Shaykh Ishaq ibn Muhammad il-Qurawi, O Great Sir, you've seen how reliable my friend is. May Allah grant that he solve your problem as promptly as he solved mine." Then Mahmoud nodded to me, turned, and left. Evidently, I wasn't high enough on the social ladder to be actually introduced to Ishaq ibn Muhammad il-Qurawi.

I motioned to the leather chair. Il-Qurawi made a slight wince of distaste, then sat down.

I put on my professional smile and uttered another formulaic phrase that meant, roughly, "You have come to your people and level ground." "Welcome," in other words.

"Thank you, I—"

I raised a hand, cutting him off. "You must allow me to offer you coffee, O Sir. The journey from the Budayeen must have been tiring, O Shaykh."

"I was hoping we could dispense with—"

I raised my hand again. The old me would've been more than happy to dispense with the hospitality song-and-dance, but the new me was playing a part, and the ritual three tiny cups of coffee was part of it. Still, we hurried through them as rapidly as social graces permitted. Il-Qurawi wore a sour expression the whole time.

When I offered him a fourth, he waggled his cup from side to side, indicating that he'd had enough. "May your table always be prosperous," he said, because he had to.

I shrugged. *Allah yisallimak.* May God bless you.

"Praise Allah."

"Praise Allah."

"Now," said my visitor emphatically, "you have been rec-

ommended to me as someone who might be able to help with a slight difficulty."

I nodded reassuringly. Slight difficulty, my Algerian ass. People didn't come to me with slight difficulties.

As usual, the person in the leather chair didn't know how to begin. I waited patiently, letting my smile evaporate bit by bit. I found myself thinking about the office bottle, but it was impossible to bring it out again until I was alone. Strict Muslims looked upon alcoholic beverages with the same fury that they maintained for the infidel, and I knew nothing about il-Qurawi's attitudes about such things.

"If you have an hour or two free this afternoon," he said, "I wonder if you'd come with me to my office. It's not far from here, actually. On the eastern side of the canal, but quite a bit north of here. We've restored a thirty-six-story office building, but recently there's been more than the usual amount of vandalism. I'd like to hire you to stop it."

I took a deep breath and let it out again. "Not my usual sort of assignment, O Sir," I said, shrugging, "but I don't foresee any problem. I get a hundred kiam a day plus expenses. I need a minimum of five hundred right now to pique my interest."

Il-Qurawi frowned at the discussion of money and waved his hand. "Will you accept a check?" he asked.

"No," I said. I'd noticed that the man was stingy with honorifics, so I'd decided to hold my own to the minimum.

He grunted. He was clearly annoyed and doubtful about my ability to do what he wanted. Still, he removed a moderate stack of bills from a black leather wallet, and sliced off five for me. He leaned forward and put the money on my desk. I pretended to ignore it.

I made no pretense of checking an appointment book. "I'm certain, O Shaykh, that I can spare a few hours for you."

"Very good." Il-Qurawi stood up and spent a few moments vitally absorbed in the wrinkles in his business suit. I took the time to slide the five hundred kiam into the pocket of my *gallebeya*.

"I can spare a few hours, O Shaykh," I said, "but first I'd like some more information. Such as who you are and whom you represent."

He didn't say a word. He merely slid a business card to the spot where the money had been.

I picked up the card. It said:

Ishaq ibn Muhammad il-Qurawi
Chief of Security
CRCorp

Below that was a street address that meant nothing to me, and a commcode. I didn't have a business card to give him, but I didn't think he cared. "CRCorp?" I asked.

He was still standing. He indicated that we should begin moving toward the door. It was fine by me. "Yes, we deal in consensual realities."

"Uh-huh," I said. "I know you people."

We went downstairs to his car. He owned a long, black, chauffeur-driven, restored, gasoline-powered limousine. I wasn't impressed. I'd ridden in a few of those. We got in and he murmured something to the driver. The car began gliding through the rubble-strewn streets, toward the headquarters of CRCorp.

"Can you be more exact about the nature of this vandalism, O Sir?" I said.

"You'll see. I believe it's being caused by one person. I have no idea why; I just want it stopped. There are too many clients in the building beginning to complain."

And it's beyond the capabilities of the Chief of Security, I thought. That spoke something ominous to me.

After about half an hour of weaving north and east, then back west toward the canal, then farther north, we arrived at the CRCorp building. Allah only knew what it had been before this entire part of the city had been destroyed, but now it stood looking newly built among its broken and blasted neighbors. One fixed-up building in all that desolation seemed pretty lonely and conspicuous, I thought, but I guess you had to start someplace.

Il-Qurawi and I got out of the limousine and walked across the freshly surfaced parking area. There were no other cars in it. "The executive offices are on the seventeenth floor, about halfway up, but there's nothing interesting to see there. You'll want to visit one or two of the consensual realities, and then look at the vandalism I mentioned."

Well, sure, as soon as he said there wasn't anything interesting on the seventeenth floor, I immediately wanted to go there. I hate it when other people tell me what I want to do, but it was il-Qurawi's five hundred kiam, so I stayed shut up, nodded, and followed him inside to the elevators.

"Give you a taste of one of the consensual realities," he said. "We just call them CRs around here. We'll stop off first on twenty-six. It's functioning just fine, and there's been no sign of vandalism as yet."

Still nothing for me to say. We rode up quickly, silently in the mirrored elevator. I glanced at my reflection. I wasn't happy with the appearance I'd had to adopt, but I was stuck with it.

We got off at twenty-six. The elevator doors opened, we stepped out, and passed through a small, well-constructed airlock. When I turned to look, the elevator and airlock had disappeared. I mean, there was no sign that elevator doors could possibly exist for hundreds of miles. I felt for them and there was nothing but air. Rather thin, cold air. If I'd been pressed to make a guess, I'd have said that we were on the surface of Mars. I knew that was impossible, but I'd seen holo shots of the Martian surface, and this is just what it looked like.

"Here," said il-Qurawi, handing me a mask and a small tank, "this should help you somewhat."

"I am in your debt, O Great One." I used the tight-grip straps to hold the mask in place, but the tank was made to be worn on a belt. I had a rope holding my *gallebeya* closed, but

it wouldn't support the weight of the tank, so I just carried it
in my hands. We started walking across the barren, boulder-
studded surface of Mars, toward a collection of buildings in
the far distance that I recognized as the international Martian
colony.

"The atmosphere on this floor only approximates that of
Mars," said il-Qurawi. "That was part of the group's consensus agreement. Still, if you're outside and not wearing the
mask, you're liable to develop a rather serious condition they
call 'Mars throat.' Affects your sinuses, your inner ears, your
throat, and so forth."

"Let me see if I can guess, O Sir," I said, huffing a little as I
made my way over the extremely rough terrain. "Group of
people in the colony, all would-be Martian colonists, and
they've voted on how they wanted the place to look." I gazed
up at a pink-peach-colored sky.

"Exactly. And they voted on how they wanted it to feel and
smell and sound. Actually, it approximates the reports we get
from the true Mars Project rather closely. CRCorp supplies
the area, for which we charge what we feel is a fair price. We
also supply the software that maintains the illusion, too."

I kicked a boulder. No illusion. "How much of this is real?"
I said. Even using the tank, I was already short of breath and
eager to get inside one of the buildings.

"The boulders, as you've just discovered, are artificial but
real. The buildings are real. The carefully maintained atmosphere is also our responsibility. Everything else you might
experience is computer or holo-generated. It can be quite
deadly out here, but that's the way this group wanted it. We
haven't left anything out, down to the toxin-laden lichen,
which *is* part of the illusion. For all intents and purposes, this
is the surface of Mars. Group 26 has always seemed to be very
pleased with it. We've gotten very few complaints or sugges-
tions for improvement."

"Naturally, O Sir," I said, "I'm looking forward to interviewing a few of the residents."

"Of course," said il-Qurawi. "That's why I brought you here. We're very proud of Group 26, and justly so, I think."

"Praise Allah," I said. No echo from my client.

After more time and hiking than I'd been prepared for, we arrived at the colony itself. I felt like a physical wreck; the executive with me was not suffering at all. He looked like he'd just taken a leisurely stroll through the repro of the Tiger Gardens in the city's entertainment quarter.

"This way," he said, pointing to an airlock into the long main building. It appeared to have been constructed of some material derived from the reddish sand all around, but I wasn't interested enough to find out for sure if that were true or part of the holographic illusion.

We cycled through the airlock. Inside, we found ourselves in a corridor that had been painted in institutional colors: dark green to waist-level, a kind of maddening tan above that. I was absolutely sure that I would quickly come to hate those colors; soon it proved that they dominated the color scheme of the most of the hallways and meeting rooms. The people of Group 26 must have had a very different aesthetic sense than I. It didn't give me great hopes for them.

Il-Qurawi glanced at his wristwatch, a European product like the rest of his outfit. It was thin and sleek and made of gold. "The majority of them will be in the refectory module now," he said. "Good. You'll have the opportunity to meet as many of Group 26 as you like. Ask whatever you like, but we are under a little time pressure. I'd like to take you to floor seven within the next half hour."

"I give thanks to the Maker of Worlds," I said. Il-Qurawi gave me a sidelong glance to see if I were serious. I was doing my best to give that impression.

The refectory was down the entire length of the main building and through a low, narrow, windowless passageway. I felt a touch of claustrophobia, as if I were down deep beneath the surface. I had to remind myself that I was actually on the twenty-sixth floor of an office tower.

The refectory was at the other end of the passageway. It was a large room, filled with orderly rows of tables. Men, women, and children sat at the tables, eating food from trays that were dispensed from a large and intricate machine on one side of the front of the room. I stared at it for a while, watching people go up to it, press colored panels, and receive their trays within fifteen or twenty seconds each.

"Catering," said il-Qurawi with an audible sigh. "Major part of our overhead."

"Question, O Sir," I said. "Who's actually paying for all this?"

He looked at me as if I were a total fool. "All these people in Group 26, of course. They've signed over varying amounts of cash and property, depending on how long they intend to stay. Some come for a week, but the greater portion of the group has paid in advance for ten- or twenty-year leases."

My eyes narrowed as I thought and did a little multiplication in my head. "Then, depending on the populations of the other thirty-some floors," I said slowly, "CRCorp ought to be making a very tidy bundle."

His head jerked around to look at me directly. "I've already mentioned the high overhead. The expenses we incur to maintain all this—and the CRs on the other floors—are staggering. Our profits are not so great as you might think."

"I ask a thousand pardons, O Sir," I said. "I truly had no intention to give offense. I'm still trying to get an idea of how large an operation this is. Maybe now's the time to speak to one or two of these 'Martian colonists.'"

He relaxed a little. He was hiding something, I'd bet my wives and kids on it. "Of course," he said smoothly. I thought back on it and couldn't recall a single time he'd actually called me by name. In any event, he directed me to one of the tables where there was an empty seat beside an elderly man with short-cropped white hair. He wore a pale blue jumpsuit. Hell, *everyone* there wore a pale blue jumpsuit. I wondered if that was the official uniform on the real Mars colony, or just a group decision of this particular CR.

"*Salaam alaykum,*" I said to the elderly man.

"*Alaykum as-Salaam,*" he said mechanically. "Outsider, huh?"

"Just came in to get a quick look."

He leaned over and whispered in my ear. "Now, some of us *really* hate outsiders. Spoils the group consensus."

"I'll be out of here before you know it, *inshallah.*"

The white-haired man took a forkful of some brown, smooth substance on his tray, chewed it thoughtfully, then said, "Could've at least gotten into a goddamn jumpsuit, *hayawaan.* Too much trouble?"

I ignored the insult. Il-Qurawi should've thought of the jumpsuit. "How long you been part of Group 26?" I asked.

"We don't call ourselves 'Group 26,'" said the man, evidently disliking me even more. "We're the Mars colony."

Well, the real Mars colony was a combined project of the Federated New England States of America, the new Fifth Reich, and the Fragrant Heavenly Empire of True Cathay.

There were no—or very few—Arabs on the real Mars.

Someone delivered a tray of food to me: molded food without texture slapped onto a molded plastic tray; the brown stuff, some green stuff that I took to be some form of vegetable material—as nondescript and unidentifiable as anything else on the tray—a small portion of dark red, chewy stuff that might have been a meat substitute, and the almost obligatory serving of gelatin salad with chopped carrots, celery, and canned fruit in it. There were also slices of dark bread and disposable cups of camel's milk.

I turned again to the white-haired gentleman. "Milk, huh?" I asked.

His bushy eyebrows went up. "Milk is the best thing for you. If you want to live forever."

I murmured "*Bismillah,*" which means "In the name of God," and I began eating my meal, not knowing what some of the dishes were even after I'd tasted and chewed and swallowed them. I ate out of social obligation, and I did pretty well, too. When some of the others were finished, they took their trays and utensils to a machine very much like the one that dispensed the meals in the first place. The hard items disappeared into a long, wide slot, and I felt certain that leftover food was recycled in one form or another. CRCorp prided itself on efficiency, and this was one way to keep the operating costs down.

I still had my doubts about the limited choices in the refectory—including the compulsory camel's milk, which was served in four-ounce cups. As I ate, il-Qurawi turned toward me again. "Are you enjoying the meal?" he asked.

"Praise God for His beneficence," I said.

"God, God—," il-Qurawi shook his head. "It's permissible if you really believe in that sort of thing. But the people here are not all Muslim—some belong to no organized religion at all—and they're using whatever agricultural training they had on 'Earth,' and they're applying it here on 'Mars.' They grew a small portion of these delicious meats and vegetables themselves—it came from their skill, their dedication, their determination. They receive no aid or interference from CRCorp."

"Yeah, you right," I said, and decided I'd had enough of il-Qurawi, too. I hadn't tasted anything the least bit palatable except possibly the bread and milk, and how wildly enthusiastic could I get about them? I didn't mention anything about CRCorp's inability to reproduce the noticeably lower gravity of the true Mars, or certain other aspects of the interplanetary milieu.

I spoke some more to the white-haired man, and then one of the plainly clothed women further down the table leaned over and interrupted us. Her hair was cut just above shoulder-length, dull from not having been washed for a very long time. I suppose that while there was plenty of water in the thirty-six-story office building, in the headquarters of the CRCorp, and on some of the other consensus reality floors, there was extremely little water available on floor twenty-six—the Mars for the sort of folks who yearned for danger, but no danger more threatening than the elevator ride from the main lobby.

"Has he told you everything?" asked the filthy woman. Her voice was clearly intended to be a whisper, but I'm sure she was overheard several rows of tables away on either side of us.

"There's so much more I want you to see," said il-Qurawi, even going so far as to grab my arm. That just made me determined to hear the woman out.

"I have not finished my meal, O *fellah*," I said, somewhat irritably. I'd called him a peasant. I shouldn't have, but it felt good. "What is your blessed name, O Lady?" I asked her.

She looked blank for a few seconds, then confused. Finally she said, "Marjory Mulcher. Yeah, that's me now. Sometimes I'm Marjory Tiller, depending on the season and how badly they need me and how many people are willing to work with me."

I nodded, figuring I understood what she meant. "Everything that passeth in this world," I said, "—or any other world —" I interpolated, "is naught but the expression of the Will of God."

Marjory's eyes grew larger and she smiled. "I'm a Roman Catholic," she said. "Lapsed, maybe, but what does *that* do to you, camel jockey?" I couldn't think of a safely irrelevant reply.

In her mind, the CRCorp probably had nothing to do with her present situation. Perhaps in her own mind, she *was* on Mars. That may have been the great and ultimate victory of CRCorp.

"I asked you," said Marjory with a frown, "are they showing you everything? Are they telling you everything?"

"Don't know," I said. "I just got here."

Marjory moved down a few places and sat beside me, on the other side from the white-haired man. I looked around and saw that only she and I were still eating. Everyone else had disposed of his tray and was sitting, almost expectantly, in his molded plastic seat, politely and quietly.

The woman smelled terrible. She leaned toward me and whispered, "You know the corporation is just about ready to unleash a devastating CR. Something we won't be able to manage at all. Death on every floor, I imagine. And then, when they've tested this horrible CR on us, may their religion be cursed, they'll unleash it on you and what you casually prefer to call the rest of the world. Earth, I mean. I grew up on Earth, you know. Still have some relatives there."

By the holy sacred beard of the Prophet, may the blessings of Allah be on him and peace, I've never felt so relieved as when she discovered a sudden interest in the gelatin salad. "Raisins. Rejoicing and celebrations," she said to no one in particular. "Consensual raisins."

I slowly closed my eyes and tightened my lips. My right hand dropped its piece of bread and raised up tiredly to cover my tightly shut eyelids, at the same time massaging my forehead. We didn't have enough facilities for mentals and nutsos in the city; we just let the ones with the wealthier families shut 'em away in places like Group 26 in the CRCorp Building. *Yaa Allah*, you never knew when you were going to run into one of these bereft cookies.

Still with my eyes covered, I could feel the man with the close-cropped white hair lean toward me on the other side. I knew that son-of-a-biscuit hadn't liked me from the getgo. "Get Marjory to tell you all about her raisins sometime. It's a fascinating story in its own right."

"Be sure to," I murmured. In the spring with the apricots, I would. I picked up the bread with my eating hand again and opened my eyes. Everyone within hollering range was staring at me with rapt attention. I don't know why; I didn't *want* to know why then, and I *still* don't want to know why. I hoped it was just that I was an oddity, a welcome interruption in the daily routine, like a visit from one of Prince Shaykh Mahali's wives or children.

I'd had enough to eat, and so I'd picked up the tray—I'm quick on the uptake, and I'd figured out the disposal drill from observation. It wasn't that difficult to begin with, and, jeez, I'm a trained professional, *mush hayk?* Yeah, you right. I slid the tray into the proper slot in the proper machine. Then, il-Qurawi having nothing immediate to do, he chose to be nowhere in sight. I slumped back down between Marjory and the old, white-haired man. Fortunately, Marjory was still enchanted by her gelatin salad—the al-Qaddani moddy, a Palestinian fictional hardboiled-detective piece of hardware I was wearing, gave me the impression that Marjory was like this at *every* meal, whatever was served—and the old gentleman gave me a disapproving look, stood up, and moved away, toward what real people did to compensate society for their daily sustenance. For a few moments I had utter peace and utter silence, but I did not expect them to last very long. I was correct as usual in this sort of discouraging speculation.

Almost directly across from me was a woman with extremely large breasts, which were trapped in an undergarment which must have been painfully confining for them. I really wasn't interested enough to read if they were genuine—God-given—or not; she must've thought she had, you know, the most devastating figure on all of Mars, and of course we understand what we mean when we speak of Mars. She wore a long, flowing, print shift of a drabness that directed all one's attention elsewhere and upwards; bare feet; and a live, medium-sized, suffering lizard on one shoulder that was there only to extort yet another sort of response from you. As if her grotesque *mamelons* weren't enough.

"Oh," you were supposed to say, "you have a live, medium-sized lizard on your shoulder." Now, when someone has gone to *that* amount of labor to pry a reaction from me, my innate obstinacy sets in. I will not look more than two or three times at the tits, casually, as after the first encounter they don't exist for me. I won't even glance furtively at her various other vulgar accoutrements. I won't remark at all on the lizard. The lizard and I will never have a relationship; the woman and I barely had one, and that only through courtesy.

She spoke, in a voice intended to be heard by the nearby portion of mankind: "I think Marjory means well." She looked around herself to find agreement, and there wasn't a single person still in the refectory who would contradict her. I got the feeling that would be true *whatever* she said. "I know for a fact that Marjory never goes beyond the buildings of the Mars colony. She never sees Allah's holy miracle of creation. Does it not say in the Book, the noble Qur'ân, 'Frequently you see the ground dry and barren: but no sooner do We send down rain to moisten it than it begins to tremble and magnify, putting forth each and every kind of blossoming life. That is because Allah is Truth: He gives life to the dead and has power over all things.'?" She sat back, evidently very self-satisfied. "That was from the sûrah called *Pilgrimage*, in the holy Qur'ân."

"May the Creator of heaven and earth bless this recitation of His holy words," said one man softly.

"May Allah give His blessing," said a woman quietly.

I had several things I might have mentioned; the first was that the imitation surface of Mars I'd crossed was not, in point of fact, covered with every variety of blooming plant. Yet maybe to some of these people that was beside the point. Before I could say anything, a young, sparsely bearded man sat beside me in the old white-haired resident's seat. The young man said, "You know, Umm Sulaiman, that you shouldn't hold up Marjory as a typical resident of the Mars colony."

Umm Sulaiman frowned. "I have further scripture that I could recite which supports my words and actions."

The young man shuddered. "No, my mother-in-law"—clearly an honorific and a title not to be taken seriously—"all is as Allah wills." He turned to me and murmured, "I wish both of them—the two old women, Marjory and Umm Sulaiman—would stop behaving in their ways. I admit it, I'm superstitious, and it frightens me."

"Seems a shame to pay all this money to CRCorp just to be frightened."

The young man looked to either side, then leaned even closer. "I've heard a story, O Sir," he murmured. "Actually, I've heard several stories, some as wild as Marjory's, some ever crazier. But, by the beard of the Prophet—"

"May the blessings of Allah be on him and peace," I said.

"—there's one story that won't go away, a story that's repeated often by the most sane and reliable of our team." "Team," as if they really were part of some kind of international extraterrestrial project.

I pursed my lips and tried to show that I was rabidly eager to hear his bit of gossip. "And what is this persistent story, O Wise One?"

He looked to either side again, took my arm, and together we left the table and the others. We walked slowly toward the exit. "Now, O Sir," he said, "I've had this directly from bin el-Fadawin, who is CRCorp and Shaykh il-Qurawi's highest representative here in the Mars colony."

"Group 26, you mean," I said.

"Yeah, if you insist on it, Group 26." It was obvious that he didn't like his illusion broken, even for a moment. It cast some preliminary doubt on what he was about to tell me. "Listen, O Sir," he said. "El-Fadawin and others drop hints now and again that CRCorp has better uses for these premises, that they're even now working on ways to turn away and run off the very people who've paid them for long-term care."

I shrugged. "If CRCorp wanted to evict y'all, O Young Man, I'm sure they could do it without too much difficulty. I mean, they got the lawyers and you got, what, rocks and lichen? Still, you and all the others have handed over—and continue to hand over—truly exorbitant amounts of cash and property; and all they've really done is decorated to your specifications a large, empty space in a restored office tower."

"They've created our consensual reality, please, O Shaykh."

"Yeah, you right," I said, amazed that this somewhat intel-

ligent young man could be so easily taken in. "So you're telling me that the CRs—which the corporation has worked so
hard to create, and for which it's being richly rewarded—will
start disappearing, one by one?"

"*Begin* disappearing!" cried the young man. "Have Shaykh
il-Qurawi—"

"Did I hear my name mentioned, O Most Gracious Ones?"
asked my client, appearing silently enough through the door
of the refectory room. "In a pleasant context, I hope."

"I was commenting, O Sir," I said, covering quickly, "on
the truly spectacular job CRCorp has done here, inside the
buildings and out. That little lizard Umm Sulaiman wears on
her shoulder—is that a genuine Martian life form?"

"No," he said, frowning slightly. "There aren't any native
lizards on Mars. We've tried to discourage her from wearing it
—it creates a disharmony with what we're trying to accomplish here. Still, the choice is her own."

"Ah," I said. I'd figured all that before; I was just easing the
young man out of the conversation. "I believe I've seen
enough here, O Sir. Next I'd like to see some of the vandalism
you spoke of."

"Of course," said il-Qurawi, moving a hand to *almost* touch
me, almost grasp my elbow and lead me from the refectory.
He gave me no time at all for the typically effusive Muslim
farewells. We left the building the way we'd come, and once
again I used the mask and bottled air. However, we didn't
make the long trek across the make-believe Martian landscape; il-Qurawi knew of a nearer exit. I guess he'd just
wanted me to come the long way before, to sample the handi-
work of CRCorp.

We ducked through a nearly invisible airlock near the buildings of the colony, and took an elevator down to floor seven.
When we stepped in, I removed the mask and air tank. The air
pressure and oxygen content of the atmosphere was Earth-
normal.

I saw immediately il-Qurawi's problem. Floor seven was entirely abandoned. In fact, except for some living quarters and outbuildings in the distance, and the barren and artificially landscaped "hills" and "valleys" built into the area, floor seven was nothing but a large and vacant loft a few stories above street level.

"What happened here, O Sir?" I asked.

Il-Qurawi turned around and casually indicated the entire floor. "This used to be a re-creation of Egypt at the time of the Ptolemies. I personally never saw the need for a consensual reality set in pre-Islamic times, but I was assured that certain academic experts wanted to reestablish the Library of Alexandria, which was destroyed by the Romans before the birth of the Prophet."

"May the blessings of Allah be on him and peace," I murmured.

Il-Qurawi shrugged. "It was functioning quite well, at least as well as the Martian colony, if not better, until one day it just . . . went away. The holographic images vanished, the specially-created computer effects went offline, and nothing our creative staff did restored them. After a week or ten days of living in this emptiness, the people of Group Seven demanded a refund and departed."

I rubbed my dyed beard. "O Sir, where are the controlling mechanisms, and how hard is it to get access to them?"

Il-Qurawi led me toward the northern wall. We had a good distance to hike. I saw that the floor was some molded synthetic material; it was probably the same on floor twenty-six. All the rest was the result of the electronic magic of CRCorp —what they got paid for. I could imagine the chagrin, then the wrath, of the residents of floor seven.

We reached the northern wall, and il-Qurawi led me to a small metal door built into the wall about eye-level. He opened the door, and I saw some familiar computer controls and some that were completely baffling to me, slots for bubble-plate memory units, hard-copy readout devices, a keyboard data-entry device, a voice-recognition entry device, and other things that were completely strange and unrecognizable to me. I never claimed to be a computer expert. I'm not. I just didn't think it was profitable to let il-Qurawi know it.

"Wiped clean," he said, indicating the hardware inside the door. "Someone got in—someone knowing where to look for the control mechanisms—and deleted all the vital programs, routines, and local effects."

"All right," I said, beginning to turn the problem over in my mind. It had the look of a simple crime. "Any recently discharged employees with a grudge?"

Il-Qurawi swore under his breath. I admit it, I was a little shocked. That's how much I'd changed since the old days. "Don't you think we checked out all the simple solutions ourselves? Before we came to you? By the life of my children, I'm positive it wasn't a disgruntled former employee, or a current one with plans for extortion, or any of the other easy answers that will occur to you at first. We're faced with a genuine disaster: someone is destroying consensual realities for no apparent reason."

I blinked at him for a few seconds, thinking over what he'd just told me. I was standing in what had once been a replica of a strip of ancient civilization along the banks of the Nile River in pre-Muslim Egypt. Now I could look across the unfurnished space toward the other walls, seeing only the textured, generally flat floor in-between. "You used the plural, O Sir," I said at last. "How many other consensual realities have been ruined like this one?"

"Out of thirty rented floors," he said quietly, "eighteen have been rendered inactive."

I just stared. CRCorp didn't have just a serious problem; it was facing extinction. I was surprised that the company hadn't come to me sooner. Of course, il-Qurawi was the chief of security, and he probably figured he could solve the mess himself. Finally, with no small degree of humiliation, I'm sure, he sought outside help. And he knew I knew it. It was a good thing I wasn't in a mood to rub it in, because I had all the ammunition I needed.

Il-Qurawi showed me a few other consensual realities, working ones and empty ones, because I asked him to. He didn't seem eager for me to get too familiar with the CRCorp operation, yet if he wanted me to help with his difficulty, he had to give me a certain amount of access. He and his corporation were backed against the wall, and he knew it. So I saw a vigorous CR based on an Eritrean-written fantasy-novel series almost a century old, and a successful CR that re-created a strict Sunni Islamic way of life that had never truly existed, and two more floors that were lifeless and unfurnished.

I decided I'd seen enough for the present. Il-Qurawi thanked me for my time, wished me luck in my quest for the culprit, and hoped it wouldn't take me too long to complete the assignment.

I said, "It shouldn't be more than a day or two, *inshallah.* I already have some possibilities to look into." That was a lie. I was as lost as Qabeel's spare mule.

He didn't think it was necessary to accompany me back to my office; he just put me in the limousine with his driver. I didn't care.

I got a scare when I got back to my office. In the time while I'd visited the CRCorp Building, someone had defeated my expensive, elaborate security system, entered, and swiped my own CR hardware and software. The shabbiness had disappeared, replaced by the true polished floors and freshly-painted walls of the building. I'd worked hard to reproduce the run-down office of Lutfy Gad's detective, al-Qaddani, but now it was clean and new and sleek and modern. I was really furious. On my desk, under a Venetian glass paperweight, was a sheet of my notepaper with two words on it: *A warning.*

In the name of Allah, the Beneficent, the Merciful. I took out my prayer rug from the closet, spread it carefully on the floor, faced toward Mecca, and prayed. Then, my thoughts on higher things than CRCorp, I returned the rug to the closet. I

sprawled in my chair behind the desk and stared at the notepaper. *A warning.* Hell, some guy was good at B & E, and
cleaning out CRs, large and small. But he hadn't made me
afraid, only so angry that my stomach hurt.

I didn't want to look at my office space in its true, elegantly
modern, fashionable form. Changing everything back the way
it had been would be simple enough—I'd been wise enough to
buy backups of everything from the small consensual reality
shop that had done up al-Qaddani's office for me in the first
place. It would take me what? Half an hour to restore the
slovenly look I preferred.

I was certain that Shaykh il-Qurawi had backups to his dys-
functional floors, as well; it was only that CRCorp had tried
to pass along the costs of restoration to the residents, and they
had balked, perhaps unanimously. I recalled an old proverb I'd
learned from my mother, may Allah grant her peace: "Greed
lessens what is gathered." It was something CRCorp had yet
to learn.

It also meant that everything seemed to be close to its final
resolution. I tipped a little from the office bottle into a tum-
bler and glanced at the setting sun through it. The true meaning—the actual one, the one that counted—had nothing to do
with resolutions, however. I knew as well as I knew my childhood pet goat's name that things were never this easy. Mark
this down, it's a free tip from an experienced operative (that
means street punk): things are never this easy. I'd known it
before I started messing around on the street; then I'd learned
it the simple way, from more experienced punks; and finally
I'd had to learn it the hard way, too many times. Things are
never this easy.

What I'm saying is that Simple Shaykh il-Qurawi knew perfectly well that he could do the same as I had, and chunk in
the backup tapes, programs, and mechanisms. His echoing,
forlorn floors would all quickly return to their fantasy factual-
ities, and they'd probably be repopulated within days. CRCorp
would then lose just a minimum of cash, and all the evil time

could be filed away as just one of those bad experiences that had to be weathered by every company now and then.

Begging the question: why, then, didn't CRCorp use the backups immediately, but instead suffer the angry defection of so many of its clients? And did il-Qurawi really think I was *that* stupid, that it all wouldn't occur to me pretty damn fast?

Don't ask me. I didn't have a clue.

As the days went by, and the weeks, I learned through bin el-Fadawin—CRCorp's plant on floor twenty-six—that in fact some of the other floors had been restored, and some of their tenants had returned. Great, wonderful, I told myself, expecting il-Qurawi himself to show up with the rest of my money and possibly even a thank-you, although I don't really believe in miracles.

Three weeks later, okay? I get a visitor from floor three. This was a floor that had been changed into a consensual reality replica of a generation ship—a starship that would take generation upon generation to reach its goal, a planet merely called D, circling a star named in the catalog simply as Wolf 359. They had years, decades, even longer to name the planet more cheerfully, and the same with "their" star, Wolf 359. However, the electronics had failed brutally, turning their generation ship into the sort of empty loft I'd witnessed in the CRCorp building. The "crew" had gotten disgusted and resigned, feeling cheated and threatening lawsuits.

After CRCorp instituted repairs, and when the science fiction-oriented customers heard that floor three had returned to its generation-ship environment, many of them reenlisted at the agreed-upon huge rates. I got another visit, from bin el-Fadawin this time.

"CRCorp and Shaykh il-Qurawi are more grateful than they can properly express," he said, putting a moderately fat envelope on my desk. "Your work on this case has shown the corporation the techniques it needs to restore each and every consensual reality."

"Please convey my thanks to both the shaykh and the corporation. I'm just glad everything worked out well at the end," I said. "If Allah wills, the residents of the CRCorp building will once again be happy with their shared worlds." I knew I hadn't done anything but check their security system, but if they were happy, it was worth investigating just for fun.

El-Fadawin touched his heart, his lips, and his forehead. *"Inshallah.* You have earned the acknowledged gratitude of CRCorp," he said, bowing low. "This is a mighty though intangible thing to have to your credit."

"I'll mark that down in my book," I said, through a thin smile. I'd had enough of il-Qurawi's lackey. The money in the envelope was spendable and good enough; the gratitude of CRCorp was something as invisible and nonexistent as a dream djinn. I paid it the same attention, which is to say, none.

"Thank you again, O Wise One, and I speak as a representative of both CRCorp and Shaykh il-Qurawi."

"No thanks are necessary," I said. "He asked of me a favor, and I did my best to fulfill it."

"May Allah shower you with blessings," he said, sidling toward the inner door.

"May God grant your wishes, my brother," I said, watching him sidle and doing nothing to stop him. When I heard the outer door open and shut, and I was sure that I was alone, I picked up the envelope, opened it, and counted the take. There were three thousand kiam there, which included a sizable bonus. I felt extravagantly well paid-off, but not the least bit satisfied. I had this feeling, you see, one I'd had before . . .

It was a familiar feeling that everything wasn't as picture perfect as il-Qurawi's hopfrog had let me suppose. The feeling was borne out quite some time later, when I'd almost forgotten it. My typically long, slow morning was interrupted by, of all people, the white-haired old gentleman from floor twenty-six. His name was Uzair ibn Yaqoub, and he seemed extremely nervous, even in my office, which had been rendered shabby and comfortable again. He sat in the red-leather chair opposite me and fidgeted for a little while. I gave him a few minutes.

"It's the Terran oxygen level and the air pressure," he said in explanation.

I nodded. It sure as hell was something, to get him to leave his "Martian colony," even for an hour or two.

"Take your time, O Shaykh ibn Yaqoub," I said. I offered him water, some fruit, that's all I had around the office. That and the bottle in the drawer, which had less than a slug left in it.

"You know, of course," said ibn Yaqoub, "that after your visit, the same trouble that had plagued other consensual realities struck us. Fortunately for us, they found out what was wrong on Mars, and they fixed it, and we're all back there living just as before."

I nodded. That was chiefly my job at this stage of the interview.

"Well," said ibn Yaqoub, "I'm certain—and some of the others, even those who never agreed with me before—that something wrong and devious and possibly criminal is happening."

I thought, what could be more criminal than the destruction—the *theft*—of consensual realities? But I merely said, "What do you mean, O Wise One?"

"I mean that somehow, someone is stealing from us."

"Stealing what?" I asked, remembering that they produced little, some vegetables, maybe, some authentic lichen . . .

"Stealing," insisted ibn Yaqoub. "You know the Mars colony pays each of us flight pay and hazardous duty pay during our stay."

No, I hadn't heard that before. All I'd known was that the money went the other way, from the colonist to the corporation. This was becoming interesting.

"And that's in addition to our regular low wages," said the white-haired old man. "We didn't sign up to make money. It was the Martian experience we longed for."

I nodded a third time. "And you think, O Shaykh, that somehow you're being cheated?"

He made a fist and struck my desk. "I know it!" he cried. "I figured in advance how much pay to expect for a four-week period, because I had to send some to my grandchildren. When the pay voucher arrived, it was barely more than half the kiam I expected. I tried to have someone in the colony explain it to me—I admit I'm not as good with figures as I used to be—and even bin el-Fadawin assured me that I must have made an error in calculation. I don't particularly trust el-Fadawin, but everyone else seemed to agree with him. Then, as time passed, more and more people noticed tax rates too high, payroll deductions too large, miscellaneous costs showing up here and there. Now we're all generally agreed that something needs to be done. You helped us greatly before. We beg you to help us again."

I stood up behind my desk and paced, as I usually did when I was thinking over a new case. But was this a new case, or just an extension of the old one? It was difficult for me to believe il-Qurawi and CRCorp needed every last fîq and kiam of these poor people, who were already paying the majority of their wealth for the privilege of living in "the Mars colony." Cheating them like this was too trivial, too cruel, even for CRCorp.

I told ibn Yaqoub I'd look into the matter, accepted no retainer, and quoted him a vanishingly small fee. I liked him, and I liked most of the others in Group 26.

I returned first to the twenty-sixth floor, not telling anyone I was coming—particularly not il-Qurawi or bin el-Fadawin. I knew where to get a mask, oxygen tank, and blue coverall. Now I also knew where the control box was hidden on the "Martian" wall, and I checked it. I made several interesting discoveries: someone was indeed bleeding off funds from the internal operation of the consensus reality.

I returned to my office, wondering who the culprit was. I was not terribly surprised to see my outer office filled with three waiting clients—all of them from other consensus realities. One, from the harsh Sunni floor, threatened to start taking off hands and arms if I didn't come up with an acceptable alternative. The other two were nowhere as bloodthirsty, but just as outraged.

I assured and mollified and talked them down; then I waited until they left, and I opened the bottom drawer and withdrew the office bottle. I felt I'd earned the final slug. A voice behind me spoke: "Got a gift for ya," the young man said. I turned. I saw a youth in his mid-twenties, wearing a *gallebeya* that seemed to shift colors from green to blue as he changed positions.

"For you, 'cause you're so damn smart," he said, coming toward me, setting a fresh bottle of gin on my desk.

"Bismillah," I said. "I am in your debt."

"We'll see," said the young man, with a quirky smile.

I built us two quick White Deaths. He sat in the red-leather chair and sipped his, enjoying the taste; I gulped the first half of mine, then slowed to his speed just to show that I could do it.

I waited. I could gain much by waiting—information perhaps, at least the other half of the White Death.

"You don't know me," said the young man. "Call me Firon." That was Arabic for Pharaoh. "It's as phony a name as Musa. Or your own."

The mention of Musa made me sit up straight. I was sore that he'd broken his way into my inner office, eavesdropped on my clients, and knew that I was out of gin on top of it. I started to say something, but he stopped me with a raised hand. "There's a lot you don't know, O Sir," he said, rather sadly, I thought. "You used to run the streets the way we run them, but it's been too long, and you rose too high, and now you're trapped over here on this side of the canal. So you've lost touch in some ways."

"Lost touch, but still with connections—"

Firon laughed. "Connections! Musa and I and our friends now decide who gets what and how much and when. And then we slip back into our carefully built alternate personalities. Some of us make use of your antique moddy and daddy technology. Some of us slip in and out of consensual realities. The rest of us—how many ways are there of hiding?"

"One," I said. "Just one good way. The rest is merely waiting until you're caught."

Firon laughed brightly and pointed a finger. "Exactly! Exactly so! And what are you doing? Or I? Can we tell?"

I sat back down wearily. I didn't want another White Death, which was a bad sign. "What do you want, then?" I asked.

Firon stood and towered over me. "Just this, and listen well: we know who you are, we know how vulnerable you are. You must let us continue to make our small, almost inconsequential financial transactions, or we'll simply reveal your identity. Reveal it generally, if you take my meaning."

"I take it precisely," I said, feeling old and slow. But not *too* old and slow. Firon, this young would-be tyrant, was so certain of his power over me that he wasn't paying very close attention. He was a victim of his own pride, his own self-delusions. I took the nearly full bottle of gin and put it in the bottom drawer; at the same time I took a small but extremely serviceable seizure gun—the one that used to belong to my second wife—from my ankle holster and I showed it to him. "Old ways are sometimes the best," I said, with a wry smile.

He sank slowly into the red-leather chair, a wide and wobbly grin on his face. "In the name of Allah, the Beneficent, the Merciful," he said.

"Praise Allah," I said.

"Now what?" asked Firon. "We're at one of those famous impasses."

I thought for a moment or two. "Here," I said at last, "how's this? You're ripping off people in the CRCorp building who've become my friends, some of them. I don't like that. But I don't have a goddamn problem with you and Musa and whoever else you've got pulling this gimmick all over town. You don't turn my name over to Shaykh Reda, and I let you guys alone, unless you take on my few remaining friends. You do that, I'll turn you over to the civil authorities, and you know—Musa sure as hell knows—what the penalties are."

"We can trust you?"

"Can you?"

Firon took a deep breath, let it out, and nodded. "We can live with that. We can surely live with that! You're a kind of legend among us. A small legend, an ignoble kind of legend, but if you were our age . . . !"

"Thanks a hell of a lot," I said, still holding the seizure gun on him.

Firon got up and headed for my inner door. "You know, CRCorp knew about me, and let me be. It just wanted to test out its security department and its alarm programs. You care more about those people in that building than *they* do."

"Somebody's got to," I said wearily.

"People's lives are their own, and there are no corporations, man!" He made some sort of sign with his hand in the gloomy outer office, and then he was gone.